THE AUTHOR

Geoff Lee was born in St Helens in early September 1939, on the first full day of the war, but it is believed that this was just a coincidence. He lived in Lancashire for the first part of his life, but has lived in Yorkshire since 1972. He first worked at Prescot for BICC (British Insulated Callender's Cables), but often referred to locally as the Biggest Individual Collection of Comedians. Since then he has worked in many drawing offices, the source of much of the content of this novel. He is a leading member of the Rugby League Supporters' Association and is responsible for the distribution of its magazine, *The Greatest Game*. His debut novel, *One Winter*, was published in 1999 to much critical acclaim. *One Spring* is its sequel.

WHAT THE CRITICS SAID ABOUT 'ONE WINTER':

"An evening spent within its pages is like an evening spent in a snug somewhere, with a pint at your side and some friendly old bloke with a tale to tell. A tale you want to hear."
TONY HANNAN

"...warm and authentic and an enjoyable read."
STAN BARSTOW

One Spring

Romance, Rock 'n' Roll and
Rugby League in the 1970s

by Geoff Lee

The Parrs Wood Press
MANCHESTER

First Published 2002

THE PARRS WOOD PRESS
St Wilfrid's Enterprise Centre
Royce Road, Manchester, M15 5BJ
www.parrswoodpress.com

© Geoff Lee 2002

ISBN: 1 903158 28 1

This book was produced by The Parrs Wood Press
and Printed in Great Britain by:

MFP Design and Print
Longford Trading Estate
Thomas Street
Stretford
Manchester M32 0JT

CONTENTS

1. The Great Escape 7
2. The Australian Connection 14
3. Les Earnshaw and his first book 23
4. The Death of a War Hero 31
5. The Girl from Cumberland 38
6. The Storming of Stafford Gates 45
7. Uno's Dabs 52
8. Les Earnshaw and his second book 59
9. Philosophy in the Colliers Arms 66
10. Visitors from Outer Space 73
11. The Tragic Death of Little Sophie 82
12. Les Earnshaw: TV Superstar 88
13. "Us English and Welsh have got to stick together" . 95
14 The Foremen's Fiasco 102
15. The Naked Apprentice 108
16. Two Fat Ladies 116
17. Where's My Pub Gone? 122
18. Dorothy's Dinner Party 129
19. Edward Holding 1891-1972 R.I.P. 136
20. Wyt ti eisio thi achub ti oddi wrtho fo? 144
21. Spending a night in Sowerby Bridge 152
22. I liked Grandad. He was funny.. 159
23. War and Peace 167
24. A Little Girl is Lost 176
25. I thought Murphy was the Referee 184
26. Poppel Doomer Mini-Stars 192
27. Hanky Panky in Smart Street 199
28. "Do you still put water in the beer?" 206

1.

THE GREAT ESCAPE

"Semper in Mira. Solum Profundum Variat."

"Eh."

"Always in the shit. Only the depth varies."

"What language is that?"

"Latin."

"A dead language. That's just about right for you."

"Rubbish. What language do you think they speak in Latin America?"

There were six of them in the Horse and Jockey for their regular Friday lunchtime drink. Keith, the latest addition to Wilkinson's Drawing Office, was sat between Charlie, the office comedian, and Yorky, the man from Mytholmroyd, looking very miserable.

"Have you heard what's happened on that job he's been working on for ages?" said Charlie, with a big smile on his face. "They've just run an armoured cable from the Sub-station to the Refinery and it won't reach the main fuse board."

"It's only ten foot short," muttered Keith forlornly.

"Aye, but it still won't reach."

Suddenly the pub door burst open and in walked George, foreman in the Works Maintenance Shop. He took his flat cap off his head, waved it in the air and shouted out "pint of mild" to the barmaid Mavis, then turned round to where the draughtsmen were sat in their usual corner and continued in the same loud voice so that the rest of the pub could hear.

"A bit of good news, Keith, old lad. That cable we've run for you, you'll be pleased to hear we've managed to cut a couple of corners."

Keith's face lit up. "Great."

Then, with a bigger grin on his face, George went on: "Yes, it's only five foot short now."

Keith sunk back into his seat. He was not having a good day. In fact, he was not having a good week. He was a likeable sort of lad, but the sort that others had always liked to play tricks on, right from his first day at the Jarratt Machine Tool factory in Hemsley. Sixteen years old and still wet behind the ears, he had spent the first two hours of his apprenticeship at the counter in the Maintenance Stores waiting for a long stand. Later that afternoon his mentor and alma mater, Billy Ramsbottom, told him to go to the Research Laboratory to get a new bubble for his spirit level! Fortunately for Keith he had been able to turn a bad thing into a good one. While waiting for the bubble to be calibrated, he had made the acquaintance of the well endowed office girl Sonia, the outcome of this being that for the next three months he had gone out with her and been the envy of all the other young lads in the place.

His five year apprenticeship had been one disaster after another, usually because the rest of the electricians' shop were always setting him up. The worst occasion had been a year later on his seventeenth birthday. One of Keith's many failings was that he was always falling asleep, sometimes in the most unlikely of situations and locations. Not surprisingly this got him into all sorts of bother. On this particular occasion, he had been helping Billy run a cable along the roof of the Welding Shop. All he had to do was keep his foot on the ladder that Billy had climbed up. But within minutes he had nodded off. As soon as Billy saw that he was lost to this world, he crawled along the ceiling boards to the next stanchion, shinned down it and lay down on the ground a few feet away from Keith with jam smeared all over his face. Then the shop foreman shouted at Keith, who woke up and saw Billy lying on the floor. At this point two nurses appeared carrying a stretcher; one felt Billy's pulse and announced he was dead. They lifted him onto the stretcher, covered his face with a blanket and told Keith that they were taking him to the morgue! The shop foreman then told Keith to go to the Divisional Manager's office, where the secretary asked him if he was the lad who was responsible for the death of that electrician.

"Oh his poor wife and children and another on the way," she said solemnly. She told him to go into the office and wait for Mr. Bridge and be prepared to meet his doom. Keith trudged in there and stood in front of the empty desk waiting to hear his fate. After a few minutes he heard moaning from under a large white sheet behind the desk. Suddenly Billy emerged from under the sheet shouting loudly, to the amusement of the three girls next door.

"You won't fall asleep again will you, you dozy pillock!" And from that day forth, Keith had managed, albeit it with great difficulty, to keep his eyes open all day every day.

Back in the office, as was normally the case on a Friday afternoon, little work was being done. This lack of productive activity was aided by the fact that the Chief Draughtsman, John Battesby, and their section leader, Alan Groves, were somewhere on the East Lancashire Road heading back from visiting Agecroft Power Station on the outskirts of Manchester.

"Don't look so miserable Keith," said Charlie. "It's not the end of the world."

Then Yorky chipped in: "Why don't you suggest they build another wall and put the fuse board on it."

"He could even put it in the suggestion box and get ten bob for it," said Len.

"They could move the sub station," laughed Alan. "Just a few yards."

Keith was not impressed.

"Come on Keith, cheer up. It's Friday, the whole weekend to look forward to, intoxicating beer to sample, Rugby to watch or play, good food to eat, pools coupons to check and women to chase and catch if you're lucky," said Mick.

"Don't talk to me about women. I'm in enough trouble there as well."

"Why?"

"You wouldn't believe me if I told you."

"We might."

"It's summat that happened last night."

"Go on then, tell us."

"No, I can't."

"Go on, we won't tell anybody."

Keith ran his hand across the back of his neck, smiled, and went on:

"You know when I used to work in Jarratt's Drawing Office. Well, there was a right sexy tracer there called Mary. She was in her forties, and a right nosey thing as well, but what I liked about her was she was brilliant with her use of language. No matter what she said, it either had a double meaning to it or was a clever play on words. She was a bit like that comedian Ted Ray."

"Anyway, last night I was walking down Dob Lane on the way to my mate's house when I saw her getting off the bus with a big heavy suitcase. So me being the perfect gentleman I am, I offered to carry it for her. When we get to her house I carried it into the hall and quite innocently asked her where did she want it. Straight away she smiles and says 'I'd like it in the bedroom', so I lugged the thing upstairs and when I came down she asked me whether I wanted a beer or a whisky or something else."

"I'd like a beer first and maybe something else later, I jokingly said."

"Then she started giving me all the juicy gossip about the goings on at work. This went on for about twenty minutes, although it was probably fifty per cent truth and fifty per cent her making it up. She always had a vivid imagination did Mary. Then she asked me about Wilkinsons so I told her what you lot were like and then she asked me whether I was getting my rations regularly. Now I knew whatever I said would get blown up out of all proportion the following day, so I told her I was probably getting about as much as she was."

"That's not very good," she replied, "because I've lost my ration book."

"So I asked her where her husband was and she told me that he was up in Scotland and not coming back for another month."

"He's working on an oil rig in Aberdeen and left his dear little wife here with nothing to do at night."

"So he's not going to turn up and find me here engaging in linguistic semantics with you, is he?"

"Is that what we're doing?"

"Only verbally."

"She went on a bit more about who was doing what to whom and where at Jarratts and then she took hold of my hand and said, 'Let's see what the future has got in store for you, young man' and starts running her finger over my palm. She was always doing that at work. 'Oh this looks interesting.' she continued, 'I can see that you've been working too hard recently and had no time for play. But fear not, new opportunities are on the horizon and an old friend is going to come back into your life: but beware of an unknown stranger.'"

"And then you woke up," shouted out Mick.

"No."

"Go on then, what happened next?"

"She kept hold of my hand and then she started licking it."

"And that's when you woke up," laughed Mick.

"So I said to her, 'Do you know Mary, when I was at Jarratts there were six women in the world that used to drive me wild.'

'Who were they?'

'Bridget Bardot, Sabrina, Anita Ekberg, Sally who used to serve the chips in the canteen, the red head who used to wait on in the Glass Blowers and you.'

'What, in that order?'

'No, reverse order, you were always the top of my list.'

'Don't you say the nicest things. You really do have a lovely way with your words.'

'That's one thing I've learned from listening to you.'

'Well be that as it may or June, don't be getting any big ideas just because I'm sat here on my own in this empty house all vulnerable and with no one to protect me.'

'But you're not on your own, you're with me, your great admirer.'

'Keith, don't you dare start anything. If you touch me, I'll scream', and then she leaned forward, put her hand on my knee and whispered, 'but I'll only do it very quietly.'

So I said to her, 'Do you know there's one thing I've done that I bet that no one at Jarratts has ever done?'

'What's that?'

'I've been in your bedroom.'

'What did you think of it?'

'Very nice. I liked the look of it and I have to declare that your wallpaper epitomises the gregarious life-style and outlook of a bohemian free-thinker.'

'Would you like to have another look at it and explain what you mean?'

'What do you think?'

And then she shouts out 'Geronimo, saddle the horses, we're riding into town' and runs up the stairs. So I chased her into the bedroom and of course we both trip over that bloody big suitcase I'd left there. Well, we messed about on the bed for a bit but before very long we were in it. And then disaster struck.

I couldn't be sure but I thought I heard the back door being opened. I definitely heard footsteps on the stairs and then the bedroom door opened and a little girl burst into the room and shouts 'Boo'. It was her grand daughter."

The whole office burst out laughing.

"So what did you do?" asked Charlie.

"We both got dressed right quick. Mary told the girl not to tell Mummy what she had seen and we both managed to get downstairs before her daughter Gillian came into the house. Mary told her that I was an electrician giving her an estimate to rewire the house and then I left, promising to telephone her with a price as soon as I could, a bit of a stupid thing to say because she hasn't got a phone."

"You can just imagine it, can't you?" laughed Charlie. "Her loving husband comes home from Scotland, he goes to see his little granddaughter and she asks him to read her a story. So he reads her the Three Bears and when he gets to that line when the baby bear asks 'Who's Been Sleeping in My Bed' she blurts out: 'An electrician's been sleeping in your bed, Grandad.'"

"It's not funny."

10

"I think it is."

"So when are you seeing her again?"

"I'm not, I'm keeping out of the way for a bit. If her husband finds out, I'm dead."

Then Mick chips in: "I'll have to tell Les Earnshaw about this. He can put it in his next book, with the names changed to protect the guilty."

"Where's he working now?" asked Len.

And much to Keith's annoyance Mick replied, "Jarratts!"

Despite what he had just said, Keith's intention, not surprisingly, was to carry on with what he had started. But he knew that weekends were always a time when those who were working away might just come back home. He couldn't be absolutely sure whether a six foot two fifteen stone welder was not already on the train somewhere south of Aberdeen and heading direct for Ashurst. On the other hand Mary had told him that he wouldn't be coming back for another month. So he decided to chance his luck. Unfortunately what had started badly finished badly too. As it turned out it could have been a life-threatening situation if Mary's rather uncultured husband, Cyril, had not arrived home from the Granite City absolutely paralitic.

Cyril was a bit of a hard man, not a person to cross or upset. Because of his extremely short temper, he had made a lot of enemies around the town, which partly explained why he frequently had to find employment out of town. When he was younger he had played for Gillarsfield Labour Club as open side prop. In appearance he looked uncannily like Ab Terry, who used to play at number eight for the Saints a few years earlier. But Cyril had neither the skill nor the fitness level of the former international and during his two seasons there, he had been either been sent off or booked at least a dozen times. His best, or perhaps better described as his worst, game had been in a "friendly" against the East Ashurst Social Club.

Cyril had once been a heavy-drinking member of that club until he had a dispute with one of the waiters over the philosophical meaning of the concept of time and its symbiotic relationship with the purchase of alcohol just after half past ten. His interpretation of the rules for membership of the club led to the committee having to ban him, a decision they could only enforce by taking on three extra doormen. And from then on, Cyril had born a grudge against anything or anyone associated with the East Ashurst Social Club.

In the opening exchanges, the opposing number eight had got the first punch in, much to the surprise of Cyril who believed that since it was a home game that should have been his prerogative. As a result Cyril went hunting for his opposite number. Unknown to Cyril however, the lad had his two brothers on the field and more relatives on the touchline. And since the game was only a friendly the referee was the bar steward who literally had turned up without his glasses! After half an hour or so, Cyril finally managed to get at the lad. But as they began to scrap, his seventy-two year old grandmother ran onto the pitch and hit Cyril with her umbrella, knocking him out stone cold. This was achieved quite easily because it was a rather unusual umbrella, since to help keep the rain off its owner incorporated a short piece of lead piping welded into the handle.

Sometimes a blow like that could have knocked some sense into the injured party. In Cyril's case, it was the opposite. Five minutes after regaining consciousness and returning to the field of play, he committed acts of an anti-social nature both to opponents on the field and spectators off it and was accordingly sent off and the following Tuesday banned sine die by the Ashurst District Referees Society. On returning to the dressing room, he only made matters worse both for himself and everybody else. After having had his shower, he turned off the main switch and cut the wiring to the water boiler so that later many of the players found that in addition to the usual collection of bumps and bruises, they were also suffering the first stages of frostbite.

Cyril was also known to have caused various people in the town to become accustomed to eating hospital food. And on one very stupid occasion, when lodging in Hull and working for a while at the BP Oil Refinery at Saltend, he had stood in the middle of the Threepenny Stand at the Boulevard and hurled abuse at anything associated with the fair county of Yorkshire. Fortunately for Cyril it was only an 'A' team game so he was able to get out of the ground before the wrath of the small number of spectators present, and the twenty-six Hull and Doncaster players, finally boiled over.

But even though Alan knew all this he still decided to risk it. As soon as they finished work, he went into town and waited in a telephone box outside the Town Hall, where the works buses would soon disgorge their passengers. Ten minutes later he began to believe that his luck had changed when he saw Mary on her own walking towards him. When she saw him in the telephone box, she walked towards him and immediately said that she had been sat by the phone all day expecting him to ring. Then she apologised for the previous night's unfortunate interruption and told him it wouldn't happen again, because if ever she was in the same situation, she would take the precaution to lock the doors first.

And then much to his delight she asked him if he would like to have another look at her bedroom wallpaper and explain what he meant about it's symbolism. As a result he found himself back in Mary's living room three hours later, drinking whisky and listening to her tell him that she had hardly told a soul about what had happened the previous night - well, only a couple of the other tracers. There was Jean, who never believed anything that Mary told her, Stella, who was more interested in telling Mary about some rather titillating activities that were going on in next door's shed, and Mousey Margaret, usually known behind her back as Margaret the Mouth!

He told her that he hadn't told anybody either and their little secret was safe with him. Then, as she had no shoes on, she asked him to get a bottle of ginger ale from the garden shed. It was a request that may have saved his life, for as soon as he was inside the shed, he heard an enormous commotion as the garden gate was flung open and in walked Cyril wearing a kilt and tam 'o' shanter, carrying two suitcases and an enormous shoulder bag. A petrified Keith watched him as he staggered across the lawn and headed straight for the shed. He pulled the door open, threw his bag and one suitcase onto the floor, then bleary-eyed saw this strange young man stood there and slurred out:

"Who the hell are you, Jimmy?"

"The milkman. It's an early delivery."

"Well, leave an extra pint. I've come home."

And with that he staggered into his house to meet his charming little wife, who would immediately tell him how pleased she was to see him and how lonely she had been all the time he had been away.

And half way through the following afternoon, by which time Cyril had finally sobered up, Mary had had to convince him three or four times that he must have been seeing things in the shed since the milkman only ever delivered at seven in the morning and always on the front door-step. And by that time Keith had paid a visit to the barbers where he said goodbye to his Beatles haircut and started growing a beard and wearing dark glasses and a Che Guevera beret. But two weeks later he received an unexpected telephone call at work telling him that the coast was now clear from Ashurst up to the Scottish border and could he deliver some milk that evening. And for the next two months, Keith was frequently seen by Mary's real milkman walking home down Dob Lane just as the dawn was breaking.

And luckily for him, one wet morning he was nearly run down by a maniac driver on Carlton Lane; well, lucky because although he didn't see the face of the driver, he did see the Aberdeen address on the back of the large white van. After that he proceeded to lay low for a while, taking his night school studies more seriously and considering whether life might be a little less fraught with danger if he were to join the Army, the Merchant Navy or even the French Foreign Legion. But before long, and while he was thinking that he might just telephone Mary one lunch-time, he looked out of the Drawing Office window and saw below a motley crew of case-hardened labourers pulling an armoured cable into a trench. And among them, wearing a thin vest, baggy tartan trousers and a Tam o Shanter was a face from the past, unfortunately in this case the quite recent past: Cyril McIntosh!

2.

THE AUSTRALIAN CONNECTION

"Aaaaaaaaaaaaaaaaaaaaaaaaaaaaaaaaaaaaaaaagh."

"What the bloody hell was that?"

"It's only me, Charlie" said a voice from behind a drawing board. It was Jason, the apprentice, who was in the last week of his two month stay in the electrical section of the Drawing Office.

Tea breaks in Wilkinson's Drawing Office were normally a time for heated discussion on some important issue or another. Rugby, Women, Wages and Politics being the four most common topics. But not today. It had been very quiet at least until that outburst. Alan was reading the Rugby Leaguer, Charlie was trying to repair an alarm clock, Len was checking the union subs he had just collected and Mick was staring out of the window at a large seagull attacking a small seagull on the roof of the Foundry. Yorky was doing his pools, Dickie was enjoying the last crumbs of his bacon butty and Keith had disappeared to no one knew where - as usual.

"You know what your trouble is Argonaut," said Charlie. "Too much bed and not enough sleep."

"Lucky me," laughed the Scouser.

Jason Reynolds led a very hectic life. It would have been much more convenient for him if there had been around thirty hours in every day and ten days in every week. He lived at Huyton on the outskirts of Liverpool and travelled ten miles to Ashurst every morning on his old and not very trusted motorbike. He would spend the weekend earning more money for beer by rewiring houses. He also regularly visited his sister in Alder Hey Hospital, and made infrequent appearances at his night school class. On top of all this, he would regularly drive ten miles in the opposite direction to Wallasey on the Wirral where his girl friend Ulrika lived.

Ulrika Petra Morgannson was from Malmo and so typically Swedish: eye-catching blonde hair often done up in pig tails, long slender sexy legs, deep blue eyes and a very distinctive Scandinavian style of dress. But she had a very un-Scandinavian way of speaking, because as soon as she opened her mouth she sounded just like Cilla Black.

"I'll just go and get a breathe of fresh air. I'll be all right, you lot can carry on without me for a bit if you want to."

As the lad walked out of the office, Alan put his paper in the drawer and his cup on the tea trolley and asked: "What are you doing tonight, Charlie?"

"I'm going to be pretty busy, old lad. I'll be reading the next chapter of Tolstoy's War and Peace as soon as I've had my tea. I've got to a right interesting bit. The peasants are revolting. And at nine 'o' clock there's a chess match on the radio that I want to listen to. And if it doesn't run into extra time I want to go out and have a look at Uranus before I go to bed. It looks as though it may be running off its orbit, just like I predicted it would. Why? Did you want some more furniture moving."

"I thought that you might like to come and meet my great Uncle Len."

"And what's so special about him that you want to drag me away from the my well-appointed residence in Thatto Heath to return to this barren cultural desert?"

"Because he knows a load about the origins of Rugby League, a subject that is close to your heart I'm led to believe, and he's going to tell me about it tonight."

"You've never mentioned anything about him before."

"That's because I know next to nothing about him. He has literally just come back from Australia. He's been living there for the last fifty years."

"And is he going to tell us that the Aussies invented it?"

"No, but he'll be worth listening to and it'll be free."

The previous afternoon Alan had met his great Uncle for the first time when he had visited the house of his Uncle Jack and Auntie Doris in Rivington Avenue. Len Holding was a name on the family tree that Alan had drawn up a few years earlier, but little was known of him by the rest of the family. In 1919 and unable to find work in Ashurst, he had gone to London. A month later he sent a letter informing his mother that he was about to board a ship for Australia and for the next fifty years, little was heard from him. Then, right out of the blue he had written to his sister Doris telling her that he was returning to England and asking if he could stay with her for a few days.

"So you're Doreen's lad, are you?" were his first words to Alan after he had been introduced. "Well, I can see you've got her eyes, that's for sure. And how are your brother and sister doing. It's Paul and Joan isn't it?"

He then told them about his life in Australia. He told them about how he had first settled in a place called Parramatta and there met a nurse from Wollongong. After getting married they had moved into Sydney and had raised a family, three sons and later seven grandchildren, one of whom had played briefly for Cronulla.

"I bet he'll know Tommy Bishop," said Alan. "He used to play for the Saints."

"Oh, I know Tommy," said Uncle Len, "he used to live quite near us."

He told them about some of the places he had worked at and what it was like living in the Sydney suburb of Marrickville. Then he talked about his playing days as a rough, tough second row forward for his local footy side, the Newtown Bluebags, but only in the reserves for a season. Then he had broken his leg and had to finish playing the game he loved. It was at this point that he returned to an interest he had developed when he was still living in Ashurst, the origins and early history of the game. This was in no small way due to Mr Aspinall, their next door neighbour in Bolton Street and the father of his best pal, Ernie Aspinall.

After Ernie had been killed in an accident at Mather's foundry, Mr Aspinall had acted almost like a father to Len, whose own father, William Holding, had been killed down the pit. In this way Len had got to know much about the history of the old Northern Union. After her husband had passed away, Mrs Aspinall had given Len the large and battered suitcase in which were stored the minutes and notes of meetings stretching as far back as 1889. In this way Len became the possessor of some very important historical records, which he had read and studied with great interest. As a result, he began asking questions about how the game had split into two codes in Australia. As soon as other members of the Henson Park club heard about his interest, they and their older relatives and friends began to feed Len loads of historical information and tell him stories about what they knew and had done in their own good old days.

Sensing Alan's immediate interest, Uncle Len then invited him to come round the following night when he could tell him more about it. And when Alan had asked if he could bring his mate from work, his new found relative said that he would be very pleased to meet him, especially since Charlie came from Thatto Heath, where Len had once courted a young pit brow lass, a very long time ago.

"So Charlie, do you want to come?"

"Definitely. Tolstoy will have to wait."

"And what about the chess match?"

"I'll get the wife to listen to it and she can tell me about it when I get back. It was only Getyourkitov versus Plonkovich. I don't suppose it'll be much good."

And so that evening the pair of them had listened with great interest as Uncle Len talked about events that occurred around the turn of the century. He told them about the first season after the split, when they had continued to play to the old Rugby Union rules, fifteen-a-side, three points for a try and a penalty goal, four points for a dropped goal and five points for a conversion. Then he hastened to add that he hadn't been playing then. "I was only a school lad," he laughed. "I'm not that bloody old."

He told them about how he had played half a season for Widnes in 1914 and once got sent off for scrapping with a spectator at Rochdale. He told them how he had worked from six until twelve one Saturday morning and then gone in the club charabanc straight to Wigan for a cup tie, and the twice a week training sessions when sometimes there might be a couple of hundred people watching them.

Then he moved on to his time Down Under and particularly his time living in Marrickville with his beloved wife Joyce, who sadly had recently passed away. He gave the two Lancashire lads a fascinating account of life in Sydney in the Thirties and told them much about his links with the Newtown club, which he obviously had a great affection for. He introduced them to some of its many characters: "Ricketty" Johnson, the famous Ellis family, Joe Bugler, "Chicka" Cahill, "Bumper" Farrell and more recently the legendary Johnny Raper, and explained just why the club was known as the Bluebags. Now and again he would glance at the door to make sure his sister wasn't listening and then tell them about some of the scrapes he had got into, some of the women he had known and some of the things he had done and shouldn't have.

He talked and talked; they just couldn't stop him, and as he did his old Lancashire accent became stronger, sweeping away the Aussie twang he had picked up. And by the end of the night to Alan he sounded increasingly like his Uncle Billy, who had died ten years earlier and to whom Len bore an uncanny resemblance.

And then he just dried up. Literally. His voice had gone and with little more than a good night, he left them and went up to his bed. A few days later and fully recovered he sent a message to Alan asking him to come again and bring that young man from Thatto

Heath with him. And that evening, after another fascinating account of life in Marrickville and then in a bigger house in the nearby district of Erskineville, just as they were getting ready to leave, Uncle Len had walked into the back kitchen to make a cup of tea for them, tripped over the cat, fallen to the floor and spent the next six weeks recovering from a blow to the head in Victoria Hospital.

On his way into work the following day Charlie had the misfortune to witness another accident, this time outside the factory's Warrington Road gates. A Ford Zephyr had shot out of Grove Street and hit a Morris Minor driven by their section leader, Alan Groves. There were enough witnesses around to prove that their boss had been completely blameless, but that was of little comfort to him as he lay in a bed in the same Victoria Hospital. Fortunately things did not turn out as badly as was first feared, but it was over a month before 'Grovesy' returned to work.

Much of the conversation that morning was over who would take on his job while he was away. Some felt Len would be a good section leader, since he was such a good organiser as chairman of the Office Committee. Some thought Charlie had such a good way of dealing with everybody he came into contact with. He would be able to sort out all problems with the minimum of fuss or social altercation. Mick quickly declared that the job was not for him since if he became a manager he would have to start wearing a suit and the only one he had was his old demob suit, which appeared to upset or amuse everybody in the place. He suggested Yorky would be the man for the job with all the experience he had gained from his time in the Merchant Navy.

"I'm not taking orders from a Yorkshireman," said Charlie. "If he's in charge, I'm just doing detailing."

"Nothing personal against you Sam," said Len, "but Yorkshire has only just entered the Twentieth Century. You people just don't have the cultural, technical awareness and intellectual finesse for such an important position."

"If Yorky becomes the boss, I'm going back to being an apprentice," said Alan.

"I thought you still were an apprentice," said Keith, "judging by most of your drawings."

"Eh, lads, it's not a time for laughing and joking," intervened Mick. "We don't know how badly injured 'Grovesy' is. Let's show him some respect."

As a result the Drawing Office was a very quiet place for the next couple of days until Alice Groves rang Charlie to tell him that her husband was now out of danger and would be pleased to receive visitors at the hospital, although no-one had to make him laugh since he had broken his ribs, one of which had punctured his lung.

For Charlie this was another example of the Law of Coincidence, Uncle Len having an accident and being taken to hospital and the next day their boss finishing up in the same place. It was always happening, maybe it happened to everybody, it was just that Charlie was very conscious of the fact. Sometimes they were quite insignificant. Grade Two coincidences he labelled them, like the previous week when one of the apprentices had told Charlie that he had just started going out with a nurse from Carlisle who now worked at Providence Hospital in St Helens. That night, parked in his street in Thatto Heath, was a large white van with a Carlisle address written on its side! The following day Mick had been telling them about his son who was working in Athens. That night Charlie's wife had told him that she had been looking through some holiday brochures and fancied going to Greece. And then on Saturday morning he had seen the daughter of one of his neighbours with her husband in Nevins. And half an hour later he had seen her twin sister, although it might just have been the same one on her own!

Friday lunch time saw Alan, Charlie, Mick, Len and Jason in the Horse and Jockey for their regular lunch-time session along with Frank Taylor, a chargehand from the Outside Contracts Division, accompanied by the Two Yorkshire Clowns. Arthur Smith and Bill Atkinson were installation engineers who were based in Wilkinson's O.C.D. Depot in Leeds and who from time to time visited the main works in Ashurst. 'Einstein', as the former was usually known, was surely the best person to work with on site. There was nothing he didn't know about electrical installation work. Unfortunately, away from work there was little he knew about the real world. "Atko" on the other hand, like most other people, only went to work to earn money. When out on site with his mate, he just got on with the job in hand and then when everything had been switched on and shown to be working, he took charge of filling out the time sheets and expense forms. Away from work he liked to invest his hard-earned money in brewery products, exotic food and following the Leeds Rugby League team to the ends of the earth, which meant Workington in the North, Widnes in the West and at Craven Park, the home of Hull Kingston Rovers on the East Coast. With Smithy keenly tucking into his meat and potato pie and reading the latest issue of The Electrical Review, the conversation soon moved on to what Uncle Len had been telling Alan and Charlie.

"Eh, Billy, did you know that when the Northern Union first started they played to the Rugby Union rules and after every tackle they restarted the game with a scrum."

Billy knew his history of the game, not surprising since three members of his family and his wife's grandfather had all played around the turn of the century. "Oh aye. I remember my great Uncle Maurice telling me about it. It was quite a few years after the split with the other lot before they introduced the play the ball after you'd been tackled."

He then talked about his uncle playing for Manningham and some of the teams he had played against in the very early days: Heckmondwike, Holbeck, Brighouse Rangers and, in Uncle Maurice's opinion, one of the roughest teams in Yorkshire, Leeds Parish Church.

Then Frank, a Warrington fan, having polished off his pie and peas, joined in the conversation. One thing about Frank was his amazing memory. "When did you hear that the War had started?" "What was your first day at school like?" "Who were playing for the Wires when you first started watching them?" "Where were you when Kennedy was shot?" To questions like this he could quote chapter and verse with complete accuracy. He was just as amazing, being able to recite lists of vaguely interesting bits of information, like the names of all the neighbours in the street in Latchford where he grew up. Another of his tricks was to list all the people in his class when he was at the junior school, first in alphabetical order and then in the position of the desk they sat at. On one occasion, he had won a bet in a pub by reciting the names of all the football teams in the First, Second and Third Divisions, North and South.

On another occasion he had got into a big row when arguing with Keith Sanderson about the 1959 Lancashire Cup Final when Brian Bevan won the game for the Wires with a hotly disputed try. In the course of the argument, Les went through all the moves that had occurred in the build up to an act of bare-faced robbery. In the thirtieth minute, the other Warrington winger, Terry O'Grady, fielded the ball on his own twenty-five, made a sixty-yard run and then passed to the supporting Bobby Greenough, who kicked towards the corner. The other three wingers on the field, Tom Van Vollenhoven, Jan Prinsloo and Bevan, all chased the ball, with the Australian claiming he had got his hand to it before the two South Africans. But as everybody at the dressing room end could see, his hand went nowhere near the ball, although in the eyes of the blind Pudsey referee, Matt Coates, it was a try and so the Wires won by five points to four. And Les told it as though it had only happened the previous day when actually it had been well over ten years ago. He then went on to recount other events from that day, including the weather conditions and the size of the crowd, 39,327 to be exact. But Keith would have none of it. He had seen it with his own eyes, even though he was stood at the back of the Kop at the opposite end of the ground, well over a hundred yards away.

Not surprisingly they were all back late into work, but then they always were on a Friday. As soon as they got back in the office, Keith told them that the boss Basil Wilkinson had rung to say he was bringing the new section leader round. It was obvious that someone from outside had been appointed. If it had been Len, he would have had to negotiate with himself over the annual wage increase, which would no doubt have been astronomical. Charlie would never have been able to convince anybody that he was telling them off and if it had been Yorky they would all have complained that he was discriminating against Lancashire people no matter what he decided had to be done.

At two 'o' clock Basil appeared, accompanied by a dead ringer for Norman Wisdom. Basil introduced Raymond Sewell, who had been seconded from Head Office in London as it was still unclear how long Grovesy would be away. He smiled at Basil, stepped forward, clenched his hands behind his back and made a neat little speech that contained nothing of substance. And then he and Basil departed.

Shortly after, Len rang a draughtsman who worked at the Head Office to find out a bit about their new boss. R.Sewell would appear to be hot on three things: time-keeping, preventing more than two men ever being stood round one drawing board at the same time and forever asking what percentage of the job had been completed. When asked about his technical knowledge, Len's friend told him he didn't have any. He had simply worked his way up the company ladder by crawling. He also told Len that 'arsehole', as he was known, treated everybody beneath him as though they were children. It was clear that they would have to draw up a strategy to deal with him and quickly.

Firstly, they decided on a policy of absolute silence to unnerve him. Secondly, they decided to make sure their many visitors had to ask permission from him to spend any time with a draughtsman. Thirdly, when they wanted to go down on the shop floor they decided to ask his permission. It seemed a bit of a risky strategy, they could easily have made a rod for their own backs, but Len was sure it would see him off.

On his first day in charge, he called them all together and told them how he intended to run things. He emphasised the need for good time-keeping, not wasting the master's time, keeping costs down, meeting deadlines and finished off by saying that whenever he looked out of his office window, all he wanted to see was heads down and bottoms up. Then Len provocatively said that he wanted to ask a few questions just to make sure right from the start about the new working practices.

Mr Sewell looked at him with total amazement and then muttered yes.

"People come up from the shop floor with all sorts of queries. Usually we'll break off what we're working on to sort the problem out. But sometimes sorting one job out might make problems on another job. Should we carry on like this or do you want anyone coming in here to see you first."

"I want to know exactly who is in here and why. Yes, they must come and see me first."

"What about sorting problems out over the phone. We often get the O.C.D. lads ringing us up from site. Sometimes it may be a technical problem and sometimes the wrong parts might have been sent, which is really nothing to do with us."

"All outside calls will have to go through my phone. I don't want every Tom, Dick and Harry stopping you working for whatever reason."

"We also need to go down on the shop floor from time to time or go out on site. Do you want to know about this?"

"I want to know exactly where each one of you is all day."

"And will you decide the priorities?"

"Yes, and if ever I am not here there are to be no changes to them. What I intend to do is see you all individually every Monday morning and then on Friday afternoon to see how much has been done during the week. I intend to keep a firm check on what everybody is doing."

Then he told them he was meeting Basil in his office for the next hour and after that would be round to find out exactly what each one was working on.

"Who is this man?" asked Charlie, imitating the American actor, Jack Palance. "He's still in the Dark Ages."

"He's not a Yorkshireman is he, Sam?" said Mick.

"He won't last a month," laughed Len. "We'll run him ragged. I'll tell you what I'll do. I'll get Billy Kilshaw to keep sending his wiremen up with queries on the drawings I've modified for that job at Ellesmere Port. If I had had time I would have done four separate drawings, one for each transformer, but John Barker told me to do just one and sort it out on the shop floor. I'll also tell Dave Birchall to keep ringing in from Agecroft complaining that the parts lists for that rush job are incomplete. It was John Barker's last instruction before he went away to get all the major items listed and for me to sort the rest of the gear out after the cubicles were on site. And if we all use our heads and keep going to see him we'll just slow everything down. But we'd better keep a record of all the dead time he's caused, for when the shit hits the fan."

For the rest of his first day in charge, their new boss appeared very pleased that he had been put in control of such an obedient group of subservient draughtsmen. They almost seemed like children, he thought. But by the end of the third day he was exhausted. There always seemed to be someone knocking on his door, either to ask if he could speak to a draughtsman, or a draughtsman asking permission to go down on the shop floor. Then there were loud-mouthed individuals ringing up from site wanting him to check parts lists and delivery schedules. Charlie and Mick told him that they could not agree over the best way to lay out the control room at Blyth Power Station and asked him to advise them whose scheme was the most suitable bearing in mind possible future changes to the lay-out of the Turbine Hall. And whenever he went through the Mechanical section, one of the section leaders there would inevitably buttonhole him over some trivial issue or another.

Before the month was out he had gone. According to Basil, he had been called back to London for a far more important assignment. As a result he had decided to put John Battesby, the Chief Draughtsman, in overall control of the Electrical Section, with Charlie acting section leader until Alan Groves returned.

"Well here's a toast to Brother Len. Your plan worked. The end of an era, seventeen days all in," said Mick as they all raised their glasses at the next Friday lunch-time session in the Horse and Jockey.

"I bet there were loads of bosses like him in 1895," said Charlie.

"Why 1895?" asked Keith "What's that got to do with him?"

"Oh, it's something you won't be interested in. It's about when Rugby League got going."

"Too right. It doesn't interest me. I don't agree with blood sports."

Then Frank Taylor, who had just joined them again, told them about him visiting his grandfather in hospital the previous week and the long conversation they had had in the absence of any other relatives.

"He would be a bit older than your Uncle Len, Alan, and he's got a great memory. He told me a hell of a lot about the early days. It was either that or talking about his operation! Did you know after the split, they kept the line-out for another three years and only reduced it to thirteen-a-side in 1906."

"That's right," said Alan. "I read about it somewhere. Some teams wanted to reduce the number of players to fourteen, some to thirteen and some down to twelve. And Bradford wanted to go back to all the old Rugby Union rules. That was when they introduced the play the ball after you'd been tackled."

"So really, 1895 was the time of the administrative break, but 1906 was when the rule changes gave birth to Rugby League as a totally separate game," said Charlie.

"Do you know what would be really interesting? To watch a match played under the old rules as a curtain raiser."

"I think watching a hundred scrums in an hour would be a bit boring," said Mick.

"Listening to you talking about the Pie Eaters every day is boring but we've learned to put up with it," laughed Charlie.

"Anyway, what's this I've heard about your new boss packing it in?" asked Frank.

"That's right. He just couldn't handle our over-excessive co-operation."

"Basil won't like it."

"Basil doesn't like anything we do."

"We all know that."

"Look, Frank. He knows he's got a good bunch of lads up there. We've got experience of working on site and on the shop floor, technical qualifications and knowledge, enthusiasm, drive and imagination, good looks, charm and charisma. And that's just me."

"What skills do the rest of them have, Charlie?"

"Greeno is tri-lingual. He speaks unreconstructed English, passable Belgian and unlimited gibberish. Len knows the price of every draughtsmen from here to Hull. Yorky has perfected the art of drawing vertical lines that don't drop off the end of his drawing board, Keith can set it all to music and Mick has got his demob suit."

"What the bloody hell has that got to do with it?" growled the man from Platt Bridge.

"For when we want to impress any important visitors that are brought round from time to time," answered Charlie, and then directly to Len, he continued, "and particularly those from St Dunstans."

3.

LES EARNSHAW AND HIS FIRST BOOK

"I bumped into Les in Wigan on Saturday," said Mick the following Monday morning.
"Did you tell him about Keith's little escapade with Mary?" laughed Charlie.
"No, I didn't get chance, he was with the wife."
"How is he? Is he a rich man yet?" asked Yorky.
"He's all right. He must be worth a few bob now that he's had his book published, otherwise he wouldn't have been wasting his money buying Elvis Presley records."
"Has he really written a book? What's it called?" asked Keith who had never met Les, but had heard enough about him.
"It's called 'The Draughtsman's Tale'; it's all about things he's seen or heard about at the various places he's worked. A lot of it's based on this place." Then he went on: "You know he always seemed to get involved in the most bizarre situations."
"Do you remember that interview he had after he got finished at Wallworks?" laughed Charlie. Then, turning to Keith, he continued: "He'd been out of work for weeks and he was pretty desperate with another baby on the way. There was nothing round here so he went for an interview at a firm in Salford. The bloke who interviewed him was also in charge of Research and Development and so Les had his interview in a laboratory. As soon as he met him, Les thought there was something funny about him. The first thing he noticed was that the bloke kept walking round the lab, turning bunsen burners on, pouring chemicals into tubes and looking at charts on the wall. So Les followed him round, answering his questions. Now Les was a sheet metal man and the job was for a mechanical draughtsman with experience of designing special purpose machinery, so Les didn't rate his chances very highly."
"Some of the questions Les got were daft. The bloke asked him did he have experience of fire drills, but Les didn't know if he meant some sort of high resistance cutting device or evacuating the building. Then he asked him if he could fly, again Les wondered whether he wanted to know whether he was all right going in a plane or overcoming the law of gravity. Then the bloke pointed to some machinery on one of the benches and told Les to find out what was wrong with it. He then leaves Les and walks out of the room. Well, Les didn't have a clue how the thing worked. He must have been there half an hour, trying to fathom it out when a young lad comes into the lab and asks Les what was he doing. When Les told him he was waiting to finish an interview with Mr. Cross, the lad replies, 'You'll be waiting a long time for that bugger. He's just walked into the Wages Office took his shirt and tie off and started singing opera.'
"Strange as this sounded, it was true. What Les and everybody else there didn't know at the time was that the man was having a complete nervous breakdown."
"So did Les get the job?"

"He played it clever. He went back to the Personnel Department and told them that Mr Cross had asked him to start the following Monday. So he got a start and of course once you are in, it's that bit easy to fool them. He got three month's work before they found out he knew next to nothing about the design of lathes and milling machines."

Then Len chipped: "His book isn't only about things at work. It's about anything he'd seen or done that was funny or dramatic. One of his tales was about an old guy who used to live near him up Billinge. Well maybe it was the way Les used to tell it that made it so funny."

"What was that?"

"This old man smelled summat rotten and he was always spitting and touching you. Everybody who knew him, kept as far away from him as they could. Finally he dies, doesn't leave any money, so the vicar arranges for the local church to pay for the funeral. And being young and keen, the vicar also convinces a few of his flock that they should go to the funeral and pay their respects. So there must've been about twenty people in the church, all facing the coffin, except for the vicar who had his back to it as he faced the congregation."

"Now because it had all been done on the cheap, the wood that the joiner had used was warped. And he hadn't screwed it down either, he'd nailed it. Slowly the nails started popping out. The vicar carries on extolling the virtues of their dearly departed brother, but everybody else had their eyes on the coffin lid as it starts to open. Then a woman in the front row screams and runs down the aisle and out of the church, followed by all the others, including the vicar who is of course the last to get away. As he runs down the aisle, his cassock gets caught on one of the pew doors and as it does he shouts out: 'Get off me, you ugly, hump-backed bastard.'"

"That was a typical Les story," said Yorky. "They were always unlikely, but then again they could've been possible."

"Like that story he told about his grandfather working at Pilkington's glass works in St Helens."

"Go on, tell him."

"He and this other bloke had the job of lifting plate glass off a conveyor belt and carrying it over to the packing shop. These sheets were about six foot long and two or three foot high. Now there wasn't a lot of work on at the time and the foreman was a right little Hitler. If he found anybody talking or not working, he would just send them home, even if there was a hold up on one of the kilns and no glass was coming out. His grandfather had seven mouths at home to feed and couldn't afford to lose a penny and neither could the other fellow. So what they used to do if there was any delay and they could see the foreman up in his cabin above the kiln looking at them was to pretend to be carrying a sheet of glass. Of course, from where the foreman was stood he couldn't tell the difference.

"Unfortunately, one day the Divisional Manager comes walking through the shop and stops to talk to him. So he just stands there listening to him with his two hands in the air holding nothing. And what made it worse for his grandfather was that the other bloke had walked away."

"How long did it take Les to write this book?"

"Years. Every time he heard or saw something interesting, he'd write it down on a bit of paper. He just kept going on and on with it."

"And then he managed to get it published?"

"After a long time. He must have tried every publisher in the land before he could interest anybody. It's a good book. I still laugh when I read it, even though I must have heard most of these tales a dozen times over."

"He's writing another," said Mick, "but I think he should put a few more smutty stories in it."

"If he's working at Jarratts now that shouldn't be a problem," laughed Keith.

"There was a bit of a saucy one, about Gordon and Peggy. Do you remember them two?" enquired Yorky. Then, turning to Keith, he went on: "Gordon was in charge of the High Voltage Test Bay when they had it behind the Iron Foundry. Peggy was a chargehand in the Accessories Department and every day she had to take insulators down there to be tested. Now the two of them had been carrying on for months. He used to take her into the small test bay, lock the door and turn on the red lamp so anyone outside would think there was a test in progress. It was pretty much a case of everybody suspecting what was going on without anybody knowing what was going on. Anyway, one Friday afternoon they were in there together. Usually the old punching machine was banging out brackets so you couldn't hear yourself think, never mind hear what was going on in the Test Bay. But that particular afternoon it had broken down. The only other person in there at the time was this young apprentice. He was working away on the bench when he hears Peggy moaning and groaning and then scream out. Him, being only sixteen, doesn't know much better and, having a bit of a vivid imagination, thinks someone is either being electrocuted or murdered. So he picks up the phone and rings all the numbers that had to be rung in an emergency and telling them that there is a woman trapped in the Test Bay. About five minutes later, having had their bit of fun, Gordon and Peggy emerge looking a little flustered to an audience made up of the works fire brigade, two nurses, a security guard and a St John's ambulance man."

"Has he got anything in about Ronnie Garner and that girl Lorna who worked on the switchboard that Christmas Eve?" asked Yorky.

"What about Ronnie and that nurse from Widnes who worked at Whiston Hospital, and then that Sally whose boyfriend played for Ashurst Social, unsocial in his case," laughed Charlie, "or when he met a woman in a pub in Oldham and took her home thinking she lived in Leigh and she lived in Lees in Oldham."

"Les has got to be careful, if he writes too much about folk that are still around some might come and give a good thumping if they think they've been maligned."

"That's a posh word for a Wiganer," said Alan. "Have you started going to the library again?"

"Now he can put something in about a young draughtsman and a grandmother. He could call it the Kevin and Maria affair," said Yorky, "or maybe The Great Escape!"

Many draughtsmen had worked in Wilkinson's Drawing Office over the years. But there had never been one like Les. It was always said that after he had been born they had thrown away the mould. In addition to his vivid imagination, his ability to use and misuse the English language, both spoken and written was amazing. He would frequently use words that few had ever heard or understood, particularly when telling the Chief Draughtsman why he hadn't finished a drawing or the Machine Shop foreman why it couldn't be understood or worked to on the shop floor.

He was also extremely erudite when it came to imitating the various local accents of the area. Some times he would spend all day talking like a Wiganer and particularly when he was having one of his disputes about electrical drawing standards with Mick, who he often referred to as the Tsar of Platt Bridge. But he was at his funniest when he reverted to his own daft language. Often in the middle of a sentence, he would throw in his own totally meaningless and ridiculous words. The rest of the office varied between admiring his skill and ignoring him. But how others who didn't know him, reacted when he started was a continual source of amusement.

One day a wireman had come up from the shop floor to ask about the modifications to one of his drawings. Les explained what changes he had introduced by saying "I've moved the two GEC contactors to the back of the panel so there will be plenty room for a furgel bruker on the board, vladitsh. And can you leave a bit of room for an extra English Electric fuse to supply a huppel dinger if they need one, porin perritts."

So it came as no surprise a year after he had left Wilkinson's to read in the Lancashire Evening Post that his book had finally been published. However this news caused consternation among some members of the staff who feared they might be in it and how to make sure their wives would never get round to reading it if they were.

"Have you ever heard Johnny Morris on the wireless. Les was a bit like him, especially when he started imitating the noise of different bits of machinery" said Charlie. "I remember once we were in the Gas and Electric club one Saturday night and the comedian and the singer hadn't turned up. The Social Secretary was really worried, the place was full and the same thing had happened the previous week. I knew him well because he used to live near us in Owen Street. So I went and told him that one of the lads with us could entertain them for half an hour because he used to entertain the Drawing Office all day, when he worked with us. By this time Les had had a few and was quite keen to have a go. So he stands up and announces that he is going to do imitations. Well he starts off making all these funny noises for about two or three minutes, stops and asks does anybody know what it was. Well nobody did so he says I'll do another one. So we get a load of more funny noises and again nobody knew what he was on about; then he does a third one, they all thought he was hilarious and when he asked them what did they think it was, they started saying things like, "It's the mother in law after she's had pie and peas."

"So then Arthur, the secretary comes onto the stage, quite pleased because by this time all the audience are laughing and joking and he announces there will be a prize for the best guess. So Les has to do the first one again; no-one had a clue what it was until he tells them it was the old Churchill Redman lathe at Wallworks, cutting a groove in brass. The second one was the boiler at Jarratts starting up on a winter's day and the third one was the overhead crane in Wilkinson's Iron Foundry. So then he suggests that members of the audience should come up on stage and do their own imitations of machines where they work.

It was a great night, talk about audience participation. They were fighting to get on the stage at the end."

"I'd love to see him on television. He'd have the place in stitches."

"He could be quite serious, could Les" said Len.

"Aye, but not for more than five minutes" laughed Charlie.

"Did his book have any Rugby in it" asked Cliff, an apprentice who had been stood there listening to them talk, while waiting for Dickie to find a drawing.

"Yes. "said Charlie " but that was another funny thing, there was just one chapter with Rugby in it. It described a works outing to the 1968 Wembley Final between Leeds and Wakefield Trinity, you know when Don Fox missed that conversation right at the end."

"Ee, poor lad."

"In this chapter, there are thirty of them on a coach going down and thirty coming back, but not the same thirty. One was a Cornish bloke they had met in a pub and they offered him a lift back because they thought he wanted to go to St Helens, when he actually wanted to go to St Austell, but they couldn't understand his accent. Another one they collected at a petrol station was a bloke being chased by his mother in law in a Zephyr. And there were also two women of dubious character who they had met in a strip club in Soho and couldn't get rid of when they got back home. If you read his book but miss out that chapter, it doesn't make any difference. But when you do read that chapter, it doesn't have anything to do with the rest of his story. I bet somebody told Les after he had finished writing it that he would have a better chance of finding a publisher if it could be called a Rugby League novel so he must have put this extra chapter in."

"He was never what you could call a big Rugby League fan" said Mick. "he played a bit but he was a poor watcher."

"He always went to the Challenge Cup at Wembley, he always watched the Lancashire Cup Final, and the games on Boxing Day and Good Friday but that was about it" said Charlie.

"I didn't know he played. Who did he play for" asked Alan.

"He had a few games with Pearsons until he appeared in the Ashurst Works Final against Delaney's. I think he broke his neck: I can't remember exactly. It might have been his finger. I know he was off work for a couple of days and he packed it in after that."

"No, you're wrong" said Mick. "Don't you remember he made that great comeback and it lasted about ten minutes."

"When was that" asked Charlie.

"It was when he was working at Jarratts. He was knocking round with a couple of lads from Clock Face and these two both played for Liverpool City. Les starts going down training with them and then one Saturday he goes with the 'A' team up to Whitehaven, just for the ride, he thought. Anyway they stop off for some lunch on the way and a couple of the team must have eaten something dodgy, because by the time they get to the ground, they were not fit to play. So the coach tells the reserve and Les they were both playing. As they were stood outside the dressing room, one of the Whitehaven players was walking past and he comes over to one of the Liverpool team and passes the time of day with him. He must have known him. When he had gone, Les says something like "Bloody hell, their prop's a big 'un.'"

"Prop be buggered" said his mate. "that's the scrum half."

"Well, when Les sees the size of the rest of the Whitehaven team, he must have had a heart attack. Luckily he was playing on the wing and his opposite number was a bit on the small side: well small for a Cumbrian, only fourteen stone and six foot tall. First time he comes at him, Les was wondering which way he was going to side step but he didn't. He just ran over him. So Les lay there until this St John's Ambulance man runs on the field. The first thing Les asks is, 'where's your stretcher'; he convinces the bloke he's broke his ankle so they took him to hospital and after that Les announced that he had been forced to retire."

"Do you remember when he used to have them great long religious arguments with Norman."

Norman Wilkinson had once been one of the key members of the management team. Well at least he had a key to open the main safe in the General Offices where many important documents were stored. He was frequently known as the Do Gooder, forever trying to right the wrongs in the world, without having a clue to how the world functioned, And for a time he had been on an evangelical mission to save the members of the Drawing Office from spending the rest of their time in hell after having drawn their last line and their last breath. But his presence in the office only acted as another excuse to have a good laugh.

"I remember one day Les had got Norman to say that to understand the issues of the modern world, it was essential to take your guidelines from what was written in the Bible. Les then picks a sheet of paper out of his drawer and says that he had written down a number of questions which he hoped Norman would be able to answer, from a Christian perspective, though not necessarily straight away. And for the benefit of all the others in the office who were almost certainly agonising over them as well, he would read them out first."

"Question number 1. In chapter 1 of Leviticus, it appears to recommend that I should burn a bullock on the altar as a sacrifice to the Lord. This will create a pleasing odour for him. Unfortunately I am having problems with my next door neighbour who tells me it is not pleasing to him. What should I do?

Question number 2. In chapter 15 of Leviticus I read that I am not allowed any contact with a woman while she is in her period of menstrual uncleanliness. How can I tell. Most of the women I have asked seem to take offence at this.

Question number 3. In Exodus chapter 21 verse 7 it appears to say that I am allowed to sell my daughter into slavery as a maidservant. In this day and age what do you think would be a reasonable price for her."

"Well as usual Norman couldn't answer. He said that he was not too familiar with the books of Leviticus or Exodus. Then Tony shouts out that it was a good film, giving Norman his chance to leave the room."

At that point the door burst open and in walked Basil with a visitor so for the next hour, silence and work dominated the office until Joan appeared with the tea trolley and her latest bit of news and gossip from around the town or from the General Office. And totally unaware of what they had been talking about, she began by telling Charlie that she had been in Wardle's book shop in town at the week end and bought a copy of Les's book.

"You'll like it" replied Charlie. "It's partial esoteric representation of things ephemeral and perceptive transcends the borders of human enlivement."

"And there was me just thinking it was a story book."

"Ignore him" said Alan. "He's only jealous that Les has been able to quantify the spirit of the early modernist period of renaissance industrialism before he did."

"What do you lot have for your breakfast. What ever it is, it's addled your brains."

"I usually have oysters in mushroom sauce, served with Clermont de Standish 58" said Mick "except when the butler is away and then I have to do with cornflakes in sour milk."

"Does that explain why all your jokes are so corny."

"Do you only have one butler, Mick" said Alan. "I really feel sorry for. Now I can understand why you are like you are, coming from such a deprived background. Is everybody in Wigan as under privileged as you."

"When I was a kid there was my mam and dad, my grandad and five children in our house" said Yorky.

"When I was a kid there were my parents, my gramma and grandad and six kids in our house" said Dickie.

"You did a lot better than us" said Len."there was my mother and father, both sets of grandparents five kids and a dog where we lived."

"Was it a big house then" asked Charlie.

"I suppose it was. It did have an upstairs."

"Well you lot were all very lucky" laughed Joan. "when we lived in Leigh, there was my mum, an auntie, three kids and a gold fish."

"That's not so many."

"It was for a big cardboard box. Mind you, we did have running water. Usually five minutes after it started raining."

"Is that where you learned to make this Indian tea" asked Alan. "today it's quality reminds me of the lower reaches of the Ganges accompanied by the pungent odour of what flows into the brook at the back of Wallworks."

Tea breaks were always the same in the Drawing Office. Joan's appearance was the signal that the worst part of the day was now over, the first two hours. It was a time to hear what was happening around the rest of the factory, engage in some light hearted banter with her and then either attempt to resolve the economic, political and astronomical problems of the world or have a dig at someone's recent misfortune. Without doubt in years to come historians would discover that the most important social forms of human intercourse that industrial man made in the twentieth century would be in the morning between ten and ten fifteen, or ten and ten thirty or forty or even fifty. In fact one day their tea break went on for so long that by the time they got to the canteen they found themselves right at back of the queue.

Strangely enough although so much importance was attached to the morning tea break, little enjoyment was obtained from its afternoon equivalent. Mick wanted to have it stopped, partly because the arrival of Joan always seemed to wake him up just as he had nodded off. But then to compensate for this inconvenience, she usually fed them some little gem of information she had gleaned from other departments, during the course of her daily round that morning. And one afternoon they were particularly intrigued to hear her tell them that she had seen that John Rigby who used to play with the Beatles on her way home from work the previous night, looking like something out of a Sergeant Pepper film. It was unanimously agreed that this was good news all round. It was also worked out that collectively John still owed without the interest, around four pounds seven shillings and sixpence ha'penny. It was also decided that it would be a good idea if they stopped blaming him for all the mistakes and cock ups that had occurred over the last seven years, since he had been away.

4.

THE DEATH OF A WAR HERO

In 1963 John Rigby, an inhabitant of the ancient village of Prescot, that lies on the linguistic and cultural divide between Liverpool and St Helens, had started work in Wilkinson's Drawing Office. He soon added a new dimension to it's social side. He always maintained that his main occupation was musician, being a draughtsman was only his part time job. He was the lead guitarist in The Rainmen, a Merseyside rock 'n' roll band that was always on the brink of stardom but never quite made it. Then, after two years of him drawing electrical schematics, control panel assemblies and wiring diagrams by day and the band drawing enthusiastic and sometimes quite large audiences at night, it was decided they would try their luck in London. There they did not quite achieve the success they had hoped for, although on odd occasions their names would appear in the Melody Maker and the New Musical Express and their careers were followed with great interest by most of the Wages Office where two of John's ex-girlfriends worked.

After that there had been possible sightings of him in Times Square, in Greenwich Village and then on the Golden Gate bridge in San Francisco. Charlie reckoned he had seen him as an extra in a gangster film set in Mexico and Mick was sure he had appeared in a documentary about wildlife in Alaska, although he, Mick that is, was a little inebriated at the time. So they were all surprised but pleased when John had turned up the following Friday lunchtime in the Horse and Jockey. They were even more surprised when he bought them all a drink; speed at getting to the bar when it was his round had never been one of his strong points.

"So to what do we owe this honour. I thought you would've forgotten all your old mates by now."

"How could anybody forget you, Mick."

"His rich Uncle Ernie from Orrell did when he made his will," laughed Charlie.

"So when will we enjoy the pleasure of your absence again."

"Sorry to disappoint you Mick, but I've come back for good. D'you know of any jobs going anywhere?"

"I thought you'd have retired by now with all the money you must have made," said Yorky.

"No. I made a lot and I spent a lot."

"Well you wasted it, if them daft clothes you've got on is anything to go by," said Charlie.

"Did you meet anybody famous in London," asked Alan.

"John Lennon, Mary Hopkins, Sandy Shaw, Dusty Springfield, Mick Jagger to mention a few."

"And were they pleased."

"They were pleased when they heard he wasn't staying," laughed Yorky.

"You didn't go straight down to London when you left here, did you?" asked Mick.

"No. I went working with the O.C.D. at Cockenzie Power Station up in Scotland. And when that job finished, I transferred to the Overhead Lines Group. That was a great job, climbing up and down half erected pylons, fitting the insulators to the cross arms and stringing the conductors from one pylon to the next. I was on that job for ages; it was like being in the Wild West up there and then I had my little accident."

"Go on," said Charlie.

"I fell off a pylon."

"You're joking."

"Luckily I only fell from the second arm to the third, about twenty foot. I still broke my collar bone but if I'd fallen from the third one, it would have killed me. That's when I decided overhead lines weren't my speciality and it might be better going back to being a draffie. So when I was better , I went down London, which is where I've been ever since."

"I couldn't climb up a pylon," said Alan. "I just couldn't do it."

"Climbing up and down them was all right and even going out on to the cross arms. What is pretty scary is climbing down the insulator to hook it on to the conductor and then having to climb up again, especially if it's wet. Anyway what's been going on here while I've been away?"

"Well, Stan has retired, Greeno and Thelma got married and they've got two children, Mick has learned to do joined up writing and Dickie has bought a suit."

"From Oxfam," added Alan.

"Oh and there's a new lad with us now, Keith. He's a bit like you, always getting into trouble with women, just like you."

"I didn't misbehave myself at all while I was in Scotland."

"As if."

"Well, when I was working with the Overhead Lines Group, I was lodging in Brechin, between Aberdeen and Dundee. And in Brechin there's not very much to do at night."

"So what did you do?"

"Stayed in most nights and counted my dosh. Fortunately the landlady liked to play games, so that's what we did."

"What sort of games."

"All sorts, cards, draughts, Monopoly and then I showed her how to play chess."

"I bet that was nice for her."

"I'll tell you what was nice for her. She was a widow and her name was Mrs Rigby. So one night I suggested playing at being Mr and Mrs Rigby."

"And did you?"

He just smiled.

"How old was she?"

"Let's just say her birthday came before mine. Anyway, what about Len? You haven't mentioned him. Is he still the union man?"

"You have to call him sir now, he's the chairman of the Divisional Council. Oh, and 'Grovesy' got injured in a car accident and was on the danger list for a few days, but he's all right now."

"And do you still spend half the day talking about the Saints?"

"Yes, we're still very religious," laughed Charlie.

"Eh, we've forgotten Tony. You won't believe this John, him and his Dad are running a pub."

"Where?"

"In Halifax. Don't worry, he's all right. We send a food parcel over every month."

"And what about you," asked Mick, "are you pleased to be back in the land of the great unwashed?"

"That depends on whether I can get a job. I've got three mouths to feed now."

"You've not brought them two twins from France back with you, have you?" laughed Charlie, but before he could say anything, knowing his somewhat unusual interest in marine life, Mick said that he must mean that he had added two goldfish to his collection. Then Yorky said he hoped he got a job soon and hopefully at Mathers, or Jarratts, or Wallworks or Vulcan or Vicars or UGB or British Sidac or Stoves or Crone and Taylor or preferably back at the BI in Prescot."

"Eh Sam, I think he should have his old job back here and get rid of you. It's not right, you people coming from over the hills and taking our jobs and our women and living in our houses."

"I'm sorry to disappoint you all but it's half one. We don't want another bollocking. Let's be off," said Alan. Then, turning to his old mate, he said, "Can you meet us in the Junction tonight and we'll have a few?"

"If Thelma lets him out," laughed Yorky.

And as they dashed out Alan shouted out, "Eight o clock."

Back in the office the conversation ranged over the usual Friday afternoon topics like who was going where that evening, who Saints were playing over the weekend, who had managed to get some overtime in on Saturday morning and, of course, the return of their musical friend. But the whole mood of the office was shattered when John Battesby came out of his office, asked them all to gather round and told them he had just heard that Stan had died of a heart attack.

Stan had worked at Wilkinson's since 1932, first as an electrician and then on his return from active service in the War as a draughtsman. He had a phenomenal memory of all the different jobs he had worked on over the years. He had also amassed an enormous collection of technical manuals and catalogues of equipment within the electricity supply industry, and was an invaluable source of knowledge. This usefulness however had never been recognised by the management, who had always considered him as no more than a detail draughtsman. Then, two weeks before he was due to retire, he had received a message from on high informing him to get rid of all his plants that festooned the place along with the rest of his paper work as new desks and reference tables would soon replace the furniture they had had since the year dot.

Stan had never been one to challenge authority, his years in the Army had conditioned him to do just what he was told. So, during his last week, he took great pleasure in making innumerable journeys to the Boiler House where all his historical records were transformed into ash. His only regret was not being present to see the look of anguish on the face of John Barker when he rushed in a few days later to check the size of a 1932 Ferranti Transformer from one of Stan's catalogues and discovered they were no longer available.

Unfortunately, in his last year, Stan had become a bit of a pain. Few of the younger lads could stand him due to his continual criticism of the moral decline of the youth of the nation and their lack of respect they gave to their parents and to those who had fought for their freedom. But for the older ones who had known him for years he was, in Charlie's own words, "an ace guy".

Stan had joined up in October 1939 and had arrived in France three weeks before the evacuations at Dunkirk, where he had nearly drowned. He had fought with Montgomery at Tobruk, where he had had two of his toes blown away, and right at the end of the War had taken part in the liberation of the Belsen concentration camp, something that he never spoke about but which had clearly affected him. On top of that he had come home on a 48 hour pass in 1941 to discover his house in Liverpool had suffered a direct hit during the blitz, killing his sister and leaving his wife with burns which she would suffer from for the rest of her life. And in the winter of 1951 he had saved a young lad from drowning in the Sankey Canal and caught pneumonia.

Two months earlier he had retired with great plans to build an extension on to his house in Gillarsfield and play an active part in the running of his local British Legion club. But before a brick had been laid or a meeting attended, he had run for the Earlestown bus one afternoon, struggled breathless up the stairs, sat down on the first seat he could find and dropped dead.

Among those most visibly upset was Charlie, particularly when he heard one of the younger draughtsmen called Stan, a grumpy sod, was to take his place. But his faith in humanity was soon restored when around twenty draughtsmen took a morning's holiday to go to the funeral, which was attended by over a hundred people including a car load from Coventry and a man who had come down from Barrow in Furness and who, at the reception later, told how Stan had risked his life to drag him to safety in the desert.

As a result of things that had been said at the funeral about Stan's war record, it became even clearer that he was something of an unsung hero. The man from Barrow was fulsome in his praise of his old comrade and even went so far as to suggest that it was a pity Stan had never told anybody about all that he had seen and done. "It would have made a fine book and maybe even a film," he said as everybody nodded sincerely. As the man talked, Alan's thoughts went out to his own father who he had never known and who had been killed at Monte Cassino in Italy in 1944. He realised just how little he knew about him, and how he had never really asked his mother about him in case it upset her.

Later that afternoon Yorky made the comment that the man whose name no one could remember had made a big impact on him: "He made me think I should write down some of the things I saw and did when I was in the Merchant Navy, being half crippled by a U-Boat and then on that Murmansk run."

At the same time ideas were now circulating in Alan's head. He wondered how he could find out more about his own Dad's life, an effort that would be made more difficult since the details of his childhood in Preston were pretty vague. But as he thought about one relative, his mind wandered to another, his Grandad who was now turned eighty but still very much alert. And moreover he was full of stories about his somewhat unusual war record as well as working down the pit and surviving a roof fall. As the ideas moved around in his head he decided that he could write a novel based on Edward Holding's life and times. Perhaps he could bring in other relatives, remembering that a few years ago he had constructed his own family tree, going back as far as 1791 when his great, great, great grandfather, Arthur Silas Holding, had been born at Collins Green. So the following Sunday afternoon when he, Thelma and their two children were sat in his grandparent's house in Silkstone Street, he decided to ask Grandad what he thought.

But as soon as he raised the idea, his Granny chipped in: "Well, if he's going to be in a book I want to be in it as well. Ee, it'll be a best seller. They might even have it on the pictures." Then, turning to Thelma, she nodded at her grandson and said to her, "He's still a dreamer. Always has been, always will be."

"No I'm serious, Granny. After all the things I've heard about different members of this family, it could be a best seller."

"Will you retire when you've done it? Will you go and live in a big house in Southport? Ee, he'll forget about his old Granny when he's rich and famous and on the wireless."

As she was speaking Grandad left the room and a few minutes later marched back in wearing his A.R.P. tin helmet with three medals pinned to his shirt and blowing his air raid warning whistle. And as he sat down he said, "When I heard about this war, I said to Lord Kitchener, what are we going to do about it?" Then for the rest of the afternoon he regaled them with stories of his time on the Western front. As it turned out, and as Alan knew full well, the length of time he actually spent in the trenches was quite short. Within three months of his battalion arriving in France he, along with a large number of other members of the South Lancashire Prince of Wales Volunteers, was captured and spent the next three years working down a lead mine in East Prussia. One hour and a dozen stories later, Granny, who had been sat all this time cuddling her little great grandson Robert as though he was the first baby she had ever seen, interrupted him:

"If I'm going to be in Alan's book, then I'm going to tell some stories." Then, turning to Thelma, she said, "It's all right. I didn't go to France. I didn't agree with it. No, it's about our Billy when he came home one time." She passed little Robert back to his mother brushed her pinny down and said: "He'd been wounded in France and brought back to England. He was in a hospital down South somewhere and when he got better before he went back to the fighting, he managed to get a pass for a few days. He came up on the train and all the way up all he could talk about was how much beer he was going to drink. When the train pulls into George Street station, the Mayor was there to greet them all, but Billy had no time for any ceremony. He jumps out of the carriage on the wrong side, runs across the track, climbs over the wall and while all the others are listening to patriotic speeches, Billy thought he would be starting on a great long drinking session. He walks straight into the Nags Head and saw a few blokes in there supping. He goes up to the table - that's all it was then - and asks for a pint. The barman looks at him, shakes his head and said, "Sorry old lad, we've just run out". Billy couldn't believe it. Now he always had a short temper and that day was no exception. So he takes his rifle off his shoulder, bangs it down on the table and slurs it along and swipes about fifty glasses on to the floor, smashing them all and shouting, "Well if th'ave no beer, th'all not be wanting them glasses, will tha?"

And as they all burst out laughing, Granny then put a whole different slant on things when she said: "It's all wrong really isn't it. Here we are laughing and joking about that war and it was terrible really." Then, turning to her husband, she said: "You were lucky Ned, four years away from home and just a few scars on your leg. And yet not a mile from where we're sat there are men still suffering from it."

It was true. In nearby Frances Street, Ken Rainford still found it a struggle to walk to New Street library less than two hundred yards away following a mustard gas attack at Paschendale in 1916. Joe Anders, who lived in Katherine Street, found it even more difficult just to walk since both his legs had been blown off on the Somme around the same time. And Mrs Kavanagh, who had been in the same Sunday school class as Granny, had spent the last fifty years asking everybody she met if they had seen her husband of three months, Arthur, who she could not accept or comprehend had been blown to pieces at Ypres. And Alan also remembered hearing about a reunion of players from a football team in Huddersfield in 1920, when all those still living had turned up, all four of them with only seven arms and three legs between them. And all for what.

As they walked home Alan mulled over what he had heard and knew. He began to work out a plan for writing what he was convinced could be a best seller. It would be wrong to only stress the humourous side as his Grandad usually did, although that probably was to block out all the bad things he had seen. He thought it could be called "Three Men, Three Wars" and based on the exploits of members of his own family. It would obviously start with his Grandad and his experiences mainly as a prisoner in the war and then as a miner after the war, living in a land fit for heroes, which was totally and absolutely untrue, certainly on the South Lancashire coalfield. The second part would be based on his great Uncle Jack, whose experiences on the dole in the Twenties had led him to join the International Brigade fighting on the Republican side in the Spanish Civil War in the mid Thirties. And the third part would be based on his own father who had lost his life in the liberation of Italy from the grip of Mussolini and his Black shirts. He worked out a plan to achieve this goal, maybe a month on research of each of the three main characters, then maybe two months to write each part. Then maybe another month deciding who would be the best people to publish his novel and the rest of his life living off the royalties. Unfortunately the life of an author is not so simple and twenty five years later he was complaining bitterly to himself that there were still one hundred and one questions to ask and now no father, grandfather or Uncle Jack around to answer them.

At work the following day he mentioned his thoughts on the matter to John and Charlie. But before they could go much further with the discussion they were interrupted by Len informing them that that military war might be over but the economic war was still on and Basil was up to his old tricks again. He had just issued details of his latest plans, which were to introduce a payment by results scheme on the shop floor to replace the hitherto measured day work: and for the staff he was considering presenting the union with an offer he felt they couldn't or wouldn't be allowed to refuse; no redundancies for a year based on having no wage increase for a year. Once again consternation raged. It was always the same with Basil. His twofold aim in life would appear to be to upset as many members of the lower orders as he could and to increase his bank balance as much as he could. That lunchtime a meeting of members was held. A resolution was passed and on the strength of it, the office committee was given the task of working out what had to be done, threatening to do it and then, as often as not, having to do it. Two or three weeks of industrial action would then follow, usually a clever plan of working to various rules as laid down in the company handbook. Then a compromise would be worked out and all would return to what was considered to be normal working until the next time that Basil felt like upsetting them again. And as was to be expected things were no different this time.

As usual it was Stephen Williams, the Managing Director, who gave them their opportunity. He had come up to discuss a job with John Battesby and Dave Ainsworth, a mechanical draughtsman. Unfortunately, or fortunately as the case turned out to be, just as John asked Dave to come into the office, Dave received an urgent phone call from one of the installation engineers who was working on a job at the Giants Hall colliery in Wigan.. It took Dave nearly twenty minutes to explain the changes he had made to the new layout of the colliery winding room. Then, on entering John's office, Williams's first words were something to the effect that "I thought we paid draughtsmen to draw and not spend hours gabbing on the phone". As soon as the committee heard this, they decided that from now on draughtsmen would ignore the phone, since it was not written in their contracts that it was one of their duties and also because it upset their managing director.

Allied to this was the business of sending notes. Because they refused to communicate by phone, the draughtsmen began going down on to the shop floor much more frequently to discuss various aspects of their drawings with the foremen, inspectors and wiremen. This prompted Stephen Williams to tell John Battesby that he wanted this stopped, because he knew they only went down there to talk to their mates. So whenever a problem arose, the draughtsman concerned would send a note. Unfortunately the post was only collected twice a day, meaning that every job that had a problem got slowed down. Doing exactly as you were told, no matter how stupid it was, resulted in some rather bizarre situations, although Alan spoiled it all when he refused to respond to the Works Progress Manager's comment that he could jump off Runcorn Bridge for all he cared. But as Alan couldn't swim very well he felt that the Office Committee should have taken this into consideration before declaring him an enemy of the working class.

Then there was the bog-in when everybody would down pencils and rubbers and go to the toilet at the same time. From time to time they would have a reading day when they spent the first hour scouring the pages of the Electrical Review and other trade papers after Stephen Williams again had told Charlie that he should keep himself up to date with the developments in the field of electrical control systems. And on other days, particularly when visitors were being shown round, they would all come to work dressed in the oldest and scruffiest clothes they possessed, just to show just how poorly paid they were. Mick, however, never took part in this particular protest. He just wore what he usually wore, but then it was on days like this that for once it was generally agreed that he didn't look out of place.

5.

THE GIRL FROM CUMBERLAND

Stan's untimely death was the first thing that Alan and John talked about in the pub that evening. During his time at Wilkinson's, John had worked with Stan on a number of jobs and although they would often engage in bitter exchanges over what did and didn't constitute acceptable forms of music, civilised behaviour and relationships with members of the opposite sex, they formed any unlikely pair of mates. Then John asked about Tony, with whom he had also been very friendly despite Tony's complete lack of interest in anything that could in any way be considered cultural or artistic.

"About a year ago his Dad won about thirty thousand quid on Littlewoods. The first thing he did was pack his job in at the Coal Board and buy a car for Tony to drive him and his wife round. They start going all over the place looking for a nice house to buy and one day they set off for a ride round the Trough of Bowland. Unfortunately his Dad had forgotten his glasses so his mother had to read the map. As a result they finished up near Halifax about three hours later.

"They had their lunch in a pub on the outskirts of the town and while they were there they find out that the place was for sale. Tony's Mum asks the barman if she can have a look round so his wife gives them the grand tour. There's five bedrooms and two attics upstairs, an outhouse and a greenhouse and a great big cellar. On top of that there was a bowling green and two full size snooker tables. So then his dad says, 'Should we buy it, Agnes?' 'Why not,' she replies, 'and if we don't like it we can always go and live with our Edna for a bit.'"

"And what did Tony think?"

"He wasn't too sure at first. He wanted to carry on living in Ashurst, which he could have done if he'd wanted to. But then if he was on his own he would've had to learn how to operate the sink and switch on the frying pan."

"So he went with them?"

"Aye. The following Saturday he drove them over there again to check a few things out. He gets introduced to one of the barmaids, a right cracker she was. She tells him that she and two of the other barmaids were wanting to start a women's rugby team and use the pub as their headquarters. She went on to suggest that his Dad could be the nominal President of the club and Tony could be the vice chairman, organising the social activities of about twenty fit young women. Then she took him down into the cellar to see how many barrels it could store. I don't know what else she did down there to him but as soon as he came back up he had changed his mind about living in Yorkshire."

"So what's he actually doing, is he in charge?"

"Not really, the brewery has got one of their managers in for a couple of days a week while Tony and his Dad learn the ropes. And when he is not around this barmaid is very good, always giving him a hand."

"I bet she is."

"We've got a trip arranged there for next month. Tony's organised a six team sports day, would you believe it. There's loads of us going. There's the Drawing Office, the Machine Shop, the Rolling Mill and the apprentices from here, this womens' rugby team and something called Tony's Team, which will probably be him and his Dad and half the tap room. There's going to be bowling, darts, dominoes and snooker."

"And anything else these girls are game for, I suppose," laughed John.

They were interrupted for a while by Tommy Carey, a fitter from the Machine Shop, asking if any of his Friday night drinking team had been in and then Alan asked John what he had meant about now having three mouths to feed.

"You've not brought a pair of goldfish back from London with you, have you?"

"No, it's better than that. I've brought the girl of my dreams back with me."

"So it's her and one goldfish then is it. Well, let's hear about her. What's she like?"

"Magic."

"Why? Can she make your money disappear?"

"Ha Ha."

"John, all the time I've known you, you've described every woman you've ever been going out with as magic."

"But with this one it's true."

"So where did you meet her?"

"It was when I was living in Camden Town. At the end of our street there was a smashing little Greek shop. I used to go in there nearly every night to get my kolokyhakia, patates, marouli, domates, baklavas, yiaourti."

"O.K. Don't make a meal of it."

"She worked in there. She wasn't a great looker, but interesting to talk to and have a laugh with. Anyway, after a few weeks I asked her out but she just smiled and said no. Then a couple of weeks later I had a right stroke of luck. I was going up to Kentish Town to meet a couple of mates for a drink when I saw her walking down this side street. As I was crossing the road, I saw a lad come from behind her, knock her over and grab her handbag. Then him and two other lads who were with him run towards me. As they run past me, I stuck my leg out and tripped the first one up and his mate falls over him. The third one raises his fist as if to hit me, so I punched him while he was thinking about it. Then I saw the other two were getting up off the floor so I kicked one in the goolies, just as the other lands one on me. So I kicked him as well. Then I picked her handbag up off the floor, waved my fist in the air and shouted 'Who wants it next?' I know it sounds a bit brutal, but they deserved it."

"This doesn't sound like the cultured John Rigby we all used to love and cherish."

"I know. I surpassed myself. I must have been like that Rugby player you were always going on about."

"Who?"

"Vimto….. You know….. the Mad Bull."

"No you mean, Vinty: Vinty Karalius, the Wild Bull of the Pampas."

Then John carried on: "Anyway the daft buggers all ran off shouting 'Facking Borstard' at me and she comes up and thanks me and asks me how I am. So I thought this is my big chance. I gave her the handbag and then sat on the pavement holding my arm. She gets a tissue out of her bag, kneels down and starts wiping the blood off my face while telling me how brave I was. After a few minutes I struggle to my feet and said to her that I needed a drink, would she come to the pub with me. So she could hardly say no and then while we are in there I asked her again if I could take her out."

"Well it worked. We agreed to meet on the Saturday night outside the tube station. By that time, I had an enormous black eye and a plaster over my knuckles where I had hit this kid but I knew that didn't matter. Anyway she turns up bang on seven, but guess what: she had a baby with her in a push chair. She said hello, asked me how I was and then said that she was very sorry but couldn't go out with me because she couldn't get anyone to look after her little girl. She was probably expecting that I would make some excuse and bugger off, but I didn't. I said to her that I had never been out with two good looking women at the same time and as it was a nice evening why didn't we all go for a walk."

"Didn't you feel a bit strange pushing a pram with somebody else's kid in it."

"I did at first, and she seemed really nervous as well. I suppose she thought I was just being polite with her and I'd take her out for one night and then make some excuse. We went up Parkway and into Regents Park, sat on the grass and I started playing with the baby, you know tickling it and making it laugh. I really enjoyed myself and me and her talked a lot as well, about all sorts of things, dead easy it was. To be honest I felt as though she hadn't had anybody to talk to for weeks. When it started getting dark, I walked her back to where she lived in Chalk Farm and, I suppose to her great surprise, I asked if she fancied going for a walk on Hampstead Heath the next day. Her face lit up when I said that. And that was how most of our first dates were, walking round, the three of us."

"And is she from Greece?"

"No, she's from Cumberland, Maryport."

"And how old is this Mary?"

"Who said her name was Mary?"

"You did, you said it was Mary Port?"

"You daft bugger, no it's Sandra. She's actually a month older than me."

"And where's the baby's father?"

"In Italy. He was a student in London but when he found out she was pregnant, he shot off back to Milan."

"Bloody Italians."

"Eh, there are plenty English lads who would've left her in the lurch. And the other thing was when this lad's grandmother found out, she wrote to say how ashamed she was of him and enclosed some money for Sandra to buy stuff for the baby. So Sandra writes back to thank her and a few weeks later the grandmother sends some more money and asks for a photograph. So Sandra does that and then the grandmother starts sending money every month and all she wanted was a photograph of the baby each time. This went on for nearly a year and then the letters suddenly stopped. Sandra wrote back a couple of times, but there was never a reply. Maybe the old lady had died but if Sandra hadn't had that money, she doesn't know how she would have managed."

"And what's made you bring up here? Didn't she want to stay down there?"

"No. The place she was living in was bad. It was no good for a little kiddie. She was dead keen to get away. She thinks Ashurst is great."

"A bit more like Workington or Whitehaven than Mayfair, eh."

"Definitely."

"And what does your mum think about it all?"

"She's over the moon. She hit it off with Sandra straight-away and she loves having little Helen. I suppose you can say it's her first grandchild."

"And where are you living?"

"Seddon Street. It's only a poky little place, but it's big enough for my goldfish and Sandra thinks it's a palace. Well it is after where she was living before."

The following Tuesday John came in for an interview and six days later returned to his old drawing board, his old stool and his old friends. And it soon became clear that although he was now a man with family responsibilities, he still had plenty of tales to tell. But conscious of the recent sad departure of Stan, he concentrated at first on the humourous rather than the licentious.

"I worked for a firm called John Thomson Engineering when I first went down there," he said to the assembled throng at one of the morning tea breaks. "It was an amazing place; there were about thirty draffies there. It was like the United Nations. There were six Poles, three Indians, two Anglo Indians, a Canadian, two Aussies and a South African. The rest were all English; there was one from Barnsley, one from Scarborough, my boss came from Bolton and the rest of them came from all over the South of England, Brighton, Reading, one even lived on a farm near Dover. He used to bring eggs in on a Friday to sell.

"They were a good bunch of lads, except for one of them. He was a right cocky little bastard, always telling tales to the bosses. Anyway, one day me and Cockney Jack decided to teach him a lesson. He was designing a steel framework on an A0 sheet. This framework was about twenty metres long and had to join two larger frames together. On the left hand side all the holes had to line up with holes on the end of an existing building and on the right hand side it had to line up with holes on a stanchion that one of the Polish lads, Anton, had drawn. Now Sneaky Simon had one of the new drawing boards, you know the ones you can alter the angle on the parallel slide. So when he starts on this new drawing, he works at the left hand side first for a couple of hours making sure his framework lines up with the existing building. By now it was lunchtime so he goes out for a walk. While he is out Jack alters the setting on his machine from nought to two degrees. When Simon starts again, he ghosts some lines across to reference points on Anton's stanchion. He then spent all afternoon detailing the top of his framework. The following morning, Jack comes in early and changes the setting back to nought degrees. Simon comes in and starts detailing the underside of his framework. Then he tries to fit everything together, and of course none of it lines up. It was hilarious to watch him rubbing out and re-drawing, puffing and panting; then he tried to blame Anton, who had absolutely nothing to do with it. In the end he had to start the drawing afresh and wasted three days on it."

"Well if that was the funniest thing that happened, no wonder you've come back here," laughed Charlie.

"I know it doesn't sound that funny when you tell it, but it was if you were there. And of course we couldn't tell the rest of the office, because if the boss had found out he would probably have sacked Jack."

"Oh, I'll have to sit down. My sides are splitting. I've never heard anything so funny in all my life," said Yorky. "However did you stand it?"

Ignoring his comment, John went on: "It used to be good at Christmas there. We worked on the day before Christmas Eve until about eleven in the morning. Then we went to this posh hotel in Bloomsbury for free drinks until half twelve. After that we had our Christmas dinner, listened to a couple of speeches and had more free drinks from two until three. After that we struggled back to the office and one of the lads gets out a bottle of vodka and we carry on until the cleaners turn up. By this time there were only a dozen of us still standing. Now one of these cleaners had been having a load of trouble with her ex-boy friend. He owed her about fifty quid and wouldn't pay her so we decided to play a trick on him, well it was Jack's idea really. This bloke was the landlord of a pub in King's Cross so we decided to go and help her get some money out of him. Of course we were not in much shape if it came to a punch up. So Jack comes up with the bright idea of making it look as though she was about eight months pregnant."

"Now at the hotel there had been a load of free turkeys given away but Jack's uncle had a farm in Essex and he didn't really want his. I know it sounds daft but what we did was stick his turkey up her jumper and then we went down to the pub. She tells her ex that she is pregnant and it is his kid and if he doesn't pay up she'll take him for all he's worth and tell his wife as well. So he opens the till, gives her the money he owes her and tells her to disappear for good. Straight away she leaves us and goes home, but on the way she gets hit by a drunk on a bike and gets knocked out. When the ambulance turns up they see what condition they think she is in so they take her straight to the maternity hospital and there two young nurses gently undress her and deliver this bloody turkey."

"What a load of old codswallop," said Mick.

"What happened to this band I've heard so much about?" asked Keith. "Did you play anywhere famous?"

"If you mean the Rainmen well we played together for about six months and then somebody stole Billy's drum kit and Ken came under the influence of the Hari Krishna lot, so that was the end of our great dream. I started knocking around with some lads who were getting a band going in Kenton near Wembley. When they heard I had played with Stuart Sutcliffe and knew John Lennon, they were very impressed and wanted to use the fact to get some publicity. So I went down to Abbey Road studios when I knew the band were there one day and managed to get a message to John inside. They let me in and I had a chat with him and asked him what was the chance of me playing a number with them and getting someone to photograph it for publicity for this new band I had just joined. So he goes away and comes back five minutes later and says you're on. We go in the recording studio, the other three are there; I knew Paul and George vaguely. I borrowed a guitar and John says we'll play "Love Me Do". Ringo starts with a big intro on the drums and then we all come in, play one chord and then they stop.

"'What's up?' I said. 'You have now played with the Beatles. Put that on your CV,' George said and walked out of the room. So that was literally my moment of glory. But we used the photograph to get the Kenton Krew known round the society world and played a few gigs here and there. Fortunately most of the audiences we played in front of were drunk as lords by the time we got on stage otherwise we might've got rumbled earlier than we did. Mind you, I think some of them were lords, although a lot of the women were definitely not ladies."

But before he could tell them any more John Battesby was banging on the window and pointing to his watch, indicating that it was turned half past ten and their five minute tea break had just lasted thirty two minutes.

They worked for a while in silence until the regular Friday afternoon visit of the wireman, Harry Potter, the one with a foolproof method of betting. He didn't make much money but he never lost any, ever. This was because his method was literally fool proof. If Saints were playing a poorer team, say Barrow, Harry would find a keen Saints fan and say something like give us twenty points start and I'll back Barrow. Then he would attempt to set up another bet in which he would back the Saints and give Barrow a start of less than twenty points, say ten points. If the Saints won by more than twenty points he would lose the first bet and win the second. If Saints won by less than ten points, he would win the first bet and lose the second. But if the Saints won by anything between ten and twenty points he would win both bets. Of course Harry tried to keep his betting activities secret not only from the management but from the others. But since he had asked just about everybody in the place at one time or another to take part in his little scheme, everybody knew what he was up to. At the same time Len would be going round the office collecting the union subs, a most difficult task sometimes, particularly amongst the members of the Jig and Tool section who were forever finding one poor reason or another why their membership was costing them money, not gaining it for them, and also how the union was getting involved in political activities they totally disagreed with.. Harold Pennington was one of the worst complainers. Where he got his information from was a mystery to Len, unless he was a secret member of the Economic League who from time to time stood outside the main gate handing out their scurrilous anti-union leaflets. Len kept trying to get Harold to come to a branch meeting to air his views in a proper environment. But Harold wouldn't go because it was too far for him to go to the Boilermakers Social club where the monthly meetings were held. So Len half jokingly suggested that they held a meeting in his large detached house in Hemsley.

"Aye, you'll all be welcome, fetch them all. But you'll not convince me the present union policy is any good for people like me."

So Len decided to take him at his word, using the same tactics he employed to fight Basil Wilkinson, that was by following his words to the letter. He got four of the committee to go round with him to Harold's house one evening. Unfortunately another committee member who worked at Delaney's heard about this meeting. Now that very day their management had just sacked three draughtsmen, so the committee member knew that the branch would need to discuss the issue immediately. So he told the twenty or so members who worked there to come to the committee meeting.

Harold was a keen gardener and that evening was down at the bottom of his garden pruning the roses when Len and the four committee men turn up. They are let into the house by Harold's absent minded son, who then sets off to tell his dad when the telephone in the living room rings. So he then proceeds to spend ten minutes talking to one of his mates. Over the next few minutes more members of the Ashurst branch of the Draughtsmen's and Allied Technician's Association arrive at the house and are let into the front room by Len. Finally the son manages to get down to the bottom of the garden and tell his dad that he has some visitors. After finishing what he was doing Harold slowly walks back into the house and into a smoke-laden noisy front room where about thirty men are sat about on the chairs, the leather settee, the drop down table and on the floor, arguing heatedly what had to be done to protect those who had just lost their jobs.

The following day Harold officially resigned from the union, an action that actually made it that bit stronger! And for the next few weeks he was viewed with great suspicion by his neighbours, who were all extremely curious to discover just what line of business Harold was getting involved in attracting such large numbers of suspicious looking men down their secluded leafy cul de sac.

6

THE STORMING OF STAFFORD GATES

Wilkinson's Engineering Works had always been the largest factory in Ashurst since work first started on the old Atherton Lane site in 1808. In 1937 the Smethurst rubber works had been bought and demolished, which allowed the firm to expand all the way down Industrial Street as far as the canal. As a result, the factory now covered a large area near the centre of the town. Running behind the old refinery and dividing it from the rest of the place was McFarlane Street, which housed the only building on the site that was not owned by the Company, The Volunteer, a pub that shared a common wall with the back of the Print Room.

The firm had always had a member of the Wilkinson family in charge. From 1932 this had been Joshua Albert Wilkinson D.S.O., who had run things firmly until he had suffered a heart attack in 1962. Then his eldest son, the abrasive and ambitious Basil, had assumed command, but only for nine months when in rather strange circumstances the firm had been sold to the Miller Engineering and Construction Company of Cleveland, America. After that Basil had disappeared from the scene and new bosses were jetted in from the other side of the Atlantic, often with different sets of ideas on how things should be done. The first to arrive on the scene were soon dubbed the Three Stooges but within weeks they were replaced by Mr. Winston Z. Cypanski, whose mentor would appear to have been Al Capone After the incident with the locked gates, he was replaced by two quite cultured gentlemen, each knowing independently how and when to say please and thank you. But they did little that could be classed as useful and spent much of their time in England visiting such industrial centres as Bath, Harrogate, York, Stratford on Avon and, rather strangely, Morecambe. They didn't last very long and for the last eighteen months the works supremo had been Wilbur from Idaho whose style of management was based on his obsession with what he called social inter-personal communication. This involved setting up little committees and holding meetings at every possible opportunity, often when the only item for discussion was when to hold the next meeting. Not surprisingly he soon became dubbed the SIPCO Kid.

Just prior to the reappearance of their old mate, John Rigby, rumours had begun circulating around the place that there had been something fishy or even illegal about the way the factory had been sold in 1963. After Basil had assumed command, and while his father wavered between this world and the next one, he had manoeuvred his two daft brothers, Norman the Do Gooder and Cyril the Meddler, out of the way and taken complete control, installing Stephen Williams, his old chum from his University days, as Managing Director. He had not bothered one bit about what his older sister Cynthia thought, partly because she spent most of her time in cloud cuckoo land and partly because he couldn't stand her. Her father's illness and death finally worsened her mental state to such an extent that she had voluntarily entered what was known locally as the loony bin. But the one member of the family that Basil had not taken into account in all his devious plans was Cynthia's daughter Penelope, a spoiled brat who had just returned from a finishing school in Switzerland.

Penelope had soon come to realise that she would not be able to lead the pampered existence she had always enjoyed much longer, now that the employees of the firm would no longer be subsidising her expensive tastes and hobbies. With the assistance of her young solicitor boy friend, Humphrey, she discovered that Uncle Basil had been guilty of sharp practice in much of what he had done since he had taken over. He had always assumed that as the eldest son he would take over in the absence of his father. That was clearly indicated in the Articles of Ownership Documents, which he had last seen six months before his father had suffered his heart attack. What he did not know was that his father had altered a month time later to the eldest child, partly at the insistence of his wife Nora and the company lawyer, who had since died and in whose office the documents resided. So in assuming command, Basil had created a legal problem because Cynthia was older than Basil. And in selling the factory and the land it stood on, he had created another one since the land on which the new Rolling Mill had been built was actually owned in a seperate trust fund by Basil's mother and her sister Jennifer who lived in Cornwall. As a result of Humphrey's probings and Penelope's acknowledged self interest, lawyers were consulted. And when wind of the potential complexities reached the American owners, expensive lawyers based in New Jersey soon became involved as well.

Then, out of the blue, it was announced that the firm had been sold, this time to a holding company called Electrical Designs based in the Isle of Man. A little probing in the right places and an afternoon spent by Len going through the Companies House accounts in Ashurst Library revealed that one of the subsidiary companies of Electrical Designs was another firm called HV Power Design Ltd. And on the board of one of its subsidiaries, with an address in Mayfair in London, was none other than his Royal Highness, Basil Wilkinson, along with another familiar name, Stephen Williams. As the old saying went, the more things change the more they remain the same.

As soon as it became known that Basil was back on the scene, a certain mood of despondency set in among the workforce. While the firm had been run from America, those in direct charge were men who had little knowledge of British working practices, British law, or even what products were manufactured in the factory. Each manager seemed obsessed with the need to instill in the workforce the importance and necessity for competition, not only with other companies manufacturing the same products, but also within the factory itself. Every department had to stand on its own two feet. Every department had its own annual budget, its own goals to achieve in whatever way its manager deemed necessary. Survival of the fittest and little mercy or care for the under-achievers was preached with a fervour often associated with religious fanaticism. It was a recipe for disaster.

Typical of the imported style of management was what came to be known as the Storming of Stafford Gates, the one that sealed the fate of Mr Winston Z. Cypanski. From his first week in charge, which actually coincided with the election of Harold

Wilson's Labour Government in October 1964, he had complained bitterly that he didn't agree with the way things were done in Britain. If he had his way as manager of a company, he shouldn't only have the right to sack who he wanted to. If he felt the situation warranted it, he should also have the right to shoot them as well. He was a real nasty piece of work and everybody around the place soon learned that what he said was what had to be done. Literally, utterly and completely.

Early into 1966, ten control cubicles bound for an incineration plant in Hong Kong were dispatched on three lorries down to Tilbury docks in East London. According to Cypanski absolutely nothing was to prevent or hold up their journey. An important part of the general consignment was three boxes of spare parts. Unfortunately these had not been delivered from the supplier based in Stafford around the time the cubicles were being loaded in Ashurst. But this did not worry John Barker, the Works Progress Manager. One of the lorries could collect them from Stafford, in fact the lorries would drive past the depot on their way to the docks. Unfortunately one of Cypanski's sidekicks, well his son actually, who played no small part in running things, heard of this planned detour and informed his father that evening in the hotel they were staying at in Liverpool. His father, who was heading to Transfyndd power station in North Wales the following morning, blew up: "Tell Barker those lorries don't deviate one yard from their route. If they do, he is sacked."

The following day the three lorries arrived at Tilbury docks. After their load had been lifted onto the dockside, the agent for the Hong Kong company saw there were no spare parts. So he refused to accept the load, telling the three drivers that the cubicles could not be put onto the ship as a part load. Fortunately the ship was going to be delayed by a couple of days due to the need for urgent maintenance work in the engine room. On being informed of the situation John Barker immediately informed Mr Cypanski, who angrily told John to instruct the three drivers to go back to Stafford to get what was missing. On arrival around eight that evening the drivers discovered that the warehouse where the parts were stored was locked up and the keys were unavailable until the main security guard arrived in the morning. One of the drivers rang John Barker again for instructions. He rang Cypanski and was told in no uncertain terms that those spare parts had to be on the lorries by midnight come what may.

"What if they can't get through these locked gates?"

"Tell them to smash through them. We'll pay for any damage. If this shipment isn't on its way to Hong Kong this week, there will be an enormous penalty to pay out."

John carefully relayed the message to the drivers that they had to literally drive through the gates, load up and then drive down to Tilbury again.

Back at Stafford, two of the men thought it was some sort of a wind up. But Ken Blake didn't. The previous week he had nearly lost his job for not doing exactly what he had been told to. So he took great pleasure five minutes after telling the depot security man of his intentions to drive full speed through the wooden gates. And of course by the time he did it, the incident was watched by four rather bemused members of the Stafford police force. They proceeded to arrest Ken, who then had to spend the night in custody, but rather amazingly they allowed the spare parts to be loaded on to the second lorry. The third driver, Mick, was then in a quandary. Mr Cypanski had specifically said that the three drivers had to return to Tilbury. Obviously Ken couldn't. But should he? The only thing on his lorry was some sheeting and ropes. But if anything went wrong on the journey down he knew he would be blamed. So he followed the first lorry, now carrying just a few boxes of spares that could have gone in the back of a van all the way back down to the north bank of the Thames. And after that, because they had been on the road so long without a proper rest, according to standard practice they had to spend a night in a hotel.

And on their way back they stopped outside the depot in Stafford to look at the gates again and remind themselves they hadn't dreamed about the whole affair. One of them went into a shop for cigarettes and saw the local paper, which had a photograph of the gates splashed all over its front page.

A short while later, and rather mysteriously, a copy of the Stafford Evening Gazette landed on the desk of Mr J. Conon Miller, the big boss of the Miller Engineering and Construction Company, and four days later Cypanski was summoned back to America.

He was replaced by Edgar Butterworth and Miles Keating. Edgar's role was to run the place with a little more style and panache than had hitherto been the case. He had started from the bottom in his father's old firm in Baltimore and had quite quickly, and purely on merit it must be said, risen to the rank of engineering manager before the firm had been swallowed up by the Miller Engineering and Construction lot. As a technical man Edgar fully understood most if not all about the company's products. The role of Miles was slightly different. He knew a lot about renaissance architecture, 18th century French classical music and spoke seven languages. This didn't appear to have anything to do with his role in Ashurst, which was simply to ensure that Edgar carried out to the letter the weekly instructions they were each sent in duplicate from across the Atlantic.

So it was no great loss, in fact a great relief, when they packed their bags and left and all the symbols of the great American dream were removed from the various walls and notice boards around the place. And before the American presence was little more than a dream it had been replaced by the nightmare that was Basil. Fortunately he continued to spend most of his time either in London or flying round the world in search of orders, something which he was very good at and ensured that the firm continued to be busy.

One thing that Basil was keen on was the expansion of his empire. But one thing that had always irked him over the years was the presence of The Volunteer right in the middle of the site. It's general position meant that there was always a temptation for anyone going to the Rolling Mill to nip in for a quick one. It also meant that members of the public had a right to be close to the centre of his empire and was particularly worrying on Saturday evenings when the locals sometimes climbed over the wall and sent large cable drums hurtling around the yard.

The Volunteer was also the watering hole of a number of different groups in the town, mainly because of the way in which the place was laid out. There were four small rooms upstairs which could be hired out by the hour. As a result at least a dozen trade union branches held their monthly meetings there, as did the C.N.D., Ashurst Football Referees Society, the Ashurst branch of the Everton Supporters club and Ashurst Train and Bus Spotters club. Other organisations had come and gone, like Hemsley Wine Buffs

Association, mainly because everybody brought their own liquid refreshment, the local Esperanto group, who never spoke English and sounded permanently pissed, and Gillarsfield Astronomy Club. One evening they had invited a speaker from Liverpool University who told the assembled group of the development of unusual cloud formations over the North of England. To understand the point he was making, they had all stood at the window looking at the sky when the landlord had opened the door to make sure everything was all right. All he saw was about ten middle aged men stood on his best chairs craning to look out of his stained glass window. He thought that they were all contemplating some mass suicide leap and so from then on they were relegated to a corner spot in the tap room on the ground floor.

But what had particularly upset Basil about the Volunteer was the incident that occurred during the Works Shutdown. None of the shop floor were working but many of the draughtsmen were in, since they were now allowed to be flexible when they took their holidays. On the first Monday afternoon, hammering and banging was heard coming from the back of the print room. Just as Charlie went to investigate a large hole appeared behind the print machine and the face of the pub manager appeared. He had decided to renovate his store room and put some new shelving in, not fully appreciating what was on the other side of the wall. It was also a very hot day, in fact the next fortnight was to be one glorious heatwave. As soon as Charlie saw what had happened he ordered a pint of bitter, soon to be followed by the others. The same thing happened on the Tuesday and Wednesday, then on Thursday, which was a particularly hot day, most of them had two pints. Friday presented something of a problem since they always went to the Horse and Jockey. But they decided since it was a holiday, they ought to have a change and stay in work during their lunch break. They started straight after coming back from the canteen, so by one o'clock, by which time they should have been back in work, they had all had a couple. But they already were back in work. It was generally agreed that they should carry on since no bosses had appeared all week and John Battesby and Alan Groves, now fully recovered from his accident, were both off as well. So by five to three when the bar man climbed through the hole in the wall and stood in the middle of the Drawing Office and shouted "Last Orders" they were all pretty sozzled.

It was then that they heard from the gate house that Basil had just driven in and was heading their way. Quickly all evidence of their afternoon's pleasure was removed, and by ten past three Basil, accompanied by three visitors from the Zambian State Railways, strode through the office. What the men from Africa made of the smell of yeast and barley and the smiling happy-go-lucky faces of the draughtsmen was a little unclear. Basil's obvious anger at the state of the office however was no doubt minimised by the fact that his visitors were so pleased by what they had seen that they placed a large order for railway electrification equipment. But by the time the draughtsmen returned to work on Monday morning the back of the print room had unfortunately acquired a new wall and the whole incident passed into the history of Wilkinson's Engineering Company.

And this was added to later when the news of Mr. Cypanski's return to America became common knowledge. He had gone straight to Cleveland, given his highly inaccurate account of the whole affair at Stafford to the company Managing Director, then driven to his home about thirty miles out of town. As he drove the last mile, on the left hand side he saw in full bloom the long row of conifers that shielded his stately mansion from the gaze of the common hordes. As always he was speeding at sixty or seventy miles an hour, though a speed of twenty would have been far more appropriate bearing in mind the state of the dirt track road. He approached the old cottage and oak tree on the right hand side and then without losing any speed, he turned sharply to the left with the aim of continuing to drive at breakneck speed past his palatial gardens and greenhouses and screech to a halt in front of the Baroque steps that led up to his home. Unfortunately what he did not know was that while he had been in Europe, his wife had had a pair of wrought iron gates, each eight foot high and six foot wide, built across the gap at the top of the drive and into which he careered. A fitting end to a perfect gentleman!

A few weeks later the incident was repeated as part of a rather unusual publicity stunt. Harold McIntyre, a local gardening enthusiast, having won a small fortune on the pools, had decided to open up a garden centre. Over his garden wall he had discussed his plan with his next door neighbour who purely by chance happened to be Ken Blake, the driver. Harold wanted to get some famous person to open the place one Saturday morning, but Ken had a better idea.

As a result posters went up all over the place announcing that the opening of 'Mac's Garden Centre' in Wigan Lane would be carried out by a re-enactment of "The Storming of Stafford Gates", as the incident had become known in the town. It would be carried out by Ken driving a 1928 Massey Ferguson tractor. And to add a little spice to the proceedings, the tractor would be pulling a trailer in which would be seen scantily clad young girls. That was what the poster said just to make sure none of the town's moral minority tried to stop the event taking place. But as Harold and Ken had said when asked, sheer nakedness would be the order of the day.

On the Saturday morning an extremely large number of men, who one would not have considered as being interested in horticulture, were seen laughing and joking in Cunliffe Avenue outside Harold's house. Stood on his lawn were half a dozen nurses, all smartly turned out in their uniforms. It looked like being a rather interesting affair. After making a little speech, Harold told Ken to get started. He switched on the engine and slowly backed the trailer into Harold's large garage. At the same time all the nurses waved to the crowd, blew kisses and disappeared into the garage. Of course everybody assumed the next few minutes would be spent by them stripping off. Then Harold came to the end of his drive, waved a spade in the air, threw a handful of carrots to the crowd, blew a whistle and shouted "Upwards and onward to the Garden Centre".

The tractor started again and slowly came up the drive, and as it did the trailer and its occupants came into view. Then it turned left, went about a hundred yards down Cunliffe Avenue and turned left again into Wigan Lane and down to the closed gates at the entrance to the garden centre, where about a dozen photographers were waiting. Nakedness there was a plenty for all to see and take snaps of. But not quite what the majority of those assembled there had expected. The nurses were still there, smiling and waving, but they were still wearing their uniforms. But each one was carrying a small baby, each one in its birthday suit!

And ten years later four of the 'nurses' were to strip off on the steps of the Town Hall as a very public protest at the decision of the local Health Authority to close the maternity unit of Victoria Hospital. But that was quite another story.

7.

UNO'S DABS

Among the workforce at Wilkinson's, many would describe sport as one of their main interests in life. Rugby League was the most popular, with St Helens and Wigan commanding the loyalty of the majority. Not quite as many followed soccer, with five teams sharing their loyalties: Earlestown, St Helens Town and Wigan Athletic from the Lancashire Combination, along with Manchester United and Everton.

Many of the company's employees also played a sport with soccer, rugby and crown green bowls the most popular. However, except for bowling in which many of them participated at lunchtime, only four members of the Drawing Office could be placed in the category of player: Alan along with three of the mechanical draughtsmen who were members of the Rugby section. The Social Club ran three teams, unfortunately it was the fifteen-a-side code. It was just one of those strange facts of life that Wilkinsons had always run a Rugby Union section but never a Rugby League team. This was in no small way due to the very biased and negative attitude that the Wilkinson family had always shown towards the thirteen-a-side code, which they considered with near contempt.

No doubt, if the Social Club had run a team it would have played in the Ashurst Open Age League, along with Mather's Foundry, Jarratts, Havanna Miners' Welfare, East Ashurst Social Club and Gillarsfield Labour Club. But whether Alan would have risked life and limb playing in that league was another matter. He knew quite a few lads who did and he knew he was just not big enough or brave enough, or maybe daft enough, to enjoy their company on a field on a Saturday afternoon. He knew that many encounters between these clubs were sometimes more akin to a battle than a sporting occasion. Then on odd occasions there would be friendly matches against teams from other parts of South Lancashire, although the word friendly was perhaps something of a misnomer. Unfriendly games would have probably been a much better description of the event. Yet, amazingly, whenever the participants in these games met socially in the town, they were the best of mates - most of the time.

Playing Union of course required some degree of skill and fitness but it was nowhere near as hard as playing League. Playing Union also had the added advantage of foreign travel, visiting such exotic place as far away as Birkenhead, Sandbach and Fleetwood, or even going as far as Rhyl and Littleborough, which was quite close to the Yorkshire border, although not that close to catch anything infectious.

Usually games were arranged so that the first and third teams would face the first and third teams from a club of similar level of skill while the two second teams would meet at the opposing venue. On the occasion of the last game of the 1968 season, Alan was in the second team playing at home against another works team from Staffordshire of whom nothing was known. When their opponents arrived, it was discovered that not only had the third team been sent instead of the second team, they only had fourteen players, some of whom looked as though they hadn't sobered up from the night before. As a result a very one-sided game took place with Alan scoring five tries as Wilkinsons ran out winners by one hundred and eight points to nil. Unfortunately, what spoiled the whole match completely was the fact that they had to play with a flat ball since all the other balls had gone on the first team coach. This also explained why few tries were converted that afternoon.

The previous week had been memorable for a very different reason. They had visited a rather posh club in deepest Cheshire and walloped their old boys' team by sixty two points to nil. Their hosts took it badly and the atmosphere in the club house after the match was rather frosty to say the least. Losing to a bunch of rough, uneducated buffoons from a Lancashire works team was not the done thing for the Old Welmanites, especially on the day that the club captain had announced that he was to be married after courting his older lady friend Harriet for the last fourteen seasons. Then, five minutes before they decided to leave, Johnny Bradbury, Wilkinson's cocky little scrum half who modelled himself on the great Alex Murphy and who had run the home team ragged all afternoon, discovered a fire hose in the store room at the back of the club house. To liven proceedings up a bit, he dragged it into the ladies toilet, connected one end to the tap and then went back into the bar with the other end sticking out from between his legs. Then his mate Bernard turned on the tap just for a quick burst for a laugh. Johnny proceeded to spray all the home team sat in one corner of the room but unfortunately for everybody else, Bernard couldn't turn the tap off and as a result Wilkinsons were sent a bill for fifty seven pounds for water damage to the club house fixtures and fittings.

At Easter the club had taken part in a rather prestigious seven-a-side competition in Oxfordshire. Just how they had managed to get invited was a bit of a mystery really. There were thirty two teams in the knock out event, including teams representing Wasps, Harlequins and London Irish, along with a number of top teams from the Midlands and one from the Isle of Man, who in the end never turned up. When Basil Wilkinson heard about the club's participation, he agreed to contribute to their overnight stay in a four star hotel in Banbury.

On the way down a large amount of alcohol was consumed and various tricks played. When a bag belonging to one of the younger lads fell off the rack, it was opened up by Ken Rathbone, the first team hooker, who then proceeded to put on the pyjamas he found in there.

They arrived at the hotel close on midnight and marched straight into the main lounge where an obsequious, fawning waiter proceeded to take their order, which was something like twenty four bottles of Guinness, four pints of mild, a pint of mixed and a Makeson. He then sat among this rather strange group of men, the like of which had rarely been seen in Banbury's top hotel or even in the town itself before. The waiter had little interest or knowledge of the game of Rugby, League or Union, but still politely asked questions about their visit to this quiet market town. Various players told him what they did for a living and what position they played. Then the waiter pointed at Ken, still wearing the pyjamas and now fast asleep and snoring loudly in an armchair, and asked what role he played in the team.

"He's the hooker," one of the others told him, "it's his job to hook the ball from the scrum."

"Is that an important position?" the waiter asked.

"Too right it is, old lad. You can't play Rugby without the ball."

"I see," said the ever-smiling, always keen to please and accept a little tip, Cedric, "and is that why he wears the special uniform?"

The following day Wilkinson's Old Boys, as they had been described in the glossy five shilling programme, made their brief appearance. Team selection was based on who was able to stand up and tie the laces in his boots without assistance. Not surprisingly they were knocked out in the first round. By the time the final kicked off there must have been nearly five hundred spectators stood around being entertained by the antics of various members of Wilkinson's club, few if any had ever been in such an environment like this before. Then, with two minutes to go and the surprise local team Broughampton Old Boys winning by a single point, the outstanding winger from one of the top London sides collected the ball on his own line and proceeded to side-step his way round the tiring local heroes. Finally, with the line at his mercy and twenty yards to run, he had the chance to win the game and at the same time get himself noticed by a couple of England selectors who had come up from Twickenham. Then, out of the crowd and onto the field of play, still wearing the pyjamas, appeared Mr Rathbone. As the England hopeful approached him, he slowed down and attempted to side-step round this unwelcome addition to the cause of the local lads. But he tripped over the umbrella that Ken had acquired from who knows where. Then Ken whipped the ball out of his grasp and proceeded to score a highly disputed try at the other end. Not surprisingly, the club was never invited to take part in any Oxfordshire seven-a-side competition again.

And for years after the event, in Ken's little office at the back of Wilkinson's refinery where he worked as a chargehand, was the self same umbrella nailed to the wall, the symbol of Ken's opposition to the antics of upper class twits from around the world.

A few weeks into the 1969 season, Alan, now a regular member of the second team, had suffered a tiny graze to his leg, something which had made him decide to give up playing. Well, that was not quite how he explained his decision, rather it was Charlie's description of the affair.

Right from the start of the season Alan had become injury prone. Every Monday morning he would shuffle down to the Work's Surgery to get attention. At first it was a bit of a laugh, then it became more of an embarrassment. On the sixth week he decided to grin and bear it, although he did have an injury that he felt ought to be looked at. It was all innocuous really; playing as hooker without shin pads he had received a nasty looking cut on his shin. It didn't hurt much and so by half ten he hadn't strayed more than ten yards away from his drawing board.

"Did you not have a game on Saturday, Greeno," shouted out Mick, "or has Sister Broadbent banned you from her boudoir." Alan explained that although he did have some cuts and bruises, he had decided to be brave and share Mick's rivetting company for the whole day or for as long as Mick could stay awake. Then he lifted his trouser leg to show to all and sundry the cut on his shin.

As soon as Mick saw it, his usual laconic attitude to life changed as he told Alan to forget all the joking about his Monday morning absences. "Get down to the surgery straightaway, Alan. That cut is right on the bone. If you've got any infection in it, you could easily lose your leg. Remember what happened to Derek Dooley at Preston."

Then Charlie chipped in and agreed with Mick's medical advice, strange since Charlie rarely agreed with anything Mick ever said. When Yorky said that for once Mick was right, Alan began to think it was another wind up. But he decided that for once they were all being serious. Ten minutes later he was told by Sister Broadbent that it was a bad cut, worse than all the others she had treated and could easily turn septic. For the following two weeks he went to the surgery every morning for treatment. And not once did any of the others make a funny crack about his daily absence. As a result, this served as an excuse to stop playing for a bit and start watching the Saints again. So on the following Friday morning, as was always the case, the conversation moved on to the weekend's game, this time a visit to Derwent Park, the home of Workington Town on the West Cumberland coast.

"Are you going, Charlie?"

"I can't, the brother in law is getting married. I'm really annoyed with him. He's been going out with this woman from Rainhill for ten years; you'd think he could have waited a few more weeks till the end of the season."

"Well we're going. The Social Club are running a coach. It should be a good day out."

"I remember the first time I ever went to Workington. It was in the middle of winter. On the way home the coach got stuck in the snow on Shap Fell. We didn't get home till dinner time the following day. I said I'd never go up there again."

"And did you?"

"Course I did. Frost bite and hypothermia doesn't worry a lad from Thatto Heath. We were bred tough in them days, not like you young ones today. You don't know you're born." Then he continued: "That's where I met the wife, the next time we were up there."

"I thought she was from St Helens."

"She is. She used to live in Duncan Street. She was on our coach, her and her two mates from Parr. When we got back into town we all got dropped off outside the Town Hall. It was late and all the buses had stopped running. So I walked home with her in a blizzard. When we got to the bottom of Croppers Hill she asked me if I wanted to come in for a drink and get warm. It was a bit of a funny thing for her to say really because five minutes after we had sat down, she started taking all my clothes off."

Then Charlie carried on with his reminiscences of times past: "By gum, I've watched the Saints in some bloody bad weather. I remember one year we went to Thrum Hall in the middle of January. It was absolutely freezing. At half time we were chatting to this Halifax couple. We'd met them the last couple of times we had been there. They were a smashing pair. Anyway, the woman asks us who we were playing the following week. So I told her that we were just up the road at Bradford Northern. And do you know what she said. She said you'd better get wrapped up if you're going there. It's always cold at Odsal. And there was her with a big blue and white scarf, a blue and white woolly hat and her hands and face were all blue as well. If I'd put any more clothes on, I wouldn't have got through the turnstiles."

"We always used to stand with this old guy when we played at Halifax," explained Mick. "Every time we went we used to go in what they call the Scratting Shed behind the posts and he'd be there. Herbert, he was called. Then one year we went there for a cup tie and it was absolutely packed so we didn't see him. And after that we never saw him again. Every time I go there I look out for him. I never knew anything about him but he was almost like a friend."

Then he carried on: "I know we take the piss out of Yorkshire folk, and they do the same to us, but I love going to matches over there. I always like going to Belle Vue at Wakefield. That's one of my favourite grounds. I was there for that big cup tie when they filmed some of the scenes with Richard Harris for 'This Sporting Life'."

"So you're a film star then are you Mick? And you've kept it quiet all these years, or was it because you were wearing your demob suit."

Charlie smiled and asked, "Did you ever play, Mick?"

"I did for a bit, but I got a bit lazy and started watching Wigan every week instead. Then one day I was talking to one of the fitters at work about how bad the referee had been the previous week and I said to him that I had half a mind to become a referee."

"That's all it needs," said Alan.

"Jimmy was an official in the local referees' society and he encouraged me so I had a go for a while. It wasn't as good as playing but it got me fit again."

"Did you ever send anybody off?"

"A few. I was once in charge of a cup tie. It was a right needle match, Havanna Miners Welfare against a team from Widnes. We all got changed in this big hut and I could see one of the miners' team winding one of the Widnes lads up. I didn't know at the time but it was his brother in law. Anyway, one thing leads to another and next thing they're both scrapping in this hut. So I sent them off."

"How can you send a man off if they aren't even on the field?" asked Charlie.

"I told them I could do it because it was in the Wigan and District Referees Rule book, section 7, sub section 2, as amended in 1949. I told the two captains these two lads would ruin the game if they played and they both agreed. So we played twelve-a-side and as it turned out it was one of the easiest games that I ever had charge of."

Then he went on: "I'll tell you what was funny, one of the estimators that worked there was a soccer referee and we often used to compare notes on a Monday. He'd been in charge of a cup tie that weekend as well and he told me that he'd sent three off and booked four more. On top of that another finished up in hospital and two others had been seen scrapping in the pub afterwards. 'Who were playing?' I asked him. 'Astley St Mary's and Ashurst Parish Church,' he said."

"Since it looks like being one of those afternoons when we spend our time talking about the good old days, I suppose the issue of my illustrious career with Uno's Dabs should be considered."

"Uno's Dabs, what the bloody hell is that?" asked Keith, who had quietly spent the last half hour looking at pictures of unclothed ladies in a magazine, half tucked away in his drawer.

"Uno's Dabs were a famous amateur Rugby League team who played down Parr in St Helens."

"Don't you think it's strange how Rugby League is only played in the North of England when it's the best game in the world," said Alan, ignoring Charlie's last comment but knowing what would happen if he let him get started on his short career as a player.

"Well, if you know your history it's mainly because it was up here that the players wanted paying for broken time on a Saturday," responded Len.

"Yes I know that, but it's not even played throughout the North, not even throughout Lancashire. Six miles north of Leigh, you are in Bolton and there's little interest at all there in League. And if you ever go up into East Lancashire, round Blackburn and Burnley, they haven't a clue. It's the same in Yorkshire, Barnsley, Rotherham, Sheffield, it's all soccer. I can't understand why they never got a team going round there. Up Newcastle and Gateshead, it's the same there as well."

"There used to be a few teams that played in South Wales before the First World War."

"I know that, Mick," said Alan. "One time when we were in Oldham after a match and we met an old bloke in a pub who had played for Merthyr Tydfil. Just imagine what it must have been like travelling all the way down there for a match."

"Bloody hell," exclaimed Mick, "the horses must have been knackered by the time they got there."

"They would've travelled in a charabanc, Mick, with all mod cons, and whizzed down country lanes at speeds reaching nearly twenty miles an hour," laughed Charlie.

"I take it that you're telling us that from personal experience," responded the Wiganer.

"They probably went on the train. That would've been the quickest way to get down there. But it would be interesting to find out. Just imagine York or Hull KR having to travel to Pontypridd."

"You know there have been some good lads come up from Wales. Reg Blakemore, George Parsons, Reg Cale, Steve Llewellyn, Kel Coslett. We even had one when I played for Uno's Dabs," said Charlie.

"I'll tell you one of the best lads to come North," said Mick. "Billy Boston, one of the finest wingers I have ever had the privilege to watch."

"Well don't forget, Mick, his centre was a St Helens lad, Eric Ashton, and in this game a good winger needs a good centre," replied Charlie. Then he carried on, determined to get one of them interested: "I'll tell you what, I had a cracking centre when I played for Uno's Dabs." But before he could say any more, Keith shouted out:

"Look out, here comes trouble." And moments later, into the office burst Basil Wilkinson, and without as much as a "how's your father", he went over to Len and demanded to know why one of the inspectors was preventing the loading of a control cubicle on to a lorry that had been stood in the works car park for over two hours.

"If that cubicle isn't on Liverpool Docks by nine o'clock tonight I am sacking him," he shouted out, "and you as well."

"Just a minute," said Len, not quite knowing which inspector was being referred to and which control cubicle.

"Don't you point your finger at me, you Bolshie bastard," retorted Basil, pointing his finger threateningly at the Office Committee chairman. "I make the decisions round here. When I say something leaves these premises, it leaves today, not tomorrow or next Saturday morning."

"Well, why did you tell John Barker that nothing can be sent to Karlos Murnch without being inspected to the Hungarian electrical safety standards?"

"What?"

Remembering the inspectors name, Len went on, "If it's John Hunte, he's probably discovered that the wiremen have used red, yellow and blue cable on the power side."

"Well, what's wrong with that? It's standard, isn't it? It is on every other job."

"In Hungary, the earth wire is red." And then, working hard to conceal a smile, he went on: "I thought a man in your position with all your background and education would have known that."

Beaten once again by the Drawing Office, Basil stormed out and going through the top end of the office he was heard muttering such upper class University words as hell, damnation, arrogant little bastard and cards.

"I hadn't the heart to tell him they have probably got the wrong contactors in as well. You know why all this has happened don't you. Vic who looks after the supply of equipment for all the overseas jobs is off sick. Basil has probably told Roger Ellison to modify one of the cubicles that was due to go to that power station in Poland next month. Ellison will have thought that since the two countries were so near to each other, except for different languages on the labels, there wouldn't have been any other alterations called for. Still, I bet Joe Kenny will be pleased."

"Why?"

"He'll have to go out there and rewire the thing and if he does what I told him last week, he'll be suggesting that a draughtsman goes out with him to make a record of all the changes. Oh, I just love Basil's style of management."

"I wouldn't fancy going to Hungary," said Mick, "not at this time of year."

"I wouldn't fancy going to Platt Bridge at any time of year," laughed Charlie, "but if I were on an all expenses paid fortnight in a big posh hotel, I think I could manage it."

"Charlie, how many posh hotels do you know of in Platt Bridge?" laughed Alan.

"I had a good time when I went on that job to Belgium," said Yorky, "and I was only there for three nights."

"When was that" said Len. "I don't remember you going there."

"Course you remember, Len," said Charlie. "It was just before he started visiting the doctor and taking them penicillin tablets. It must have been something he ate: probably the Brussels Sprouts."

8.

LES EARNSHAW AND
HIS SECOND BOOK

"I bumped into Les again in Wigan on Saturday," said Mick. "He'd just bought himself a typewriter."

"How's he getting on with his second book?" asked Charlie.

"How long have you got. We went for a drink in the Bodega. He must have been telling me about it for over an hour."

"So what's it about, is it anything like his first one?"

"At the start it is and then it goes completely different. You remember how he created that fictional town called Garsdale somewhere between Ashurst and Wigan. And in the town there was that chemical works with one of the employees called Albert Entwistle, the one who caused all the trouble at the works dance. Well his second novel is all about him and his adventures. He's a real sports fanatic this Albert; he plays Rugby, he fancies himself as a racing cyclist and he's got his black belt at judo, which few people know about. He's also a big time gambler, well big time for Garsdale, and at the start of the book he owes money to loads of people all over town. So in the second chapter he does a runner and goes living down South. He finds himself a job on a building site and starts playing for the local rugby club. Of course he'd only ever played League before and it was all Union down there, so he has to keep quiet about his past or he'll get banned.

"He starts in the fifth team and he's so good, within two months he's in the first team. A few games later he gets invited to join a much bigger club and the same thing happens, within two months he's in their first team. Now the club chairman is a millionaire and he arranges a right cushy job for Albert in his firm. On top of that he lets Albert live rent free in a hotel he owns and which is little more than a high class knocking shop. So the first part of the book is all about Albert's dealings with the hoi polloi. Then a member of the local gambling fraternity tries to blackmail him after he finds out that Albert is playing about with the chairman's wife. Anyway, it all comes to a head one night when he finds out that Albert has had his wife in bed as well! The two of them have a right set to in the hotel car park, with this other bloke coming off second best. The next day he is found dead in the garden of the club chairman. So of course Albert is seen as the prime suspect and gets arrested."

"Sounds a bit convoluted, even for Les."

"There's more. The police soon discover the real murderer, so they release Albert but it's now common knowledge that Albert has been messing about with other women in the town. By this time the chairman has just about had enough of this uncouth heathen from the North so he tells Albert just before the last match of the season that he is going to sack him and kick him out of the hotel. Albert then proceeds to play a blinder, scores a hat-trick and with three minutes to go his side are winning by a point. He then decides to go out in a blaze of glory. He gets the ball on the half way, turns round and runs towards his own line and drops a goal through his own goal posts, leaving the referee and everybody else in utter confusion. After that he leaves the country, goes to live in France with the Chairman's wife and soon after he gets a job as a mechanic in the Tour de France with one of the top racing teams. There he discovers that one of the team is selling drugs and Albert tries to expose him in the papers but is stitched up by the boss of the local gendarmarie."

"Now this does sound a bit far fetched."

"Especially when he leaves the chairman's wife with a large hotel bill to pay and goes down to Monte Carlo and gets a job as a bodyguard for Bridget Bardot."

"He's winding you up."

Mick laughs and carries on: "One night he has a bit of a run in with the local Mafia in a casino and puts two of them in hospital. Nothing happens until a week later when some of their top hit men arrive from Sicily and try to kidnap Bridget Bardot. He prevents it and in the process kills one of them with what he calls his Billinge Lump Chop."

"He's gone over the top with this."

Mick continues laughing and says: "As a way of thanking him, Bridget Bardot, who has never met anybody like him before, asks him to take her incognito to some exotic location well away from Monte Carlo and the Mafia. So he takes her to the epi centre of Western civilisation and culture and on the Saturday night they go dancing in Wigan Emp. And while they are in there and right out of the blue, Albert bumps into his child hood sweetheart who he hasn't seen for years. He leaves Bridget on her own and goes off with Elsie back to her idyllic little terraced house in Whelley. And so one of the sexiest women in the Western world has to walk down Wallgate to the station and catch the midnight train back to Paris."

"It'd make a fine film," laughed Charlie.

"Mick, how many did you have?"

"I'm just telling you what he told me. He seemed pretty convincing to me."

"He always did."

"What's it called?"

"The Actress Goes To Heaven."

"Well I've heard Wigan called some things in my time, but I've never heard it likened to Paradise," said Charlie.

As usual with Les, there was always an element of truth in what he said he had done or seen or heard about, but this story did seem to be a little bizarre even by his esoteric standards. He had also started going to English Literature classes at night school and enrolled for a correspondence course on creative writing. But he had only been brought up in a little terraced house in Gillarsfield, and then lived in Billinge after he first got married before buying a house in Shaley Brow. His Dad had been a collier and two of his brothers still were. And neither his speech nor his dress or his attitudes had changed one bit. It was clear he had a most fertile imagination, but he was still only a draughtsman and while he clearly had talent, his feet were still on the ground, but only just.

But then Charlie remembered some of the tales he had heard about Les when he was still at school. A few months before they were all due to go out into the big wide world, their teacher had asked each of them to list in order the three jobs they would like to do when they left school. Although one or two in the class had come up with some rather unusual occupations, Les's response was the most colourful to say the least: brain surgeon, TV presenter or submariner. "There are not many of those in Ashurst," his teacher had replied. "I'm not moving away," said Les, "if that's the case I'll be a draughtsman", which is exactly what he became. And except for doing his National Service and working for Ferrantis in Oldham for six months, he continued to live within smelling distance of Ashurst. However, he even created a certain mystique about his time working on the western foothills of the Pennines. The main Ferranti Transformer works was actually located at a place called Hollinwood between Oldham and Failsworth but Les told everyone he met that he had been working in Hollywood and more than a few actually believed that he had moved into the film industry.

"Do you remember that time he thought he was Napoleon?" asked Len.

"Eh, I thought you would get his facts right before you could say a thing like that," said Charlie.

"Well it was something like that."

Then, turning to Keith, Charlie went on: "Les was always watching historical programmes on the TV. One night he was watching a programme about the war in Poland and it mentioned a small town where there had been some heavy fighting, Vlodipotsch or something it was called. As soon as Les heard this name, he was convinced he had been there before. He lay awake for hours that night and when he finally dropped off to sleep, he dreamed about being in Napoleon's army that tried to conquer Moscow in the early part of the nineteenth century. When he looks this place up on the map the next day, he remembered the names of the next two places as well. Then over the next few weeks he remembered other things. He got loads of books out about Napoleon from their library and it all convinced him that he had had a previous life as a French peasant."

"He just made it all up," said Mick. "He couldn't speak a word of French."

"And did he reckon that he actually knew Napoleon?" asked Keith.

"Aye, Napoleon brandy," said Yorky.

"He told all this to that young student we had with us for a bit, that University lad Simon from Guildford. He was convinced Les was telling the truth and he was a pretty clever lad."

"I'll tell you how clever that bugger was" said Yorky. "Les told him after the French army got back to France, Napoleon was put on trial and then sent into exile."

"Well that's true," said Charlie.

"Well Les told this lad that some of old Boney's most trusted men were sent with him, and do you know where Les said they were all exiled to, eh?.. St Helens."

"Well he was only joking with the lad," laughed Charlie.

"Les isn't the only literary genius round here, you know," said Alan. "I'm writing a novel as well."

"You've been telling us that for months," laughed Charlie. "Have you finally started it? Is it about your Grandad and how he won the War?"

No it wasn't. He was still working on that, but reading Les's first book had inspired him to do something similar. Just like Les, Alan had set his novel in South Lancashire. His main character was an apprentice electrician who played a few games for the St Helens under 19 team but didn't get signed on. Then on his twenty first birthday he packed his job in and went hitch-hiking in the South of France through the summer and had loads of adventures, near scrapes and a dance with death. Half way through the story he saved a little girl from drowning in a river. Her father was the coach of Perpignan and so the lad gets to play for a season in the French Rugby League. At the start of the following season they play the Saints in a friendly and he played a blinder, on the wing opposite Tom Van Vollenhoven, and scored a hat-trick, but in the last minute he gets laid out by his boyhood hero, Duggie Greenall, and finished up in Peasley Cross Hospital with his arm in plaster of Paris.

"Shouldn't that be plaster of Perpignan?" asked Charlie wryly.

"Is there any sex in it?" enquired Dickie.

"There's a lot early on when he gets a lift with four Swedish nurses in a removal van and he rides all the way from Lille to Bordeaux with them."

"Obviously something you made up."

"And there was one lift he got with a headmistress from Brussels who was going to Madrid for her daughter's wedding. And that was based on personal experience, you may like to know."

"And there was you laughing at Keith when he had that fling with that fifty year old tracer from Jarratts."

"Well, I'm sure you'll all be pleased to hear that I'm going to write a book as well," said Yorky.

"Not you as well. This place is getting like a library. What's it called?"

"The Nineteenth Century Revisited: Life in Lancashire To-Day."

"What about tomorrow?"

"You cheeky bugger. We've taught you all you know, we let you travel on our buses, breathe our lovely fresh air, observe the region's panoramic views, enjoy our rivetting company and that's how you treat us. Typical bloody Yorkshire folk."

> "See All, Hear All, Say Nowt
> Eat All, Sup All, Pay Nowt
> And if Tha ever does anything for Nowt
> Do it for Thisenn."

"You know I've often thought of writing about what I did in the Merchant Navy in the War. Struggling across the Atlantic in gale force winds, being chased and nearly sunk by a U-boat and then on that Murmansk run, when the temperatures were down to about minus thirty."

"Why haven't you?"

"I can never find a pencil in our house, that's why."

"Will there be any sex in it?" asked Alan.

"Yes. We had a picture of Betty Grable on the canteen noticeboard showing her knees, both of them."

But before he could say any more the sound of Alan Groves's footsteps could be heard, and so for the next couple of hours work became the order of the morning until first the five to, then the slightly shriller three to, and finally the all consuming twelve o'clock hooter, the very welcome Final Hooter, sounded informing everybody that for the next hour they were free to eat, sleep, look at the girls from the foundry sat on the wall or play bowls.

Paying five pence a week into the Social club allowed Wilkinson's employees to join a number of different societies and take part in a wide range of sports. These included football, rugby , cross country, hockey and badminton in the winter and in the summer, cricket, athletics, fishing, rounders and bowls. The last one was one of the most popular since it could be enjoyed every lunchtime. Almost every day there would be around twenty or so pairs on each of the greens that the groundsman had opened that day. Forty bowlers on one green was not only far too many, it was also extremely dangerous. You took not so much your life in your hands as you ran across the crown, rather the risk of serious injury to your ankles. One man who knew that to his cost was Roger Ellison, the senior foreman in the Rolling Mill. He had been a real creep when he had been a junior foreman; the thing that had given him the most pleasure in life was telling tales to the bosses and seeing people punished for just enjoying life. Now that he had been promoted, he had more power to upset more people. As a result whenever he went out for a walk with his friends he had to talk to himself, primarily because he would be on his own.

However, he did like a game of bowls and usually played every Monday with Ernie, one of his chargehands. Whenever he was on the green it was hilarious to watch. The normal rules of bowls were ignored. Any Drawing Office league matches were quietly cancelled. Everyone would wait until he started to follow his second bowl as it headed towards the jack, muttering "go on, go on, go on, go on", and then rather infrequently "it's a toucher". As soon as he was within five yards of the crown around half a dozen would let fly and try and hit him on the ankles. But he was so wrapped up with his game that he failed to realise that this happened every time.

The lunchtime games were a real social event. Inevitably there would be around ten men dressed in their overalls and boiler suits stood watching around each of the greens, although there were always more around the green on which Roger Ellison was in attendance. Playing or watching bowls each lunchtime and the resulting afternoon conversation was indeed a major item of entertainment for many of Wilkinsons' employees.

One of the keenest bowlers was Ronnie Garner. A few weeks earlier he had gone down to a factory at Belvedere in Kent with the electrician, Frank, another keen bowler. One afternoon they had decided to have a break from checking a batch of high voltage circuit breakers and gone for a drink at a nearby pub. Their eyes lit up when they saw that it backed on to a bowling green. Not paying much attention to the other bowlers on the green, they collected their bowls from a small shed and decided that this was how they would spend the afternoon. Ronnie put his mat on the ground and carefully bowled off the jack across the green. As he did he commented that it didn't have much of a crown, a bit like that one at Garswood that was directly over an old pit shaft and badly affected by mining subsidence. Suddenly there was mayhem. The other dozen or so bowlers all wearing white jackets and trousers or skirts and white pumps, and all probably old aged pensioners, looked and muttered at them as though they had started to dig for oil on the grass.

"You can't do that. Have you never played this before? Who are you? We'll call the police", different ones said as they advanced menacingly towards the two bemused men from the North.

"We are only playing bowls, old lad. What's the matter with thee all?"

"Well you should keep to your own line," said another. "Whoever heard of such a thing?"

Then a friendly voice from an old man sat on a bench asked them to walk over to him.

"Where are you from, lads?" he asked with an accent that sounded vaguely familiar.

"Ashurst in Lancashire," said Ronnie.

"Well round here they don't play bowls like you do. There's no crown and you have to bowl up and down the line."

So they had a go at this strange way of playing their traditional game but found it too boring and with a bad atmosphere from the other bowlers all around them. Within ten minutes they were sat with the old man. They listened to him talk and within a few minutes discovered from the way he spoke he was also from the Red Rose County, though probably from around Blackburn or Burnley by the way he sounded his r's.

Then in the heat of the hot afternoon he told them his story. Things didn't start that way, it was just as though he hadn't had any one to talk to for a long time. He had been brought up in Great Harwood as a lad, an only child rather an unusual thing in those days. He had fought in France during the last two years of the First World War and been badly injured three days before the Armistice. He had spent nearly a year recovering in a hospital near Seven Oaks and then married one of the nurses. They had raised a family of three lads, one of whom had been killed at Dunkirk, one who had died in the London blitz and the third who had emigrated to Australia and with whom they had lost touch. Then his dear wife had passed away in 1966, leaving him to look after himself and his house of happy memories at the age of 73.

He hadn't been back up North since 1938 when he attended the funeral of his last remaining relative, but he clearly still hankered for those happy days as a lad in the first decade of this brave new century. Neither Ronnie nor Frank knew much about East Lancashire, rarely having travelled any nearer than Rochdale, but they both sensed a bond of friendship with him. Then he invited them back to his neat little semi nearby and was so pleased not only to have someone in his house but also to be able to serve them tea and biscuits. He pointed out who was who on the many photographs around the walls, then showed them his war and sports medals and a pair of football boots he had worn in a 1912 Sunday school cup match at Peel Park, the home of Accrington Stanley. The time passed quickly, perhaps too quickly for the old man, and soon it was time for them to say goodbye. They shook hands almost solemnly and wished him all the best. But they were sure the next few days or months or even years would continue to see him pottering around almost certainly on his own until he was reunited with those who knew him best.

On the way back home in the works van, they talked about him and the lonely life he appeared to lead and how much more friendly things seemed to be in the North. But of course they were two Northern lads who had lived most of their lives in the same town, whereas their erstwhile colleague had been away from his home town for years and had lost contact with all his friends from the past. As they talked they agreed that despite the tyrannical Basil aiming to make their lives a misery, despite the dirty industrial environment that Ashurst was part of and contributed greatly towards, there was on the other hand a general degree of friendliness or comradeship among most of those who worked within the factory and lived within the town. Of course there were miserable ones within their ranks, others they couldn't trust, others who were boring, always on the cadge or told lies. There were no doubt some who beat their wives, stole from their neighbours or committed other forms of anti-social behaviour. Ashurst was definitely no paradise on Earth but they were both pleased that they lived there, worked at Wilkinson's and able to have a proper game of bowls whenever they wanted to.

9.

PHILOSOPHY IN THE COLLIERS' ARMS

Sunday evening found Alan and Thelma, Johnny Shufflebottom and his wife Margaret, and Ken Parr and his wife Janice sat in the back room of the Colliers' Arms. Not surprising they were all a little on the glum side, for the previous day at Station Road, Swinton, at the far end of the East Lancashire Road, Leeds had beaten the Saints by nine points to five in the Championship Final in front of over twenty four thousand spectators. After a while they were joined by Ronnie Harper and his wife Dorothy. Though also unhappy with the final score, 'Harpo' was in a very good mood. Before they had caught the train to Swinton, he had put two pounds on a horse called The Cornish Lady that was running at Haydock that afternoon and it had come in at thirty three to one.

How many times the words 'if only' were used in the next hour was unbelievable. 'If only Coslett had been able to keep hold of Hardisty before he had managed to get that pass to Atkinson.' 'If only Pimblett had been able to hold on to that pass from Benyon.' 'If only Heaton had gone himself instead of passing to Rees just before half time'. 'If only Clawson hadn't got his fingertips to that pass from Kelly to Wilson'. And of course 'if only the referee hadn't left his glasses at home'. But then Dorothy was able to put the whole thing in its proper context when she reminded everybody that seven days earlier at Wembley Stadium down in London the two teams had met again, though this time the winners had been the men from Knowsley Road by sixteen points to thirteen.

Their conversation moved on to the day itself and the people they had seen in the capital. Ken had bumped into his uncle who now lived at Greenwich in Kent. Janice had seen one of the chargehands from work with a ginger haired woman who was certainly not his wife. Johnny had met his brother on the Underground, while Alan had brushed shoulders with Frank Carlton, an old Saints star from the Fifties. Then Dorothy mentioned that she had seen her dozy brother in town the previous day and how his first visit to Wembley had not exactly got off to a good start. For once he had managed to get inside the ground in good time for the kick off. Then he decided because he was early he would go and buy himself a hot dog. Unfortunately he found himself in the queue behind a large man who wanted not one hot dog but one hot dog for every member of the Keighley Albion Rugby League club and their wives and girlfriends. So by the time he had got to his seat it was two minutes past three and he could see the Leeds captain Alan Hardisty preparing to kick off. He turned to his mate sat on the seat next to him, laughed and said, "I told you I wouldn't miss owt."

"I'm sorry old lad, but you did. They kicked off two minutes early. Hepworth tried to clear his line, Graham Rees charged it down, chased it and scored after less than a minute.

Coslett's converted it and we are winning five-nil."

And then, as if to add insult to injury, his mate went on, "Can I have a bite of your hot dog.?"

Soon it was time for another trip to the bar and as Alan was placing the drinks on the tray that Ronnie was holding, they heard a familiar voice behind them. It was Pete Slemp, who had been in their class at Lane Head Junior School but who they hadn't seen for nearly fifteen years. They shook hands and discovering that he was on his own, they invited him to join them. He immediately recognised Dorothy, Ken and Johnny, who he had once shared a desk with in Miss Welsby's class. Then he told them what he had been doing since he had last been in their company.

His father had been a G.I. at the Burtonwood American Air Base. In 1950 he had returned home to Boston taking his wife and three children with them. Shortly after, he moved into the world of real estate and property development and by buying and selling land in New Hampshire and moving financial documents around, he had amassed a large fortune. As a result, for two years after leaving high school, he had paid for his son to travel widely all over Latin America, from Mexico City down to the southern tip of Chile at Tierra del Fuego. Then Pete had gone to Yale University and excelled himself, not so much in the classrooms and lecture halls but more by playing American football. On the campus he had been able to impress others with his tales of the many touchdowns he had scored as a quarterback, but among an audience of Rugby League people in the North of England, his exploits were considered with the same degree of awe and admiration as if he had told them in graphic detail how he had won the Mid-West inter-state under nineteens indoors draughts championship. Then he went on to tell them he had been staying at his uncle's house in Gillarsfield and would be around for another week.

While he had been at Lane Head school, Pete had frequently taken part with all the other boys in the playground in what was known as scrag and bash. He had pushed and shoved with the best of them, cut his knees on the ground, banged his elbows against the walls and frequently gone home with his short trousers or pullover ripped and blood on his shirt. As a result he had some appreciation of the toughness and skill that was needed to play Rugby League.

"Did you go to Swinton yesterday, Pete?"

"No, but I saw the Cup Final on the television last Saturday."

"What did you think of it?"

"I really enjoyed it. I haven't seen anything like that for years."

"Do you remember the first time you came to watch the Saints with us?" asked Ronnie. "When we played Whitehaven and there was a great brawl just in front of the boys' pen. Jonty Pilkington was in great form and put three big Cumbrians in hospital before he got sent off."

"I do. It was when we were in Mrs Duxberry's class."

"How do you fancy having a game now?" said Ronnie. "I think you'll find it a bit tougher than your American football."

"I've not got my boots with me," said Pete with a wry smile on his face. "Maybe next time I'm in these parts, eh."

"So what are you doing for a living?" asked Alan.

"At the moment I'm involved in research work for an educational foundation in New York. We're trying to develop an ideological link between sport and philosophy."

"Why?" said Ronnie.

"Because it's important. Sport is popular wherever you go in the world. But few people are interested in philosophy, they do not grasp the importance of its links with their everyday lives. Yet the Russians and the Chinese have their philosophy and they are using it to try to change the world. We want to keep it as it is. We need to make more people, and particularly students, appreciate the wide sweep and depth of the different philosophies and philosophers that we have had in the West."

"Don't tell us you're working for the C.I.A.," said Alan.

"Special agent, Peter Slemp Junior, O.B.E.," said Johnny in a voice that sounded just like a drunken version of Burt Lancaster.

Then Dorothy chipped in: "Don't let's get on to politics Alan or else we'll be here till midnight." Then, turning to Pete, she went on: "First of all, what do you mean by philosophies and philosophers?"

"Well let me put it this way. Philosophies are combinations of ideas, which while referring to objective realities are essentially mental in character. However the tools of thought, the concepts used for intellectual production in the field of philosophy, have origins similar to the material means of production that men fabricate. These concepts have been created in accord with the evolution of man's productive powers and out of his changing social relations.

"And as to who are the philosophers, well philosophy was born in the Aegean civilisation in the Sixth Century B.C. One of the very first philosophers was Miletus, though perhaps the names Plato and Aristotle are much better known to you all."

"You knew all that, didn't you Dot?" said Ronnie. Then turning back to Pete he said: "She was only talking about it to one of the neighbours last week in the butchers."

Ignoring her husband's flippant comment, Dorothy went on: "So for example, are you trying to get students to understand Greek philosophy by comparing it to different aspects of sport?"

"Yes, sort of, in a round about way."

"Well answer me this. What is the link between Greek philosophy and Rugby League?"

"There isn't one," said Ken. "How can there be. They never played Rugby in Greece then. It was only invented in Huddersfield in 1896."

"1895 actually," said Alan.

"Sorry, I wasn't there, unlike you."

"Ignore them," said Dorothy. "Tell me about this guy Plato. What did he say?"

Realising that he had an opportunity to impress them with his knowledge, Pete decided to start with Plato's Theory of Forms. But he knew it wouldn't be easy, not on a Sunday night in a pub, least of all the Colliers' Arms, which was not well known for its appreciation of mental agility and intellectual prowess. So he began by asking if the room was warm.

"What sort of a daft question is that. Course it's warm. If it wasn't, we'd have gone to the Nags Head," laughed Alan.

"Answer the question," said Pete.

"Yes."

"What would you be if you were wearing a scarf, balaclava, two big jumpers and an overcoat?"

"Hot."

"And what would you be if you were sat here with no clothes on at all?"

"Probably fancied by every woman in the place."

Pete smiled. He'd been away from Lancashire a long time but had not forgotten the natural sense of humour that its inhabitants possessed.

"I'd be cold, if that's the answer you want."

"So at the same time this room could be described as cold, warm and hot."

"Yes."

"So what is it, all three?"

"Yes, it's hot if you stand near the fire, it's warm where we are sat, but it's cold round my feet when there's a draught from that door when it's open. So yes, Plato must be right."

They all went quiet for a moment, not quite sure of the significance, or lack of it, in what Pete had said. Then Margaret threw the cat among the pigeons when she told Pete that her cousin Kevin had studied philosophy at Leeds University and that he had introduced her to some rather strange concepts and so, with that little bit of knowledge, she asked Pete to explain Plato's idea of horse.

"Was Plato a betting man then?" asked Ronnie. "Did he ever go to Haydock?"

Pete laughed, then asked Ronnie what seemed a very simple question.

"Do you know what horse is?"

"Of course I know. A horse has got four legs, a tail and is about this high if it's a big horse."

"What colour is horse?"

"Well that depends what colour it is. It might be a white horse or a brown horse or a black horse."

"Look, when I say horse what comes into your head is the idea of horse, not any specific horse."

"No you're wrong. If you'd mentioned horse to me this morning I would tell you it was The Cornish Lady I was thinking of. I had two quid on it."

"What Plato projected in his Theory of Forms is the view that the idea represents the most ideal form of a thing and everything else is a mere copy of it. You can have the idea of horse in your head without knowing what colour it is, or whether it is young or old, or whether it is a racehorse or a carthorse."

"That's right," said Ronnie. "I thought The Cornish Lady was a racehorse, everybody else at Haydock must have thought it was a carthorse. That's why it was at thirty three to one. Good old Plato."

Ignoring the comment, Pete then went on to quote the other concept frequently used to attempt to account for one of Plato's fundamental thoughts.

"Here's another example," he said. "What is bed?"

"It's where horse goes to when it's tired," proffered Ronnie.

"A bed is like a place where you go to recover from the exertions of the day," said Thelma.

"It's also a place where you go to for the exertions of the night," laughed John as he smiled at his wife and put his hand on her knee.

"No. Bed can be seen as an idea. It doesn't have to be seen as a specific entity."

"Well, it's bound to have four legs and some blankets and a pillow, isn't it?"

"Wrong. What about a hammock in a ship, or kipping down in a sleeping bag or on straw?"

"This is all too complicated for me," said Janice, running her hand over her brow, "It's making me feel tired."

"Well you'll have to go to bed, won't you, but make sure there isn't the idea of a horse in it."

Then Alan chipped in with a seemingly odd comment when he said: "Here's a thought then. Never mind horse or bed. Take the idea of match, not what's in a match box but in sport. It might be Saints v Wigan, or Gillarsfield v UGB. Then again it could be Liverpool v Everton, or Argentina v Brazil. It could be Wales v England at Cardiff Arms Park or a tennis match in the Davis Cup. Different sports, different countries but everybody knows what is meant by a match, just the idea of the word."

"So what's that got to do with Plato?"

"Well the idea of match is like the idea of bed or horse, it's just an idea of the thing generally without being specific."

"Aren't you a clever bugger, Greeno."

"Here's another idea. When you go to a match what do you see, and do you see the same things as the guy stood next to you?"

"You must do unless you're stood behind a stanchion or a six foot six man with a trilby on his head."

"Do you remember when Wigan played Saints on Good Friday? The following Tuesday, Charlie and Mick had a right big argument about it and to listen to them talk you would think they'd both been at totally different games."

"Well you know what Wiganers are like, they only ever see what they want to."

"I remember a couple of years ago Billy Rathbone having a right ding dong with our Paul. He was blaming Dick Huddart for losing us the game against Bradford Northern and how he wasn't training and not fit. The daft thing was Huddart wasn't playing that day but Billy wouldn't have it. So he was seeing things that weren't there."

"He must have got in the Black Bull too early."

"So what's all that got to do with philosophy?"

"No, I'm just saying that things are not always what you think they are. Even watching the Saints can be viewed in different ways, your perception of the action may be clouded by different factors."

"Perception? That's a clever word for you, Greeno. Are you trying to baffle us with science? What does it mean?"

Then Margaret threw in a bit more that she had gleaned from her brother Kevin, when she told them that his favourite philosopher had been Hegel.

"I've never heard of him," said Ronnie, "but then I don't suppose he's ever heard of me. Was he big on horses or did he spend all his time in the idea of bed?"

"Or at the match," laughed Alan.

"They didn't have matches in the Duchy of Wurttemberg at the end of the 18th century," said Pete somewhat reluctantly.

"So how did they light their fires?" asked Johnny.

"To really appreciate what Hegel offered, it's first necessary to understand that there are two traditions in the field of philosophy. The Materialist tradition, those who argue that things can only be explained in terms of material causes, and the Idealist tradition, those who argue that things can only be explained in terms of mental causes. What Hegel did was to combine Idealism with Realism by means of his dialectical method in which the thought of the philosopher becomes identical with the objective development of reality."

Then, realising he had lost them, Pete went on: "The essence of his philosophy was that you start off first with the idea and from that springs the social practice, and from that emerges more advanced ideas through a linked process of thesis, anti-thesis and synthesis."

"That's pretty obvious," said Ken. "I had the idea that we'd go out for a drink tonight. And so I engaged in the action of putting some clean clothes on and came down here on the bus. Is that what can be described as social practice?"

"The philosopher who came after him had the right idea," chipped in Alan. "It was Karl Marx. He turned Hegel's ideas on their head and said you start off first with the social practice. From that emerges the ideas and they lead on to new forms of social practice.

"So that means that I had to engage in the practice of going out for a drink on a Sunday night for weeks and from that I was able to get the idea of going out for a drink on a Sunday night which led to a new form of social practice, like going out on a Saturday night for a drink, which is something I've been doing for the last six years."

"Hang on a minute," said Janice "Is that right Margaret, that in philosophy you start off with an idea and from that comes the practice. I mean I've got the idea of going on my holidays to Greece next year. Is that right? What happens if we don't go or change our minds?"

"Oh, I don't know. It's just what our Kevin told me. The only other thing I can remember about Hegel was that he was once sat in a coffee bar in Stuttgart or somewhere and watched Napoleon with his troops on the way to invade Moscow and conquer Russia. Hegel made the comment that he'd just seen the spirit of the 19th century, whatever that means."

"I thought you were going to say he'd just seen Les Earnshaw."

"And who might Les Earnshaw be?" asked Pete, now resigned to the fact that discussions on the nuances of Plato, Aristotle and Hegel could no longer be pursued that evening with any degree of seriousness.

"Les Earnshaw is a modern day writer, contemporary thinker and outstanding philosopher all rolled into one," said Alan.

"I think I have heard of him vaguely but I haven't come across any of his writings.

Does he have a chair at Harvard?"

"No, he's got them all in the living room," quipped Ronnie.

"Except when he hears that the mother-in-law is coming and he puts them all in the shed and locks the door," laughed Alan.

"So what's brought you back here, Pete?" asked Janice.

"I'm attending a conference at York University next week so I just thought I'd take the opportunity to come over here for a few days."

"And in the great name of freedom and the great American dream, have you been to Vietnam yet?"

"Oh, don't let's start about Vietnam," said Dorothy, "or we'll be here till midnight. I've only come for a drink."

"You know that our government is in Vietnam to protect the Vietnamese."

"Is that why you're bombing Vietnamese villages. To protect them from themselves. You lot go all over the world interfering in other people's affairs and causing trouble. Now I've nothing against you Pete or any other ordinary American but your Government is the cause of half the trouble in the world today. And if Plato was alive today, he'd say the same thing."

"Well I don't want to get involved in politics, my interest is only in philosophy as you have probably gathered. And it looks as though we are not going to be able to discuss things in any depth as I can see they are getting ready for the bingo. It's been very nice seeing you all but I don't want to spend the rest of the evening arguing, not in this place. So I'll say goodbye and hope to see you all again." And as quickly as he had burst into their lives after a long absence, he disappeared.

Before much more could be said, it was time for the entertainment and for the rest of the evening they listened first to a comedian from Abram and then a singer from Warrington who did impersonations of Frankie Lane, Frank Sinatra, Dean Martin, Perry Como and a host of other American singers.

And, interestingly, the next time they were out together, Dorothy surprised Alan when she asked him why there was a war going on in Vietnam. And, ironically, following their brief talk with Pete, she now seemed able to accept that everything that she read in her Dad's Daily Mail just might present only one side of an issue. But she had to admit that she still couldn't understand what relevance Pluto and Harry Stottle had to do with understanding what was going on in the world around her.

10.

VISITORS FROM OUTER SPACE

The first thing to hit any visitor to Ashurst was its smell, or rather its many varied smells. Coming out of George Street station the first quite pleasant impact on the nose came from Whitaker's brewery in Railway Street. Turning left and crossing over the railway bridge, the first thing to hit the eye was Ashurst Gas works with the accompanying all pervasive smell of gas. Proceeding down Atherton Street, the unsuspecting visitor would then feel that he had moved back into the 19th century as he walked towards Delaney's Foundry, now a shadow of its former glory and soon to be demolished. Behind it could be seen Mount Everest, a slag heap so named because it had been created by the chemical firm Everards at the turn of the century. In 1952 the firm had been taken over and moved to the North East. Unfortunately the new owners did not have the common decency to take their slag heap with them. A little further on was the Havanna colliery, with its winding gear and own tip of industrial waste dominating the landscape. And from there could also be seen the smaller and older Bank Top colliery about a mile away and now under threat of closure.

Turning right out of the station and then right again past the old trolley bus garage the first thing to be seen was the distinctive frontage of the old Rivoli cinema, now operating as the Empire Bingo club. Next to it was the Eldorado night club, temporally closed following a recent altercation between a gang of youths from Hemsley and two bouncers. Next door was a Chinese takeaway, run by a man from Manchester who spoke Mandolin, then a paper shop and a bookies. Next to it was a little park and then Wallworks, Mathers Foundry and Wilkinsons, the biggest factory in the town. Not surprisingly, and particularly when it was a windy day, there was a rare collection of pungent odours to be experienced.

Coming out of the station and walking straight ahead, any visitor would soon be in the centre of the town. Within ten minutes he or she would be through the place and approaching Sacred Heart Church on the left and Ashurst Parish church on the right, two imposing Christian buildings that both glowered at each other. Then it was derelict land on either side of Billinge Road for the next quarter of a mile and where the Bankers used to live. However, it must be emphasised that they were not those well dressed and cultured gentlemen who spend their days moving large amounts of money around and who get extremely well paid for doing so. It was because the area had once been known as Hyde Bank, having expanded in the early part of the nineteenth century around that den of iniquity, The Hyde Bank Arms. It was a well chosen name for another good reason because whenever the police, or rent collectors, or women with babies in their arms, came into the place, the men were always hidden away somewhere and could never be found.

Another half a mile or so on the left hand side was Gillarsfield colliery and behind it in the distance what was left of the Prince of Wales colliery. Opposite was Jarratts Machine Tools and then Dawson's chocolate works, from which always emanated a rather sweet smell. Another hundred yards down the road was one of the three waterways that flowed in the area, this one known as Stinky Brook, relatively clean until it flowed past the back of Jarratts.

In the centre of Ashurst was the Town Hall built in 1895. Directly in front of it was a large square dominated by a statue of Queen Victoria. Bus shelters were located all round the square and from there travellers could get to all parts of the town and to some of the major centres of population in the Western world like St Helens, Wigan, Leigh, Warrington and Widnes. Liverpool and Manchester could also be reached. And on match days it was possible to take a coach to even more exotic places like Featherstone and Castleford, Batley and Dewsbury, Whitehaven and Workington.

A small number of those who came to work in Ashurst were not that impressed with the town, particularly the graduate apprentices who often hailed from such pleasant places as Chichester, Salisbury, Stow on the Wold and Chipping Sodbury. For them, Ashurst was definitely a culture shock. On the other hand, Mick confessed that he always felt at home in the place, but then he only came from Platt Bridge in Wigan. Charlie often used to compare the town's thoroughfares with Elephant Lane in Thatto Heath, though never favourably. On a good day, Yorky was sometimes prepared to accept that the ambiance and geo-physical nuances of the area had much in common with his own childhood memories of his parents' large country estate in Mytholmroyd.

Various jokes were made about the town like how the Luftwaffe had targetted it in the early days of the War, destroyed half of it and done nearly ten pounds worth of damage. Others told how when the Roman legionnaires were marching from Chester up to Hadrians Wall, the Praetorian Guard found things so bad there that they had to run through the hamlet while holding their fingers to their noses. How true this was no one knew, though the existence of Sprint Lane at the back of Mathers' Foundry was often cited as evidence.

The town was always considered to be a bit of a backwater by its more cultured neighbours. But what it didn't have in terms of sophistication and panache, it made up for in terms of the many characters who lived there. Among these were the National Secretary of the James Dean fan club, who believed he was still alive, two sisters who lived in Virgil Street off Dob Lane and who worked on the tills in Hemsley Co-op by day and engaged in witchcraft at the weekend in Liptrot's wood, and also a small number of devotees of the Unified Church of the All Fearful, who practised celibacy, abstinence and vegetarianism, but never at the week end or on a Bank Holiday unless it fell on a Wednesday.

One of the slightly more reasonable odd balls in the town was the current Mayor, John Taylor. He had been a member of the Labour Party for years, in fact it was often said that he had recruited Keir Hardie into the Young Socialists. If ever there was a menial task to be done, John would volunteer to do it. He really had little interest in the grand sweep of politics, the thrust of a sharp ideological discussion or the excitement linked with a big public campaign, like the one that Alan had taken part in to keep the station open. All John wanted to do was serve the interests of the people of Ashurst. Maybe that was putting things a bit too widely. Really all he wanted to do was serve the interests of the people of his Moss Hill ward and particularly those who lived in Mossdale Avenue and very particularly those at twenty three, which were his wife and him, in that order. Issues like the Vietnam War, the OPEC oil crisis, the miners' strike and the three day week seemed to pass him by. What was much more important to him was being able to see the binmen doing their business before eight 'o' clock every Thursday morning and the number seven bus running on time to take his neighbours into town to pick up their pensions and visit the library which he had always taken immense pride in.

John liked to describe himself as a civil servant, a rather glowing description of his function as a wages clerk in the Town Hall. He was a Walter Mitty in the making. His belief was that once he became the Mayor he would make such an outstanding contribution to the well-being of the town that his name would go down in the history books as the great saviour of the people and particularly of Moss Hill. In particular he looked forward to what would be the greatest tribute Ashurst could bestow on him, the opening of a library in Grasmere Avenue where the old workhouse used to be and called the John Taylor Memorial Library.

Perhaps his only vice was a love of good food, particularly when he didn't have to pay for it. He knew that as Mayor he would have to attend many functions both in the town and further afield. He hoped he might even get a call to visit Buckingham Palace, certainly there would be trips to the House of Commons to see various Ministers of the Crown and the local M.P. and surely at least one trip abroad. So he looked forward with great excitement to his first engagement, meeting the residents of the Carlton Street Old People's Club in Gillarsfield at eleven 'o' clock. He wondered where he would be taken for his first banquet.

The Mayoral car picked him up from the Town Hall at ten to eleven and by driving very slowly his driver managed to arrive bang on time at Carlton Street. John was resplendent in a pin-striped suit, around which was draped his Mayoral Chain and bowler hat. As he walked into the club one of the old ladies began clapping and her equally senile friend nudged her and asked whether it was Neville Chamberlain who had come to visit them.

For the next hour he walked round the club, shook hands with everybody, shook hands with some people twice and four times with one old dear who kept asking him if he could get her some new false teeth. Finally, the club steward Horace ushered all the members of the committee into the television room and made a short speech. He spoke of their gratitude to John for honouring them with the first visit of his Mayoral year and stressed how in the world of great changes, it was their intention to maintain the old traditions that the Carlton Street Old Peoples' Club held so dearly. John of course nodded in full agreement and in his speech promised them that honouring old traditions was close to his heart and would dominate his year in office. All the committee clapped vigorously and then Horace said the words that John had been wanting to hear for the last hour.

"Well, I think it's now time to eat."

They walked out of the committee room and headed for the doors. Again just about everybody in the place succeeded in shaking his hand again. They walked along the road, with John quite puzzled as to where the most important part of the visit would be held at.

He was soon to be unpleasantly surprised. They turned down into Canal Street and proceeded to walk into Martindale's chip shop.

"It's always our tradition that we bring the Mayor here," said Horace, "and it's always our tradition that the Mayor gets served last and pays for it all."

And ten minutes later they were all stood outside the shop eating fish, chips and mushy peas with Horace telling John that he had organised a charity twenty four hour darts competition and hoped that the new Mayor would be prepared to throw the first dart and stay to watch the last one!

Another bit of an odd ball was his wife, Prudence Taylor; well she had to be, living with him all those years. The only funny thing about her, if the word funny is used in the broadest way possible, was that she had never aged. John was now fifty two years old but looked much younger, Prudence was fifty four but looked older. Back in 1950, around the time of the Great Exhibition, as an up and coming young thing in the Labour Party, he had been the leading light in converting the old Mechanics Institute in Hemsley into a library. At the opening ceremony, in the absence of anybody even slightly interesting, he had made an uninspired speech in which he had stressed the importance and joy of the written word. He had told those present how the best thing his mother had ever done for him and his career was to introduce him to Dob Lane library and the chief librarian, Miss Pennyworth, when he was only eight years old. He could even remember the first book he had borrowed, Emil and the Detectives. He then spoke about the need for a war-like effort to help those who couldn't read.

He then proceeded to trot out his latest party piece, a poem he had made up a few months ago and was now heading for its one hundredth airing:

> *"I've travelled the world many times*
> *Met many folk out on the road,*
> *Poets and beggars, kings and queens,*
> *Old hands and apprentices.*
> *I've seen magic, learned secrets*
> *Been terrified and joyful*
> *All with my ticket*
> *To my magical house of dreams.*
> *My local library."*

Then, to stress his war theme, he told the assembled throng of six people his own book choices for the first week; Tolstoy's 'War and Peace', H.G. Wells's 'War of the Worlds' and his own favourite, Robert Louis Stevenson's 'Treasure Island'.

The whole event had been keenly covered for the Ashurst Reporter by a young journalist on his first assignment and the photographer, old Henry, who was probably on his last. Back in their office the following day, young Michael, the journalist, had looked through the photographs of this very local and rather boring event and chosen quite an interesting one: John and his wife each holding a book in their hands, John with Tolstoy, Prudence with H.G. Wells. And so in his first article for the Reporter, below the photograph, Michael had written "At the opening of the new Hemsley Library on Wednesday night, local councillor John Taylor, seen above with his mother, announced his vote-catching War on Literacy."

And a few weeks later on the Warrington bus, the conductor had made a similar mistake when in all good faith, he had returned half of Prudence's fare, telling her that it was half price for pensioners after half past nine.

It was purely coincidental that another of the town's oddballs was one of the most regular visitors to Mossdale Library. The appropriately named Peter Starr had led a fairly normal existence until just after he had started work as a turner at Jarratts. Then an event occurred that completely changed his life. After a night out in the Seven Stars, he had witnessed the first arrival of aliens on planet Earth. He had been taking a shortcut home over Mount Everest when he had seen one of his mates making the earth move for Vicki who doled out the chips in Wilkinson's works canteen. A couple of minutes later, the earth definitely did move and sparks were seen coming from behind the two trees that had miraculously continued to grow on this desolate and inhospitable scar on the environment. As he looked more, he was sure that he saw three figures about four foot tall scampering away and grunting in a most weird manner. And when he reached the exact spot, the pond that they had played in for years as kids was completely dry and smoke was rising from holes in the ground. Unfortunately for Peter, that night soon became one of continuous rain so that by the time he could return, any evidence of what might have landed there had gone.

The following day he read in the Daily Mirror of the sighting of a UFO at a place called Yarov Stan in Western Siberia. That night on the television he also heard of similar sightings in Moscow, a small town thirty miles east of Memphis in America. He then dug out his Atlas and drew a line between the two places and to his amazement discovered that the exact mid-point, give or take ten miles or so, was Ashurst. From then on he became obsessed with the para normal and spent much of his free time reading up about extra terrestrial life in reference books in the library and roaming over Mount Everest in the dark. Soon he made contact with a man from Bolton who had evidence of the landing of a spaceship on Rivington Pike in 1948 and who put him in contact with a group of students in a place called Cape Disappointment on the west coast of California. After reading some of their literature, he discovered that around the same time that he had first seen alien life in Ashurst, two other significant events had occurred: at Mbizi in Rhodesia a freak rain storm had fallen for three days and in the north of Greenland, and in Mylius Erichsens Land, strange fish had been seen swimming out of Independence Fjord into the Wandells Sea. A line drawn between these two places not only ran straight through Lancashire again; but also its centre was to be found, give or take ten or so miles, in Ashurst. By now, with the knowledge and help of his new found friends in America, Peter became convinced that the Earth was about to be colonised by Zartecs. But although he made every effort to warn people in both Whitehall and on Ashurst Council of the need to do something about it, all his efforts came to nought. He did however manage to set up a branch of the World Society of UFO spotters, though the only people who showed much interest in joining it was Vicki, who would appear to get quite turned on by the prospects of being caught at it on Mount Everest by men from another planet, along with a teacher from the suitably named district of Crank in St Helens.

Another interesting person, though completely sane and well respected, was the town's literary genius, Eric Farrell. Eric had spent most of his working life underground, first at Southport Edge until it had been closed in 1938, then at the old Monty until its seams had been exhausted in 1956, and finally at Havanna until he had retired in 1970. Few people associated digging coal with writing poetry, but after they had met Eric they would ask themselves, why not? Get him in the pub, at the match or in the bookies and he would be no different than any of his other workmates. But catch him at home in the evening and he was like a man transformed. He just loved the world of literature, and of course there was nothing wrong with that.

As a result, Ashurst Council had put him on a panel of three to help organise the town's annual Literature Festival. Unfortunately the other two members of the panel did not think or behave like Eric did. Cynthia Porter was the wife of the chairman of the Chamber of Commerce and a leading socialite about the place, with little time for most of the riff-raff who couldn't even talk properly never mind read. John Sykes, a school teacher, was so wrapped up in the works of Byron, Shelley and Homer and keen to get accepted in the town's small group of theatre buffs that he always agreed with whatever Cynthia felt was suitable for the ratepayers of the borough. As a result, the festival was always held in the Conservative club in Dob Lane and was aimed overwhelmingly at teachers and the professional classes with a love for discourse on such rivetting topics as the influence of geography on Shakespeare and the role of the merchants in 17th century novelettes.

In preparation for the 1972 festival a meeting was called for the group to rubber stamp what Cynthia wanted. Fortunately, on the night in question she had been invited to a gathering of business people to meet Edward Heath in Liverpool and was unable to attend, as was John who suddenly had a strange attack of Legionnaires Disease. Instead of cancelling the meeting as Cynthia had instructed, even though she didn't have the power to do so, Eric invited a number of more imaginative-minded dignitaries with power and influence to pass comment on his suggestions. They included the Town Clerk, a Scot well known for his love of the Scottish poet William McGonigal, Stephen Queen, the owner of the new Primrose Variety and Social Club, the editor and the newly appointed media writer for the Ashurst Reporter, and Harry Leek, who had a B.A. in English literature and also owned the town's second largest furniture removal business, Cynthia's husband owning the largest.

Eric explained that he had invited them as they were all people who, in the absence of the rest of the Committee, could help make progress and perhaps be innovative in their contribution. Then he outlined his plan, which was to make the Literature festival more accessible to local people and raise the profile of reading within the town. This was something no one could disagree with. Then he suggested it be in three parts; firstly, they should invite a local writer to start the proceedings by explaining why reading was good for your health. When Harry Leek suggested asking the Z Cars actor Colin Welland, who came from nearby Newton le Willows, Eric knew he had won him over. Then he suggested a rather novel item for the second part of the programme. Anyone in the town could send in a famous poem that had been bowdlerised to make it appear to have been based on Ashurst. When the Town Clerk asked what did he mean, Eric said:

"I know that you love to read William McGonigal."

The Town Clerk nodded.

"Well do you recall that ode he wrote about Glasgow?:

> *Beautiful city of Glasgow, with your streets so neat and clean,*
> *Your stately mansions, and beautiful Green!*
> *Likewise your beautiful bridges across the river Clyde,*
> *And on your bonnie banks I would like to reside."*

"Yes"

"Well it could be rewritten something like this:

> *Beautiful town of Ashurst, with your streets so neat and fair*
> *Your stately library and beautiful Town Hall square*
> *Likewise your beautiful bridge across the River Sankey*
> *It brings tears to my eyes and then into my hanky."*

Before the Town Clerk could comment or point out that the Sankey was a canal not a river, Eric half apologised and went on:

"Maybe his most famous poem about the Tay Bridge Disaster could be re-written so that it took place where the Ashurst to Leigh railway line crosses the Stinky Brook just past Jarratts."

"I've got the idea, but maybe you could have used some better examples," said the Town Clerk, "like Blake's Battle of Culloden Moor being re-written as though it'd taken place behind Gillarsfield Labour Club."

"I think this is a very good idea," said the Editor of the Reporter, aware that this could make very good copy for Friday's paper. "What's the third part of this festival to be? It all looks very interesting."

"We'll invite anybody in the town to submit a poem but to involve as many people as possible, they'll have to do it through an organisation. For example, we could ask the Fire Brigade for one, which would mean all the firemen discussing it. We could ask each firm to send something in, the Co-op, any shop or school or pub. We could ask the working mens' clubs to join in as well. This way we would get loads of publicity and everybody would feel as though they were involved. Perhaps we might have to limit it to people who pay the rates but only as long as they pay them on time."

This pleased the Town Clerk no end.

"I can see one little problem," said the Editor. "We'll have to change the venue. You'll never get more than twenty in that room at the Conservative Club."

"You could have it in the lounge of my club as long as it's not on a Friday or Saturday night and it won't cost you a penny," said Stephen Queen. "And I'll put five pounds up for a prize for the funniest contribution on the night."

"And I'll donate a prize for the most moving poem," said Harry Leek with a smile on his face knowing he had just got one over on Cynthia and her husband, "and we could circulate it round Ashurst College and try and get some young ones interested instead of hanging round the streets all night."

"If you liase with my new media writer Terry here," said the Editor, "we could feature it in the Reporter. And here was me thinking the town had no culture."

"Just one problem though," said Eric, "do we have the authority to decide this in the absence of Cynthia and John?"

"No problem at all," said the Town Clerk, "I'll make sure of it and I'll be taking part in it as well."

And when Cynthia opened up her copy of the Reporter later in the week, she nearly had a heart attack when she saw what had been agreed in her absence.

Six months later the festival was held and was a resounding success. Over two hundred people were in attendance, and sat there on the third row was the famous Rugby League player Alex Murphy, with his wife Alice. Some who saw him thought he must have been invited to give out the prizes, but then why wasn't he on the top table? Soon all was to be revealed. The proceedings began with Eric explaining why he, as a former miner, was recommending to the audience to consider enjoying the world of literature and encouraging them to join a readers group that would be set up at every library in the town.

Then the Town Clerk, who was chairing the proceedings, said that he would now like to invite Alex Murphy, known and loved by all Saints fans, known and not loved to quite the same degree by everybody else in the world, to say a few words. Alex strode to the front of the hall, climbed up to the platform and said how pleased he was to have been invited to take part:

"In 1966 I was privileged to play for St Helens at Wembley against Wigan. It was an unforgettable experience. I was so moved by the whole event that shortly after I came home I put pen to paper and wrote a poem about it. I even put it on a telegram and sent it to Central Park for them to enjoy it as well. So this is my contribution to this Literature Festival and good luck to everybody."

Then he took a small piece of paper from his pocket, smiled and read out:

"Roses are Red.
Violets are Blue
St Helens Twenty One
Wigan Two."

"Thank you, good night and God Bless."

11.

THE TRAGIC DEATH
OF LITTLE SOPHIE

Around the time of that terrible winter of 1962/63, Alan had spent time constructing the family tree. At the heart of it, on his mother's side, was the marriage in 1908 of his grandfather Edward George Holding, born in 1890, to his grandmother, Mary Isabella Tabern, born one year later. On his Grandad's side he had been able to trace back through three generations to his great, great, great grandfather Arthur Silas Holding. He had first seen the light of day in a tiny collier's cottage at Collins Green in 1791 on the very same day that the composer Wolfgang Amadeus Mozart had died. On his Granny's side through the line of her father, Alan had information going back to her great grandfather, Billy Tabern the watch maker, who had been born in 1803 in Gillarsfield. Through the line of her mother Elizabeth Pickavance he had knowledge of her grandfather Joseph Pickavance, another collier born in 1798 at Pocket Nook in St Helens and who married Mary Frances Dagnall, born two years later at nearby Fingerpost on the day that Horatio Nelson had won a great naval victory at the battle of the Nile.

Much of the information Alan had at his command had been written on scraps of paper by Granny's brother Eric during a long period of unemployment in the Twenties. Doing this had given him some purpose and meaning in life and took his mind off the hunger that he and so many others around him experienced as an ever present fact of their daily existence.

Not only had he written down names and dates, he had also included occupations and where known their sporting interests. He had also included from who and where he had obtained the information, almost as though he expected that some time in the future someone would check it to make sure it was correct. When he died in 1947, he had left a wealth of information in his little Corporation house in Barrow Street.

From his jottings, Alan found out that three occupations dominated the family tree, labourer, bricklayer and collier. Among the latter over the years three relatives had died underground and another two had been badly injured.. There were some interesting exceptions, one distant relative was for a while the manager of a cotton mill in Bolton and another had worked on the building of the Titanic. He also discovered that his great Uncle Albert had played for a season for Widnes and more recently his Uncle Norman had played for Crompton Recs before being the subject of a big transfer deal that had taken him to Stubshaw Cross, who were one place below them in the Second Division of the Lancashire Combination.

After a lot of thinking about it, Alan had finally started on the research for writing the double biography of his Granny and Grandad. Research was perhaps a bit of a grandiose description of the work. All he ever had to do was to ask either of them a question about the old days and off they would go, sometimes contradicting each other as they racked their brains to tell their story, usually in their back kitchen in Silkstone Street.

Whenever Grandad talked about the past, he always seemed to concentrate on the humorous side, but when Granny told her tales, they seemed to deal much more with the reality of it all, the hardships and the poverty as well as the friendships and goodness in life. And it was from Granny that six months after her second child Robert was born, Thelma first heard the tragic story of little Sophie. It was a story that Granny had told many times before and would no doubt tell again whenever new people came into her circle of relatives.

Sophie Katherine Pickavance lived in Pretoria Street at the back of the station. Her father, Stanley Pickavance, and mother, who had been born Alice Harriet McGinty, had four children, one girl and three boys. She was the youngest, a little treasure, always laughing, always wanting to help others. She was indeed the apple of her father's eye and one of her daily tasks was to take his dinner to the glass bottle factory where he worked at in nearby Pickersgill Street.

She would skip past the gatehouse where Paddy the Irishman always used to make her laugh with some little trick or other. Then she would walk down the yard to the old hut where her Dad and the others would eat their jam butties. But that particular morning there had been a fire and the hut was no longer to be used and the men had been told to eat their snap in one of the warehouses. Unfortunately little Sophie had arrived very early so her Dad had not had chance to meet her at the usual spot. Not seeing him around she asked one of the labourers where he was.

"He's working on number three kiln, tha'll have to tek his butties up theer, love. We can't eat here now" and he pointed to a large chimney bellowing out smoke.

"Tha can go up them stairs and down t'other side. That'll be quickest way for thee," and as he spoke he pointed to the wooden stairs going up above a large tank from which smoke was rising, "but be careful, little one."

She was never seen again. She climbed up the rickety stairs, then walked along the walkway above the tank in which molten glass was bubbling. The steps were slippery and some were missing and she had probably slipped and........ The molten glass at a temperature of over 1000 degrees Centigrade ensured that within minutes if not seconds any evidence of her nine year life on Earth was totally wiped out.

Perhaps it was the way Granny told the tale and wiped her moist eyes that made it so powerful and moving. If she had lived, little Sophie would have now been over a hundred years old anyway but a century later her life and then sudden death still affected everybody who heard of it. And as she cradled her little son, Thelma knew that one day she would pass that and the rest of the history of her new family on to Rebecca and Robert and any other children she might bring into the world. And no doubt she would also wipe her eyes as she told the story - it was one of the saddest stories ever told.

But soon Granny was back to her usual self, regaling them with stories about her two brothers who were always in trouble, even going back to the days when they went to Sunday school one day and brought a mouse into the Church Hall and all the younger children and three teachers had run out screaming.

As she listened and laughed at the tales, Thelma sometimes felt sad that she would never be able to tell her children anything about her own relatives, but then how could she, she didn't have any or so she thought until one Friday afternoon when she had called in to see Granny and have a natter.

As soon as she walked into the house, she could tell that something was wrong. Granny looked worried and agitated; she didn't immediately take Robert out of his pram and cuddle him as she always did.

"Oh, Thelma, I'm so pleased you've come. I've been worrying. I was going to get Ned to call and tell you, but he's gone out."

"What's up Granny? What's happened?"

"We've had a visitor. He's come to see you. He's coming back. That's all I know."

"Granny, sit down and tell me exactly what's happened."

That morning Grandad had gone out on his rounds, visiting various relatives like he normally did on a Friday and calling in at the British Legion club in Pasture Lane to have his secret pint. Shortly after there had been a knock on the door. When Granny opened it she saw before her a man in his early twenties, wearing a smart green blazer and flannels. In a strange accent he asked if Thelma Johnson lived there. Granny said that she didn't but used to until she had got married. Then she asked why. The man had politely said he very much wanted to see her as he had some news for her. So Granny had suggested he came round after tea when she would make sure Thelma and her husband would be there.

At half past six Granny and Grandad and Alan and Thelma were sat there just wondering who this man could be. Then came a knock on the front door, which Alan went to answer. As soon as their visitor asked for Thelma, Alan recognised the Aussie twang. He shook his hand and welcomed him into the house where he was immediately offered a cup of tea and a scone that Granny had just baked. Then he told them a tale that helped Thelma know a little more about her own background

He began by telling her that her father came from a place called Thrakomakedhones, about twenty miles north of Athens. He was an engineer by trade and in the late Thirties had been forced into exile by the Metaxas government. The start of the Second World War had found him working as a stoker on a British Merchant Navy ship sailing out of Cardiff Docks. It was there that he had met Rebecca Johnson, a young Land Army girl, at a dance in 1942. Inevitably the war ensured their time together was very limited. But they soon fell in love and had every intention of getting married when it was all over. Then one year later, on the day his ship was due to sail, she told him she was pregnant. He wanted to get married there and then but there was no time but he promised they would do it when he next came back to Wales.

Unfortunately it was not to be. His ship was sunk by a German U-boat off the coast of Greece and as a result he spent six months recovering from gunshot wounds in a small village protected by partisans on the island of Corfu. Then, with the war finished, he briefly returned to Thrakomakedhones to see his family and there got caught up in the Greek civil war, supporting the side which was now considered the enemy by the British Government. As it came to an end, and being on the losing side, he knew he would never again be allowed back into Britain because of what had happened in that bitter struggle.

So with many other Greeks, he had to leave the country he had fought for and finally settled in Australia, along with his brother, in the Camperdown suburb of Sydney. He had never married but soon became the favourite uncle of the children of his brother and a couple of other Greek families. But he never forgot Rebecca Johnson and their child he had never seen, a part of his life that he had never mentioned to his brother. Then, in the spring of 1972 he heard that his eldest nephew Laurie had been chosen to tour Britain with the New South Wales athletics team in the summer. A few weeks later, at his brother's birthday party and after they had all drunk a great deal too much wine, he finally told them of that secret part of his life. And after they had all sobered up the following day, he asked Laurie to visit Rosemount Terrace in Tonyrefail near Pontypridd, Rebecca's last known address. He had of course written to that address on a number of occasions but never received a reply.

As soon as he had the opportunity Laurie went to Tonyrefail during the team's stay in South Wales, and there had been redirected to Silkstone Street in Ashurst on the South Lancashire coalfield .

"And what's my dad's name?" asked Thelma quietly.

"Yiorgos Angelopoulos, but most people call him Angel," his nephew replied.

"Do you have any photographs of him?" she continued, clearly moved by what she was hearing.

Laurie opened the bag he was carrying and gave her an envelope full of photographs. Most had been taken recently, mainly around Sydney but a very faded one showed Cardiff City Hall in the background and a woman she clearly recognised from other photographs as her own mother.

As she wiped tears away from her eyes she said: "He won't know that my mum died when I was a baby, will he?"

"No."

Then Laurie went on to say that her father would love to see her. He was now too old to travel. But he had told Laurie that he would pay for his child's flight and all the expenses and she could stay for as long as she wanted to. But before Thelma could reply, the door opened and in came Alan's Mum with Rebecca and Robert. They were introduced to Laurie, who then went on to say that he didn't know that she had her own children and that it would not be that easy for her to travel to the other side of the world.

"Well maybe later when they've grown up a bit. Uncle Yiorgos isn't short of a few dollars. He'll pay for you but you must let me have photographs of you all before I go. He'll be so proud of you, Thelma and all your family."

Then he told them more about her father, how popular he was due to his very affable nature, the funny way he spoke English and his work with the Newtown junior footy teams, hastening to add that by footy he meant Rugby League. He told them about the jobs he had had, working first in a foundry before moving to work on Sydney docks and then in the City Transport Department after he had been injured helping load a ship bound for Liverpool. But soon it was time to leave. Thelma walked her new-found relative back into town where he was meeting other members of the squad at a reception in the Town Hall. Just before he left , he said to her:

"He'll be really pleased when I tell him about you and all your family, Thelma. They all seem really nice."

"They are and there's a lot more of them as well. But you tell him I've always wondered what he was like. Now that I know I'm so pleased, and tell him that we'll come out and see him when the children are a bit older."

But sadly it was not to be. What Laurie did not know at the time, and would not know until he arrived back in Sydney, was that a few days earlier, Thelma's father and his favourite uncle had suffered a massive heart attack. Without properly recovering he died a month later. And when the nurse discovered that Yiorgos had passed away, she saw in his hand a crumpled photograph of his daughter Thelma, who he had never seen, and her two children, his grandchildren Rebecca and Robert Greenall.

From then on Laurie and Thelma corresponded regularly. He began to send her details about her father's life, sometimes things Yiorgos had told his friends but not necessarily his own relatives. As she grew to know more about her father, she became even more conscious that she knew so little about the young Land Army girl who Yiorgos had loved during the War. And increasingly at home as Thelma heard more about the Holdings and the Taberns and the Pickavances, she became determined to find out about Rebecca Johnson who had lived and died in a little terraced house in Tonyrefail near Pontypridd in South Wales in 1944. And the first thing she wanted to know was where she was buried.

But before she could do anything about it, most of her time was taken up with looking after Rebecca and Robert. And around this time occurred the sad death of Grandad.

It all happened so quickly. And it was so unexpected. He was the picture of health for a man of eighty two. This was partly a result of his pram-pushing activities. At least once a week he would take Robert out in his push chair to watch the trains shunting wagons on Lowton Bank. Another day they would go to Billy Fairclough's farm to look at the hens, the geese and the cows. Then, after his stint with that great grand child, he would walk over to Gillarsfield and take out Neil, the eldest son of Alan's cousin Marion. And every other week he would catch a bus to Haydock where a third great grandchild would look forward to being walked up to the East Lancs Road to watch the lorries drive by. But one bright summer morning all this came to a sudden end. He had taken Robert on an adventure on to the slag heap at the back of the old Gillarsfield colliery. By tea time they still hadn't returned. Thelma thought he had gone back to Silkstone Street. Granny thought he had gone back to Beswick Terrace. But an old miner out walking his dog proved them both wrong when he found him lying unconscious on the ground with little Robert, covered in coal dust and slack, crying and trying to wake him up.

Five weeks later, Ned Holding breathed his last breath. Despite a hard life working down the pit, fighting in the trenches and as a prisoner of war, then returning to a land fit for heroes and two long periods on strike in the Twenties fighting for the basics to enjoy a life, and then unemployed for another long period during the Depression, despite all this he had always been, certainly for all his grandchildren and great grandchildren, the funniest man in the world. And with his departure they were all the poorer for it. Much poorer.

After the funeral Granny had declared that as long as she had a few visits from the rest of them and someone to do the shopping, she would carry on living in Silkstone Street. Not surprisingly, her most regular visitor was Thelma. She would come down two or three times a week and then again at the weekend with Alan and the children. Most days she would find Granny sat in her favourite chair snoozing or watching the fire burn. Sometimes she would be a little forgetful, sometimes even a bit sharp. But this was always compensated for when she was back to her old self.

One particular Sunday afternoon would stick in their memory for a long time. The four of them arrived to find that Granny had baked a plateful of scones and a chocolate cake, something she hadn't done for ages. She immediately reached out for Robert, sat him on her lap and started talking to him. After rambling on about his newly arrived teeth and his spiky hair she went on:

"Ee, you've got Mum's eyes and mouth haven't you? But I think you're going to be a lot heavier than she is. Do you know, I can remember when I first saw her. I can still remember it, as clear as though it was yesterday."

Watching Granny talking to her great grandson was hilarious. Alan had once described it as the Little Laurie and Big Hardy show. All the time she was talking he would be looking up at her face and laughing and every few minutes, for no reason, he would give her a big sloppy kiss.

"I thought she was a bit thin and pale looking but she had a nice face, with all her freckles and that. And then do you know what the first thing she said to me was: 'Can I be of any help, Mrs Greenall'. I thought to myself here's a good little worker, and I wasn't wrong was I?"

And then Granny continued as though Robert was the only other person in the room who could understand what she was talking about.

"And then she went and fell ill. Oh, she was poorly, proper poorly she was. She nearly went to hospital but we looked after her and she soon got better, but she didn't like me putting a Kaolin poultice on her."

Thelma, Alan and Rebecca remained silent as she continued, almost oblivious to their presence in the room.

"She had such a bad cough, and she couldn't hold anything down for days. I was so worried about her and the doctor had to come every day. But then if I hadn't looked after her, I wouldn't have met you and you might have had somebody else for a Granny or a great Granny or whatever it is."

Then she looked up at Thelma and said: "Do you know you were like a little frightened mouse that first week?"

"Was I?"

"I don't think that you knew where you were in that back bedroom. And you just couldn't understand how I knew Alan. I don't think you knew how you got here."

Thelma just smiled, she could only vaguely remember her first week there.

Then Granny asked Thelma if she could remember the first time she had come downstairs to have a meal, early in the New Year.

"I do because after I had eaten it, you said there was a present for me."

One of the first things that had struck Granny about her visitor on that Christmas Day in 1962 had been the state of her clothing: the down-at-heel shoes, the ladders in her tights, the ripped skirt and the thin green summer coat she had been wearing in the depths of one of the worst winters in living memory. When Alan had brought back her clothes on the Boxing Day from where she had been living in Grasmere Avenue, Granny had seen more of the same, including the old dressing gown and an even older pair of slippers, more holes than material. So she had told Alan that Thelma would appreciate a nice Christmas present from him and a pair of slippers would be a good idea. And so, after her first taste of Granny's famous stew and dumplings, Thelma had been presented with a brand new pair of slippers wrapped in brown paper. And frequently that day Granny noticed how her lodger, as she was to become, kept looking at the slippers on her feet and stroking them.

Then, as Thelma began to get better and as Granny got to know her better, the bond between them had grown stronger. And now Thelma, the orphan from South Wales who had drifted into Ashurst and hardly knew a soul there, was a most welcome member of the family. And she knew it was all due to the loving care and attention this increasingly frail old lady had given her ten years earlier. And now that Granny was living on her own, Thelma knew that she would do all she could to return that loving care and attention. But tonight Granny was just like she used to be and how they all knew and loved her. And fortunately for them all, so it was to be until the time she finally had to leave the house in which she had lived since 1891 to go and live in the Greenfield Old People's Home in Dob Lane. And shortly after Granny moved out, four new occupants, all members of the Holding/Tabern/Greenall/Pickavance dynasty, moved in to carry on a long family tradition.

12.

LES EARNSHAW: TV SUPERSTAR

"Have you heard the news? Les is going to be on the television."

"You're joking," said Mick.

"No, it's right," and with that Alan produced a copy of the Radio Times. There, in black and white for Wednesday night on the Home Service was clearly stated under the heading of New Writers, the full and glowing details:

"David Frost interviews four up and coming regional writers; Cynthia Sanderson from Brighton, Marcus Phipps from Gloucester, Janette Close from Bristol and Leslie Earnshaw from Lancashire."

"The ewd bugger. He's managed it at last," laughed Mick. "I always knew he would."

"Oh, here we go, Mick is going to invite all their street to come and watch his telly. And he'll tell them that he was the inspiration behind Les becoming a world famous writer," said Yorky.

"There were some things that I told him that's in his first book."

"What. Like your lad blowing your shed up all over Platt Bridge."

"Will it be live?" asked Len. "I hope he doesn't start swearing."

"I know what he'll do," said Alan. "If he tells one of his funny stories, or if he gets one over on somebody, he'll raise his right hand, clench it and shake it while pulling that funny face he does."

"I hope he doesn't get into any arguments," said Charlie, "or he'll be pointing his finger at them and offering to take them outside."

"I wonder what they'll all make of his second book?" wondered Charlie. "The Actress Goes to Heaven one."

"They'll probably just talk about his first novel," said Mick. "They usually do."

"How do you know? You never have any of them intellectual programmes on in your house. Anyway, you can't get BBC 2 in Wigan."

"Mick can and he hasn't even paid his licence."

Not surprisingly it was the source of much conversation over the next few days. They all wondered how seriously Les would behave. Some thought he would be pretty nervous and so act in a quiet and restrained manner. Others thought he would have a skinful of ale beforehand and then not care a toss what he said. Those who knew him best felt that he was bound to pull at least one stunt and so they were all waiting with great interest on the Wednesday evening when David Frost's smiling face appeared on the screen.

"Good evening and welcome to this first in a series of programmes about the state of modern day English Literature," he began. "Tonight I have invited four unknown writers who in their own way reflect different aspects of the cultural life of Britain today."

He then said a few words of introduction about each of his guests. Before retiring,

Cynthia Sanderson had been the headmistress of a large private school in Dorking. Her two great interests in life were the architecture of 18th century Italy and Buddhism. Marcus Phipps was a lecturer in philosophy at London University. Previous to that he had been at Eton and then Oxford University where he first studied the classics and proceeded to carry out research on his pet subject, the rise of feudalism in Tuscany, a subject that necessitated many visits to the region.

Janette Close had been born in Holland where her father was in the diplomatic service but on the outbreak of the war had moved to the West Country. Her contribution to literature was in developing stories around the eventless and meaningless lives of some of the most noble families in Somerset, and particularly around the villages she had either lived in or in which she and her husband owned property or farmed land.

Then David spoke briefly about his fourth guest:

"My fourth guest comes from a long established industrial family in the North. His great grandfather worked on the building of the first railway line between Liverpool and Manchester, his grandfather was something of an expert on the excavation of fossil fuels at the turn of the century and his father knew much about the under utilisation of industry in Lancashire in the 1930s. Leslie himself continues to explore the problems of the alienation of mankind against the rise of modern technology and combines this with a sharp interest in the role history plays in the emergence of new practices in the working environment."

"I thought you said he was just an ordinary working class bloke from Ashurst," muttered Mrs Henderson as her husband wondered whether it was the same Les Earnshaw that he used to work with.

"He sounds like a bit of a professor to me."

Then David Frost threw the first question open for discussion: What did the panel think of the state of the contemporary literature scene? The first three rattled on in standard BBC English about matters that were incomprehensible and uninteresting to most of those listening in and around Ashurst. They talked about the absence of creative dynamism in the representation of reality, the inward negative symbolism of those who sought to comment on the cultureless lifestyles of the masses, the over-representation of the capital and its inhabitants as being true of the whole country and the intellectual challenges facing the rising school of new writers like themselves. Finally it was Les's turn. But it wasn't Les. His voice sounded more like Neville Chamberlain when he had announced on the radio on September 3rd 1939 that "from eleven o'clock this morning, this country is at war with Germany". He sounded little different than any of the others, at first an enormous disappointment:

"My initial perception of that what passes for modern day literature is too bound up with a false representation of life. Not art for art's sake, rather literature for the self projection and advance of those who know little and can appreciate nothing in the field of cultural bleakness!"

His opening comments were met by a stony silence around the table.

The next question dealt with the existence, or rather the non-existence, of humour in much contemporary literature and why this was so.

Cynthia Sanderson gave the impression that if she were to laugh her face would fall apart and answered the question by saying that the artist in society had always to be serious, detached and objective about the lives of those they wrote about. Marcus Phipps told an excruciatingly boring story about the time he had been camping with the Scouts in Devon, while Janette Close said that the English humour she encountered in her village was humdrum and childish. And in particular she indicated her displeasure with what passed for entertainment that came from across the Atlantic.

Then it was Les's turn. By now many in Ashurst and around had probably turned over to ITV, but for those who didn't a treat was in store:

"Humour has to be understood as essential to the writer as is fresh air or fresh food or a well sharpened pencil. Humour rooted in the sometimes harsh, sometimes comfortable realities of a pampered life can present the writer with the means to overcome the dross and drivel of society and meet head on and face to face the challenges of the dark non-literary forces that encapsulate the narrow mindedness of the uneducated."

Then he pulled at the top button of his shirt and tie and said in a voice that sounded very much like one of his impersonations of Mick: "This bloody thing has been rubbing against me throat all neet."

Then he continued with his previous 1930s-style voice: "Yes, he or she who does not find the time to stand and stare or sit and laugh is by the very nature of his or her existence unable to reflect the correct relationships between us that Harry Stottle perceived ultimately, without fear or family favourites as being at the heart of our relationship one with another and his brother or his sister."

And around the town those who knew him, or knew what he was like, said in different ways:

"He's starting."

Then Cynthia Sanderson asked Les whether the many long days and nights that he had obviously spent working on his manuscripts not only drew him apart from the rest of society but bred in him a purity which enabled him better to know himself. In this way the relevant insignificance of humour in matters of serious content would be personalised and would also put the rest of the population in their appointed place in the hierarchy of things.

He then replied in a St Helens accent, this time sounding very much like Charlie.

"Eh love, can I just ask you what you mean by spending long days and nights on my manuscripts. I have to go to work. Don't you? Do you not have a job?"

Then he turned to their interviewer and said: "Have you got a real job Dave, or do you just ask folk questions? You remind me of one of the managers at work."

Seeing the need to bring out a little more of his rather unusual guest, the rising star of British televison said:

"Leslie, I am sure that none of us appreciated that you were still working full time as well as being a writer in your spare time. How much inspiration do you take from your daily contact with others to create your characters?"

"Well its like this, ewd lad. In my second book you will know that the main character is a scaffolder called Albert Entwhistle. Now he's a combination of two lads I used to work with, Billy Pickles at Jarratts and Charlie Eccleston at Wilkinsons. Billy was always very physical, always playing tricks, mainly on the apprentices. On the other side Charlie was forever telling funny stories about things he had done or heard about and always making us laugh. Billy was a great sportsman, rugby, running, darts, whereas in his younger days Charlie was always getting into trouble with the women. Knowing the two of them very well, what I did was develop the character of Albert Entwhistle from a combination of the two of them plus bits based on other lads I've worked with. That is why Albert is such a human character, not like any of the bunch you've got round this table. How come they got invited, I haven't heard one of them say a funny thing all neet."

"This is not the Goon Show," protested Marcus, "surely we are hear to discuss literature, not the meaningless antics of working class Northern buffoons."

"Eh, are you calling my mate Charlie a buffoon? You'll be sorry you said that. He'll sue you." And with that he also pointed his finger at Marcus and said, "and that's after I've dealt with you if you're calling me the same, pal."

"Gentlemen, gentlemen, let's act responsibly," intervened David Frost, a little upset that things were beginning to get out of hand. "Let's move on to another issue, possibly a controversial one in view of what has already been hinted at. What do we think of the influence of American writers on the situation in Britain today? Let's start with you, Les. What are your thoughts?"

Les leaned back, looked around the table and said: "I've just finished reading the American writer Ezra Poundnote, and his Confucius: the Unwobbling Pivot and the Great Digest. It juxtaposes well against his earlier work, "The Impact, Essays and the Ignorance and Decline of American Civilisation", which I am sure everybody here will be familiar with. In it he displays a virtuosity that Martlew describes as a style that ranges from laconic formulations to fluid associations with his subject matter. But I think the question that should be asked is what do we think about the influence of English writers on the situation in Britain today."

"What do you mean?" asked David Frost as the others looked rather bemused at the man who was slowly taking over the show.

"When you read most novels about this country, well it's not the country I've lived in for the last hundred years. Have you noticed how most of the characters never seem to go to work; they are either members of the upper class, criminals, civil servants, M.P.s or layabouts who have never done a day's work in their lives. And most of the stories are based in London or some posh little village in the Cotswolds."

Then Cynthia Sanderson raised the temperature a little when she suggested that that might be because there were few people in the North who had the talent to write successfully, or maybe those that did preferred to write about more interesting places than could be found 'oop North'.

"Do you know many writers from the North, love?"

"No."

"So do you think us Northerners are all thick?"

"No, I didn't say that."

"You might as well have."

"Ladies, gentlemen please. Literature can describe passion, it can even evoke passion, but let's rise above this here and now."

Then Marcus interjected with a rather interesting comment when he said: "I've never met a writer like Les before. In fact I don't think I've ever met anyone like Les before. I think I am slowly beginning to understand the essence of his novel."

Then David Frost jumped back in and mentioned the incident in "The Actress Goes To Heaven" when Bridget Bardot was left on her own in the Wigan Emp dancehall one Saturday night.

"A little bizarre, wouldn't you say Les, but quite imaginative, I thought?"

"You have got to write about what you know. Wigan Emp is the best dance hall in the country. I could just imagine Bridget Bardot in there. I bet half of Wigan could as well. So what's wrong with my imagination. A bit more interesting than setting a love story in Little Much Binding on a March, or La spaghetti di milano o ristorante, over two hundred years ago."

And with that he stared at Cynthia, raised his right hand in the air, clenched it and pulled one of his funny faces.

Keen to regain control of his programme, David Frost then asked the panel how much their environment had moulded their writing, both its style and content. By this time the other three had become rather silent, not wanting to feel the sharp invective of Les hurled against them. So he jumped in again and told them how his own background had not only made him but had made many more like him.

Then, for no apparent reason, he picked up again on the question about the importance of humour in life and quoted some of the great comedians that Lancashire had produced, Tommy Handley, Sandy Powell, Ted Ray, Al Read, Ted Lune, Ken Dodd and Ken Platt. "I won't take my coat off, I'm not stopping". And then he began to explain how that had come from Ken's days working as a cable drum pusher at the B.I.C.C. cable factory in Leigh. But before he could say much more, David Frost had to draw the programme to a close:

"Well, tonight's programme has been a little different to say the least and I would like to thank the four members of the panel for their contributions. Next week we will be looking at another aspect of the contemporary English literature scene - the emergence of women writers."

And as the credits began to appear on the country's television screens, Les was heard to shout out:

"I'll fetch the wife."

The following day, in places as far apart as Hanging Heaton, Wath Brow, Wath on Dearne, Shelf, Oswaldtwistle, Little Lever, Bailiff Bridge, Mount Tabor and Egypt (near Queensbury), comments were made about Les's stunning performance.

"That fellow from Lancashire was a bit of a rum bugger on the television last night. I couldn't work out whether he was on the right programme."

"He put everybody in their place did that lad, especially that woman from Brighton with the big earrings. He made me laugh when he shook his fist in the air and pulled a funny face at her."

"I thought he talked a lot of sense, but I don't think I could put up with him for too long."

And back at work at Wilkinsons and all the other factories in the town, the main topic of conversation was the same.

"I thought he did very well," said Mick, "but I don't think he'll get invited again."

"I wonder what David Frost thought of him," said Len. "I thought he only just managed to keep control of the programme."

"It made me laugh when Les called him Dave and then ewd lad," said Alan.

"It's not the first time he's done that," said Charlie. "When he was working at Wallworks, Harold Wilson came round to look at that new gear cutting machine they had designed. Les had done all the sheet metal work on it and so he was one of those who was introduced to Wilson. And he called him Harry. A few weeks later Prince Phillip came as well so they sent Les to Agecroft Power Station for a couple of days to keep him out of the way."

"You know we ought to start a Les Earnshaw fan club. It could be really big," said Alan. "After that performance, somebody is bound to see his potential as an entertainer. He could easily put a show on doing impersonations."

"Oh that really would bring the house down, Greeno. Les Earnshaw and his impersonations of three phase electric motors operating at different voltages," said Mick.

"We might even see Mike Yarwood imitating him on the telly, just like he does with Eddie Waring."

"Now that would be a good one to listen to, Mike Yarwood imitating Les impersonating Mick."

"They could just have Mick on being himself and save us all a load of money. It would be quite funny, especially if Mick wears his demob suit for it."

A couple of days later Charlie announced to everyone that there was a letter in a BBC envelope waiting for him when he got home the previous evening. He then opened it up and read the following notes from their old workmate, the new television superstar:

"Dear Charlie and anybody else who is awake,

I hope you all enjoyed my performance on the television last night. I went out with David Frost for a pint after the show and met a few of his mates in some right posh club, a Welsh bloke called Tom Jones who used to work down the pit, Marianne Shaw, Sandie Faithfull, Norman Wisdomtooth and loads more. Anyway, no more name-dropping, other than to tell you that Engelbert Humperdink bought us a pint, that's me and Petula Clark, who I had a dance with. Anyway you'll all get the chance to meet them as I've invited them up to Ashurst next Saturday night. There is about thirty of them coming in a charabanc. We can go to the Gas and Electric club or Gillarsfield Labour Club. It should be a good night out. So Charlie, can you arrange for some of them to kip in your front room and the rest at your Auntie Elsie's?

One other thing, to show that success has not gone to my head. I know that Greeno still likes to go trainspotting (secretly). Well on the journey back we were an hour late leaving Euston station so I've collected a load of namers for him. Those I have put a tick against I spotted twice so he can swap those for any he hasn't got.

Hope he has managed to draw straight lines and mastered the art of producing vertical lines. And does he still draw cables with twelve wires in at one end and thirteen out at the other?

Yours, Les Earnshaw M.B.E.

P.S. M.B.E. means Master of Bloody Everything."

And below was a list of twenty or thirty locomotives which Les had written down, though how he had managed it was a bit of a mystery since many of them had been sent to the scrapyard a couple of years earlier. Or was it that Les was also a secret trainspotter, or maybe he had a Trevor Allan trainspotters book tucked away somewhere with his football programmes, school reports and prints of his first drawings. They would have to find out when they next saw him. At the weekend maybe, with all his new-found friends from London.

Or, knowing Les, maybe not.

13.

"US ENGLISH AND WELSH HAVE GOT TO STICK TOGETHER"

They all waited with great interest, but little hope, that they would see Les and his new coterie of chums on the Saturday night. And, of course, they didn't, although one of the Work Study men was sure he had seen him on the number 39 bus going to Leigh on the Friday evening. They all watched the David Frost programme the following week too, hoping that he might make some comments about the previous week's show. One or two hoped Mrs Earnshaw would be one of the guests, but they were to be disappointed, particularly after Mick had told them that he reckoned that she was funnier than Les and certainly a lot better looking.

So life in the Drawing Office moved into a rather settled period for a few weeks. Basil was away most of the time and they were so busy they even worked overtime and at the enhanced rate of time and a third during the week and double time at the weekend, thanks to the skilful negotiating tactics of Len and the Office Committee. Then a tragedy hit the town.

"Have you heard about that accident at Havanna last night?" said Len as he walked into the office. They all looked up at him as he went on, "three men have been killed and another twenty trapped for over four hours. Charlie's lad was one of them, he's broke a couple of ribs and his ankle."

"Where is he now? Is he all right?" asked Mick.

"They've took him to Peasley Cross Hospital. That's where Charlie is. He'll not be in today."

"Do you know who got killed?" asked the apprentice Ken anxiously, since both his brother and a couple of his mates worked at the Havanna pit.

"Two men from Widnes and a lad from Dublin who lived in Hemsley."

"You know, they take their lives in their hands every day they go to work, don't they?" said Mick.

"I wouldn't work down the pit for all the tea in China," said Keith, a comment that the rest of them appeared to concur with by their silence. Then, shocked by the three deaths, they all started work and maintained the silence pretty much until Joan appeared with the tea trolley just after ten o'clock. As always she knew a little bit more about the incident and after her departure the general conversation was about the working conditions underground.

But it was not too long before the latest addition to the Electrical Section began to make his usual disparaging remarks about the human race. Nigel Stannington-James was one of six graduate apprentices who had joined the company the previous September.

After spending a week in the Brass Foundry and another in the Iron Foundry, he then graced the Machine Shop, Wiring Shop, Assembly Shop, Tinning Shop and the Winding Shop with his presence. After that the red carpet was rolled out for him at the entrance to the Refinery and after that the Rolling Mill. In each place he had mainly observed others working rather than engaged in work himself but reckoned that by the end of his week in each department he had become an expert on what others had spent a lifetime learning about. Then he had spent a week on days and another on nights in the Works Maintenance shop, where individually and quite independently, three electricians had each attempted unsuccessfully to electrocute him. And then it was the turn of the Drawing Office to put up with 'His Lordship'. During his time in the factory a few of those who had come into contact with him thought he was an extremely bright young man, with the potential to go far, but most people saw him as a toffee-nosed upper class twit who had raised arrogance to an art form.

He didn't seem to come from anywhere in particular, since his father had moved the family at least three times before he even reached the age of five. Then his parents demonstrated their great love for their darling little offspring by sending him to boarding school two years later. After that it was Eton and University, followed by a year in South Africa where an uncle owned a large farm before returning to "the finest country in the world". It was rather a funny description of the land of his birth since he appeared to dislike, distrust or just plain hate most of those who lived in it. He didn't like the Irish or the Welsh, though strangely Scottish people did not appear to upset him, except of course for those from Glasgow. He disliked all those who worked in the media, most though not all politicians, those who lived on council estates, bus conductors, people who worked on the market and of course the trade unions and in particular the Liverpool dockers, the Ford car workers and, most of all, the miners, one of whom it appeared had once given him a good hiding in a nightclub.

His general arrogance was accompanied by a total lack of awareness of the people around him, as shown by his early negative comments about those who dug the coal out of the ground. He clearly did not comprehend that the people who he was currently working alongside might have relatives, neighbours or friends who worked underground for the National Coal Board. Or perhaps geography was not one of his best subjects and he did not know that Ashurst was based right at the centre of the South Lancashire coalfield.

"Why should the miners always get this sympathy for doing what they get very well paid for?" was his opening gambit. "I don't hear many people expressing any concern for the farm workers who get killed on the land helping to feed us all."

No one said anything as he continued:

"It's a free country, isn't it? They don't have to work down the mine. I suppose it's because you don't need any brains to dig coal that they go there.

"Look, I am as sorry as anybody else that three men have been killed, but it is happening all the time. Would any of them be at all upset if I or any of you dropped dead or were killed in an accident in the foundry. I don't think so."

No one said a thing and the rest of the morning proceeded in a state of general silence.

The afternoon strangely enough began with a laugh. An electrician had come up to see Alan about one of his drawings and when his questions had been answered, Charlie asked Gary whether he was going to the match at the weekend. There was then a fairly short conversation about the current St Helens team and then the lad went back to the Wiring Shop.

After he had gone Charlie said to Mick: "Red hot Saints fan, that lad."

"I know."

"Do you know how he first got interested?"

"No."

"You know he comes from North Wales, don't you? Well, him and all his family used to follow Bangor City Football Club. About three years ago they were drawn against St Helens Town in the F.A.Cup. A coachload of them came up to watch the game. They drove through the Mersey Tunnel and when they got to Prescot they turned left at the lights for St Helens as you would expect. When they got to Grange Park Golf Club, the driver stopped to ask directions to the ground. He got told to go as far as a pub called The Bird I' T'hand and then find somewhere to park. Since it was only about one o'clock they all went into the pub and had a few and then walked down Dunriding Lane and got on the ground about half two. But when they see the shape of the goal posts they realise they had come to the wrong place. Well it was too late to go over to Hoghton Road so they stood and watched the first bit of live Rugby League most of them had ever seen. And that's how Gary changed codes and now he's living here; there isn't a bigger Saints fan in Ashurst than him now."

Then Nigel decided that he would pass some anti-social comment about Welsh people as a result of hearing this tale.

"Typical bloody Welsh."

"What do you mean?" asked Len.

"To come all that way to watch the wrong game. If they had had anything about them, they would have found out where they were going before they set off."

"It was just a mistake," laughed Len, "I thought it was quite funny."

"Shagging sheep, that's all the Welsh are good at."

Suddenly Alan shot across the room, grabbed Nigel by the neck and pushed him up against the wall, knocking a bottle of ink all over his reference table.

"We've just about had enough of you, you little Fascist bastard. We're sick and tired of your continual ranting on about just how many people you hate. Well we all fucking hate you, so you had better change your attitude, or better still just keep your fucking mouth shut while you are in here, or you'll go home with your teeth in a bag."

Charlie quickly moved over to separate the pair of them but not before the whole incident, which had taken little more than half a minute, had been witnessed by Basil Wilkinson, who just happened to be coming to see John Battesby, the Chief Draughtsman.

Pointing at Alan, he shouted: "You get off the premises. You're sacked." Then, turning to Nigel, he said "You, go down to the surgery and get that cut on your face checked and then come to my office, sharpish." And before anyone else could say or do anything he stormed out of the room.

"What are you going to do, Alan?" said Keith.

"No," said Len. "What are we going to do. He's not getting away with that. Alan was provoked. I'll get one of the committee and we'll go down and see Basil in his office. You stay here, Greeno, and don't start fighting with Yorky while I'm out."

"What have I done?" said the man from Mytholmroyd.

"Not a lot, well, since Christmas," muttered Mick. But the humour fell rather flat, the possibility that Alan might lose his job was serious.

Ten minutes later Len was back in the office.

"He wouldn't even talk to me about it. He just shouted at me across the main office that he was employing no brawlers in his works. I tried to explain the background to it and told him that if he went ahead with the sacking, I would have to go and get legal advice from the Union Office in Liverpool and I would have to take members of his Committee with him.

"'You can take all your bloody members to Liverpool if you want and go and jump in the Mersey', he shouted and then slammed his door shut. So it looks as though we'll have to do what he told us to."

"What?" said Mick.

"We'll all have to go down to Liverpool. I'll take a couple of the committee in to see Ken Glover, and then we'll all meet on the Pier Head. It's a nice day and we are only doing what the boss wants us to."

Within ten minutes all the members of the Draughtsmans and Allied Technicians Association had left the building. Alan's reputation as one of the lads and the universal dislike of Nigel Stannington-James made the decision an easy one to make. And generally Basil was upsetting more and more people. But before the first car was able to leave, one of the security men had been instructed to lock the car park gate.

"Should I break it?" asked one of the lads from the Laboratory. "I could do it with a karate chop."

"What time is it?" asked Len.

"Ten to two."

"And what happens at two o'clock?"

"The afternoon shift comes on."

"But they won't be able to get into the car park will they. So they'll block the road outside, all the way up to Warrington Road, and within ten minutes we'll have the police here because of the traffic and they can go and sort Basil out. And he'll lose production as well. I just love negotiating with him sometimes."

By three o'clock, the police had come and gone, the morning shift shop steward had negotiated an extra hour's pay for the time his lads had been "imprisoned", the afternoon shift had been paid an hour for waiting to get parked and the draughtsmen just went back to work as though nothing had happened and the threat to Alan's continued employment at Wilkinson's was removed. Once again Basil had shot himself in the foot, but surely he wouldn't carry on being such a fool for much longer? Or would he?

Needless to say, Nigel did not return to the Drawing Office. He had been there just three and a half days, so he couldn't claim to have become a fully qualified draughtsman.

In his estimation that would probably take at least a fortnight.

"I thought you handled that jumped up get very well yesterday, Greeno," said Charlie the following morning. "I couldn't've done it quicker or better myself."

"Was Thelma proud of you?" asked Len.

"She was very pleased with you Len, the way you saved my job."

"Well give her my regards, won't you. Us English and Welsh have got to stick together."

"Well, not English people like that little get," said Alan.

"Would you have done the same if he'd been having a go at the French or the Irish."

"I don't know. Probably. It just made my blood boil. I've been wanting to stick one on him ever since he's been here."

"You can just imagine what his Lordship will be saying about Lancashire folk when he gets down to Head Office."

"Is that where he's gone?" asked Mick.

"Apparently," said Len, "he'll be saying they're all short-tempered, uncivilised, uncouth, evil bastards."

"That sounds quite an adequate description," laughed Yorky. "I could go along with that."

"Weird, isn't it? How many people say they hate the Welsh or the Irish or the Frogs or the Germans, but when challenged they won't be able to tell you why, or maybe they'll say that all the Welsh or Irish or French they have met have been all right," said Charlie.

"You are just as bad. That last time we all went down Liverpool for a night out and that barman short changed you out of a ten pound note, you said all Scousers were thieving gets."

"Well he was."

"Exactly, but that of itself doesn't make every other person in Liverpool the same. A few maybe, but not everybody. You would never have called Stan that would you, or that Jason we had in here for a bit."

It was a fair point, like saying all Yorkshiremen had short arms and long pockets. Charlie frequently said that about Yorky but in reality Sam was one of the most generous men in the office, particularly when there was an office collection for some other group of workers in trouble. And of course Charlie knew it and often admitted it, but never in the presence of his best mate.

Later on in the day more details emerged about the accident at Havanna. The death toll had risen to five, a deputy and another miner had failed to recover from the injuries received when the roof had caved in and two more were in intensive care and would be so for another three weeks. And the whole incident had cast some doubt on the continued existence of the Havanna colliery itself. In fact, if the pit was closed that would only leave Bank Top and Gillarsfield still working, and accountants were already considering whether to close the former as well. This was not because there was little coal left in its seams. It was due to the way they did the financial calculations in London that would determine whether another landmark in the town would disappear. It was probably also influenced by the way that the miners had pressed their case for a well-deserved wage increase earlier in the year and in doing so had upset important people, both in the Government and in Whitehall, generally.

"I reckon that if this Government gets its way, there'll be no pits left in this country in ten years," said Charlie the following afternoon.

"That'll make sense if we can go over to North Sea gas," said Mick. "And it'll mean your lad won't be risking life and limb every time he goes to work."

"It'll also mean he'll be out of a job," said Len.

"Well if there isn't the work there, it's inevitable, I suppose."

"If there's not enough work around, why don't we all go on a four day week then?"

"Could you manage forever on four days pay? Look how much you moaned when we were on that three day week."

"I think we should still get the same pay and be on a four day week. Isn't that what this so-called progress is supposed to be for instead of all the benefits going to the faceless shareholders every time."

"Well they took a risk investing their money, that's why they have to have a return on their investments."

"And don't the miners take an even bigger risk every day?"

It was just another variation on a familiar theme, a discussion that was frequently held not only in Wilkinson's Drawing Office, but in many other drawing offices up and down the land. Sometimes opinions were changed, sometimes they were hardened, not immediately but over the course of time. Attitudes also changed as people grew older; there seemed to be something of a golden rule that the older you became, the more likely you were prepared or even happy to put up with things as they were. Strange but true and unfortunate. But at the same time whenever Basil made some major decision that directly affected the wages or working conditions of the workforce, it would all be back to square one. And so it was to prove again on the following Thursday.

To get to the Rolling Mill, Basil would come down the stairs in the Main Office and then cut through the back of the Pensions Office and go through the locker room used by some of the shift workers for making a brew and eating their sandwiches when the canteen was shut. On the morning in question Basil had gone through the place around half nine and seen two men drinking tea. An hour later, and in a foul mood after having had an altercation with the Works Maintenance foreman George Carr, who he had lambasted for doing exactly what he had asked him to do the previous day, Basil had seen the same two men still sat there.

"Have you men no work to do?" he shouted. "You've been here over an hour drinking tea."

"So what?" said one of the men who Basil had never seen before "It's a damn sight warmer here than stood outside waiting about."

"So, you admit you've nothing to do. Well you can do that in your own time. You're sacked."

"So what do you want me to do about it?" the man asked very aggressively in a strange accent

"What's your name and which department are you in?"

"Smith, Transport."

"And what about you?" he said to the other.

His name was also Smith though he worked in the Tinning Shop.

"Right, the same for you, Smith. Get off the premises."

So with that, the first Smith left the room, walked down the main yard, got into his lorry and drove back to report to his own boss, the Transport Manager of a large haulage firm in Gateshead. The other Smith walked down to the Tinning Shop to talk to his shop steward. He had just been told five minutes earlier by his foreman to go down to the locker room and tell the Geordie lad that the load he was delivering to Stella North Power Station on the banks of the Tyne would be ready early in the afternoon.

Unfortunately Basil had assumed two things. Firstly that the first Smith he had sacked worked for Wilkinsons. Well, he didn't. Secondly he had assumed that the second Smith he had sacked was the same man he had seen drinking tea an hour earlier. Unfortunately it wasn't. That was actually his twin brother who an hour earlier had spent all of four minutes getting the man from Byker a drink before returning to his own job in the store room in the same Tinning Shop where his brother worked.

Another classic piece of management by Basil.

Another classic example of talking before engaging the brain.

Another classic to go in the Wilkinson book of great cock-ups of our time.

"Manager. He couldn't manage a hot dinner."

But he could certainly manage to regularly upset most of the people whose very livelihoods he controlled.

14.

THE FOREMEN'S FIASCO

Despite Basil Wilkinson's sometimes clumsy attempts to antagonise whichever of his employees came into his presence, away from work he could be quite charming. He had always made a point of attending the first hour of each of the dances that were organised by the Staff Association. During the course of the year these would be held at the Wigan Empress Ballroom at Christmas, the Floral Hall in Southport in the Spring, the summer dance at Rivington Barn and the Bonfire Night fancy dress ball in Dob Lane Conservative Club. Each had its own character and attracted quite different audiences. Then Basil decided to introduce a new event to the Wilkinson Social calendar, the Foremens' Weekend, which was to be held at the Norbeck Hotel in Blackpool. Unlike all the other dances to which any employee could attend, as long as he or she had obtained a ticket the Norbreck do was by invitation only. Most of those invited would be either foremen or managers, along with their wives. However, from time to time a chargehand might also receive an invitation, a clear indication that the person was being considered for promotion.

After the second one was held in 1971, various rumours began to circulate about some of the hanky panky that went on at these events after the formal dinner had finished. But since none of those who attended these events were likely to spill the beans, it was all conjecture, but still the subject of much nodding and winking. Then out of the blue, Tony Hanson, a chargehand in the Iron Foundry, was invited to join the party for the 1972 visit to Blackpool. Tony was clearly the last person anyone would have expected to receive such an invitation. He was a good chargehand, an ideal man for the foundry where most of the moulders did not always respond immediately to the word 'please' from anybody in authority. He was however a heavy drinker and somewhat coarse in his use and frequent misuse of the English language.

His wife, Alma, was also built in a similar mould. She had once been barred from the Derby Arms for fighting with a warehouseman and a bus driver over a comment that the latter had made about her breaking the mirror in the ladies toilet by looking in it. So when it became known that the Hanson heavyweights were going to the Norbreck, this became a source of much amusement around the factory. But then anything the Hansons did was a source of much amusement around the factory, like the time she had gone to watch her husband playing in a friendly for his local against a team from Salford. Shortly before the kick off, with the home team three players short, volunteers had been called for from among the crowd. When only two young lads came forward, Alma decided to have a go herself and followed the other two into the dressing room. Whether she would have been allowed to play was never discovered because as she began to strip off, one of the Salford lads said in a loud voice that he wouldn't mind having an early bath with the Karalius lookalike. A second Salford lad asked her if she was the hooker, and then a third, who had played a few games for Batley, made the comment that it now looked as though he wouldn't be the only old pro on the field. As a result the first melee took place five minutes before kick off. Unfortunately, as the referee tried to break it up, he received a blow to the face, his whistle got stuck in his throat and he had to be rushed to hospital, causing the game to be postponed before it had even started.

At first the lads that Tony was in charge of tried to convince him that he was soon going to get a foreman's job. Then they began to tell him that they had heard that one of the sales managers fancied his chances with Alma. One of the stories circulating on the shop floor was that wife-swapping was de rigeur at the Norbreck. But there was no proof of this because of the way everybody who attended this event kept very quiet about it, not surprisingly. And when Tony mentioned this to his own foreman, all he was told was that as long as he and their Alma kept their mouths shut they would both be in for a good night out, one that might even help his future career at work - but only if he behaved himself.

Unfortunately things started badly for Mr and Mrs. Hanson. For whatever reason they found themselves on the top table along with Basil Wilkinon and a number of senior managers, plus the highly honoured guest from the London Institute of Electrical Engineers and his buxom, haughty wife, Dorothy Helsome-Giles, a lady of impeccable taste and social etiquette. As soon as the drinks waiter appeared it became clear that the Hansons were not only on the wrong table, they were really in the wrong room. Most of the guests ordered a particular wine, often quoting the year and vineyard, one or two chose an aperitif, but nothing so fancy was asked for by Tony and Alma. He asked for a pint of mixed and she a pint of mild, which is what she always drank.

As the guests proceeded to eat the first course Alma chatted with Dorothy Helsome-Giles, who she called Dot. Well that was what she called her sister who had also once been christened Dorothy. And at first they appeared to be talking the same language when 'Dot' told Alma of her love of horses.

"Oh, I love the horses," replied Alma. "Sometimes if I get on a winning streak, I'll spend all day in the bookies."

Then she went on: "Do you ever go to Haydock; it's good there. I never go to Aintree though, there's too many toffs there for my liking."

"Dot" then told her somewhat unusual companion that her love of horses really only extended to those she owned on her large farm in the Cotswolds. Then she attempted to broaden the content of their chat by asking Alma if she ever went to the opera or the theatre.

"Yes, we do actually, well not a lot but we were there last week at the Theatre Royal in St Helens. It's really nice now that they have had it done up. Have you been there?"

Much more likely to have been found at the Strand Theatre or the Haymarket in the West End, "Dot" ignored the question and asked whether it was one of Samuel Becket's recent plays that she had seen.

"No, it was the Merseysippi Jazz Band," said Alma. "They've got a new drummer, he really gives it some welly."

Suddenly their conversation was interrupted by Basil Wilkinson tapping on the table and then proceeding to tell them all that he had just heard that the Prime Minister, Edward

Heath, had accepted an invitation to visit the Company's prestigious new headquarters in London.

Meanwhile, Tony Hanson had been chatting away to Roger Ellison, the Senior foreman in the Refinery, not someone he would normally pass the time of day with, but in the present company a relatively friendly face in a potentially hostile environment. With the main course on the table before them, the assorted guests began to take the vegetables from the dishes and place them on their plates. Then one of the managers mentioned that the pickled walnuts were particularly recommended. Tony had seen the others lift them from the dish with the silver tongs, so he decided to try them. Unfortunately he was not too skilled with the use of these tongs. The walnuts seemed to allude his every attempt to lift them on to his plate. Then, with his final attempt, the chosen walnut shot up into the air and slipped down the cleavage of "Dot's" dress. At this point Tony was faced with the decision what to do next. In these situations do you (a) ignore it and hope no one else has seen it, or (b) apologise and in doing so make everybody round the table aware of what has happened, or (c) quickly remove the offending walnut by a quick sleight of hand, or should one use the tongs and not be misinterpreted as trying to fondle the breasts of the important guest's wife. Fortunately it was all resolved for him by the quick action of "Dot", who removed the walnut herself. But things were then made worse when Alma turned to her husband and said in a loud voice:

"That wouldn't've happened if you hadn't used them stupid pliers. Why didn't you use your fingers like you do when you're at home." Then, turning to "Dot", she shook her head and said, "Ee, some men just have no manners, do they? You'd think he'd been dragged up."

By the time the dinner was over Alma had consumed four pints of mild along with a double brandy, which Cecil Helsome-Giles had bought everyone, and a gin and tonic, thanks to the generosity of Basil who seemed in excellent form and who in Alma's wild thoughts was continually glancing her way. Tony had also had more than his fair share, well there was nothing fair about it, he hadn't put his hand in his pocket once and had managed to consume two pints of mixed to start with then three pints of bitter, Cecil's double brandy and a pernod, which he had never sampled before. He was now feeling very relaxed and, seeing "Dot" smiling at him, began to think about trying to lob another pickled walnut down her cleavage. Fortunately the waiter managed to remove them while he was thinking about it. Then Basil stood up and suggested a fifteen minute break to freshen up, after which they should all reassemble in the bar where the drinks for the first hour would be on the company.

Tony and Alma returned to their bedroom, at which point they were convinced that it would be in the bar that partners would be chosen, not just for the dancing but hopefully for the rest of the night. By this time Tony was sure that by the end of the weekend, "Dot" would not remember him by his initial clumsy performance at the table, rather by his seductive skills in her bedroom. He also remembered what one of his chargehands had told him about these events, how everybody who was keen to join in reappeared suitably dressed for the second half of the evening. So he proceeded to put on his pyjamas while Alma donned her nightie plus a pair of red slippers and a beret. Then, along the corridor they walked and pushed open the double doors that overlooked the bar just as Basil was calling for quiet once again. As they began to descend down the stairs holding hands, with Tony looking around the assembled guests for "Dot", Alma tripped and the pair of them rolled down the rest of the stairs.

Fortunately it was Roger Ellison who helped the pair of them get up and as he did he whispered in Tony's ear that the fancy dress ball was in November and to piss off back upstairs and get dressed. And the following Monday a copy of the week's menus for the Senior Managers' section of the works canteen was pinned up on the noticeboard in the entrance to the Foundry. And on it, underlined in red biro for Thursday, was the chef's speciality, Beef and Onion Pie and Cabbage with Pickled Walnut.

Wilkinson's canteen had to be seen to be believed. It was an enormous place, but for its main purpose, that of feeding the hungry, it represented an unbelievable divided structure. Firstly there was the Rose Room, where only the very top managers ate. It had just five tables, a large drinks cabinet, a head waiter, four waitresses and a young man who came from Chester every day to serve the drinks. Next to it was the Bluebell Room where around fifty or so senior managers were served. Then there was the Hyacinth Room where a hundred or so of the Middle Management team were expected to dine. Next was the Small Hall which could seat up to five hundred and where the members of the Junior Staff and the foremen ate. Here it was still waitress service, unlike the Main Hall where the shop floor had to queue up to get their grub. But even here there was division with the charge-hands all expected to sit at the top of the room next to the bandstand.

At the top of the building, overlooking the football pitch, was the kitchen, well to be more accurate the three kitchens. A chef who had once worked at the Grosvenor Hotel in London was responsible for the food that appeared in the Rose Room. Another maitre de cuisine, who had cooked food for the high and mighty in Paris, looked after the needs of those who ate in the Blue Bell and Hyacinth rooms. And the health of everybody else was in the hands of around a dozen cooks, most of whom had obtained their qualifications and knowledge of preparing food at Ashurst Technical College (Food and Catering Department).

Another source of division was not surprisingly the quality of the food, which actually came from three different suppliers, but perhaps the biggest complaint was about the birds in the Main Hall. Due both to the main doors always being open and the cracks in the roof, pigeons and seagulls were forever flying around and frequently dive-bombing the men as they ate their food. Attempts to get the management to do something about the problem were rarely successful, until one Monday morning when a trade delegation from China visited the factory, interested in buying equipment for the modernisation of their Power Generation industry. At a rather grand reception on their arrival, Basil had told them that there were no class divisions in this factory. Everybody belonged to a great team who all pulled together and, swayed by the power of his own voice, he went on to say that any employee could join any of the company's social clubs, which was true, anyone could save for his prosperity through the firm's saving schemes, which was also true, and those who wanted to advance themselves would have their night school fees paid, which was also true. And then after emphasising that all Wilkinson's employees worked for one common goal; he went on to say that they all breathed the same air, they all enjoyed their social life together and they all ate together.

It was not quite clear why he had said that. Perhaps he had meant to say that they all ate under the same extremely large roof. Perhaps it was because he was trying to make a political point after having visited Russia a couple of years earlier and visited a factory where the managers ate in a canteen some distance from where the rest of the workforce ate.

As soon as news of this statement leaked out, a dozen or so moulders in the Iron Foundry decided that they would take this as a change in company policy. They made a point of being the first to get to the canteen that lunchtime and headed straight for the Rose Room, where they convinced the head waiter Terence of their right to eat there and then proceeded to empty the drinks cabinet. A short while later Basil was seen eating in the Works Canteen along with his important guests from China and whose visit coincided with the arrival of around half a dozen very anti-social seagulls from the Pier Head in Liverpool who proceeded to dive-bomb their table all the time they were eating!

Two days later the factory was graced by the visit of a delegation from the Department of Trade and Industry. At a reception on their arrival, Basil had said the very opposite to what he had told the men from the East. He told his visitors from Whitehall that there were social divisions within the factory, divisions that actually encouraged those with talent and ability to work harder to get to the top. And this was one of the main reasons for the success of the company at a time of increasing competition, particularly from China and South East Asia. After a short walk round the Refinery and Rolling Mill, the party then headed for the Rose Room where no expense had been spared to entertain these important visitors from the City. Unfortunately for Basil, one of those who had witnessed the NATO-inspired attack by reactionary right wing seagulls on the revolutionary Chinese workers was Joe Atherton, an electrician who was becoming fed up eating pigeon pie three or four times a week. That week he had been rewiring the lights in the kitchen and so had every right to be in the canteen along with all his tools and equipment. While no one was paying much attention to him early that morning, he had clambered up into the ceiling area above the Rose Room and drilled a few holes over the spot where Basil's party would be sat. As lunchtime approached he went back up there with a bag of white pellets and as the important guests began to eat the first course, a highly original tomato soup flavoured not surprisingly with sage and basil. Joe began to drop these white pellets into the soup of the under Minister for National Research and Development and his associates. Unknown to Joe, Basil had been dragged away to answer the telephone in the office of the chef Terence. And so for the first few minutes the visitors, all well-groomed to a man, used the stiff upper lip approach to pretend nothing was amiss. From his little spy hole, Joe could see that no one was paying attention so he seriously considered bringing out the heavy artillery, which in this case would have been 6BA screws, then 4BA screws and if none of this influenced events, six inch nails. But in the end he chickened out and decided to drop just one drawing pin, hoping that this would throw suspicion on the Drawing Office before making a quick retreat back through the labyrinth of passageways in the roof and climbing down the ladder into the store room that led into the back of the kitchen.

Immediately after the meal was over, Basil summoned George Carr, the Works Maintenance foreman, to find out what was immediately above the table at which he and his guests had been sat. George knew Joe was working in the canteen kitchen so told him to have a look. And so Joe was able to destroy all the evidence of his attack on the Rose Room by blaming it on rats and putting his boot through the six inch square area in which he had drilled his holes. As a result of both incidents, by the end of the following week the canteen roof was totally repaired and made rat-free, pigeon-free and seagull-free. And after that everybody ate much better, thanks it seemed to Basil's concern for his workforce, although really all of it was down to Joe, although he didn't dare tell anybody about his heroic attack on the forces of reaction and parliamentary privilege.

Joe's reticence in telling anybody about what he had done was understandable. Although he and all the others who had worked at Wilkinson's over the years had never been told directly that dropping things into the food of guests was a sackable offence, it probably was. In fact, on reflection he began to think it was a stupid thing to have done, not because of the action itself but because he could not tell anyone about it. He couldn't tell his wife, she couldn't keep something like that to herself, well she probably could all week until Saturday night in the club after she had had a couple of Babychams. He couldn't really tell any of his other relatives either, although none of them would have believed him anyway. But in the end he decided that he would tell his Uncle Herbert. He was the only one who Joe could trust completely, but only because Uncle Herbert was bedridden and stone deaf. But then three days later Joe heard some rather disturbing news from his foreman, George Carr.

Along with a number of other foremen, George had been summoned to a meeting to discuss Basil's proposal to knock down the old Maintenance Shop and relocate most of the maintenance men to two smaller buildings, one behind the Refinery and the other on the floor above the new Rolling Mill. The meeting was held in the Board Room, one indication that the subject was important; the second indication being that all present were invited to stay on and enjoy the buffet. But by half twelve the only food that had appeared was a large plate full of bread rolls.

While they were waiting for the rest of the food to arrive, George had jokingly said that it looked as though they might have to finish up eating fresh air butties. Basil then commented that he hadn't always been as comfortably off as he was now and how he could remember a regular meal in their large detached house in the Thirties being "bread and pull it". But imitating Basil's upper class accent George told the lads back in the shop that afternoon that their boss had actually said it was "bread and pellet!"

15.

THE NAKED APPRENTICE

"Eh, Greeno do you still collect stamps and go train spotting?"

"He certainly does," said Mick; "but he only does it in the dark now so nobody can see him."

"How can you collect stamps in the dark?"

"Doesn't your lass get annoyed when you nip out every night after the news to see what's pulling the Blackpool train?"

"I bet she thinks he's seeing another woman."

"No, you're wrong. What really annoys Thelma is when she finds out he's come back five minutes later and not gone to paddle in the sea."

"Do you still read comics, Greeno? What's your favourite one? Is it the Beano or the Dandy?"

That morning Alan had made a mistake on one of his drawings. It could easily have been sorted out with the assistance of a friendly wireman. Unfortunately it was Terry Foster, who had spotted the error and blown the thing up out of all proportion, as he always did. On hearing about it, the rest of the office decided they would make it "Have a Go at Greeno Day".

"All right, I made a mistake. I'll put my hand up for it. The first one this year."

"The first one this morning."

"Eh, joking apart Greeno, have you still got any of your old comics?"

"Why?"

"Because if you have you might be sitting on a fortune. I read in the paper last week about a bloke in Coventry who was prepared to pay up to ten quid for any copies of Radio Fun before 1949."

"He must have money to burn."

"He has. He's just won a fortune on the pools."

"I could think of a few other things I'd spend my money on if I'd won the pools."

"You never know; he might be going on a world cruise on a luxury yacht and want them to read for a bit of relaxation."

"If I were going on a world cruise I'd think I'd have an all female crew and have a lot of relaxation," said John.

"Would you have any oars on your boat?"

"I'd have two crews, one for the day shaft and one for the night shaft."

"Where would you go?"

"We'd set off from Liverpool, go down through the Mediterranean, spend a few days at Nice or Cannes, then on to Sicily and call in at St Helens."

"St Helena, you pillock."

"That's where Napoleon was exiled to."

"What, St Helens; the poor man."

It was definitely going to be one of those days.

"Would you take any of us, John?"

"I'd definitely take you Charlie, but you'd have to get off at our first main port of call."

"And which erotic place in the world would that be?"

"Birkenhead."

"I'll tell you what I've got at home," said Alan.

"The early onset of senile dementure," laughed Charlie.

"No, the first copy of Eagle. I bet that's worth a few bob now."

This led on to comparisions being drawn between that glossy comic and earlier favourites like Adventure, Hotspur, Rover and Wizard. Then Mick began to talk about the adventures of Dan Dare and Digby against the Mekon, which would appear to have amused and interested him immensely even though he was nearly thirty when Eagle made its first appearance in 1953.

"Dan Dare was much better on Radio Luxembourg," said Len. "Like Journey into Space, with a bit of an imagination it was a lot more frightening."

"Do you remember that time the Mekon captured Digby and made him send a message back to Dan Dare telling him it was safe to come to visit him?" asked Mick. "Well, as you all know very well, Digby was from Wigan and like most Wiganers very clever. So he sends this postcard back to Earth and tells Dan Dare that he was having a wonderful time, just like when he went to visit his Auntie Beryl in Heckmondwike. Now Dan Dare knew that Digby couldn't stand her or Heckmondwike and so knew that it was a trap."

"Crikey, that's really exciting Mick," said Len. "However, did you manage to go to sleep that night. I would've been terrified."

Totally bored by this story John then asked if anyone knew what he would do if he won the pools. But before he could tell them which famous Californian nightclub he would arrange for his latest band to perform at, the door opened and in marched John Pickles, the Engineering Manager. And the rest of the morning was spent in urgent discussion about how to get a Mark IV speed control box redesigned in order to use a larger load-sensing device.

At lunchtime Charlie, Yorky, Mick and Alan were sat on the wall outside the Brass Foundry watching the world go up and down Warrington Road when an old man slowly walked up to Charlie, put his hand on his own head, opened his mouth widely and then said:

"Haven't you been put down yet, you old bugger."

A broad grin appeared on Charlie's face as he stood up and shook the man's hand. Then, turning to the others, he introduced Tommy, the bane of his life when he had been an apprentice at Pilkington's Ravenhead works.

"So how are you doing? I haven't seen you for ages."

"All right for an old un."

"Have you had your telegram from the Queen yet."

"Eh, watch it, I'm only eighty three."

"And what are you doing round here?"

"My granddaughter lives in Platt Street. I'm just going there for my dinner."

Then he turned to the others and asked them how they managed to put up with Charlie all day. After a few minutes chat, he sat down on the wall next to Yorky and said:

"Are you from Yorkshire, lad?"

"Aye."

"Is it near Halifax?"

"Aye."

"I thought so, it's the way you pronounce your t's."

Then, turning to Charlie he went on, nodding at the man from Mytholmroyd:

"Is he any good, Charlie? Can he run errands and come back with what he went for?"

"For a Yorkshireman he's not bad, which is not to say he is much good, but when he's finished his apprenticeship, he'll do."

"Charlie, you were the worst apprentice I ever had with me and I'd a few over the years."

Then he laughed and went on: "Do you remember that time when you were in the showers with me."

Charlie most certainly did. It was the first week that he had been with Tommy. They had spent all afternoon wiring thermocouples that were used to measure the temperature of molten glass. It was an energy-sapping job, working in an environment where the temperature was well over a hundred degrees. Around twenty to five, they had collected their tools, dumped them in the electricians' locker behind the foreman's office and gone downstairs into the showers for a well earned wash. As they were stripping off, Tommy made a big point of telling Alan that the boiler was on its last legs and likely to blow up at any time. However, he need not worry because Tommy had fitted an alarm if it was going to overheat but if they did hear it, they had to run down the corridor and go straight out through the door at the end.

Alan was first in the showers when Tommy disappeared to get some more soap from his locker. The next thing the alarm went off and straight away Charlie did what Tommy had told him. Not stopping to collect his clothes or even his towel he ran towards the door, pushed it open and ran out into the yard. As he did he looked round and saw Tommy about thirty yards behind him running. But he never appeared through the door which had now shut. Charlie tried to open it but it wouldn't budge. So thinking Tommy was trapped inside, he ran all the way round the block to the main entrance door, which was also locked. So he ran across the road to the electricians' shop to get help, ignoring the fact that he was completely naked. He looked around and suddenly saw about fifty women from the Wages Department heading for the main gates and their bus home. And when he saw a couple of them holding a large magnifying glass he knew he had been tricked. And over the next few months he would be frequently tricked.

Back in the office Charlie told them a bit more about his old mentor. Of course it started off with a funny one:

"I remember a few years ago when we all went to the funeral of one of the old timers. We were all waiting around for the cars to pick us up at the cemetery to take us to the reception when he sees an old mate there. Now you think at a funeral everyone would be on their best behaviour, but not Tommy. He says to this bloke, 'Eh Fred, how old are you now?'. So this old guy tells everybody within earshot that he was eighty four, at which point Tommy says to him with a dead straight face, 'Is it worth you going home?'" Then Charlie continued: "I remember once he told me that his neighbour had died. The previous Sunday morning his wife had just started making their Sunday dinner and asked him to go and get a cabbage from his allotment. Well off he went and never came back. According to Tommy the bloke went into his little shed he had there, sat down and dropped dead. And so his wife who was in a wheel chair most of the time was left at home waiting for him. So I then asked Tommy what did she do. And he replied, 'She had to open a tin of peas'.

"You know he never had any qualifications, but he was good at anything he turned his hand to, plumbing, bricklaying, mending cars, you name it he could do it. And whenever he got a new apprentice with him he used to help them with their night school work. D.C. motors, that was his special forte."

"And what was his special fifte?"

"History, that was something else he knew a lot about."

"What, 1066 and all that?"

"No, 1895 and all that. He reckons he saw the first ever Northern Union game that Saints played: it was against Rochdale. Now here's a question for you, Greeno. How many players took part in that game?"

"Thirty."

"How did you know that it was still fifteen-a-side?"

"Because my Uncle Len told me and you. Have you forgotten?"

"Oh aye."

"Well here's a question for you, what colours did Saints play in?"

"Blue and white striped shirts, knee length shorts and black socks."

"Very good. Well I bet you don't know where they used to get stripped?"

"The Talbot in Duke Street, and they used to get taken up to the ground in a horse-drawn wagon."

Then Mick chimed in: "Aye, and I bet they made the away team walk it there!"

Then came another another historical question from Charlie:

"When did they first start using the clubhouse?"

"Don't know."

"They built it in 1920 and Lord Derby opened it before the Boxing Day derby against Wigan."

"Who won?" asked Mick.

"I don't know."

"That must mean Wigan did," laughed Mick.

"Look out, that sounds like Basil on the warpath," muttered Yorky, and immediately everyone assumed the keen to be at work position, one which they had to maintain with some difficulty for the rest of the afternoon while listening to Basil shouting and bawling both at John Battesby, Alan Groves and Ronnie Garner in John's office. Judging from what they could hear it would appear that Basil had once again been the cause of a problem that he was now trying to blame everybody else for.

In the past the factory had been known as Butlins. But with the reappearance of Basil at the helm, things had gone down the pan. One of the reasons was associated with the newly-appointed accountant that Basil had taken on, the suitably named Mr. Temple. He was quite prepared to admit that he knew absolutely nothing about engineering. All he was interested in was sorting out the finances and ensuring Wilkinson's made a large profit. As a result all the managers had been instructed by him to exercise much tighter financial control over what went on in their departments. Some managers did this with enthusiasm while others ignored his guidelines, at least until Basil found out. John Battesby in particular was quite offended by the degree of importance that "that jumped up clerk" was now afforded. Perhaps that was why his budget for office supplies was cut quite drastically. And it was around this time that the issue of the rubber rations arose.

The basic things that any draughtsman needed to carry out his work were paper on his drawing board, a pencil, set square, scale rule, erasing shield and rubber. Around the time that John Battesby was being instructed into how to organise the office finances, something he had been doing for nearly ten years, John Meredith found that he needed a new rubber. But when he went to get one from Rita she found that she only had three left. So without more thought to the matter she gave John one and then walked down to the Main Stores to have a chat with her friend Maureen and bring back whatever stationary the D.O. was short of. But she was more than surprised when Maureen told her that she would have to fill out a R11 form and have it signed by her Manager before she could have anything. So on returning to the D.O. she went to see John Battesby, only to discover that he was out for the afternoon at Fidlers Ferry Power Station.

When she asked him the following morning if he had any R11 forms, he told her he hadn't a clue what they were and before she could ask him what to do about getting stationary, he had put on his coat and disappeared back to the North bank of the Mersey. So she decided to go down to the General Office and sort things out. Two hours later she returned empty handed, having spent the best part of the morning trying to find out exactly what R11 forms were and where they could be obtained but without any success. By this time, and purely coincidentally, another five draughtsmen had just rubbed the last of their rubbers away. This shortage was beginning to take on the status of a national emergency.

In the absence of John Battesby, Alan Groves was called on to make a major decision. In his view the only way to handle the problem in the short term, at least until John returned, was to share the rubbers out. So he instructed every draughtsman to put his rubber on his desk. Then, knowing the layout of the office, he gave one rubber to every fourth draughtsman. It was not a very good working arrangement, and quite soon what became known as the war of the rubbers started. And shortly after Basil heard about it, he let it be known that for small amounts of stationary the old arrangement that had existed since the year dot would continue to operate, much to the distress of Mr Temple with all his qualifications in business accounting.

But before he could do much more damage, he was suitably tricked and embarrassed.

Mr. Temple, no one ever knew his first name, was a bit of a fitness freak. Each morning he would run to work in his London Business School Athletics Section vest, shorts and trainers from his large detached house in Orchard Lane, usually arriving a good half hour before any other members of the Finance Department. Then he would collect his clothes from his office and go down to the Refinery showers and wash away the exertions of his three mile run, get dressed and put his running tackle back in the locker. One morning later that week, when he had come out of the showers, he discovered that his tie and one sock had disappeared! He looked high and low for them. It could not have happened on a worse day; he was due to address a meeting of the board an hour later. He went straight up to his office as furtively as possible and told Betty the office junior to come in. He then gave her a five pound note and told her to go into town and buy him a pair of socks and a tie and to be quick about it. One hour later Basil was somewhat shocked to see his so-called financial whizz-kid wearing a bright yellow tie on which a shadowy and tastleless picture of a naked woman was imposed and a pair of bright red socks. Betty had clearly been keen to apply Mr Temple's financial principles of always paying the least possible for products and services and so maximising the financial gain either for the company or the individual. She had gone straight to the nearest charity shop and on return had proudly returned four pounds thirty pence to the company financial guru along with his "new" clothes.

And fortunately for most of those concerned, the incident convinced Mr Temple that his presence was not thoroughly appreciated in the engineering industry and within the month he had left. However, before he did go he managed to upset Peter Warner, an engineer in the Outside Contracts Department. Until recently most of the O.C.D. site work was in England, Scotland and Wales, usually at power stations, collieries and heavy power plants. But due to Basil's ability to win orders, particularly from abroad, more and more of the O.C.D. work involved foreign travel, firstly in Belgium, France and Germany and then further afield. With his somewhat limited knowledge of French and Italian, mainly learned on holiday at the Club Mediterranean camp near Nice, Peter had been able to wangle himself into becoming the O.C.D. Overseas Manager. As soon as an order was won he would shoot off to the site and begin to sort out all the necessary details. On his first visit to Tunisia, to a cotton mill, he had worked out how he could save Wilkinson's a substantial amount of money by changing a few things in the contract. To do this he had to convince the local site engineer and this involved wining and dining him a bit. This was something Peter was very good at. Unfortunately there was a slight linguistic misunderstanding and the site engineer brought along his brother and two other engineers from the plant to a meal in a very expensive hotel restaurant.

After the meal they went down to the bar where they just happened to meet up with three girls who worked in the mill. During the course of a rather raucous evening, one of the girls had a bit of an altercation with the waiter. Despite this Peter was able to get a receipt for all he had bought and which he duly included with the rest of his expenses. Compared to all his other expenses it was rather large to say the least. And to make matters worse it was in Arabic. So Mr Temple, slightly suspicious, gave it to a multi-lingual acquaintance who translated it and told him that it actually said: "This bill was for five drunken fools to consume a small amount of food, a large amount of alcohol and be entertained by three whores."

Surprisingly nothing was said about the matter. Mr Temple told Basil but all Basil could see was the money that Peter had saved the company. All that Basil wanted was more and more orders coming in, and if that was done by fair means or foul he didn't care. And another beneficiary of Basil's wordly view a few weeks later was Alan.

He had just removed the cover from his drawing board when Alan Groves called him into his office and asked him how good his French was. "Not bad," replied Alan. "Why?"

"I've just had Basil on the phone. You know we're hoping to get a big order from the French Railways. Well three of their engineers were due here today, but only one has arrived and he doesn't speak much English. Basil wants someone to look after him. Can you take him round and keep him amused?"

"If you've got a job number for it, oui monsieur le President."

As soon as the rest of them heard about it, they of course started pouring scorn on his ability to speak French, but he needn't have worried because actually Jean Pierre Villancourt did speak a little English - and he was also a treiziste.

As soon as he walked into Basil's office Alan could tell by Basil's body language that it was essential that the visitor had to be given a good impression of Wilkinson's, both its products and its personnel. The boss then told Alan to take him round the factory, spending all day if necessary, eat in the Hyacinth Room at lunchtime and generally act as an ambassador for the company. So the morning was taken up visiting the most spectacular parts of the factory, the Refinery, the new Rolling Mill and the now disused old Rolling Mill and the Brass Foundry. As soon as they were alone, Jean Pierre told Alan that he could speak some English but had difficulty understanding it when spoken by an English person. Alan told him that he could speak French but likewise had difficulty understanding it when spoken by a French person. As a result they got on very well. And when right out of the blue Jean Pierre asked Alan did he like the football or the rugby, well conversation soon moved on to Jean Pierre's favourite sport, rugby a treize as the greatest game is known over the Channel.

As dinnertime approached Alan decided that he would rather eat with all the lads in the junior staff canteen rather than being listened to in the Hyacinth Room by the managers. It was a wise move. By the time they had finished eating it was clear that Jean Pierre felt that he was among friends. Then it was over to the bowling green for his first ever game of crown green bowls. After that they went round the Iron Foundry, Tinning Shop, through the Accessories Workshop, where he introduced the chargehand, Bertha, to her very first Frenchman, and she nearly fainted when he took her hand, kissed it and said "enchante" to her. Then it was back to the Drawing Office for the afternoon tea break where he was very pleased to meet their tea lady Joan. Then, as they sat there, Charlie chatted away to Jean Pierre as though he had known him for years. He started by asking their visitor if Greeno could actually speak any French.

"Yes, bien sur, better than everybody else here, I think. I do understand his words. But he sometimes says somethings which is wrong, but yes he is good for me."

"He tells us that French people think he is from Belgium," said Mick.

"Yes, I think so. I think he has a strong accent in English and so it comes again when he speaks French."

"Can you tell that we all speak with strong accents, Jean Pierre?"

"Yes, it is like Scotland accent I think."

"Can you tell the different accents in this room?"

"In this room? I do not understand."

Then Len tried to explain what he meant by pointing out the differences among them. Charlie was from St Helens, Mick from Wigan, Alan, Dickie and he were from Ashurst and although the three towns were very near the accents were different.

"I don't know, you all sound the same I think, but not like in London or TV people."

So then Len suggested that each of them read a couple of paragraphs from Mick's paper, but despite that Jean Pierre could still not tell the difference.

"Jean Pierre, you listen to Mick say the words down, out, round. Listen to how he pronounces the 'o', more like an 'e' - dewn, ewt, rewnd."

So Mick then obliged.

"Now listen to Charlie, his 'o' sounds much more like an 'o'."

Likewise, the lad from Thatto Heath obliged.

"Now listen to Alan, his 'o' is not as strong as Mick's 'o', but it doesn't sound like Charlie's pure 'o'."

The Frenchman listened carefully, totally bemused by what he was hearing them say.

"Now listen to Mick say 'Are you not going out tonight?', listen how he drops the last word in the sentence. Then listen to Charlie, the way he says it, the words begin to rise as he says them." It was all getting a bit surreal. A few more efforts were made to highlight the linguistic differences found in such a small area when the door opened and in walked the owner of another very distinctive accent, Jason the Scouser.

So they made him talk to Jean Pierre and then asked him where he thought he came from. To their amazement their visitor replied that he thought Jason sounded like the Beatles. Then it was the turn of Jean Pierre. He said a few sentences in his own accent from Lezignan, then he imitated a Parisienne, then a Breton and finally a man from Marseilles. But as they say, time flies when you are having a good time and particularly when you are being paid to have a good time and so finally Jean Pierre had to take his leave of them. But Charlie made sure there was no embarrassment right at the end when he said:

"I hope you're not going to kiss us all, and especially not me, mon ami."

By the time they returned to Basil's office, it was nearly five o'clock. And by this time Alan had arranged to take Jean Pierre to a match at Knowsley Road when the Frenchman came again. Unfortunately for all, Jean Pierre never returned to Ashurst, but a few weeks later a large crate was delivered to the Drawing Office containing half a dozen bottles of Vin de Lezignan in appreciation for the good time Jean Pierre had enjoyed "avec les ouvriers de Ashurst".

16.

TWO FAT LADIES

Over the years, there had always been plenty of work at Wilkinson's. Anyone joining the firm in the Fifties and Sixties knew they had a job for life as long as they did nothing stupid. But with big changes coming about in the world economy and the fourfold increase in the price of oil in the early Seventies, the engineering industry began to suffer and no more so than in the town of Ashurst. And over the following few years the whole area was to see many of its long-standing industrial landmarks disappear.

Ever since assuming the position of chairman of the company after his father had suffered a massive heart attack in 1962, Basil had combined this role with that of head of the sales team. At least once a month he would fly off to somewhere in Europe or further afield and return with orders either for immediate delivery or some time in the future. But more recently he had not been achieving the success he had once enjoyed. Increasingly the other managers began to ask each other why he was spending so much time away from the factory. What they didn't appreciate was that Basil secretly liked to combine business with pleasure. This was why he planned most of his journeys abroad so that he had to change flights at the Dutch airport at Schipol. This gave him the opportunity frequently to stay overnight in Amsterdam, for reasons that had nothing at all to do with engineering or business.

On one occasion, flying back from a visit to Iran where he had once been introduced to the Shah, he had looked forward keenly to an overnight stay in the city of bicycles, canals and naughty ladies. After checking in to his favourite hotel on Marnixstraat, he had made one telephone call, then changed into casual clothes, eaten at a Vietnamese restaurant near to the railway station and walked down to Brankendom Straat in the red light district of the city to meet an old acquaintance, Dietra van Poofen, who held a position in the city's entertainment and leisure industry. In fact, over the years she could be said to have held many positions in the entertainment and leisure industry of Amsterdam.

Dietra was quite a large lady, in fact she was very large. She was good company, certainly in the physical sense with soft silky skin that Basil loved to take hold of and play with in his hands as though it was putty. He met her as usual at the back of the bar in the Hotel der Plaaq. They chatted for a while, drinking pernod with Amstel beer chaser and then just as she was about to take him upstairs to show him her latest trick, Basil froze. Into the bar stumbled a noisy group of drunken Englishmen. Round the corner he saw them plonk themselves down adjacent to the stairs that led up to where he would soon be heading. He waited to hear them speak and immediately by their accents he could tell that they were from the North of England. He listened more carefully and picked out at least two Wiganers, another from Widnes, a Sintelliner and, horror of horrors, the dulcet tones and intonations of a man from Ashurst. As the time passed they consumed more beer and became even more boisterous. Then, as one went to the bar, Basil took a quick peek at him and vaguely recognised the face.

By this time Dietra's equally large friend Petra had joined them, happily eyeing up the group, some if not all she hoped she would be entertaining later in the evening. It was clear he had to get out of the place because if he stayed there much longer the lads would soon start roaming round the place, possibly to put money into the jukebox they were sat near to. So he asked Petra to go up to her room and take a large sheet off her bed. As she walked past them they all made various suggestions to her, ones that she would normally have been more than pleased to take up. The same thing happened on the way down, more lewd comments and questions of what she would do for five guilders. Then she put the sheet over Basil, tied it up with yellow ribbon and then with Petra in front and Dietra behind, the three of them had walked past the lads and up the stairs, thirty plus stone of unequalled ugliness about to have their way with some unfortunate twelve stone nothing.

"Eh, lad it's your girlfriends that should have a bag over their faces" and "I'd be embarrassed too if I was seen with them two" and "I hope you're going to be on top, old lad or you'll get crushed to death" being some of the many ribald comments the lads made.

Back at work a couple of days later, with little to show for his time away and aware of the growing decline of the national economy generally, Basil decided that it was an opportune time to get rid of some of those who clocked in and out every day but who in his opinion, did little else. He just regretted not having embarked on this course of action a couple of months earlier, before he had made that stupid speech to the Manchester Chamber of Commerce when he said that he considered his workforce to be his most prized asset. This had been given great prominence in the local papers and particularly the St Helens Reporter, the Ashurst Reporter and the Wigan Observer.

After a long session with John Pickles, the Engineering Manager, he had been eating his lunch in the Rose Room when he heard a great deal of laughing and guffawing from one of the other tables. That afternoon he had asked John Barker, who had been sat at that particular table, what all the noise had been about.

"Ronnie Garner was telling us about some of the things one of his fitters had done while him and his mates had been in Amsterdam for a dirty weekend. I'm not sure how true they all were, particularly the ones involving a donkey, but one story seemed to ring true. He said they were in a bar having a right good laugh when a very large woman comes down the stairs carrying a bed sheet. A few minutes later she and an even bigger women go back upstairs with this sheet tied up over a little bloke. They thought they must have kidnapped him, because they were sure no decent man would have gone with either of them willingly, unless he was kinky. After a while the first women comes back down the stairs and so they invite her to join them, buy her drinks and ask why the bloke was under the sheet. She says if they each paid her five guilders, she would tell them. So they do. She tells them that he was an Englishman and often slept with her friend when he was over from England on business. He had told her that he knew one of them, which is why he had to have the sheet put over his head so whoever it was wouldn't recognise him. Then she said if they all gave her another five guilders she would tell them more about what she knew of him. So of course they did and she told them that he came from near Manchester where he owned a large engineering firm and his name was Brazil."

"Well it certainly wasn't me," stuttered Basil. "I was nowhere near the place. I spent all night in a Vietnamese restaurant."

The phrase 'He who protesteth' ran through John's head as he smiled to himself. "You dirty old bugger," he thought.

And with this on his mind Basil decided that it would be better to let things lie for a while, until some other major incident occurred or his visit to Amsterdam had been forgotten.

As a result he spent a week down in the London offices before deciding that now was the time to act. The banks had no morals when it came to high finance, neither did the oil sheiks in the Middle East or his competitors in the engineering world. Moreover, many other firms were laying off their workers, at least he wouldn't be the first to do it. And so the following week he announced that around one in twelve of the workforce would be made redundant.

The news did not come as a complete surprise. Over the last few months, the size of the workforce had been slowly going down. Whenever anybody had left or retired he or she had not been replaced. The intake of apprentices had dropped from twenty four to six, the night shift in the Iron Foundry had been laid off and some of the Technical Publicity work transferred to London. Redundancies had also been announced at Mathers, Jarratts and Wallworks, while at Delaney's there were now only two draughtsmen where once there had been a dozen, and Smithson Power Design had closed down completely.

In fact, across South Lancashire and most of the North of England, the situation did not look promising. Those on the wrong side of fifty began to talk about what it had been like in the Thirties. Younger ones like Alan and John with young families could not see much of a future in engineering. Len pointed out that they all had to stick together and fight for their jobs. Most agreed with him, though unsure just how successful they might be. Everybody began to look for someone or something to blame. Ted Heath and his Government came in for a lot of stick, equally OPEC was blamed for raising the price of oil. Others thought it was all because of the miners, the dock workers the steel workers and the postmen striking for higher wages than the country could afford. Then Charlie put things in a different light by blaming the big companies like GEC, Pilkingtons, ICI and Ford for wanting higher profits for their shareholders than the country could afford.

Inevitably the tea break discussions began to take on much more of a serious dimension. Everybody knew that they had little job security any more and so it was either a case of look after number one and bugger everybody else, or stick together and fight to keep their jobs. Various meetings were held at which a strategy for dealing with the issue was hammered out. Unfortunately, as always, the six members of the Jig and Tool took a very selfish attitude since they were pretty confident their own jobs were safe. The Sheet Metal men were also against any militant action since in their opinion the shop floor was grossly over-manned and refusing to work normally would only make things worse.

Then Basil called the Office Committee to a meeting and gave them the details of how the redundancies would affect the white collar staff. He was going to close down the Metal Fatigue Lab, the High Voltage Test Bay and Technical Publicity, twenty two people in total.

He was going to move the Contracts Specifications office to London where they would have their job titles altered and he was going to get rid of twelve draughtsmen, made up of two Electrical men, three Sheet Metal men, three Mechanical men and four Jig and Tool with the other two being moved into what used to be the old Store Room at the back of the Sand Wash. And finally he was getting rid of his Personnel Officer and the four useless women he kept amused at no small expense. And before the Committee could ask any questions, Basil told them they would all be receiving any further information through their letter boxes at home and to go back and get some work done for once.

As they walked down the corridor on their way back to the Drawing Office, the Personnel Manager, John Walker, asked Len to come into his office. He was sixty three and soon due for retirement. Being made redundant was just the thing for him, he would do very nicely out of it financially. But he was also a man of strong principle, a Methodist lay preacher, one who had always practised what he preached, albeit in a very old fashioned way. Over the last couple of years he had been appalled at some of the things Basil had said and done. He then told Len about Basil's overall plan, which was to maintain the same level of output with a reduced workforce, instal a climate of fear and get rid of all the Office Committee. While it was true there was overmanning in some sections, an eight per cent reduction in the total number employed was well over the top. Neither was it true there were no orders; there were quite a few, Basil just hadn't put them into the Planning Office and wouldn't do until he had got rid of those he didn't want.

"How do you know all this, John?"

"I daren't tell you who it has come from, Len, so keep this under your hat. But you'd be very surprised if I told you who it was. All I will say is that some of those who work nearest to Basil dislike him the most."

And as Len prepared to leave, armed with some powerful ammunition but not exactly sure how best to use it, John went on:

"If anybody wants to know why you were in here, it was because I was asking your union to sponsor a charity event that our chapel is putting on for starving children in Ethiopa."

Straight after lunch, a meeting of the union members was held on the football pitch. By now Len had worked out his plan. He spoke briefly about what Basil had said but without any of the details. Then he had asked one member from each section to say what they generally felt had to be done. First it was the Mechanical Section, then the Sheet Metal men, followed by the Jig and Tool and Charlie who spoke for the Electrical section. Then various other groups had their say. Except for the Jig and Tool and the Wages Office there was a general consensus that they had to do something, but this varied from walking out straight away, or even occupying the place, to those who felt that the best course of action was to write to the town's Labour M.P. a man not known for doing very much that was useful.

Then Len spelled out the details. Soon some of those who hadn't been that keen on any action began to realise that it was their jobs that were on the line. Cleverly Len had not mentioned what Basil had said about the Jig and Tool. He looked at them all stood together, George Pennington their section leader was actually laughing at something his side-kick, Ernie Broadbent, had just said. Then, as planned, Ray Hewitt pointed out that Len had forgotten something.

"We all know what you two are up to," shouted Ernie. "You're trying to drag this meeting out so it goes past half one. Well, some of us have got jobs to go to so I suggest we have a vote."

"What's the vote for?" shouted Yorky. "You lot are only concerned about yourselves." At that point even the man from Mytholmroyd didn't know the full story.

"Hang on just a minute," said Len. "There was one other thing that Basil said."

"Come on then get on with it," said George.

"As part of the redundancy package, he is also making four of the Jig and Tool redundant and moving the other two into the old Sand Wash Storeroom."

Everybody burst out laughing. It would now be hilarious to watch them try to wriggle out of what they had been saying for the last week.

"Welcome to the real world George. And there was you thinking the sun shone out of Basil's backside," said Mick. "So are you going home for good, or are you going to try and save your jobs?"

As a result the meeting dragged on until turned two when it was agreed unanimously that they were all against the redundancies, at least until there had been full discussions and the order book had been seen. On top of that no one would work any more overtime, and it was also agreed with one or two dissenting voices that the office committee would co-operate fully with the shop floor committee. They also decided to inform the press and have another meeting on the following Monday at the same time. Then Len proposed that they all line up and march back into work, going through the Machine Shop en route. And as they walked past all the drillers, borers, millers, shapers, sawmen, inspectors, turners, lathe operators, fitters, storemen and labourers, they received a rapturous round of applause, particularly when it was seen that the march was led by John Meredith carrying the red flag. Well it wasn't really a red flag, it was just a red football jersey that he held aloft.

Had the revolution begun? Would the march through Wilkinsons' Machine Shop by around one hundred white collar workers be one day likened historically to the storming of the Winter Palace in Petrograd in 1917, or even the Bastille in Paris in 1789?

However, the significance of their action would only become clear after the weekend was over since by the time their meeting had ended, Basil was on his way to Manchester Airport, this time with his wife making a short weekend trip at everybody else's expense to watch the dancing girls in Montemarte in Paris. And when he returned on Tuesday he was very annoyed to see a large poster hanging from the offices above the Iron Foundry proclaiming "No Redundancies Here" and next to it was another one that said "Paris for the Boss, Nelson Street for the Workers. No Way".

By the end of the day he had met the shop floor committee and office committee together, something that had never happened before, and told them that he had just won a large order to supply electrical switchgear to a power station in Istanbul. As a result, although there would still be need for some cutbacks, the figure of eight per cent was now history and any redundancies would be on a voluntary basis.

There was however one final twist to the tale. Ken Jaundrill, one of the sheet metal draughtsmen, decided to take voluntary redundancy and go to work in Holland. Before he left, he got hold of some pictures of Basil taken at various company functions. He also found out which bar the incident with the man called Brazil had occurred in. During his first week there he had visited the bar, shown Basil's picture to every fat lady in the place and found the one who Basil liked to be entertained by. Then he had sent pictures of her back to Ashurst where just about everybody in Wilkinsons saw them, although it was rather cruel of one of the electricians to send one on to Mrs Wilkinson with the caption, "Proof that when your husband is working away he is missing you".

The outcome of the whole affair was that only around thirty employees left and not the two hundred that Basil would have liked. But three weeks later all but one of the Refinery 'A' shift left in rather humourous circumstances. Every week without fail, the twenty men put a pound into a kitty. This money would then be put on horses, greyhounds, football teams or anything else that could be bet on. For two years they hadn't won a penny. Then finally, on a week when there were only nine draws on the coupon, they discovered they had them all in the right set of permutations and so won an absolute fortune. To celebrate their win, they decided to begin with a joint holiday, a weekend away, and decided on Amsterdam.

"If it's good enough for the boss to go there and have a dirty weekend, its good enough for us."

"You mean, if it's good enough for our former boss to go there and have a dirty weekend, its good enough for us."

"Well, even though we don't have to work here, we can still send him a postcard telling him how much we are missing the bastard."

"Don't you mean, even though we don't have to work now, we can still send him a postcard."

And while they were in Amsterdam, and particularly when they were drunk, which was most of the time, the lads thought of all the ways they could get their own back on Basil. Inviting Petra and Dietra to Ashurst was one idea. Getting them to appear at the Dob Lane Working Men's club to talk about Amsterdam, its buildings, waterways and night life would no doubt attract an enormous attendance. Sneaking them into one of Wilkinson's Staff Association dances was another. But in the end it all fell flat. With all the attention being given to the issue, the two ladies began to believe that Basil was actually a member of the Government, or even part of the Royal Family, and so their price for having a week's holiday in Ashurst doubled and then trebled. In the end all that happened was that they had their photographs taken with each member of the syndicate on location so to speak. They were funny to look at when drunk, not quite so funny in the cold light of day and in the end the ones that were not 'lost' were confiscated on their return to England a few weeks later by Passport Control. That was except for Ken who kept his safe for possible future use if he ever wanted to return to Ashurst and get his old job back in Wilkinson's Drawing Office.

Which happened about three months later and shortly after he had been introduced to the local delicacy, Badhoevedorp carrot cake, with its sweet smell and highly enjoyable, though mind-bending, side-effects.

17.

WHERE'S MY PUB GONE?

As a result of being found out, all during the summer Basil spent most of his time in London at the company's Head Office. There he made the acquaintance of Lady Phillapa Delcourt, whose husband worked at the Foreign Office and spent much of his time travelling in the Benelux countries, and somewhat ironically frequently visiting the city of Amsterdam. Lady Phillapa on the other hand preferred to stay in London, where her time was divided between doing charitable work for the poor, which usually took up the best part of a morning a week, and enjoying her visits to the ballet, opera and charity events, which took up the rest of the week. As a result the months of June, July and August 1972 were fairly uneventful at Wilkinsons.

Things were very quiet just before the Works Shutdown, quite an ominous sign for Wilkinson's, and a few wondered whether they might return to discover the place had been closed down or sold. But it was still there when they came back from resorts as far apart as Seville and Southport, Brighton and New Brighton, Paris and Pensarn, Malaga and Morecambe. All seemed as normal as they clocked on and readied themselves to tell each other what sort of a holiday they had had. And before very long, after they had all remembered just what they had been doing before their holidays, Charlie made the expected comment that the new season was about to start.

Alan had been following the Saints ever since he had first stood in the boys' pen at Knowsley Road one Wednesday afternoon and saw New Zealand beat the men in red and white by eleven points to five. He could still recall the game. There was an enormous crowd in attendance that day, well over twenty thousand, and the team included the names of some who were soon to become his boyhood heroes: Jimmy Stott, Duggie Greenall, Reg Blakemore and Len Aston. At first he was taken by his Uncle Norman, and when he was a little bit older he began to go with his two friends Ken Parr and Geoff Platt. Then, one bitter cold, memorable day in March 1950, he remembered going to watch them draw nil apiece against Bradford Northern in the Third Round of the Challenge Cup in front of another enormous crowd and then the great disappointment when his Mum said he couldn't go to watch the replay four days later. And ever since then, except when he played soccer for Astley United and then Rugby Union for the works third and second teams, he had rarely missed a home game. And to prove it, he had n large collection of programmes, some whose value was increased by autographs of various players. Over the years he had seen many great games, although perhaps one of the most memorable was not at Knowsley Road and not even in Lancashire but at the Odsal Stadium in Bradford to see his team win the Championship Final against Hunslet in 1959 in front of over fifty thousand spectators.

At the start of the previous season he had started going with his brother Paul. Usually,

Paul would pick him up in his Fiat 126, not a very powerful car but good enough to get them from Ashurst to Knowsley Road in twenty minutes flat, even if it did mean having to drive on the pavement from time to time. Parking was never a problem for them, there was always a place on the drive of the house in Mulberry Avenue where Paul's mother-in-law lived.

Blood is thicker than water it is said, but in some respects that did not seem to apply to the two brothers' views on watching the match. Paul always stood in the Edington Stand behind the posts, Alan preferred the half-way line. Each had their own mates to stand with. That's how they liked it and it also provided them with more points to discuss on the way home, having seen things from different vantage points.

Alan found the rest of the gang in their usual place for the opening match and soon they were discussing the prospects for the coming season. Today's visitors were Featherstone Rovers and a good game was expected. As usual music blared out from the tannoy, quiet enough to allow their conversation to proceed relatively smoothly without having to keep resorting to the word "eh". Of course it hadn't been like that when he had first started watching the Saints. Then there was no tannoy, no announcements and certainly no music unless a local brass band had been invited to play, usually before a big cup-tie. In those early days after the war, the only noise that could be heard would be the sound of around twenty thousand men and women talking. A great, naturally-produced build up, which would move into overdrive when, ten minutes before kick off, a small boy walked round with a blackboard on which the changes to the programme were chalked.

But when the two teams finally emerged from the tunnel, all hell would be let loose. It was at the point when the away team appeared that you could tell by the sound of the cheers just how many fans they had brought with them. Today's opponents had come from over the Pennines, from a mining town somewhat similar to Ashurst. As usual, there were a couple of altercations early on between the two front rows, but the referee was having none of it. And except for a good old-fashioned punch up just before half time, the game was as good as over when full back Geoff Pimblett sliced his way through some slack defence by the men from Post Office Road to seal victory with twenty minutes to go.

As he had been watching the game, Alan noticed a face that seemed familiar, about twenty yards away. When the final whistle went, he moved over to the man but before he could reach him, the man had gone. He was probably still only about ten yards away but in a crowd like that impossible to find. Alan waited for the others and together they walked out of the ground, passed the training ground and onto Dunriding Lane. They turned right to walk up to Thatto Heath, he turned left, crossed over the bridge over the old railway line that once ran up to the Triplex works and as he crossed the road, he saw the man again stood waiting for a bus.

It was at that point that Alan realised who it was: Ian Astbury, who had once lived at the top of Chisnall Avenue. He had been a big mate of his brother Paul but had left the area in 1955 to do his National Service and never returned.

"Hello, Greeno."

"Hello, Ian. Long time, no see, where have you been hiding?"

"I've been living down South."

"And where are you going now?"

"Back to Ashurst. I'm living with my mum and dad for a bit."

"Do you want a lift?"

"Have you got a car then?"

"No, but our kid has, come on."

They soon turned into Mulberry Avenue and saw Paul in his mother in law's garden. As soon as he saw his old mate, Paul's face lit up.

On the way back to Ashurst, Ian told them about his time away from the town. He had done much of his National Service at an Army camp in the West Country. Just before he was demobbed, he had started going out with a local girl and had decided to stay down there. Soon after they decided to see the world and spent six months traveling around Europe. Then they had come back to England, got married and settled about ten miles from his old Army camp. But recently she had died and so he had decided to come back up North with his two children and make a fresh start.

"How old are your kids?" asked Paul.

"David is ten and Jennifer five."

"What school are they going to?"

"Lane Head Juniors, where else."

"Have they settled in all right?"

"Luckily they have, one of the girls in Jennifer's class lives next door and they are getting on really great. David had a bit of trouble at first. They thought he was a bit stuck up because of his accent. I thought they might have a problem as soon as they opened their mouths. Compared to the way Ashurst folk talk, they both sound pretty posh, not la di da, just different really. I suppose they will soon pick up an Ashurst accent."

"You might pick one up as well."

"Do I sound different then?"

"A bit."

"Well I'll have to go for anti elocution lessons, won'ta eh, ewd lad."

"Have you seen many changes around the place?"

"A few. I see our old house in Peter Street has gone and Platt Lane school. And they've stopped running the trolley buses."

"They stopped during that terrible winter in 1962," said Paul

"Delaney's has been knocked down and the old Montague pit has gone as well. And there's a load of new houses where that tip was where we used to go collecting cig packets up Hyde Bank," said Alan.

"That high rise block of flats at the back of the Town Hall is a bit of an eyesore, isn't it? Whoever built them?"

"Probably Cheshire Constructions. They've got loads of work off the Council. Everybody reckons a couple of councillors on the Planning Committee are getting backhanders, but nobody can prove it."

They told him about some of the other changes about the place and then Alan asked him if he had watched any Rugby Union while he had been living in the West Country.

"A bit," he laughed. "I once went to one of their big derby games. Bristol versus Bath, I nearly got thrown out of the clubhouse."

"Why?"

"Well after twenty minutes I was so bored with it, I went into the bar, bought myself a pint and asked the steward if I could go on the snooker table until the lads I had come with had finished watching the headless chickens running round on the field. He didn't like it one bit. But then neither did I."

"You haven't lost your sense of humour then."

"No, but I don't think many of them down there understood it. It got me into trouble more than once. I almost got into a fight at one place when one of the lads came back from having his hair cut one lunchtime and all I said to him was, are the barbers working to rule then?"

As they drove past Bold Colliery he asked Alan if he had started going out with girls yet.

"He's married and got two kids, Rebecca and Robert," said his brother.

"And do you still go trainspotting?"

Silence.

"He does, I'm sure of it," said Paul. "But no one has ever caught him in the act. Well not yet."

"It's no good now that they are getting shut of the steam locos."

"Some of my happiest days were spent trainspotting," said Ian. "Do you remember that summer, we all went on Wigan station four days running and got loads of namers?"

"I do," said Paul, "and then on the Friday we decided to go somewhere totally different, and finished up at Golbourne on the East Lancs Road, watching all the same trains about five miles down the same line."

"I'll tell you where I liked going," said Alan. "Carr Mill. We used to know the signalman there. He used to let us work the levers."

"You wouldn't get many namers there," said Ian.

"You did on a Saturday night. There was always a goods train going up to Scotland from Pilks. If we were lucky it would be a double header with two Scottish engines, those with the big round boilers and no windshields."

At this point they had reached the bottom of Martin Avenue and Ian told Paul to stop as he wanted to go in Wilcock's newsagents.

As he got out of the car, Paul asked him what he was doing the following evening.

"Nothing special. Probably playing Ludo. Why?"

"It's our Dot's birthday and we're having a bit of a party. Why don't you come? You'll know most of them who'll be there."

He didn't take much persuading.

Back home that evening Alan began to think about what the town must have been like when Ian had left it. Then he thought about his earliest recollections of it around the time he was five years old, the earliest that he could remember: incidents from the last few months of the war and then the early days of peace time. The first thing he recalled was the ration books, which his mum guarded as though their lives depended upon it, but then in a way they did. Having to spend hours queuing in shops, carrying a gas mask round in a cardboard box, endless jam butties and then after he started at Lane Head school, those horrible school dinners and particularly mince made from horse meat. He remembered fondly the frequent visits that his Auntie Kitty used to make to their house. More often than not, whenever he saw her coming up Chisnall Avenue she would be carrying something wrapped up in a brown paper parcel. And after she had gone he or Paul or his sister Joan would have some nearly new item of clothing to wear or toy to play with.

He remembered the first time he had ever been lost, surrounded by hundreds of other children in the middle of the night and then been found again. It was when he was six and the British Legion had organised a childrens' party to celebrate the end of the war. Everybody from around Chisnall Avenue had assembled at the bottom of Martin Avenue and had been taken from there in a coach to the old Pearson Engineering works. Somehow, in their large canteen, he had got seperated from Paul, Joan and the rest of them and had finished up with a group of children he didn't know all eating the celebration meal: one ham paste sandwich, one corned beef sandwich, a small cake, an apple and a glass of orange juice to drink or spill. Then they had watched a juggler followed by two acrobats and finally a magician. After that a man with what looked like a polished bicycle chain round his neck had made a speech and the vicar had said a prayer. Then they all sang God Save the King and after that everybody began to leave the hall and he was left stood on his own, until somebody had taken him by the hand and led him outside and put him on a bus, Twenty minutes later he was put off it and to his utter amazement the first person he saw was his mother. However all that had been managed he hadn't a clue; he just stood there and said nothing as they waited another ten minutes until another coach drove up and from which Paul and his sister Joan and all the others alighted.

He remembered his early days at school when his Mum used to walk the three of them there and then he was taken alternatively by either Joan or Paul, both of whom wished they didn't have to. Then he remembered proudly the first time he had walked home on his own. After that, as long as he was home by five o'clock he was allowed to mess about with the other boys in his class on their way home. He never missed the five o'clock deadline because that was when Children's Hour started on the wireless and there was always something good on it.

He remembered that terrible winter of 1947. Well it wasn't terrible really because it was so exciting having to fight your way through the snow. But it was so cold and sometimes their mother and the three of them would have to sleep downstairs in the living room because it was the only warm room in the house, at least until the fire went out. He also recalled another of his tricks to beat the cold; he would lie on the bed just wearing his pyjamas and count up to ten. Then he would get under the first blanket and count to fifteen. Then under the next blanket and count to twenty, then the next one and then under the sheet so that by then he was a lot warmer than when he had first entered the frozen bedroom. He remembered also skating about on Mill Dam at the back of Taylor's Yard. Then on a warmer day, a young lad from Gillarsfield, who should have been at school, was skating on it, went through the ice and drowned.

He thought what the centre of the town was like just after the War. Although Ashurst was on a direct line between Berlin and Liverpool, luckily it received few direct hits. One building that did disappear however was Kiln Lane foundry. It had been there since the beginning of the Industrial Revolution, then one night a bomb had landed in the road and the walls of the foundry had collapsed.

He remembered the first party he had ever been invited to but never went to. It was Alan Shuttleworth's who lived up Bankside Avenue at the back of the Griffin Inn, famed throughout the North of England for its immaculate bowling green. On the Friday at school, he had told Alan that he was invited to his seventh birthday party and to bring his football boots. As Alan didn't know exactly where he lived, he somehow assumed that 'Shutty' would come for him. But that was a wrong assumption and so Alan had spent the whole Saturday afternoon sat in the living room holding his Albert Stubbins boots which he had specially dubbined that morning. Instead of being at a party he had been entertained by the dulcet tones of Kenneth Wolstenholme, commentating on the FA Cup Final between Burnley and Charlton Athletic, a game he could still well remember.

Then his mind wandered on to his first visit to the Hemsley Arms, which must have been one of the strangest pubs ever. If seen from the sky, it would have looked like a triangle with the narrowest angle at thirty degrees. So at what was known as the bottom end there would be just enough room for a small man to stand. This was the tap room and would be full when six people were in it, packed if ten were there. In the middle of the pub were two doors opposite each other facing out on to two separate pavements. To go out of one door into Pemberton Street you walked down three steps on to the pavement. To go out of the opposite door into Clyde Street you had to walk up four steps. On the other side of these doors was the best room which not surprisingly sloped. To anyone on their first visit, being in the best room was a bit like being in a ship, with all the paintings and photographs of the sea on the walls. This was a much bigger room and could house up to maybe twenty people as long as they were all on the thin side.

Over the years many unusual things had happened or were alleged to have happened in the Hemsley Arms, usually involving loose women, illegal betting associated with arm wrestling and an unusual form of darts in which the dartboard was fixed on the ceiling, horizontally! This however had led to the pub being closed for a week in 1938 when a local dignitary in the place for the first time had a dart fall from the board and embed itself in his head.

Unfortunately thirty years later, almost to the week, a car being driven by a seventy two year old man, having his second driving lesson had skidded into the top door just after the pub had closed one Monday afternoon. Old Harry who had run the place for years walked off into town to get his mate, a joiner, to come and see if he could repair it. As he banged the other door to, he heard a cracking sound but thought little of it. While he was away, the bottom wall started to collapse and then the end wall began to go and within about twenty minutes the roof fell in. On his return about half an hour later Harry, on seeing an enormous pile of bricks, was heard to say those memorable words:

"Where's my pub gone?"

Other famous landmarks Alan remembered were the many cinemas the town had once had but with the advent of television had now disappeared. The Rivoli was still there with its distinctive Italian Baroque frontage in Standish Street. The Capitol in Bridge Street was now divided into two halves, so you could now watch one film and hear two. His favourite was the Oxford, usually known as the Occhy and now a carpet warehouse, and the Gaumont which had been turned into a highly unsuccessful bowling alley and then almost certainly burned down by its owner for insurance purposes. The Hemsley Dog was now a garage and the Hippodrome demolished to allow the construction of a traffic island, which had existed for about three years before being dug up to make way for an underpass. The Plaza he remembered fondly was still there. In 1961 it had been converted into a dance hall but had retained its old name. The owner had tried to get some big name band to play at the opening, but nobody in the musical industry appeared interested. So in the end he finished up with a group of lads from Liverpool with the quite ridiculous name for a rock 'n' roll band, the Beatles!

He remembered also Miss Blanchard's shop in Bridge Street. There you could get all sorts of interesting things, dinky cars, balsa wood to build models with, stamps from foreign countries, Gillick cards, football programmes, second hand jig saws, Meccano and a whole range of other toys. Then there were large collections of comics and adventure books, 78 R.P.M. records and postcards from every city thinkable. And for a penny you could buy a piece of malt bread or three large sweets or a small packet of sherbet. Sometimes Miss Blanchard sold Spanish. This was very popular and she usually sold out quite quickly. When this happened she would tell anyone who wanted some that the man was bringing some more from Spain in a few days time.

He also remembered how she had died after being hit by a runaway horse in Dob Lane and a few months later, her old treasure trove and Edwina's wool shop next door had been turned into an Italian coffee bar called Marios. And Alan remembered fondly how it was in there on Christmas Eve 1962 he had first discovered that Thelma, the somewhat mysterious print room girl at work, had nowhere to go on Christmas Day. And so he had invited her to his Granny's for the day and there she had fallen ill and within a month had been virtually adopted by his grandparents. And ten years later, she was now Mrs Greenall. Yes he remembered Miss Blanchard well, she reminded him of a character out of a Charles Dickens novel. He also remembered Mario too: Mario who spoke English with a broad Bolton accent because that was where he had always lived until he had moved to Ashurst to serve coffee and spaghetti bolognese made just in the way it was done in his native Italy - which he had unfortunately never visited!

18.

DOROTHY'S DINNER PARTY

Paul's wife, Dorothy, was well know for what she liked to call her little soirees. She loved to have a dozen or so friends sat round their large table in the living room of their house in Kenyon Avenue, eating, drinking and having a good laugh. She always liked to experiment on these occasions, usually helped by her elder sister Pam who would always arrive two hours early carrying two bottles of wine, an expensive one for her and Dorothy to consume while they were preparing the meal and a cheap one to use in the meal irrespective of what it might be. Invariably it would be based on some variation on scouse or lobbies: potatoes, carrots, onions, Oxo cubes, Worcester sauce, mint sauce, a dash of vinegar, and a large piece of lamb or beef drowned in a Vin de Perpignan or Hausfraumilch von Bremenhausengeplonk. And every time Dorothy laid the meal before her assembled guests, one of the others would say that it looked good and smelled good. Then Dorothy, usually quite inebriated by this time, would announce that it was Ragout de Bollichelli, or Vienna Esprit de Corpse, or some other exotic title based on something she had just read in the Radio Times or Woman's Own earlier that day.

But tonight things were not like they usually were. Pam had started on her latest recipe which required a third of a bottle of red wine. Unfortunately she poured the wine from the wrong bottle and then, on discovering her mistake, had thrown her hands up to her face and knocked the bottle all over the floor. And since the other bottle she had brought was labelled as only suitable for cooking purposes, the two of them were still sober by the time they started the meal. After they had finished eating, they sat back as Paul brought in a bottle of Napoleon brandy. Then, as she always did, Dorothy threw her napkin on the table and announced with a flourish of her hand:

"Gentlemen, you may now smoke, but only in the garden."

She didn't like cigarettes.

Then she turned to Ian and asked him what he had been doing since he had left the town nearly twenty years ago.

He began by telling them of his courting a girl from Taunton while he had been doing his National Service. When he had been demobbed, the pair of them had spent six months travelling round Europe, getting as far East as Istanbul in Turkey and as far South as the Italian city of Sorrento. Then, on their return to England, they got married and settled in Wiltshire. While they had been abroad, Diane had been a real free spirit without a care in the world. But back home she soon fell under the influence of her mother. At first things went along quite well. Ian earned good money, working first as a draughtsman and then as an installation engineer, though having to work away a lot. They had two children and lived in a detached house on a very upper class estate. Fortunately Diane's mother lived about fifteen miles away, and more importantly three bus rides away. Then Diane's father was promoted and given a company car and so Mama was able to visit them whenever she wanted to, just to help with the children she would say.

As time went by, she began to act as though his household could not exist without her. Soon he realised that although there had been no formal declaration, a state of war existed between the two of them, with Diane always agreeing with what her mother suggested. Soon his wife was turning into a carbon copy of her mother. And the more she went that way, the more Ian went the other way. And then, as he had suspected for some time, he discovered that she had been playing away while he had been working away. One thing led to another, she stormed out of the house after a big argument and later that evening her and a local solicitor were killed in a car crash.

"Oh, I am sorry," said Dorothy, not quite expecting to hear such a seemingly sorry tale.

"Well I'm not," Ian said. "I'm a lot better off without her. I didn't realise just how devious and conniving she was. She certainly fooled me and her mother, although her Ladyship would never admit it, not to me anyway. And I'm certainly glad to be away from that estate. I hated it there."

"Why?"

"It was a right snooty place. I think there was only me had a real job. The rest of them all seemed to have private means. Some were retired, some were retired at bloody fifty. One was a bank manager, I never knew what most of the others did. I don't think I managed to speak to half of them. They probably thought I was a bit too lower class for them."

"So how did you get to buy a house in such a posh place?"

"It belonged to my boss at work. He'd always had plenty money and then his rich uncle died and left him a load more. So he decided one day that he wanted to go and live on a Greek island. I jokingly offered him twelve grand for his house for a quick sale. He shook my hand and that was it. About a month later, after we had moved in, the house next door, identical to ours, went for nineteen thousand. So that's how we managed it, with a great slice of luck, although looking back I wished we'd come to live in Ashurst after we got married. So you don't need to feel sorry for me. I'm back where I want to be. I've got a couple of interviews lined up for next week, and I can start watching the Saints again."

Then he laughed and said, "And the greatest thing of all, I'll never have to see her bloody mother again. She was an absolute pain. Super snob that's what she was. I'll give you an example what she was like. It'll make you laugh if nothing else.

"We once went to Barnstaple in Somerset for a day out. When we got there we went in this very smart hotel for a drink. A few minutes later, about half a dozen lads came in and sat near to us. They had obviously had a few and as soon as they started talking I could tell they were from Yorkshire, though I wasn't quite sure whereabouts. They were only in their early twenties, noisy, but quite harmless. After a bit I could see the mother-in-law getting annoyed at them. And then she asks me to tell these oafs to behave or leave the room, so that we could have our drink in peace. But by this time I was enjoying myself listening to them, they were really funny. So I turned round to one of them and laid my accent on a bit and said:

'Where are you from, lads?'

'Featherstone, where tha from?'

"Well I just felt at home with them straight away, so of course I said, Ashurst, near St Helens. And then she pipes up in her awful shrill posh voice and said 'and we are from Stow on the Wold'. The way she pronounced the place you could tell she thought it was a far superior place to Featherstone, though I doubt if she had ever been there before.

"Then one of the other lads shouts out: 'I'm from Glasshoughton on the Wold', and of course they all burst out laughing and another shouts out 'and I'm from Sharlston on the Wold'. And then the little one in the corner stands up and says 'And I'm from Allerton Bywater on the Wold'. At this all the others start booing him and the lad next to me tells me he was a Castleford fan and not really with them.

"So we started talking about Rugby. At this point she snorts like she usually did when someone had disobeyed her and then her and Diane announce they were going out for some fresh air. Well after that I had a right laugh with these lads. One of them kept saying 'We are from Stow on the Wold' and every time he said this we all fell about laughing. It's the sort of thing you laugh about when you've had a few. Needless to say the atmosphere in the car on the journey back home was a little frosty to say the least.

"You couldn't ever have a discussion with her. She just knew she was right and of course she had Jesus on her side. And that was her downfall. She claimed to be a Christian, but the number of people or countries she hated was amazing. She didn't like blacks or Asians or the French or the Germans. The Americans were too loud-mouthed and had no culture and the Scots, the Welsh and the Irish were always sponging off us long-suffering English. But among her own people she hated Scousers, Brummies and Cockneys and thought people from Cornwall were a bit thick and Bristolians common. I assume by the incident in that pub, Featherstone, Sharlston and Glasshoughton would have been added to her list. I know Ashurst and all the places that bordered onto it were damned as well as the Isle of Man, though I could never work that one out.

"So as you can imagine family life wasn't too good when she was around. But then it was just as bad at work when I was working in the Drawing Office. I've never come across a more miserable bunch of morons. I've known loads of draughtsmen over the years and that lot were the worst ever. All the time I was there I never heard any of them ever make serious comment about anything. Every hour or so one of them would burp loudly and then say to the apprentice 'stop that John', and he would say, 'which way did it go'. Every lunchtime, when one of them went home for his dinner, he would say I'll go and entertain the wife now, and when he came back, he would walk into the office pretending to do up his flies and say, 'I've just left her smoking in bed'. Every bloody day they had the same standard set of phrases, funny the first time, but after that," and he shook his head.

"How long where you there?"

"Too long, the wages were only average but there was a big bonus at Christmas which made it worth staying. It used to make me laugh the way they got their annual increases. The first Monday in March everybody would receive a letter telling them what they were getting. There were no negotiations or any discussion. And then they all had to send a letter to the boss thanking him and pledging their continued loyalty and how much they appreciated his generosity. They must have thought the revolution was starting when I told them I wasn't writing any daft letter, not for a seven and six increase.

"Still I got my own back on them all at the end. They used to have this table tennis competition, it was a handicap event but everybody knew that the winner had to be the manager's secretary. It always had been. Well I was pretty good at table tennis so I started going down for a game during the lunch hour. But what I did, I made out that I was hopeless so when they made the draw I had a starting handicap of twelve. In the first two rounds my opponents were not much cop so I easily got through to the last eight. Then I decided to turn it on and I beat the Shipping Manager twenty one three, twenty one four. In the semi final I played one of the other draffies and beat him twenty one two, twenty one five. And then it was the final against Miss Hepplethwaite. I beat her twenty one nineteen in the first game, then let her win the second quite easily and I suppose everyone was thinking that she would be allowed to win as normal. But then I really played well in the grand decider and beat her twenty one nil and won the competition in total silence. And do you know not one of them congratulated me."

"I once heard of a firm in Chester where you were expected to thank the boss in writing for your annual increase," said Alan. "This mate of mine went working there and when he got a four shilling a week increase, he wasn't too pleased so he sent the boss a poem:

Roses are Red
Violets are Blue
How the hell can I manage
On twelve pounds sixteen and two"

"You've just made that up, Alan," said Thelma.

"Well, it wouldn't rhyme if he had put twelve pounds sixteen shillings, would it?"

Then he carried on: "I'll tell you a story that is true. Last year at Jarratts the Office Committee put in a wage claim for six pounds a week. There were six on the committee and they had all agreed whatever the first offer was, they would refuse it. They had a new Personnel Manager and he comes across with a load of tough talk and finally says that he was going to make them an offer, but he wasn't going to be messed about with protracted discussions. The offer was only on the table until two o'clock that afternoon. Then he announced it would be one pound five shillings for the over thirties and seventeen shillings for all the others."

"Before they could reject it, one of the young lads on the committee said that as far as he was concerned that seemed reasonable but could he ask a question. So of course the Personnel Manager, quite pleased with this response, agreed.

"Now that you're in charge, is it company policy to negotiate on a daily instead of a weekly basis?" the lad asked.

"You know, Alan, that is really funny," said Thelma again.

"I think your Catalonian Choux de Guerre has gone to his head," said Pam turning to her sister.

"I thought it was very nice," said Dorothy. "It must have been the expensive French wine that gave it that flavour."

"So why is it a Catalonian dish if you made it with French wine, Dot?" asked Paul. "And where is Catalonia?"

"I don't know," said Dorothy. "It's probably abroad somewhere."

"You are without doubt a chef extraordinaire," carried on Paul, now intent on winding her up, "so can you tell me from your knowledge of European cuisine, where do Brussels sprouts come from, is it Brussels?"

"And does Turkish Delight come from Turkey or Yorkshire puddings from Yorkshire?" asked Alan.

"Well they must have originally," said Dorothy. "Lancashire hot pot comes from Lancashire, doesn't it?"

"Where was the first ever Lancashire hot pot made, who made it and who ate it?" asked Alan.

"I don't know," said Dorothy, "I'm only thirty five."

"Well I know that Napoleon marched on Moscow in 1802 and I'm not one hundred and seventy," said Alan.

"How did you know that"

"Les Earnshaw told me, he was there."

"How could he be?" asked Pam.

"Because in an earlier life he was a French peasant."

"Is he that bloke from Gillarsfield that was on the telly?" asked Joan, Dorothy's next door neighbour. "I thought he was hilarious."

"Alan used to work with him," said Dorothy proudly.

"I've never met anybody famous," said Joan.

"Nobody?"

"Well that Rugby player Tom Van Vollenhoven once served me in Rothery's shop in St Helens. But I didn't know he was famous, not then."

"I once met John Taylor, the Mayor," said Paul. "He was in the chip shop in Dob Lane."

"He used to be my boss when I worked in the Town Hall," said Carol, another of Dorothy's neighbours. "When I first met him I thought that he had the charm of a wet haddock. After he had been in charge of us for a bit, I realised that I had under estimated him, he actually had the charm of two wet haddock."

"No codding," said Alan, "well he certainly knows his place."

"I remember when he was the chairman of our Nalgo branch," continued Carol. "One lunchtime we had a big meeting about a wage claim. It was held in the Town Hall, there must have been about two hundred of us there. He was chairing it and at bang on half one, he closed the meeting very abruptly and shot off. So I walked back to our office with a couple of the others, we were on the second floor then and when we got back there, he tells us off for being late. And it was his flipping meeting."

"He's not involved in this bribery and corruption with Cheshire Constructions, is he?"

"Not John. I'll tell you what, if he found a penny lying on the floor in the Town Hall, he'd put a note on the notice board asking whoever thinks he has lost it to come and see him and describe it."

"That might be part of a cunning plan to give the impression he is squeaky clean on small things and been involved in some big style fraud. He wouldn't be the first."

"Who's looking after the kids, Thelma? Is it Grandma?"

"Yes."

"And how's Granny?"

"Not too bad. She's eighty one next week."

"And still behaving like a seventy nine year old," laughed Alan

"You know, Thelma, you still haven't lost your Welsh accent."

"Where are you from?" asked Carol.

"I was born in Tonyrefail, but I was brought up in Cardiff."

"Do you know Pontedu?" asked Joan.

"Not really, it's about twenty miles from Tonyrefail. Why?"

"One of the lads at work has gone living down there. It's where his girlfriend comes from."

"Does he like it?"

"He reckons they've got better slag heaps than we have."

"They've started pulling them all down, haven't they?"

"Dorothy, how can you pull a slag heap down."

"Well you know what I mean, taking them away."

"Only in bits."

"Have they started on Mount Everest yet?" asked Ian.

"They have at the bottom end, near where the spaceship landed."

"Eh?"

"Oh, you won't have heard about Peter Starr, will you?"

"No."

"Going home one night he reckoned he saw a spaceship there."

"Had he been drinking?"

"Yes, but he said that had nothing to do with it."

"Well as Christine Keeler often used to say, he would do, wouldn't he?"

The evening carried on in similar vein, with Ian feeling increasingly at home. He smiled to himself when he thought about the various dinner parties or social gatherings small cliques of his former neighbours had held but rarely invited him and his late wife to. But he knew that even if they had he would not have enjoyed himself there one hundredth part as much as he had that evening. And he was more than happy at the reception he received from his children's other grandmother when he finally arrived home, much the worse for wear.

Back at work the following day, after Alan had told the others about Ian and his mother-in-law and the bit about "We are from Stow on the Wold", a big discussion began on the role of mother-in-laws in society. In general they had a bad press and it was easy to stereotype them. But as Yorky pointed out to Alan, Thelma's mother-in-law was at the same time his own mother.

Then Charlie chipped in about when he had been working on a job in Nottingham for a couple of weeks and lodged in a guest house along with a group of lads from the city of Wakefield.

"It was a rum place was that. There were about twelve of us there at the time, these four lads, me and Ronnie Garner and about half a dozen business types from London. The landlady ran the place with an iron fist. She let everybody know right from the start that she was the boss. She had her husband and her son there as well and she treated them just the same."

"Now her son Nigel didn't go out much, except to the local church club to play badminton, and sometimes have the odd pint, without his mother knowing. So he wasn't very clued up about the way of the world. Anyway, on their last night, these Wakey lads told Mrs Revis that they were going to have a bit of a celebration and would Nigel like to come with them. They led her to believe that they would be going to the cinema or maybe the theatre and after that they might go for an Indian meal. Well they had been pretty well behaved all the time they had been there, so Mrs Revis virtually told her son to go out somewhere different for a change and maybe learn something from these very cultured Yorkshiremen.

"So they all get dolled up and off they go. They go in one pub and have a pint, and then another and then another and of course before very long Nigel gets drunk. Finally they finish up in a bit of a rough night club by which time all Nigel is wanting to do is drink coffee and get sobered up before he goes home to face the wrath of his mother. At this point the lads introduce him to Hazel, in whose bed three of them had already spent a night during their four weeks stay in the town. After a couple more drinks, she tells Nigel she's got something in her flat that will help him sober up so they go back there and she introduces him to the pleasures of the flesh.

"She throws him out of the place about three in the morning and he staggers back home. But because he rarely went out, he didn't have a key to get in the house. He didn't want to wake his mother up, so he threw some pebbles against one of the bedroom windows, just like he had seen them do in the films. No response from the two lads who shared that room. They were probably still out on the town. So he did it again. No response. And again. Still in a drunken stupor, he steps back a few yards and picks up a larger stone and throws it with a bit more force. Unfortunately he slipped as he let go and as a result the trajectory of the stone did not head for its intended target, but ten yards to the left of it, the window of the room in which his parents were sleeping. And of course when it made contact with the window, it went straight through it.

"When his mother came down to let him in, she was not amused. He was smelling of beer and his speech was slurred. On top of that there was lipstick on his face and on the collar of his shirt and down below where you tuck it into your trousers."

"And had the lad enjoyed himself?" asked Alan.

"I'm sure he did, because the next week, he went out every night. I don't know where he was going, but I know he didn't take his badminton racket with him."

"No, but I bet he took his shuttlecock," said Yorky.

19.

EDWARD HOLDING 1891- 1972 R.I.P.

It was the fifty eighth anniversary of Granny's wedding. Thelma and Alan had walked down to Silkstone Street, expecting that their visit would be a rather sombre affair. But as they approached the house they saw an amazing sight. Granny was kneeling down washing the front door step with a donkey stone. Before Grandad had died that would have been nothing unusual, but now it never got done, not until today of all days. As soon as their seven year old daughter Rebecca saw her great grandmother, she ran up to her shouting "Granny, Granny", the term Great Granny somehow seemed quite inappropriate really. She stood up, ran her hand up and down her side like she always used to and then held her arms out to greet her great granddaughter and kiss her. The smile on her wrinkled and lined face reminded Thelma again of the first time they had met on Christmas Day over ten years earlier when Granny had said those first loving words to her: "Hello Thelma. I'm very pleased to meet you. You're very welcome, love."

Then Granny threw the water from the bucket over the overgrown tiny front garden and led them into the house. It was clear that she had been busy that morning, the kitchen was like a new pin, the windows had been washed and she had even baked a cake. And before they could even hang up their coats, the kettle was on and Rebecca's little brother Robert was sat on her lap.

After she had talked to him for a few minutes and Thelma had made a pot of tea, she said to Alan, "I wonder what your Grandad is doing today", and then, turning to Thelma, she went on, "I want to know whether he's been behaving himself."

Neither quite knew how to respond to her comments so Alan responded with the general bland statement that he really didn't know.

Then she carried on, "I've been clearing out the drawers and I've got something to show you both", and with that she lifted Robert down, went into the living room and came back with a box full of photographs. They all sat round the kitchen table as she gave one to Thelma and said, "Can you see him on this one?"

It was a photograph of about twenty soldiers, mainly British Tommies from the First World War, a couple from the Black Watch and others with unrecognisable uniforms. Grandad was there right in the middle, with a big grin on his face and a German officer's helmet on his head.

"Where did he get that from?" said Thelma.

"Did he never tell you about it? Well he told everybody else in Ashurst."

She brushed a few crumbs off her pinny, took hold of little Robert again, kissed him and went on: "It was just before they all got captured. There were a few of them in no man's land, early one morning. Suddenly the Germans started firing and Ned dives for cover in this awful muddy hole. He lay there for ages, making himself as little as he could, with his eyes shut. Then he slowly opened one eye and then the other to see where he was. The first thing he saw was the spike on the top of this German helmet, about a foot away from him. He must have been petrified. Then he slowly looked down the helmet and into the face of the enemy. He had never been that close to a German soldier before. He saw an eye and a nose but no mouth or jaw and he looked further down and saw half a body and all the man's stomach hanging out and bleeding. It was awful. Then he saw he was about twenty yards from our trenches so he waved to one of our lads, he shouts to the others and then he waves for Ned to crawl back. So he brings this helmet with him as a souvenir. And I don't know how he managed it but he carried it around with him all the time he was in that prisoner of war camp."

Then she passed a crumpled sepia coloured photograph of a lady in crinolin with a baby on her lap to Thelma.

"Who is it?"

"This little baby is Alan's mum, and this is me. Do you know Ned carried this photograph with him all through that war. Doreen was only three when he went away Ee, I remember how excited she was when I told her that her daddy was coming home and we all went down to the station to meet him. She wouldn't let go of his hand for days after he came back. She must have thought he was going away again."

Then, as Granny turned to stop Robert crawling under the table, Thelma picked a postcard from out of the box. On the front was a poem, written in black against a glossy white background. Granny smiled as she saw it and said, "very nice words, read it out, love."

"Absence makes the heart grow fonder"

Though the saying is not new,
Every hour I from you wander
Makes it seem to me more true,
Makes me long to see you, kiss you,
Look into your loving eyes,
Teaches me how much I miss you,
And how much your love I prize.
So when once again I meet you,
In that happy day in store,
You will know, dear
When I greet you
Absence made me love you more.

Then she turned it over and on it she saw what Granny had written nearly sixty years earlier:

My Dear Husband,

Just received your letter and was glad you got the box alright. Your Len joined the

Royal Engineers this morning. Jack Decon has listed in Kitchener's Army but Willie is going mad to join something but I don't know what. Will close now with fondest love from Doreen and myself.

Your loving wife Mary.

"Oh that was lovely, Granny."

Granny smiled with tears in her eyes and nodded. "I remember writing it and when I finished it, Doreen kissed it and said 'Come home Daddy'. And a month later I got a letter to say he was a prisoner of war."

"Do you know Granny, I was a little bit frightened of him at first."

"Were you, love."

"I don't know why, I just was."

"Well he was always a bit gruff with people. It was just his way. They were all like that in Alfred Street, it was a funny place where he used to live."

"What were his mother and father like?"

"His father was a collier at Lea Green, he worked hard but he loved to give his money away, particularly to whoever was serving beer in the Black Horse. His mother, her name was Catherine Tunstall before she was married, she was a lovely lady. She loved to read to herself, then to her children and to anybody else who wanted to listen to her. She came from Lacey Street off Dob Lane. It's not there now. They knocked it down a long time ago."

"Granny, can I have one of your chocolate biscuits, please?"

"Course you can love. You know where they are."

As Rebecca walked over to the pantry, Granny commented on how quickly she was growing up and then said:

"Ee, I can still remember the first time you walked into the house, as clear as though it was yesterday." It was a statement that Granny often made.

"So can I," said Thelma. "Do you know Granny, I knew I was going to like you from the moment I set my eyes on you."

"And do you still like me?"

Thelma just nodded, then got up and gave her a big hug.

"Does anybody round here like me?" asked Alan rather dourly, but before anybody could reply there was a loud crash as the box of biscuits fell to the floor in the pantry and Rebecca reappeared with the words: "I think I've dropped the biscuits, Granny."

"It doesn't matter, love. They'll all get broken when you eat them, won't they?" and with that she got up from her chair and helped Rebecca put them back in the tin.

"Do you want to have a look at the encyclopedias?"

She did, she always did and so off she went into the living room to work her way through volume three of the well thumbed Arthur Mee collection that Granny had been given as a wedding present in 1909. Since then, every child, grandchild and now great grandchild that had ever visited the house had derived enormous pleasure from them. The blue and brown sepia-coloured photographs had an attraction all of their own. Many of the photographs were of places and people that no longer existed. But it had a fascinating appeal, a vivid account or description of how things were when Granny was a little girl and Grandad a little boy. Thelma too had spent hours working her way through them. By the time she had opened her first page she was turned nineteen. But she would still sit there curled up on the floor in front of a glowing warm fire with her thumb in her mouth maybe as Alan's mum had once said, "catching up on a childhood she had never had."

"Can I have a read as well?" she jokingly said.

"Go on with you" laughed Granny. "You must have read them ten times over the amount of time you spent with them. You were always reading them."

"Where did you get them from?"

"It was a wedding present. It was from Grandad's eldest brother Thomas and his wife, Agnes. He was the one who got killed at Paschendale and the same week Agnes died in childbirth. They were a really nice couple." Then she went on: "You know when Grandad came back from the war, he would spend hours reading them, well he couldn't get a job at first and then they were on strike for a long time. He liked to read them in the front room, he never bothered if it was cold in there, he'd just put his overcoat and his flat cap on. I think they were all good readers in his family."

"How many brothers and sisters did he have?"

"Well there was Doris, and Thomas and Frank and Leonard. Frank was always a bit of a handful. He worked down the pit at first and then he went to live in Burnley and started playing football for them. I think he was very good at it, but I never saw him play. But that didn't last long and then one of his pals got him fixed up working in a bakery over there."

"Let me see if I can remember all your brothers and sisters."

"Go on then, I'm not sure if I can now."

"Well there was Doris, Hilda, Kitty and you."

"You forgot Eric."

"Oh yes, what happened to him?"

"He went to live near Rhyl in North Wales when he was twenty one and married a farmer's daughter. Then in 1947, in that very bad winter I think it was, he died from a heart attack. He was always the silent one, you could never work out what he was thinking."

"And what about your mother and father?"

"My father worked for the Corporation as a joiner. My mother worked on the pit brow for a bit, then she decided that she wanted to be a nurse. But by the time she had started doing her training she had met my father and before very long she was expecting our Hilda so they got married instead and after that she had another four of us and then died when I was thirteen. And so that's when I had to finish school and start looking after everybody at home."

Then Alan piped up, "And you've been doing it ever since."

It wasn't the first time that Thelma had asked these questions of Granny. Ever since she had first gone to live in Silkstone Street she wanted to know about all the members of the family who had come to accept her as one of their own. The oldest relative she knew about was Grandad's great grandfather, Arthur Silas Holding, born in a little miners' cottage in 1791 at Collins Green. She felt a great affinity with them all and particularly with Rebecca Kenilworth, who had been born somewhere in Wales in 1809 and died ninety years later and a strong influence on her great granddaughter, Isabella Mary Tabern, Granny.

Then into the house came Granny's second child Stanley carrying a bunch of flowers. After greeting the others, he asked her if she would like to go up to the cemetry to lay them on the family grave. His offer demonstrated the harsh reality of it all. Granny would never see Grandad again, but in her head she could still see him now as clearly as she had first seen him on that Whit Monday church walk from Ashurst Parish church to the playing fields at the back of the old Pearson Engineering works.

It was decided that they would all go up together in Stanley's car, Granny in the front and the Greenalls all packed in together in the back. They laid their flowers on the grave and looked around at others doing the same. Cemeteries were always such sad places, thought Alan, particularly at times like this, although Granny didn't seem too bothered. No doubt when she got back home and on her own again she would have a little weep, but stood there reorganising the flowers, some of which were equally fresh and obviously placed by other relatives or maybe by some of Ned's old comrades from the war or other pals he had known.

As they gathered around the grave, it began to rain. It had been threatening to do it all morning. They each buttoned up their coats and slowly began to move away, with Granny leading the way. Alan was thus the last to leave. He stood for a minute on his own, remembering his Grandad, oblivious to the rain and the cold, remembering a wonderful old man. He wiped a tear from his face and turned away and quickly walked to catch the rest of them up.

Edward Holding, Rest In Peace

Stood on the terraces that afternoon everything about the morning was soon forgotten as the home team turned on a scintillating display of Rugby League football against the men from Watersheddings. At half time, stood in the queue to get a Pimblett meat and potato pie, he had seen his old friend Eric Yates, the one whose trickery that Christmas Eve had led to his meeting Thelma. Eric was now a big union man, that is he was the Regional Organiser for the General and Municipal Workers Union, although in his Granny's words he was still best described as 'that scruffy pants Eric Yates'.

They hadn't met for a long time and so Eric expressed his sorrow at hearing of Grandad's death a year earlier.

"Do you still ride round on that old bike you had?" Alan asked.

"On no, I'm moving in high circles now. The union's provided me with a car and I've even got a phone at home. Ashurst 779988. Give us a ring some time. If I'm not in the secretary will take a message."

"You've not got a secretary as well have you?"

"I certainly have. This job is so hectic. I've got to go all over the place. I was up in Hartlepools last week for three days negotiating with ICI."

"And did the secretary have to go with you?"

"She did and do you know the union are so tight with the expenses we even had to share a room up there."

"My heart bleeds for you."

"Well, it's tough at the top."

At this point the two teams had reappeared on the pitch. Eric repeated the numbers 779988 and disappeared into the crowd.

Eric was a week younger than Alan and had a very similar background, although due to his religion he had not gone to Lane Head Juniors, but St. Theresa's school a mile further away. Like Alan, he also had a sister and a brother, his father had been killed in the war at Dunkirk and he had also served an apprenticeship, but as a bricklayer with the Corporation. They had also played together in a skiffle band in Johnny Shufflebottom's garage in Manor Avenue, though clearly Eric hadn't a musical note within him. They had been good mates over the years, whenever their paths had crossed though with them going to different schools, their interests had often varied.

The second half was a lot better than the first, Oldham had obviously been given a right rollicking by their coach in the dressing room, but they could make little headway against a well-drilled Saints team who in the end had won quite easily.

After the game was over Alan had to get back home on the bus as his brother Paul was still recovering from having his appendix removed. As Alan stood in the queue in Knowsley Road outside the paper shop, he watched the large crowds disperse, seeing a familiar face now and then. Upstairs on the bus he listened to all the discussion about the game from those sat around him. They were clearly all Saints fans, happy with what they had just seen. Different people analysed the game from different viewpoints, one or two argued over who had scored the first try, who was their man of the match and the general style of play of their opponents. As the bus went past Rivington Road he saw all the coaches stretching right up to the top of the hill, rapidly filling up with the away fans ready to be transported back to such exotic places as Mumps, Werneth, Shaw, Lees, Failsworth and Chadderton. But this general mood of euphoria and pleasure of being among Rugby League folk disappeared when he changed buses in town and got on the Ashurst bus. There wasn't a soul on it who looked or sounded vaguely like a Rugby League fan. The atmosphere was totally different and he was glad to get off and walk down Manchester Road and then turn into Silkstone Street and find his wife and children finishing their tea.

"Did they win?" Thelma asked, but before he could tell her much more than the result she told him that his tea was in the oven and that they were in the sitting room watching the television. As he ate his tea he thought about his grandparents, how he had loved going to visit them when he was a small boy. He thought what it was like when his Grandad was still working and how he loved to hear the sound of his clogs as he came down the yard after a hard day's work at Mather's Foundry. He remembered as a small boy all the stories Grandad had told him and his other grandchildren. Strangely, he had never been much of a sports fan. In fact he had never been to watch the Saints, except once when they had played Huddersfield at Wembley in 1953. But he had been one of the funniest men Alan had ever known and he had now been dead for over a year. And Granny, who had known and loved him for over sixty years, would now probably be fondly remembering him and missing him.

After he had finished his meal he picked up the Sunday Observer and began by looking at the previous day's football results. Then he took his football coupon off the mantelpiece. He was in two syndicates, one at work with over twenty draughtsmen each putting in twenty pence a week and one he did with his brother Paul. He flicked through the first set of numbers; there was no chance of success, he could tell that after he had got as far as the fifth number. Then he started on the other. The first number was two and a draw, the second one was five and a draw, the next three were all homes but then three draws all together just like the numbers, nineteen, twenty and twenty one: five draws so far and another four numbers to check. Number thirty two was a draw thanks to a late equaliser by Newport County: only two more and they were in the money; the next one was a home and then a draw and finally another draw. They had got eight and there were only eleven on the coupon.

"What's up?" shouted Thelma as she dashed into the room hearing his shriek of joy.

"We've won the pools, I'm sure of it. Here, check these numbers."

Yes, it was right, yippee they would be able to pay the gas bill on time and the rates and the electric bill and buy Rebecca a frock and Robert a new pair of shoes and have change out of it to go out for a meal and, and, and......But only if Paul had sent off the coupon! He rang his brother straight away. Dorothy answered the phone, Paul was still in bed but he struggled downstairs and heard his brother ask if he had sent the coupon off before he had gone into hospital on the Thursday. "I didn't," he replied, "I asked our Dorothy to do it. Hang on."

A minute later Dorothy, his sister-in-law, came back on the phone. "What is it, Alan?"

"Did you post the pools coupon on Thursday?"

"No, I gave it to our Pam. Why, have we won?"

Alan groaned. Pamela should really have been christened Dorothy and then she could have been known as the dotty one. The odds were something like five to one on that the envelope was still in her handbag.

"Can you ring her and find out? Yes, I think we've won."

An hour later, Dorothy rang back to say that Pamela wasn't sure whether she had posted it or given it to her husband to post. And she couldn't ask him because he had gone to Workington to watch his brother playing for Widnes 'A' team that afternoon and probably wouldn't be back before midnight.

It was a long evening, a very long evening indeed until finally at ten past twelve they were woken by Dorothy with the news that Pam's husband Kevin was ninety per cent sure he had put it in the post box outside the Labour Exchange, but he wasn't sure when.

It was another eighty hours before the postman delivered the mail from Vernons Pools in Liverpool fifteen miles away to Kenyon Avenue. And it was another nine hours before Dorothy arrived home from work to discover an envelope containing a cheque for almost twelve thousand pounds. Unfortunately for the two brothers, that week they had decided to include Paul's next door neighbour. So what would have been six thousand pound each was actually only four thousand pounds each. But what the hell, four thousand pounds is..... four thousand pounds. It could just have easily been nothing if the third man hadn't appeared on the scene. So goodnight Vienna.

One of Alan's first suggestions on what they should spend the money on was a holiday, abroad. Then Thelma suggested they had a joint one with Paul, Dorothy and their two children. And then she suggested taking his Mum and Granny!

Mum yes, but Granny? Not that they wouldn't have been pleased to take her but at eighty one, flying for the first time, well not really. And when they asked her she said that she would be quite happy to be taken to Southport and New Brighton and if the money would stretch to it, Hoylake as well: just as nice as any of those funny places abroad, she thought.

And so they spent some of their winnings on a week's holiday in Brittany in late September and with money to spare, and with Rebecca and Robert under the careful supervision of Granma, Alan and Thelma had a night in a hotel thirty kilometres away and slept in the same bed they had slept in together ten years earlier in 1963 at St Quay Potrieux. And much to their surprise the old French maid who had been there before was still there, and no doubt had seen a few more saucy things just like what had happened before.

20.

WYT TI EISIO THI ACHUB TI ODDI WRTHO FO?

It had been in August 1963 that Alan and Thelma had enjoyed their first holiday together, hitchhiking round Normandy and Brittany. The following year they had hitched as far as St Jean de Luz in the South West corner of France and in 1965, they had managed to cross the French Italian border at Venti Miglia and reach Milan in Italy. Later that year they got married, bought a house in Beswick Street and started to spend money on other things. In 1966, young Rebecca Greenall appeared on the scene and three years later her little brother Robert, who would one day become one of the finest sheet metal draughtsmen the Western world had ever known. So the week they spent in Brittany brought back many happy memories for them. And with money still left over from the pools win, they decided they could easily manage to have another week's holiday in late September and spend it in South Wales and see if they could find anything out about Thelma's mother. Fortunately Thelma had kept in touch with Mr and Mrs Morrison who had bought the house in Rosemount Terrace that she had first lived in as a small baby.

When Thelma wrote to tell them they were coming to spend a week in the area and would like to pay them a visit, Mrs. Morrison immediately wrote back to invite them to stay there and where they were treated like long-lost relatives. In fact they couldn't have been treated better if they had stayed in a five star hotel.

On the Sunday night, with Mr and Mrs Morrison quite happy to look after Rebecca and Robert, they had gone into a nearby pub for a drink. As they were chatting away, working out what to do on the next day, a man at the adjacent table leaned over and said to Alan in a strong Welsh accent:

"Excuse me, are you from St Helens?"

"No. Ashurst, but it's quite near."

"I know. Are you on your holidays?"

"Yes."

"Come and join us if you like."

They moved their chairs across and the man introduced his wife, her sister and her husband.

"I lived for a couple of years at Haydock, not far from the racecourse. I enjoyed myself up there. The Lancashire people were very good to me. So whenever I hear the old twang, I always like to make them feel welcome down here in the Valleys."

He then asked Thelma where they were staying and on hearing her reply he said, "I don't think you are a Lancashire lass. I think you are one of us." And then he smiled and continued in Welsh: "Wyt ti eisio thi achub ti oddi wrtho fo?"

144

Thelma just smiled and shook her head. Then she told them about her links with the place, living in Rosemount Terrace and then being brought up in a home in Cardiff and now coming back to find out something about her mother.

She told them that all she knew about her was her name and that she had been a Land Army girl. Then she told them about her father. That was the key. As soon as she mentioned that he was a Greek sailor in the Merchant Navy, bells began to ring in their heads.

The man's wife was particularly helpful.

"I remember a Greek man, yes definitely. He came to my sister's wedding in 1943. I remember him because he had a funny looking guitar with him and sang us a lot of Greek songs. A good looking man he was, and he was with a girl with long black hair and freckles, a bit like you."

"Where's your sister now?"

"She lives in Pontypridd. I'll ring her tonight when I get home and ask her to come over in the week." Then she went on: "I don't think your mother came from Tonyrefail or else I would have seen her around more. Maybe she didn't live long in the town."

"My mother use to live in the next street," chipped in the other man. "She's living in a home now, but I'll go and ask her. She used to know everybody round there. She was a nurse at the hospital."

They talked for a long while about the subject. You could see the four of them racking their brains to remember things from nearly thirty years ago. Then one of the man's friends in the pub was roped in. He used to keep the records at the local cemetery and offered to go through them over the next few days.

The beer was flowing quite nicely when the former resident of Haydock changed the subject and asked Alan if he was a Rugby fan.

"You won't throw me in the river if I told you I was a supporter of the thirteen-a-side code, would you?" he laughed. "It's been done before."

"When I was up North, I used to watch the Rugby League every week. Wigan, St Helens, Warrington, Leigh, whereever the best game was I would go there. It's much better than Union and I played Union for years before the War. The others won't have it."

"Too much stopping and starting in Rugby League," said the other man. "That play the ball. I can't stand it."

"But in Rugby Union, the spectators handle the ball as much as the players do," protested Alan. "Kick and clap, we call it."

"Your scrums are a farce," Dai went on, "and how can it be called a sport when you get paid for playing it."

"There are plenty of amateurs playing Rugby League," replied Alan, "and there are plenty of lads playing Union who can't afford to lose money by going North."

Dai appeared unaware that many people played Rugby League as amateurs in the North of England. He was also not easily prepared to accept that many of the top players in Union had made a fortune out of the game. So Alan pointed out another home truth.

"In the North it's the working class who play League and it's the professional types who prefer Union. Why is it so different in Wales? You used to play League down here until the Union people managed to crush it."

The man was obviously working class himself and probably quite proud of it. Alan's point had obviously hit a raw nerve, so he confessed that it was probably because the way they ran the game in Wales was not like it was in England. He shrugged his shoulders, put his arm round Alan and declared that he didn't want to fall out over the matter. And the next half hour or so was spent remembering the names of those Welshmen who had gone North and become stars in the Northern game, people like Billy Boston at Wigan, Trevor Foster who played for Bradford Northern and a whole host of Saints players. And they discussed how some had returned to the Valleys and been respected for what they had achieved and others had been treated disgracefully by former colleagues and fellow Welshmen.

During the course of the next few days, Thelma was visited by Harriet Davies, the sister from Pontypridd. Yes, she had been a friend of Rebecca Johnson a long time ago. The last time they had been together was at Rebecca's wedding but after that she had only heard of her through another friend who now lived at Nant-y-moel. The following evening, Mr Morrison drove them to their house about fifteen miles away, met the lady, who was also called Rebecca and who told Thelma more about her mother and how she was now buried in Oystermouth cemetery in Pontypridd. She told Thelma that her mother had been brought up in Llantrisant as a child before moving to Cardiff just before the outbreak of war when she was twenty one and then, when she was expecting Thelma, she had moved up to Tonyrefail.

Thelma now knew a little more about her mother, and where she was buried, so that was their next port of call. Much to her surprise not only was the grave reasonably well looked after, there was a fresh bunch of flowers on it. Whoever could that be from? When she told their new-found friends, Harriet offered to keep an eye out for her, no great problem since her house overlooked the cemetery.

But despite her kind offer, she never found out just who Thelma's mother's mystery friend was.

The following year, while they were considering visiting South Wales again, Thelma heard that Mr Morrison had died and that Mrs Morrison had gone to live with her sister at Clydach in West Glamorgan. And it was around this time, while they were thinking it might have to be Southport, New Brighton and picnicking at Carr Mill for their holidays, that a little cash donation from Ernie in Lytham St Annes to Alan's Mum gave them the opportunity to travel abroad again. Greece would have been an excellent place to visit thought Thelma, but at the time the country was under martial law and no doubt asking questions about her father might not be that convenient, so instead they all had another fortnight in Brittany at St Quay Potrieux.

When Alan had first mentioned to the others they were going to rent a large gite there, Yorky's first words were "I told you so". One thing the Yorkshireman had taken to was making predictions. Over the years he had developed the capacity to predict what was going to happen in the future. The first prediction that he made was that the Labour Party would win the 1964 General Election, but without a proper majority and so would have to call another election shortly, which actually happened. After that he predicted that Ken

Dodd's version of 'Tears' would make it to the Top of the Pops, a statement that the rest of them had laughed at. He also said it would stay there for three weeks and it did. A few weeks later he predicted that a lad from Leigh would be at the top of the charts some time in 1966, and it happened, Georgie Fame with 'Get Away' just before the Works Shutdown. He also backed England to win the World Cup, which of course they did by beating West Germany.

Of course he wasn't able to predict things absolutely, like which games would be draws on next Saturday's coupon, or what would be the result of Saints' next game. But he seemed to have some insight into the future, although sometimes he would go for months without coming up with anything startling. When Alan had told them about their intended holiday, Yorky proceeded to tell him an amazing tale, one that went right back to shortly after Freckles, as she was known then, had come to work at Wilkinson's.

"I never said anything at the time, but just after she started in the Print Room, I kept getting this picture in my head of you and her getting married. Then, after she came back to work after being so ill at your Granny's, I said to myself that I bet you go on your holidays together, hitch-hiking like you always did. And three weeks later you told us you were going to Brittany. And a few weeks after that I was watching that famous Jacque Tati film, 'Mr Hulot's Holiday', and I got this picture in my head of you and Thelma and some children there on holiday."

"Do you ever get these pictures of other people in the future?"

"I thought Stan wouldn't be long retired. It was just a feeling, but I was right there. I can't explain it, I just sense that something is going to happen in a certain way. The latest thing is that the war in Vietnam is going to end soon and the Americans will pull out."

"Watch this space. And what other predictions have you got for me?"

"Rebecca is going to dance, Robert will play football, Thelma will grow old gracefully and you'll finally get one of your drawings right first time."

"You can't argue with that Greeno," said Mick. "Though I think Yorky has stuck his neck out on the fourth one."

"What's going to happen to Mick, Yorky?" said Charlie. "When is he going to get a new suit?"

"You know Yorky, you're pretty clever for a Yorkshireman. That answer you gave Alan then about his family," chipped in Charlie again. "You know Rebecca goes to a dancing school every week, so you're right Rebecca will dance, probably tonight. Robert likes to play football with his Dad on the lawn every night. You had to say that about Thelma and with the design of computers and space age technology, Greeno is bound to get one of his drawings right first time, even if it's only on an A4 sheet."

"I will make one prediction, old lad. About computers. They'll put us lot out of work and thousands of others too."

"No, you're wrong there," said Mick. "With computers coming in, we'll all be on a three day week and a four day weekend."

"We were on a three day week when the miners were on strike, Mick."

"I tell you something else, with computers and new technology the big companies will start transferring their production to the Third World countries where the wages are much lower. All the heavy industry will go in the next twenty years from this country, I'm sure of it And it won't just happen here, it'll happen right across Europe."

"You're a bit of a pessimist today, what's up with you?"

"It's just the way I see things developing. The bosses are only in it to make profits. You don't think Basil cares one bit about us lot. If he can get our control gear made abroad at one tenth the cost of doing it here, what do you think he'll do. He look after number one and bugger us lot. It's the name of the game for them."

"Yorky is right, for once," chipped in Len. "This place will get like America, multi millionaires and folk on Skid Row living less than a mile from each other. And this Government will probably encourage it too."

As he was talking he looked over to Charlie, expecting him to agree with him, but he was engrossed in reading something he had just brought out of his bottom drawer. Then he started laughing.

"What is it Charlie?" Mick asked.

"I haven't seen this for years. It's McTaggish's Golden Rules."

"Who's he?"

"He was one of the section leaders at Wallworks. Listen to this, I take it you lot aren't busy -

Problems Linked to The Behaviour of Inanimate Objects in the Field of Engineering Design.

The more innocuous a design change appears, the further its influence will extend.
The necessity of making a design change increases as the fabrication approaches completion.
Any error that can creep in will do so, and in that direction which will cause the most damage.
Any material cut exactly to length will be too short.
Identical units tested under identical conditions will not be identical in the field.
The availability of components is inversely proportional to their need.
If n components are required, n minus 1 will be available.
A dropped tool will land where it will do the most damage. This is also known as the Law of Selective Gravitation.
A device selected at random from a group having 99% reliability will be a member of the 1% group.
The probability of a dimension being omitted from a plan or drawing is inversely proportional to its importance.
Parts that are supposed to be interchangeable, won't be.
Components which must not, and cannot, be assembled improperly will be.
A failure will not appear until the unit has passed its final inspection.
After the last of sixteen screws have been removed from an access cover, it will be found to be the wrong cover.
After a device has been fully assembled, extra components will be found on the bench.

148

In a device characterised by a number of plus or minus errors, the total error will be the sum of all the possible errors in the same direction.

"I think I've heard them before," said Mick. "I remember when I first started here, they used to have something called the Value Analysis Team. Three Unwise Men who always looked at any design changes and see how good they were. I think it was Les Earnshaw who coined what he called the Law of Diminishing Usefulness. What was it now? Oh, yes:

"Suggestions made by the Value Analysis Group will increase costs and reduce capabilities. And another one was: in any given miscalculation, the fault will never be placed if there is more than one person involved in that miscalculation.

"And then there was that classic one: important original drawings will always get mangled in the copying machine."

"Especially if Small Joe was doing it," said Charlie.

"Who's he?" asked Alan.

"He was one of the labourers that used to work here. His actual name was Joseph Small. He was bloody useless. Absolutely."

"I'll tell you how bad he was," said Len. "He once got told to clean out the store room at the back of the Pattern Shop, which he did. Then he was told to sweep the floor clean and paint it, which he did. Unfortunately he started at the door and worked his way inwards and painted himself into a corner. And then he stood there for about two hours while it dried."

"Do you remember that time he got that foreman jammed in his office?" said Charlie. Then turning to Alan he went on: "Billy Phillips had his office at the top of the stairs above the Machine Shop. It was a right dingy place and next to it was where they used to store all the dies, drills and cutting tools. One day Billy tells Joe to give it a good cleaning. So he starts first thing and then just before dinner time he drags this big heavy table out on to the landing so he could sweep the floor, intending to do it in the afternoon. Now it was only a small landing and Billy's office door used to open out onto this landing. Well Billy was in there looking for something and of course when he tries to open the door he can't. It was no use him shouting because the milling machine was far too loud for anybody to hear him.

"Then, in the afternoon straight after dinner, one of the chargehands sends Joe over to the Laboratory to get something. Now Joe's attitude to life was always the same, 'Obey the last order'. When he gets to the lab, one of the engineers in there told him that he would have to wait for half an hour so Joe watches them doing some High Voltage Testing. Well it's about half three before he comes back to the Machine Shop. Billy wasn't very pleased, first because he had been stuck in there for about four hours and secondly because nobody had missed him. He always thought he was indispensable. Clearly not."

"You've missed the best bit," said Len. "After he had been stuck in there about twenty minutes, Billy gets the bright idea to send a message to the outside world calling for help. There was a hole in the wall about ten foot up, big enough to take a large washer. So he ties a piece of string to a couple of washers and attaches a note to it, then pushes it through the hole and lowers it down. After a bit the string goes loose so Billy reckons it had reached the ground. So he starts pulling it up about two foot and then letting it go. Then it gets pulled out of his hand, so he assumed somebody had found it. But nobody came. What he didn't know was that there was a lorry parked directly underneath the hole in the wall and just at that moment, with the string caught on some machinery, the driver had driven off to Preston."

"I'll tell you another tale about Joe," laughed Charlie. "One day he was told to drive to Ashurst station in one of the company pool cars and pick up an important visitor who was coming on the train from Liverpool and arriving at half ten. So after he had had his tea break, Joe drives down to the station and gets there about ten past ten. He parks it in the station yard just as a train pulls in. Joe is sat there wearing a chauffeur's hat he had found in the glove compartment when the back door opens and an old bloke with a suitcase gets in and mutters something to Joe which he didn't quite hear. So he replies by saying yes it was a nice day and then proceeds to drive back to work. When they stop outside the Main Offices , this bloke says:

"Where are we?"

"Wilkinson's," said Joe.

"But I want to go to go Victoria Hospital."

"Why, are you poorly?"

"No, I'm a doctor there."

"So Joe has to drive the man to the hospital and then back to the station and pick up the real visitor who had been standing there for ten minutes and bring him back. The daft bugger."

"He wasn't that daft. Both of his passengers thought it was a private taxi so they paid him," laughed Charlie.

Then he went on, "Do you know what his nickname was. TL14B?"

"Go on, tell us," said Keith. "This must be good."

"It was just after the war. Joe's brother had an old motorbike and he was forever repairing it. Anyway, he needed a spare part making, a special washer which he couldn't get anywhere for love nor money. So he asked one of the draughtsmen to draw it up and then get it made in the Machine Shop. But of course it wasn't that easy. With all the restrictions on because of the War and that it had to have a part number and be on a drawing parts list. The draughtsman had just finished drawing some complicated spring mechanism assembly so he added this washer to it and to make it look official he gave it a part number; TL14B.

"A few weeks later the lad gets called up for his National Service. By now this drawing was made the standard for spring mechanisms on the old speed control unit box, so a TL14B gets called up every time. But nobody ever knew what it was used for, maybe they just thought it was a spare part for use in an emergency. About five years later, one of the chargehands, looking in the stores for some large washers, finds about a thousand of these TL14B's. So he gets it deleted from the drawing, but not from the spares list that goes out with these boxes, so all over the world can be found these bloody washers that nobody has ever fitted to anything."

150

"Is Joe still here?"

"No, he retired a few years ago. He was quite a likeable bloke. They even had a collection for him in the Fitting Shop when he left."

"Did they get much for him?" asked Keith, half expecting what the answer would be.

"Oh, aye. Seven pounds six shillings and a dozen bags of TL14B's."

21.

SPENDING A NIGHT
IN SOWERBY BRIDGE

"Look out. Here comes Billy Cotton," said Alan.

"What, you mean the band leader?" asked Keith.

"Yes, and he's got Alma Coggan with him, you daft bat," replied his mate.

Before he could explain, the door burst open and as Alan and the others knew he would, the first words their visitor uttered were:

"Wakey, Wakey. Is there any one here who's awake or even still alive?"

It was Terry Robledo, just one more of the many characters from the shop floor, although now that he was working with the Outside Contracts Department, not much was seen of him either in the factory or around the town.

"Hello Charlie. I thought you'd retired. Then turning to Mick he said, "Keep moving around Mick. Don't you know they're stock-taking today. I don't want you being put in a cardboard box, well not until you've paid your debts."

"What debts?"

"Seven and six or whatever it is in this new-fangled money."

It was a debt based on a complicated bet they had had over eighteen months earlier, too complicated to go into.

Then he told Yorky not go outside for a bit as the binmen were collecting the rubbish, rubbed Alan's head roughly as he said "Hello Dad" and asked Keith, who he had not met before, what heinous crime he had committed to be sentenced to work in this madhouse.

"So, are you all right then?" asked Len.

"Only down one side."

Terry sat down on a vacant chair, folded his arms and said, "You might all be a little surprised to hear that I've come here today in order to apologise. I've just returned from the Land of the Aztecs and the Incas. I've swum across the Gulf of Mexico and climbed up the Andes. I've seen some amazing sights, could spend the rest of the day telling you about them and showing you photographs of me in old Monterey. But I won't waste my time. I'll come straight to the point. I'm now prepared to admit that I've been a little harsh on you lot, made insinuating comments about your parentage and cast doubt on your technical ability."

They all waited for the punchline. There had to be one. There always was one with Terry.

"Three weeks ago I was in the ancient and historic city of Lima installing the latest range of the very fashionable 33kV air blast switchgear. And with me I had an electrical schematic diagram with matching wiring diagram and cubicle assembly drawn by one

Senor Pedro Greenall. And would you believe it, the drawings were actually useful. For the first time ever there was not one mistake on them. Greeno, I'm proud of you. You're an absolute star. And there was me thinking by being here you were depriving some small village of an idiot."

And with that he gave Alan something that he had no doubt collected ten minutes earlier from the back of the Iron Foundry:

"So here's a little momento from my day on the beach at Chorillos and which has been washed by the Pacific Ocean for over a million years." And with that he deposited a handful of sand on Alan's reference table.

"Thank you, Terry. You've made my day."

Then he looked around the room, opened a couple of drawers and went on: "Whenever I come in here, do you know what famous piece of classical music always springs to mind."

They all waited, ready for his next crack

"'Lazing on a Summer's Afternoon' by the Kinks" he laughed. Then he stood up, walked round the office looking at every body's drawing board and went on: "I don't know how you lot manage it. You always have the same drawing on your board. Look at this one of Mick's. He's even got the date on when he started it. Over a year he's been on it. It isn't a rush job is it, Mick?"

"There's been a few changes to the original scheme," said Mick.

"One thing's for sure, there's been no changes with you. You're still wearing the same suit you had when you came here."

"It's good material."

"So where have you been?" asked Charlie.

Terry sat down again and went on:

"We were supposed to start off in Mexico, installing the second generator at Rosario power station, but just before we arrived they had an earthquake there, so they sent us down to Lambayeque in Peru to replace that 400 MVA transformer. We were there nearly three months. It was a hell of a job. Then the rest of the gang went back to Mexico and I went to commission the control desk at the refinery at Matucana. Then, the night before I was due to fly back home, John Barker rings me up and asks if I could call in at Paysandu in Uruguay on the way home and sort out the second half of the railway job that Billy Pilkington was working on. Bloody hell, it was about a thousand miles away. It was a good job I had a fit lhama to carry me."

"How come you get all these good jobs?" asked Alan enviously.

"Because I'm good at making things work, not like you lot who only draw pictures on bits of paper."

"I think we're all in the wrong game," moaned Yorky. "I bet he makes more on expenses than we get paid."

"Eh, it's not all dead cushy," said Terry. "Some of the places I've stayed in were pretty rough and the food isn't much kop either when you get right off the beaten track."

"Where are you off to next?"

"Three right miserable jobs I'm lined up for now. Stapi in Iceland at a fish canning factory, then Alesund in Norway, another fishy place, and after that I've got to go to Halifax."

"What, in Newfoundland?"

"No, in bloody Yorkshire. I've heard it's really primitive over there. And they don't speak English either."

"You can go and stay with Tony if you're going to Halifax" said Charlie. "In his pub."

"How's he getting on?"

"I think he's having the time of his life."

"Why, what's he doing? Is it missionary work?"

"It's certainly the missionary position. He's only become the coach, trainer and masseur for a womens' Rugby team."

"How did he manage that? I didn't think he liked Rugby."

"He didn't, but he does now."

"I bet he does."

"You know his Dad bought the pub over there, after he won all that money on the pools."

"Yes."

"Well it was only because he fancied living in a place that had its own bowling green, snooker table and loads of free ale. He certainly didn't fancy all the work, so he's employed a manager to run the place. Tony helps him and four barmaids all help Tony."

"To do what."

"You'd be surprised."

"Knowing Tony, I don't think I would be. And is he still working on the board?"

"No, he's full time in the pub now."

"Give us his phone number. I'm going over there next Monday, to look at a job at Butler's."

"That's right near Thrum Hall," said Alan.

"What's that, some stately home?"

Alan explained.

"Oh that's really made my day," replied Terry, "knowing that I'm going to be spending a whole day next to a bloody Rugby field."

"A bit more interesting than a magnetic field," laughed Yorky.

"Or Huddersfield," chipped in Len.

"Is it anywhere near where you were brought up, Sam?" And then Terry had three or four attempts at pronouncing the nearby town of Mytholmroyd. But before Sam could respond, Charlie butted in and said:

"It's funny, isn't it, how things change. Two years ago you thought that going to Trafford Park was an adventure."

Terry's introduction to the world of foreign travel had come about quite by chance. After completing his apprenticeship he had spent three years working in the Assembly shop on the bench with just the odd day trip out around Merseyside or as far east as Salford or Rochdale or on one forgettable occasion to Scunthorpe. Then one morning his foreman had called him into the office and told him that he wanted Terry to fit an extension bracket he had just made to a rolling mill in the French town of Nancy: and he wanted it doing that afternoon! So he had been driven straight home in Basil Wilkinson's car by Basil's personal chauffeur, Horace, collected his passport and some extra clothes and then been taken to Manchester Airport and on to his first trip abroad. At the mill in Nancy, he had carefully fitted the bracket, an act which had greatly increased the machine's efficiency. The following day he had rung in to report on his success, only to be told by his foreman to spend a couple of days making another two brackets and then fit one to an identical rolling mill at Metz about thirty miles away and then repeat the exercise at Buste Arsino just to the north of Milan before returning to Nancy to check on the first machine's progress.

Around this time he had not been seeing eye to eye with his girlfriend, Nora. She didn't like the idea of him being away, and when she heard from his brother John that Terry was looking forward to going back to see Nancy, she decided that she had had enough of it. Unfortunately for her, Terry had by this time decided that he had had enough of her and so on his return to work he had got himself transferred to the Outside Contracts Department. The world had become his oyster and boy did he make a meal of his all expenses paid trips around the world.

His next three visits were to places that could not be said to be the most exciting in the world: a cotton mill in Accrington, Hull Docks and Dolgarrog Hydro electric power station in North Wales. Then followed a period in the O.C.D. fitting shop until one of the erection fitters fell off a ladder two days before a gang were due to depart for a contract in Tunisia. It was at this point that Terry's introduction to the O.C.D. Foreign Holiday Club really started. Strangely enough the place the installation team stayed at was a holiday camp! As it was only February, there were plenty rooms available at the holiday resort at Hammamet just south of Tunis and less than ten miles from a water treatment plant at which Wilkinson's were installing a couple of electrical control cubicles.

There were not many holiday-makers there at the time, although there was a group of twelve young ladies from the University of Stockholm Geology Department, resting for a week after trekking in the Sahara desert. There was quite a social interchange of cultures over the week the two groups lived there. The Swedes were taught the game of Rugby, at least its touch and pass variety - plenty touching and many passes being made. In return, the girls from the land of the midnight sun encouraged the men from Ashurst to enjoy the benefits of swimming naked in the ice cold sea, ready for the time when they would be invited to come to Stockholm and run around the health and nature club and frolic in the sauna at their University sports complex in the middle of a harsh Swedish winter.

Yes, working for the OCD had proved to be the making of Terry. He quite quickly mastered the creative skill of filling out time sheets and expense claim forms, and more importantly getting them signed. He soon came to realise that compared to some of the major cities of the world, Ashurst was a little on the dull side, though no doubt in some far flung corner of the globe he would describe the town in most glowing terms.

In fact, no matter where he went, he always returned with a vivid description of the place and the people who lived there, the night life and the incidents that he had witnessed or mini adventures that he had enjoyed. As a result his visit to the Drawing Office, officially to discuss all the cock ups he had had to put right on site and to discuss the corrections to their drawings, was a most enjoyable experience for all who had the good fortune to hear him.

Interestingly, he had the same ability to entertain as two other characters who lived in Gillarsfield, Les Earnshaw and Mick Ellison, a chargehand in the Rolling Mill and an executive class member of the Done Everything, Met Everybody, Been Everywhere club. Just like them, Terry was also brilliant at impersonations, with Harold Wilson, Eddie Waring and Basil Wilkinson being his most entertaining. Yes, the water they drank in Gillarsfield certainly had some magical properties, or was it the pungent air they breathed there.

He stayed until lunchtime, during which time he received three phone calls, one of which particularly pleased him. It was from John Barker telling him that he could forget Stapi in Norway and Alesund in Iceland. After completing the job at Butler's, he was going back to South America to a country he had not yet visited, Chile, where he could expect to stay until Christmas! There he was about to witness at first hand the traumatic earth-shattering events that overtook that country with the overthrow of the Government of Salvador Allende and the imposition of martial law under General Augusto Pinochet.

Then he graced them with his presence in the canteen where he continued to regale them with stories about some of the places he had worked at, the hotels he had stayed at and the ladies in whose houses or sumptuous palaces he had eaten breakfast at. Then it was over to the bowling green and not surprisingly a late return to work. Yes, an hour spent listening to Terry was a treat indeed and a good part of the afternoon was spent discussing who was the funniest, Terry or Les Earnshaw, about whom various stories were circulating around town.

It was generally agreed that nothing on this Earth could ever be as funny as the two of them in company. Charlie suggested that they should all chip in a fiver each and hire the Theatre Royal in St Helens and have what he called an evening of industrial humour. It would certainly be a sell-out, particularly if they had a couple of warm-up acts, maybe getting the old Saints star Duggie Greenall to do his Al Jonson repertoire and Alex Murphy to recite his poem. John Rigby could organise a reunion of his Sixties band the Rainmen to attract a few of the younger ones, and he finished by suggesting that Mick should be the compere, wearing his demob suit to bring back happy memories for the Old Age Pensioners.

Three weeks later, before setting off for Chile, Terry had a couple of days back in the factory. He had stayed at Tony's dad's pub in Halifax, met some of the women's Rugby team, drunk an enormous amount of Webster's best bitter and still made over fifteen pounds on his expenses. He then told a hilarious tale of a night out in a pub in Sowerby Bridge with a couple of the fitters and where he had had the place in stitches with his dead-pan humour and impersonations. There he had also met and impressed Delia, the barmaid. After taking her for a highly spiced Indian curry, nothing this much-travelled Marco Polo Mint couldn't handle, he had then walked her home, encouraged by the fact that she had told him at least three times that she lived on her own. On arrival at the house, she discovered she had left her keys at her sister's where she had been earlier that afternoon. In the yard Terry spied a pair of ladders, so without thinking any more of it he placed them against the wall and went up to an open window on the first floor, Delia's bedroom as it turned out and where Delia then proceeded to keep him awake for the rest of the night.

Around half past six the following morning, they both heard knocking on the front door.

"Hell, it's my husband," she said.

"I didn't think you had one."

"He left me about six months ago but he's probably come for some money I owe him. He'll be on his way home from work."

"Should I go?"

"Yes, go down that bloody ladder and don't come back."

And so, literally according to Terry, he clambered half-naked down the ladder carrying his jacket, trousers and shoes, dressed himself in the back entry, much to the amusement of a small boy delivering papers, and made his way back to Tony's pub.

Terry then proceeded to tell them about Tony's new life in Halifax. It was clear he was enjoying himself, both with Sandra and Felicity, or Fay as he called her. Sandra was his favourite barmaid and a keen Rugby player; Fay lived in a hippie commune near Hebden Bridge and was totally uninterested in sport. In fact, she was not only unable to tell the difference between Rugby League and Rugby Union, she could not even tell the difference between Rugby League and basketball. In fact, she would have had difficulty in explaining the difference between Rugby League and the Temperance League, but to compensate for this gap in her knowledge she was something of an expert on the benefits of organically grown vegetables.

Sandra was a real beauty. To look at her you would think that butter wouldn't melt in her mouth. She was tall and slim and played on the wing. She also had a husband, which didn't really cramp her style because he lived in Leeds, in the district of Armley to be more precise; in Armley prison to be exact. He was there due to the way he had dealt with a bus driver on the 508 route from Leeds to Halifax and who he insisted had short-changed him late one night. And unless there was a mass break out from Armley he would be there for another three years. Unfortunately for Tony, the man's brother was also in the same state institution but due out in six months time, able and prepared to look after his sister-in-law, and if not allowed to, to find out what she had been doing during the absence of the two brothers from the town!

Fay had been brought up in Chelsea and educated at Roedean public school for young ladies. Actually, the name was a little misleading. Few of the public actually ever got into the place. After finishing that period in her life she had spent a year at a finishing school in Switzerland and returned to England where, at the age of twenty one, she decided to retire to the country and settled in an old converted barn on the outskirts of Hebden Bridge. She was a naturalist, a health freak, teetotal, vegetarian and a free thinker, and also liked to dabble in the occult. She rarely came down into Halifax, and of course rarely into a pub, and it was in the Piece Hall in the middle of Halifax that she had met Tony and where she helped a girlfriend run a stall selling a rather dubious assortment of expensive carrot cake.

Terry then talked about his forthcoming trip to Chile, where he would be installing a turbine generator in a power station and heating and ventilating equipment in a hospital on the outskirts of Santiago. "I'd better not tell them I play snooker in the Conservative club," he laughed, "or they'll have my guts for garters."

"If you get into any trouble, you'll just have to tell them you know Comrade Greenall, chairman of the All Lancashire Soviet Federation of Landless and Hopeless Peasants," said Yorky. "That'll impress them."

"You'll be seeing a bit of history being made when you're out there," said Alan seriously. "I'll want a full report when you get back."

"Oui, mon capitaine," said Terry, clenching his fist and also indicating that he would let the M.P. for Huyton know as well. But when they did next see him, he had a deep cut across his cheek where a soldier had hit him with his rifle and a bitter story to tell that made no one laugh.

22.

I LIKED GRANDAD. HE WAS FUNNY.

Without fail, over each weekend Alan and Thelma and the two children would call in to see Granny at the old peoples' home in Dob Lane, where she now lived. Then, one beautiful afternoon, they decided to take her up to the cemetery to lay flowers on Grandad's grave. Paul drove Granny up in his car, it was only a short distance but a long way for an old lady who was now nearly eighty two. As soon as they came into view, Rebecca rushed over to hold her hand and help her along. Then, as the others began to tidy the grave, she began asking questions, not an unusual thing - she was always doing it.

"Granny, where's Grandad? I thought we were coming to see him."

Quickly her mother came in to point out that they had come to remember Grandad by visiting the place where he had been buried.

"So is he here under all this dirty old soil?"

"Yes," said Thelma. "Well his body is there, but he's gone to another land now."

Rebecca thought for a while and then asked if he knew that they had all come to see him.

"Oh, he'll know," laughed Granny. "He knows everything."

Rebecca looked at the headstone and then at the grave and the flowers they had laid and then said:

"Can I have a look at him?"

Once again her mother tried to provide a satisfactory answer, but with difficulty.

Then Rebecca said: "Will you die one day Granny?"

"Everybody has to die one day," said her mother.

"Yes, little one," replied Granny. "I'll die one day but don't you worry, it won't be until you're a big girl."

"Will they put you in this place as well?"

"Yes."

"How will they put you in it? Will there be any room for you?"

"Oh I'm sure they'll find some room for me."

"Well if there is no room will one of these other people have to get out?"

Then she pointed at the names on the headstone and asked: "Does Grandad know any of these people, Granny?"

So again her mother explained who the people were that were buried there. It was the Holding family grave and in it were Grandad's parents, William and Catherine Holding, his grandparents on his mother's side, William and Frances Tunstall, along with three of his aunties and a great uncle.

She looked at the names again, working her finger over them, and then turned to her mother and asked:

"Where is your Mummy buried? Is she not in there as well?"

Thelma explained quietly that her mother was buried in Wales, which was a long way away.

Then the little girl passed a comment that brought tears to their eyes when she said: "I liked Grandad. He was funny."

Then, in an act of child-like innocence, having probably forgotten all the questions she had been so pointedly asking, Rebecca waved at the gravestone and shouted out "Bye bye Grandad" and asked if they could go now.

They decided to invite Granny back to their house for the rest of the day and later, as they were eating their tea, Thelma noticed that by her general behaviour at the table Granny was clearly losing her eyesight. It was the way she picked things from her plate or moved her spoon from the sugar bowl to her cup. She said nothing, perhaps Granny just needed some new glasses, she thought. But then it might just be that old age was really setting in. And as she looked at her, Thelma's thoughts went back to another old lady she had once known and whose eyesight was much worse than Granny's, Mrs. Thomas who used to live in Beech Street in Cardiff, many years ago.

When she was fourteen Thelma had been very friendly with a girl in her class called Megan. Megan lived with her parents and her three brothers and sister quite near to the home where Thelma had been brought up. Every week Megan had to visit her grandmother and run errands for her and do any little jobs about the house, something that she didn't want to do. One day she had taken Thelma with her and after they had left, Thelma told Megan that she wouldn't mind helping the old lady. And so it was agreed and in this way Thelma began to visit Mrs Thomas. And soon the old lady became almost like a grandmother to Thelma.

Mrs Thomas had been brought up in West Wales until at the age of sixteen she had been put into domestic service in Cardiff and she had lived in that city for the next sixty or so years, and there had brought up her three sons and a daughter. The old lady quickly discovered that her new found young friend was much more interested to hear about her own childhood days in Carmarthen than anything her own family had ever done. And she also discovered that Thelma was quite keen to learn to speak Welsh and so had begun to teach her. All during that summer of 1958 Thelma would visit her maybe two or three times a week and after running any errands for her or doing any little jobs around the house, they would just sit and talk. Then one sad day Thelma had been unable to get into the house and had run to tell Megan. On the doorstep Thelma had been told the sad news that Megan's grandmother had had a heart attack a couple of days earlier and had died that morning.

A few days later, after the funeral had been held, Megan gave Thelma a large envelope in which were found a ten shilling note, a broach and necklace and a note from Mrs Thomas thanking her for all the help Thelma had given her and a fervent hope that one day Thelma would have her own family. And when she asked Megan where the old lady had been buried she had been told that it was miles away at a place called Llandyssul, north of Pembroke, and where the old lady had been born.

Until she had first walked into the house in Silkstone Street and set her eyes on Alan's

Granny, Thelma had often thought about old Mrs Thomas. But after that eventful Christmas Day in 1962, well she then had a real Granny to look after her. But from time to time she did recall the old Welsh lady and the way she liked to hold Thelma's hand while they talked, something of course that Granny rarely did. But then Granny had always had good eyesight, at least until now.

That night Thelma thought a lot about Granny and her fading health and eyesight. She remembered again fondly Granny's first words to her in the living room in what was now her own home: "Hello, Thelma. I'm very pleased to meet you. You're very welcome, love."

Thelma remembered again how Granny had taken her into the kitchen on that fateful morning to look at the turkey roasting away in the oven and then they had had a little drink of sherry together and started to get to know each other. During the course of their Christmas Day celebrations, Granny had looked after her, not that she really needed to since the rest of the Holding family had made her more than welcome. And then, just as things seemed to be going so well, she had fallen ill and for the next six weeks or so, Granny and Grandad had cared for her and nursed her back to health. And at the time they hardly knew a thing about her.

Now Grandad was no longer with them. She did have many happy memories of him as well, even though she had been a little bit frightened of him at first. There were other relatives too who were no longer alive, Auntie Hilda and Uncle Eric who had gone down with the flu just before that Christmas Day; Uncle Albert, who had died after being hit by the crane at Mathers' Foundry three weeks before he was due to retire, and Auntie Eunice, the schoolteacher, the only one in the family that Thelma had never taken to. And others had moved away, like Alan's cousin Trevor, who had been a student at Hull University and on graduation had decided to settle in that city.

On the other hand some of the relatives seemed unaffected by the passage of time. Uncle Jack and Auntie Doris, now both in their late seventies but still behaving like sixty years olds, Alan's Mum and his Uncle Stan who was now in charge of the Maintenance department at the Town Hall and hoping to retire soon to a life of permanent golf. Yes, there had been many changes in Thelma's life, particularly since she had changed her name from Johnson to Greenall, and throughout all of them she had always had Granny to talk to or confide in. And now she knew that Granny would not always be there to have a little natter with. But Thelma knew that she would always have many happy memories of this wonderful old lady and all that she had done for her.

Although she was not religious, Thelma believed that if there was a place called Heaven, well Granny would surely go straight there. And no doubt Grandad would already be there, waiting for her. And after Granny had arrived and been there herself a few days, another lady would no doubt come to see her, a lady who Granny did not know. And the lady would quietly tell Granny in a strong Welsh accent that her name was Rebecca Johnson and she was the mother of the young Thelma Johnson. And then from the bottom of her heart and with tears in her eyes she would thank this old Lancashire lady for all that she had done for her daughter. And perhaps some time later, another lady with a slightly different Welsh accent would introduce herself both to Thelma's mother and to Granny; and she would also be so pleased to hear that things had worked out well for the orphan girl that she had briefly known and taught to speak a little Welsh.

And if there wasn't a place called Heaven, and if this life was not a practice run for something else but was the real thing and indeed the only thing, then it would just be like all those who had died being asleep themselves and remembered fondly by those who were still awake.

At work the following morning the morning break conversation was about what they had all done over the weekend, not very much it would have appeared except that another of Charlie's coincidences appeared on the scene. He had gone for a walk round Taylor Park in St Helens with his wife on the Sunday afternoon, and there had seen in the distance the father of an old workmate of his, sat on a park bench looking out across the lake. As soon as Charlie spoke to the man, he realised he was completely blind and discovered that he had been so for nearly five years. It was not that unusual, Ken Durham was the same age as Charlie so his father must have been well into his seventies, perhaps even turned eighty; but after what Alan had now just said about his Granny's fading eyesight, a coincidence of sorts no less.

Then Keith announced that he had started looking out for what he called Charlie's coincidences in life and had noted his first one. Listening to the radio on Saturday night just before he went to bed, "School's Out" by the Alice Cooper band had been the last record he had heard. The following morning he had switched the radio on and the first record he heard was the same record. But Charlie announced that that didn't count. The record was at the top of the charts and had been played on just about every music programme on the radio for the last month. In the end he accepted that it could be classed as a lowly Grade Three coincidence. Then Yorky joined the fray when he announced that he had had a great coincidence on the previous Friday night. They listened with interest. It was also to be Yorky's first. Seeking out coincidences in life had by now gripped the whole office.

"When I got home after work on Friday, our lass said that my tea would be in about half an hour so I decided to have a look in the garden to see how the vegetables were doing. I watered the spuds and carrots and did a bit of weeding. Then I went back in the house, had a wash and by then my meal was on the table. Now this is absolutely amazing. On the plate was a nice piece of haddock and next to it, unbelievably, were spuds and carrots."

"What a pathetic attempt," said Charlie. "None out of ten for that."

"I've got one," said Alan, "and its a Grade One coincidence."

They waited with interest. They had nothing better to do other than work.

"On Friday night I went up to Nook End on the bus and do you know who I saw on it?"

"The Halle Orchestra," said Mick.

"The Royal Philharmonic," laughed John.

"The driver," said Dickie.

"You're getting warmer."

"Another passenger," said Len.

"Do you remember when I nearly went out with that bus conductress Helen, the one who must have got pregnant a couple of weeks earlier. Well I saw her with a pair of ten year old twins."

"Very interesting," said Charlie, "but where's the coincidence?"

"Let me finish," said Alan. "Do you remember that I went to hospital after I had torn my ligaments playing football, which is why I never went out with Helen. Well when I was in the hospital there was a cracking Irish nurse there who bandaged me up. Now when the bus stopped outside the hospital, she got on, which is the coincidence. But what makes it a Grade One coincidence is that she had a pair of twins with her as well. How about that Charlie?"

"Not bad. I think you can have nine out of ten for that."

Nothing of significance happened at work or in the town for the next week or so until something of a bombshell hit them: the decision by the firm to buy out the Jarratt Machine Tool Factory. Jarratts, as it was always known, had been set up around the turn of the century and had manufactured and exported lathes, milling machines and grinders across the world. But recently it had come under the influence of alcohol, or rather the management team had come under the dominating influence of a Managing Director who in the opinion of his rather exasperated secretary was 'permanently pissed'. As a result many things went on at the place which gradually brought it to near bankruptcy and so Basil had moved in to buy the company and at the same time demonstrated his public spiritedness by investing in the town rather than elsewhere. But not long after the whole factory was flattened, the land sold to the building firm Cheshire Constructions and a sizeable amount of money deposited in one of Basil's many bank accounts.

In the classical sense Jarratts had always been an eyesore, certainly to anyone brought up on the plains of Lombardy or with an appreciation of such classical edifices as the Coliseum, the railway station at Milan or St Peters Square in Rome. But around South Lancashire, and particularly on a foggy day, the place somehow encapsulated the very essence of Northern life. Over the years no small number of photographs had been taken of its late 19th century collection of chimneys, accompanied in the background by the winding gear of the Prince of Wales colliery and the cooling tower of the old Ashurst Power Station demolished in 1937 as a result of subsidence in the area. With skill it had also been possible to include an angled view of the station and on one occasion a local enthusiast had produced a shot showing the smoke from Jarratts chimneys floating towards the West and the smoke from a moving Patriot locomotive going in the opposite direction!

Just like at Wilkinsons, no small number of comedians and characters had worked at Jarratts over the years. Of course Les Earnshaw was one of its most famous, but there had been others including Peter Starr, the spaceship freak, and also Sally, who had worked on the till in the canteen until her dancing talents had been recognised and she had joined a London dance group and appeared on TV a few times and had last been seen in the company of Charles Aznavour at the Cannes Film Festival. There was also the notorious Norman Dickson, a small time, small town gangster now resident in Walton Jail for his role in a protection racket involving chip shops, and Joe Hensingham for his attempts to molest a witness for the prosecution in the Hemsley Co-operative Bank raid trial.

In the next few weeks more details emerged of what changes would arise following the takeover. All the Drawing Office waited with great interest to see how many of Jarratts draughtsmen joined them. Keith on the other hand waited with great trepidation, wondering how many of Jarratts tracers would be coming and no doubt making sly innuendos about his special relationship with the new Head Tracer, Mary McIntosh.

Then, on the day that it was announced that the old factory was to be knocked down, the Chief Draughtsman, John Battesby, informed the office of the new arrangements. From Jarratts six men would be joining the Drawing Office, two electrical draughtsmen, a sheet metal man, two mechanical draughtsman and a planning engineer. Then came the news that made Keith's heart miss two or three beats. Three of the tracers would also be coming and would have their drawing boards placed right at the back of the electrical section. Would he and Mary be able to keep quiet about the visits he kept making to keep her company whenever her darling husband Cyril was working at least one hundred miles away? With Margaret the Mouth around, it would be with great difficulty, particularly since she had just moved house to Grappenhall Lane, a nice little cul-de-sac at the top of Dob Lane and about three hundred yards from Mary's place. But then the reason she had moved there was because her husband, a lecturer at Salford College of Technology, had just run off with a nineteen year old laboratory assistant from Eccles.

Two weeks later the two new men started work in the electrical section, and by the end of the first day the rest of them knew they were going to have trouble with the pair of them. First of all there was Walter, thirty years old, a heavy smoker with an irritating cough and accompanying sniffle and little conversational skill. His general comment about any situation that arose, whether it was in the United Nations, the House of Commons, the White House or Ashurst Town hall, was that 'they don't know what they are doing'. If a person in whatever field in life had ninety nine good points and one bad point or weakness, then it was the negative side that would receive all Walter's attention. His very presence in the room sullied the atmosphere. Fortunately within three months he was killed in unexplained circumstances.

The other newcomer was Maurice. Basically Maurice didn't have an original idea in his head. All he ever did was agree with the last comment made. One morning Charlie had taken him over to the Rolling Mill to look at a load-sensing device and in the half an hour they were away, Charlie had got Maurice to agree that with all the troubles in Ireland, the only solution was to withdraw all the British troops, send in the United Nations and let Ireland revert to being a totally independent country.

In the afternoon, Mick had taken him to the Iron Foundry to look at the controls on the weighbridge and while they were away, he got Maurice to agree that Northern Ireland was irreversibly part of the British Isles and nothing to do with the United Nations or any other foreign country, and certainly not the one in Dublin.

Then, during the afternoon tea break, with a big argument about the latest troubles in Belfast the previous night, Alan had said that in his opinion, the trouble all stemmed from the way the country had been split in two in the Twenties by the British Government. Then he asked Maurice what he thought about partition and the newcomer had merely said that he wouldn't sign any petition because he didn't know anything about it.

164

Unsurprisingly, neither were in the union and it later transpired that they were the only two non members in the whole Drawing Office at Jarratt's. "Now isn't that a coincidence?" said Charlie. "They had twelve draughtsmen there at the end, ten were in the union and two weren't and who does Basil choose to bring here, these two dopes."

However, it was quite easy to recruit Maurice. One morning Yorky had told him quite graphically just what Basil was like and how he was quite capable of trying to sack anybody whose face didn't fit. Then, sat round the dinner table with Charlie, Alan, Len, Mick and Keith that lunchtime, he had agreed with Charlie's comments about the need for everybody in the office to stick together and help each other now that Basil was in one of his foul moods.

"So are you going to join us then?" said Len. "All for one and one for all."

"Oh yes," said Maurice, not quite sure what he was agreeing to.

So Len fished out an application form to join the union from his inside pocket and asked Alan and Charlie if they would be prepared to propose and second him and before he knew it, Maurice had become a member.

Walter was quite a different kettle of fish, an evil bastard to be sure. One morning he had made the general comment that the best way to deal with the growing unemployment was to handle it like they had done in Nazi Germany.

"I don't agree with everything Hitler did, but at least under him they knew how to deal with the scum of this earth."

Len made a rather quiet reference to the setting up of the concentration camps in the Thirties and how well before the Jews, the first people to be put in them were the Communists, the Socialists and then the trade union leaders.

"Well there was nothing wrong with that. We should do that here and we'd all be a lot better off."

"And would you have them all gassed and burned like they did at Auschwitz and Birkenau and Belsen and Treblinka and Ravensbruck and a few dozen more extermination camps?"

"That old favourite. There weren't any death camps. It's an American Jewish lie. All this stuff about the Holocaust."

It was beginning to turn nasty.

Very quietly Len said: "We used to have a draffie here who took part in the liberation of Belsen. The tales he told, they turned my stomach."

"Jewish propaganda."

"So are you trying to tell us that what our old mate Stan told us was all made up?" asked Yorky.

But before Walter could answer, Alan jumped in: "You're a little Fascist bastard. I never knew my father because he died fighting scum like you."

But before any more could be said, John Battesby came out of the office to see what all the noise was about. John's great love in life was sailing. Part of that was due to his experiences on a destroyer in the Royal Navy during the War, chasing U-boats. He didn't like Germans, although to be fair to him, he knew it wasn't the fault of the younger ones. It was just those of his own generation who he could never forgive.

Not surprisingly he had turned a blind eye a couple of times when Alan had stepped out of line. But on hearing of what Walter was like, he decided to himself that he wouldn't be at Wilkinson's long enough to need to replace his 2H pencil. And as things turned out, he wasn't, and neither was Maurice.

23.

WAR AND PEACE

When Alan joined the Electrical section of the Drawing Office in 1962 it had been made up of Stan, Mick, Charlie, Len, Dickie, Yorky and Tony, all under the control of Alan Groves. Ten years later Stan had died, Tony had moved to Halifax and Dickie had become a commissioning engineer. John had come, gone and come back again, Keith had joined them from Jarratts and half a dozen apprentices had worked with them for varying lengths of time. They had always enjoyed a good working atmosphere but with the arrival of Maurice and Walter it seemed as though that would soon disappear.

Maurice was a bit of a pain, but they could put up with him. It was Walter who soured the whole atmosphere of the place. When Len had asked him to join the union he had refused. When Alan asked him to cut back on the amount of cigarettes he smoked, or at least blow his smoke over somebody else, Walter had told him that Britain was still a free country and to go and live in Russia if he didn't like it. Then "Adolf" began to force himself into their tea break discussions, bringing them down to the lowest common denominator. After two weeks they decided that they had had enough of him. He had to go, but how? As a start, they decided to send him to Coventry and so for the next month they only ever spoke to him about work. When others around the factory heard what was going on, they declared that the draughtsmen were behaving like children yet again. But when they heard that John Battesby, the Chief Draughtsman, was fully behind their action, many felt there was more to it than first appeared.

Among the other new arrivals from Jarratts was Gerald, a mechanical draughtsman. From an early age, he had suffered from a mild form of paralysis on his left hand side. This was seen in the way he walked and found difficulty in lifting with his left hand. As a result, during his school days and early youth he had spent much of his spare time reading both at home and in the library when others were messing about on the back fields or in the street. Then he had had the good fortune to meet Les Earnshaw at his cousin's wedding. After that, he read 'The Draughtsman's Tale' and 'The Actress Goes to Heaven' and as soon as he had finished them, Gerald decided to start writing novels himself.

Among his many interests were politics, history, geography and astronomy. Influenced and informed by his older cousin Steve, who had served in the British Army for two years in post-war Germany, the theme of Gerald's first novel dealt was the danger posed by the regrouping of Nazi sympathisers in South America. In his novel titled 'Fear Reappears', part of the world plan for the Fourth Reich Command Group was to set up small cells of sympathisers in Britain. And it clearly was obvious that the character Warner, the loud-mouthed technical clerk who worked at a large engineering works just outside Manchester, was based to a tee on Walter.

Gerald had given a copy of one of the chapters to Len, who had left it on his reference table in full view of Walter last thing one night. On the following day it was clear that he had read it. At lunchtime, with seemingly no one else about, Walter had gone to the top of the office where Gerald was sat reading his Guardian. In the course of a verbal altercation, Walter had threatened Gerald and prodded him on his chest. Very dramatically Gerald had shouted out and fallen to the floor. Immediately one of the mechanical draughtsmen, who appeared to have been asleep, jumped up and rushed over while another waltzed straight into John Battesby's office and told John that Walter had just attacked young Gerald. John immediately phoned the security gate to tell one of them to come and escort the man out of the office and then rang the surgery to ask for a nurse to look at the totally uninjured Gerald. Little was said about the whole affair, although it was generally felt that the whole thing had been something of a put up job. Or, as Len described it, a skilful and legitimate exercise that removed from their midst a cancer before it could affect the whole body.

If Walter's departure had been an orchestrated affair, all was justified a few weeks later when his body was found in a disused flat in the Scotland Road area of Liverpool. It was clear that Walter had other more powerful enemies, since soon after evidence was found linking him and a binman from Bootle with a shadowy terrorist group funded from a bank account in Montevideo.

For young Gerald, the whole thing was an opportunity he took with both hands. He expanded on the plan that he actually engineered with Len, and had his novel published six months later. Soon after, at the age of twenty four, he left the engineering industry and then proceeded to make his living writing thrillers, Science Fiction novels and material for television, including Coronation Street and much later Brookside. But as Charlie said of him soon after he had left, in a discussion over who was the better writer, Gerald or Les: "He was a nice lad but he never made anybody laugh."

Meanwhile Les continued to go from strength to strength. His latest piece of writing was a collection of short stories, some of which were clearly based on his time in Wilkinson's Drawing Office. Others were very moving; one dealt with a long night spent by a woman with four small children in her living room waiting to hear if her husband had survived a roof fall at the local pit. There was his passion play, titled 'The Wall'. The main character was actually a wall at the back of a dance hall and literally reported on all the things that the wall had seen or had done to it during one Saturday night. And to finish off the collection of eight stories was his tour de farce, 'Deja Vu Seen Again'. This would seem to have been influenced by his reading Finnegan's Wake by James Joyce, or at least the first chapter. But it elicited interest from the head of the Philosophy department at Harvard University, who invited Les to lecture on the relevance of his thoughts to understanding the literary fantasism of post Hegelian thought.

Les was able to visit five universities and spoke at each one, but mainly on the socioeconomic position of his scaffolder Albert Entwhistle and the juxtaposition of his class orientated pseudo-variance with his childhood surroundings and his relationship with Bridget Bardot. And to ensure that he was able to stay as long as possible, he spoke in the broadest Lancashire accent imaginable so that in the end, for whatever reason, hardly anybody could understand him. However at Yale University, warned of what he was like by a colleague from Berkeley, the professor of English, who actually came from Scotland, decided to act as a translator/interpreter for the audience. And two days later Les was asked to leave the country.

Back at the ranch, 1974 dragged on as Basil continued to act as though Britain had moved back to the economic state of feudalism. Even members of the senior staff were now complaining about his policies and the way he treated his employees. And then, right out of the blue, it was announced that Charlie Spencer, one of the top engineering managers, was leaving at the end of the August. A tough Welshman from Aberthaw, he was well respected around the factory, it being well known that he would never ask a man to do a task that he couldn't perform well himself. One of the old school, his differences with Basil were well known. And then, at his going away do, with Basil suddenly absent in London, Charlie had thanked all those he had worked with and then finished by telling a little joke.

"There was once a man who had three children. He had never been a good father to them, often away and when at home always down the pub or at the dogs. Then he wins a million pounds on the pools and decides to make things up for his past. So he asks his children what present they would like. The first was eighteen and wanted his Dad to pay for her to have driving lessons. 'I'll not only pay for them, I'll buy you a brand new car as well,' he said. The second one, aged fifteen, then came in the room and asked his Dad if he could have a guitar. 'I'll not only buy you a guitar. I'll pay for the attic to be turned into a tip top recording studio with all the latest equipment in it, as well.' Then his youngest came into the room and, never having had much bought for him and not knowing what the other two had asked for, wondered if he could have a cowboy outfit. 'You can have the biggest cowboy outfit in the North of England. I'll just ring the owner of Wilkinson's and see how much he wants to sell it for.'"

Away from work, the Rugby League season was soon upon them again. But the season seemed to get off to a slow start: the crowds were not as big as they used to be in the Fifties and there weren't as many stars around, or so it appeared. Some supporters put it down to the various changes that had been brought in, like playing the matches on a Sunday, two divisions and doing away with unlimited possession. Other supporters felt that it might be worth playing games in the summer, or maybe merging clubs that were geographically close. But if asked about this, they would of course mean other clubs merging, not their's. Some of the old timers would declare that it would never be like it used to be in the good old days. And of course it wouldn't be, certainly not for those who used to watch the game at the City Road ground in St Helens or at Belle Vue in Manchester.

Then one morning Mick bounced into the office with a big grin on his face. Surprisingly he had been very quiet during the summer, mainly because his doctor had led him to believe that he had a serious liver complaint. But the previous day he had been given the all clear at the hospital. And on coming home to tell his wife, the good Lady Elizabeth Alice Henderson of Hindley Green (on the Wold), he had heard more good news that he was shortly to announce.

"Mick's looking happy for a change," laughed Yorky, "Is he taking some new tablets?"

Of course when Mick told them of his health problem, they immediately showed their concern for him and treated him with the utmost respect for at least an hour. Then, during the tea break, he told them of his other news.

"Well you'll all be pleased to know that I'm going to become a grandad."

"Well done," said Yorky, a rather daft thing to say because in those circumstances Mick had done absolutely nothing.

"Aren't you too old to be a grandad?" said Charlie.

"He's too old to be a draughtsman," said Alan.

"I didn't know that he was a draughtsman," said John. "I just thought he lodged here."

"So what are they going to call the baby?" asked Charlie. "Johan von de Plonk Henderson."

Mick's eldest son, Paul, had been working in Holland for the last twelve months at Eindhoven where he had met the beautiful Elisia. Soon after, she was able to add Platt Bridge to her formidable list of European centres of culture that she had visited. She declared that it was quite a charming place, though quite unlike her own picturesque town of Volendam, with its windmills and inhabitants in traditional dress.

"Are they going to get married, Mick?"

"I don't know, they seem to have quite a different attitude to life over there. And what does having a ceremony and a bit of paper prove?"

"Not much if it's all written in Dutch," laughed Alan, "or Double Dutch."

"You've not been over there yet, Mick, have you?" asked Len. "When are you going?"

But before he could reply, Charlie suggested that he take his demob suit to the cleaners first, or they might think the war was still on.

"With you being a Wiganer, you'll feel at home in Holland," said Alan. "They still wear clogs over there."

"Our Paul loves it," went on Mick, ignoring the comment, "the only things he misses are going to Central Park, fish and chips and his mother's rice pudding."

"I take it he doesn't miss you, you pudding," laughed Charlie.

"I knew a couple of lads who went over there," said Alan. "They had the time of their lives. If it hadn't been for Thelma, I think I would've gone with them."

"You could have taken her with you," said Yorky.

"Maybe, but I couldn't have done what they did in Amsterdam"

"Did it include cavorting with fat ladies?"

"Fat, thin, tall, short, blonde, ginger, young and old, if half of what they told me was true."

"I fancied going to Holland," interjected Maurice, just to prove that he was still there. "I love watching the windmills."

Aye, and paint drying and grass growing, thought Alan.

"How old is he now, Mick?"

"Twenty three, Charlie. He seems a bit young for getting married, but he's old enough to make his own mind up."

"Twenty three," said Yorky." Doesn't time fly. I can still remember you telling us about when he blew your shed all over Platt Bridge with his chemistry set."

A few weeks later Maurice also left. Because of Walter, not much attention had been paid to what Maurice was doing. At the end of his first week there had been a major design change and so the drawing he had been working on was immediately made obsolete and binned. His next two weeks were spent marking up prints and doing a lot of copying so it was quite a time before he had anything original to produce. It soon became clear that his main characteristics were slowness, technical inexperience and excessive use of a rubber . When asked politely by Charlie one day after he had made a complete cock-up of an electrical schematic diagram, what he was most experienced at, he declared it was brackets. He also indicated that he quite liked doing panel assemblies, as long as he didn't have the responsibility of deciding where all the components had to be placed. He also indicated his skill at drawing junction box assemblies and his ability at showing the wiring connections into the terminal blocks.

It was clear that he was just not up to the job, never had been and never would be. Of course none of the six who had arrived from Jarratts had had an interview, they had just been picked by Basil and his good friend, Cecil, Jarratts' Personnel Manager. As a result John Battesby had to call him in and in as polite a manner as possible indicated that he was unsuitable and would have to go. But when Len heard, he knew he had to do something about it. But Maurice didn't seem too bothered; his brother had a chain of shops across the North of England and wanted Maurice to run one of them. He actually had three, one in Warrington, one in Ashurst and for some inexplicable reason one at Withernsea on the East Coast of Yorkshire.

As Office Committee Chairman, Len knew that if Maurice had left direct from Jarratts, he would have been entitled to redundancy money. On looking at the paperwork associated with his transfer, it was stated quite clearly that he would still be eligible if he left Wilkinson's for anything other than a criminal offence within sixty days. As a result Len made the firm honour the agreement and so Maurice was entitled to over nine hundred pounds. After skillful negotiating with the new Personnel Manager, Len then decided to do the same with Maurice.

He explained what he had done, without mentioning any figures, then he skillfully got Maurice to agree to show his appreciation by making a donation to one of the union's various appeals. Then Len told him of the tragic death of a union member up in Cumberland, who had left a widow and two children.

"How much do you want?" asked Maurice.

"Well if you walk out of here with eight hundred and forty two pounds, will you be more than happy?"

"Definitely."

"Well then I'm sure the family will appreciate your hundred pounds."

Then Maurice astounded Len when he said:

"Double it Len. What I never had I'll never miss."

As a result the equivalent of something like a month's pay for a draughtsman went North the following day to an address in the small town of Aspatria.

To fill the gap caused by the departure of Walter and Maurice came Colin, a young electrician. As a teenager, Colin had been something of a potential Rugby superstar. He had played for the Ashurst under seventeen's when he was fifteen and the under nineteen's when he was seventeen. Then he had played for Gillarsfield Labour Club for a couple of seasons before signing for Swinton at the start of the 1971 season. He had played twice for the 'A' team before breaking his arm; when fully recovered he had played another seven games before forcing his way into the first team. On his debut at Station Road for the Lions he had made three tries and scored one in a close fought encounter with Warrington, but on his way home down the East Lancashire Road, his career had come to a sudden and tragic end due to the antics of a stupid dog.

Some of them had known Colin before the incident, including the time he had spent a month with them as an apprentice, so they had a bit of an idea what he was like. And as soon as he limped in on his first morning they knew they would all be the better for his presence. But first he had to make his position quite clear:

"Look lads," he announced at the first tea break, "we all know what's happened. I'll never play Rugby again. I know that and I've accepted it. You know that so that's all there is to it. I'm not a cripple. I can still get round, not quite as fast as I used of course. I've got all my faculties. I could be much worse. I could be like Mick."

Once this was said and accepted, life could continue. And with Walter and Maurice gone, well it was just like the old days again, though with some differences.

Colin was very much in the Les Earnshaw/Mick Ellison mould. He came from St Helens about half a mile from the Saints ground and had gone to Knowsley Road junior school, internationally renowned in the sphere of education for its teaching of mental arithmetic. Then, at the age of eleven, his parents had moved first to Earlestown and then Ashurst. He had served his apprenticeship at Pearson's and during his first week as an electrician had been finished when the company was closed down. For the next three years he had worked on construction sites all over the North West until the onset of the summer, and then he had gone hitch-hiking all over Europe. As a result he had plenty tales to tell.

A few days after he had been with them, he was introduced to Charlie's Law of Coincidences. One of the regular topics of conversation in the office was the Second World War. There was nothing strange or macabre about this. It was part of their own history, events that had helped shape them, their thinking and identity. It had started off when Charlie had mentioned that the storeman in the Welding Shop had been hit by a bus the previous night and died. The man was well known around the town both as a billiards player and a war hero from his participation in the evacuations from Dunkirk. One thing led to another and then Colin said: "My Dad was at Dunkirk. He was lucky, he was one of the first to get away. He wasn't so lucky later, he finished up at Monte Cassino and had half his arm shot away."

"My Dad was at Monte Cassino," said Alan.

"That's a coincidence. I wonder if my Dad knows him."

"Well he won't now. He never came back."

Three weeks later, Colin discovered from his father that he had known an Arthur John Greenall before the War and then seen him in Southern Italy a few days before their battalion had arrived at Monte Casino. But he only told Charlie; he didn't tell Alan, there was not much to tell really.

Colin was a bit of a romantic, certainly a story-teller and a participant in many inci-

172

dents of international significance. In 1968 he had gone to France to join the revolutionary students. Once in the French capital, Colin had taken part in the fighting against the CRS riot police and helped paint an enormous mural on a building opposite the Sorbonne. There he had met Simone, with whom he had spent three glorious weeks, both on the barricades, at big meetings, on marches and in her room in the student quarters. But then he had been arrested and lost contact with her. Like him, she was not a member of any of the many political groups that proliferated around the city. Like him, she did not come from Paris but Marseilles until she was fourteen and then Amiens for four years until she had moved to Paris. He did not even know her second name, to him she was just Simone. During the short time he knew her, he often thought that after the revolution she might just become Simone Ashcroft and not Simone la Rouge, Red Simone as he called her. Shortly after they lost contact, he was thrown out of the country and any chances that he would ever find her again gone. His only hope was that she might just come to Ashurst and visit the famous Bentley Pie shop in Hope Street. The very last time he had been with her he had given her a photograph of the shop and told her it was one of Britain's most celebrated eating places and also where his mother worked. But she never did come and slowly, as time went by, he knew that he would never see her again. However, nearly twenty years later, watching the wedding of Charles and Diana on the television, he was sure he had seen someone who could easily have been her in the congregation. But she was dressed in a fur coat and stupid hat, engulfed by jewelry, hardly Simone's style when he had known her.

A week later, with Alan and Yorky away at Thorpe Marsh Power Station in South Yorkshire on a site visit and with Yorky acting as interpreter, Colin had asked Charlie if it was all right to talk about the war when Alan was around.

"There's no problem with Greeno. He never knew his Dad and there's no grave to go to. He just accepts it. No, the thing about Alan is that he flies off the handle if anyone tries to defend what Hitler did, or attacks some minority group." Then he told Colin how Alan had nearly lost his job when one of the graduate apprentices had slagged off the Welsh. "Greeno nearly decapitated him, but he deserved it. You see what this bloody graduate didn't know when he called the Welsh a load of sheep shaggers was that Alan's wife, Thelma, was from Cardiff."

"What was she doing up here?"

"It's a long tale," said Charlie. "She was an orphan, had drifted into Ashurst from Liverpool and Rhyl before that. Alan invites her to his Granny's on Christmas Day because she had nowhere to go to, she falls ill there and it finished up with his Granny and Grandad virtually adopting her. And she really is a lovely girl. Well she's a woman now and a mother to his two kids."

"And who is this guy Stan who seems to get mentioned so much?"

So Charlie told him about the office war hero.

"I find it really interesting talking about the war. I suppose it's because my Dad fought in the Second and my two grandfathers fought in the First, and all lived to tell the tale."

Colin then talked about one of his grandfather's experiences on the Somme, where seven of his neighbours had been killed.

"That's because they used to put everybody from the same town, or even the same street, together in the trenches. They all fought together."

"Aye, and they all died together."

"That's right. I remember my uncle telling me about the celebrations when the War was over. Behind Sacred Heart church there's Plymouth Street, Devon Street, Cornwall Street and Exeter Street He told me how they had tables out in the street and communal jam butties and flags flying there, but not in Devon Street. There were no celebrations there. Not one man who went out to fight came back to that street. And it was probably just one bomb that deprived about forty kids of their fathers."

"So where were you in the war, Charlie?"

But before Charlie could answer, the phone rang. It was Alan wanting Charlie to check a drawing of a marshalling kiosk. After he had finished, Charlie went on to tell Colin that one of the worst things for him was not seeing his kids grow up.

"Our Paul was born in '42. I saw him when he was a week old and the next time I was back home, he was turned three."

Then he went on: "I knew a bloke from Burscough whose son was three when he joined the RAF in '39. He got shot down on his first raid over France and was a P.O.W. for the rest of the war; so when he comes home five years later his wife had died and his lad was nearly ten and living with a family in Skelmersdale.

"I know it's a funny thing to say, but I really missed changing his nappy when he was little. And now he's got his own kids. I tell him to treasure their early years. You can never bring them back. I hated being away in that war. I really did. "

Then he pointed out that it wasn't all a bed of roses after he was demobbed either. There was all the rationing, that terrible winter of 1947 and never enough coal to keep the house warm, poor wages again and then the shock of hearing that an old pal had been killed or that another was back in town, but with some serious war wound that would plague him for the rest of his life. Then there were the disappointments of Attlee's Government. "We thought things were all going to change for the better. We thought the Labour Government would start to build Jerusalem in this green and pleasant land. Some things did improve, like setting up the N.H.S. despite the opposition of the doctors. Other things never changed, not really. And then America started pouring billions of dollars into Germany. That made me sick. In the War, the Germans were the enemy and the Russians our allies. As soon as it was over, the Russians became the enemy and we started helping Germany."

"What did the others do in the War?"

"Yorky was in the Merchant Navy. You want to get him to tell you about when they used to sail up to Murmansk in the Artic Circle. When he starts on about how cold it was, the bloody windows start to ice up."

"What about Mick?"

"He was a gunner in the Navy."

"And what about you?"

"I was in the Parachute Regiment."

"So together there's quite a wide range of war experiences in this office"

174

"I suppose there is. But then we only did what we had to. We didn't have any choice in the matter. And I saw a lot of things and visited a lot of places I would never have been able to, which was good. But I still missed watching our Paul growing up from being a baby."

24.

A LITTLE GIRL IS LOST

Having children can sometimes be a bit of an inconvenience. Sometimes it can be a great inconvenience. The little blighters always want their nappy changed, feeding, or their hand held for hours before they can drop off to sleep. Then, as they grow older they develop the capacity to be just plain awkward or sometimes, even with the best of intentions, a sheer nuisance. Like the occasion when Rebecca had watched her mother painting the walls in the front room. While her tea was being made in the kitchen, and knowing that her room was the next to be decorated, she had decided to help by lugging the tin of paint up the stairs. On reaching the landing she had paused for breath, the tin had twisted out of her hand and the brand new red, green and black tartan carpet they had just bought became a red, green, black and white tartan carpet. And to make matters worse, on discovering what had happened, she had run downstairs, through the living room and into the kitchen to show her mum 'flootprints'.

Then there was the occasion when Robert had attempted to wash their new kitten and had left the tap running in the bathroom while he had chased it round the house. And of course while he was doing that the kitchen flooded, just as Alan had settled down to watch the Challenge Cup Final between Featherstone Rovers and Bradford Northern. A few weeks later the little terror had demonstrated his lack of respect for those working in the public service when he had opened the window in the front bedroom, stood on a chair and with perfect timing pee'd all over the postman.

Things could be just as inconvenient outside the house, like when he was playing cricket with his Dad in the yard and had hit the ball so hard it had gone over the wall, across next door's garden and into Mr. Winstanley's new greenhouse.

But without doubt it was his sister Rebecca who had been the worst. She had begun the first day of the school holidays by dropping a bottle of milk on the kitchen floor. As a result they could not have their usual bowl of cornflakes. The jam jar was virtually empty so breakfast had to be two rounds of toast with margarine and a drink of water. Her next misdemeanor was to drop the biscuit tin on the floor just after Thelma had hoovered the place and so earned another telling off. For the rest of the morning she had been irritable and moody, which was quite unusual for her. She didn't want any dinner and when Robert had flicked some cabbage on to her frock she had pushed him off his chair and broke a plate in the process. Then she refused to go out to the shop with her mother and was generally a real pain for the rest of the afternoon. The last straw was five minutes after Thelma had put a vase of flowers on the table and Rebecca had knocked them over. Thelma had had more than enough of her. She shouted at her daughter, who had had replied with a rude word. Thelma gave her a good slapping on the leg, then turned her attention back to Robert, who had just started fighting with the cat. Rebecca disappeared from the room and no more was heard from her. Her mother assumed that she had gone up to her room to sulk, as she did from time to time, but not very often. But before Thelma could check, Mrs Pilkington called over the wall from next door. And once she started chatting, good soul as she was, another half hour had passed and Thelma hadn't even started making their tea.

By this time she expected that Rebecca would have calmed down and Robert would have forgotten that his sister had hit him and all would be well again in the Greenall household. But when Thelma went to see what her daughter had been doing in her bedroom for the last hour she was not there. In fact she was nowhere in the house. Perhaps she had gone out to her friend's house down the street, but within ten minutes Thelma had discovered that she hadn't. Suddenly it struck Thelma that she might have run away. It was the first time she had ever been away so long. On a number of occasions she had disappeared, but only into some secret place like under the bench in the shed, or in next door's garden, or at her friend's house at number twenty eight.

Minutes later, Alan arrived home from work to be greeted with the news that his daughter was missing. They immediately began to think of all the places she might have gone to: Chisnall Avenue to his Mum's house, the old people's home in Dob Lane to see Granny or to look at the fish at Uncle Jack's. Maybe she had gone to Uncle Paul's house in Kenyon Avenue. He went next door to get his other neighbour Ken to look in his shed. She wasn't there, and Ken straight away told Alan to get in his car and then drove him round to each of the likely places that she might be. She wasn't at any of them. On the way back they drove past the cemetery and looked at Grandad's grave but she wasn't there, neither was she in the school playground where some of her school friends would often play. Then they went up to Mount Everest to the pond where she had recently learned how to skim stones on the water. No sign of her there either. It was now nearly seven o'clock. It was serious, very serious. As soon as they got back to Silkstone Street, Alan went into Ken's house and rang the police and before long a major search was underway.

Back in the house Thelma was now full of remorse. It was all her fault. Rebecca was only a little girl. She hadn't dropped the milk bottle on purpose, or the biscuit tin. It wasn't her fault there was no jam in the house. Thelma shouldn't have slapped her like she did. And what were the last words her daughter had said as she left the room: "You don't love me anymore". If anything had happened to her, they would be the last words she would have heard her speak. They would reverberate around Thelma's head for ever and a day. The evening dragged on and as it began to get dark the chance of finding her would become lessened. And the forecast was for heavy rain, which would only make things worse for the army of people who were now out looking for her.

Around eight o'clock a police car slowly drew up outside the house. A young policewoman came in, with a very sad face, gave a girl's shoe to Thelma and said:

"This shoe was found by the Stinky Brook, Mrs Greenall. Does it belong to Rebecca?" Fortunately it didn't.

By now it was dark and turning cold. Where was she? Was she trapped somewhere? Had somebody run off with her? Was she even still alive? Thelma hadn't eaten since it happened. Her stomach was all knotted. Perhaps she would never want to eat ever again.

It was all her own stupid fault. Why had she hit the little one she loved so much? Why had she shouted at her? She was only seven. She went upstairs to swill her face, then looked in Rebecca's room; untidy as always. Then she walked into her and Alan's bedroom and looked out of the window. She looked down and saw a car pull up outside. Another police-woman got out, an older one this time carrying a blood-stained frock in her hands.

"We've found this at Hyde Bank, Mrs Greenall. Does it belong to Rebecca?"

Again, fortunately it didn't.

Bringing pieces of clothing that had been picked up in different parts of the town could go on all night, all the next day, forever. Never had Thelma felt so drained and so hopeless.

Uncle Stan had come round earlier and then driven off to places where there was a one in ten thousand chance that Thelma had gone to; without any success. Alan's brother Paul came straight over as soon as he had heard the news, then reminded them that she liked to chase the rabbits at the back of Ashurst Cricket club, but within five minutes of arriving they knew she wasn't there either. Mrs Pilkington came in from next door to offer her help, even though she was nearly eighty and almost blind. Then Alan remembered that a few weeks earlier he had taken Rebecca and her friend Pamela to play hide and seek in the woods at the back of the old library and where they had had a great time messing about in an abandoned car. But there was no sight either of her, or even the car, when he arrived there.

Time moved on, it never stops, neither for good things or bad things, neither for happy times or sad times, not for anything. But maybe for Thelma time would stand still at the moment her little daughter had spoken her last words to her. "You don't love me any-more". By now it was nearly half past ten and the pubs would soon be throwing out their customers. Men would be going home from an evening's drinking, to houses where they would find their children fast asleep in their beds. But nobody would find Rebecca Greenall tucked up in her bed in her untidy little room and give her a big kiss. Not tonight. Maybe never again. And no doubt many of those who had been in the pub earlier would tell those in the house who hadn't been out that evening that a little girl had gone missing. And others would be more specific and say that it was the daughter of that young couple in Silkstone Street, the Welsh lady and her husband who worked in the Drawing Office at Wilkinson's.

One young man who wouldn't be kissing any young baby that night was Peter Starr. Despite the lack of interest in alien life form by most other people around the town, he had still kept the faith. He had spent the evening in the Colliers Arms discussing the dis-appearance of the birds that normally nested on the Anticosti Island in the Gulf of St Lawrence, the drying up of the Olomanoshibo River nearby on the mainland of Canada and the sudden disappearance from Ashurst of Vicki. He walked down Onderman Street and Crimea Street and then onto what was now left of Mount Everest. He walked past the spot where he knew he had once seen a spaceship and then past the tree where he had first lay in a bush one dark evening with Vicki, just waiting for the unexpected, though with Vicki the expected came much more quickly.

He stood there looking vaguely at the scene of one of his great conquests, then walked on past the old air raid shelter. He went behind it to pay a call to nature, and as he stood there looking for Mars, he heard a strange noise coming from the wooden hut at the back of the shelter. It sounded like the noise an alien would make. He froze. Should he run or should he stay and investigate? After five pints of Greenall's best bitter, he decided he would be brave, and then he heard the noise again, a very quiet and faded cry for help.

"Who's there?" he shouted.

The wooden hut had been used by the firm who had the job of clearing the tip. But after a few weeks they had gone bust, or rather the owner had run off leaving a string of debts around the town.

It took a strong shove with his shoulder to push the heavy door open and in the dark he heard the sound of what he knew must be a child crying. He lit a match and saw Rebecca lying on the ground. He picked her up, asked her name and where she lived and then proceeded to carry her back down Crimea Street, Onderman Street and into Manchester Road when a police car screeched to a halt beside him. Five minutes later the car stopped in Silkstone Street. Little girl lost; little girl found, and shortly after the man who at first the police driver thought might be guilty of some heinous crime was recognised as a hero.

Big tears from Rebecca who was so sorry. Big tears from her Mum who was so glad, and despite all the filth and muck on the little girl, an enormous big hug followed by a bath. That night she slept in their bed and of course Robert didn't want to be left out of the action so there was not much sleep that night in the Greenall household. Needless to say Alan was late into work the following day. And Ashurst being the place it was by the time he walked through the Warrington Road gates, the news was all over the factory.

"That was the worst day of my life," he said as he sat on his stool.

"How is she?" asked Charlie.

"What happened?" asked Yorky.

It turned out that Rebecca had run out off the house intending to go to her friend's house down the street. But there was no answer when she knocked on Pamela's door. She didn't want to go back home, ever, so she decided to go and ask Granma if she could live with her in Chisnall Avenue. But as she crossed into Manchester Road she decided that she would go on to Mount Everest first and look for fish in the little pond there. As she walked on to the tip at the back of Hathershaw's garage, she saw a rabbit and carefully tip-toed behind it. Then out of the blue a big dog appeared, started barking and then chased her. She ran but she couldn't get away from it. By now it had nearly caught her so she ran into the wooden shed at the back of the old air raid shelter and slammed the door. She was now safe, or so she thought. But after she had counted to a hundred when she attempted to open the door to see if the coast was clear she couldn't move it. She was now trapped. And she would remain trapped there until Peter Starr heard her plaintiff cries for help over five hours later.

In answer to Charlie's first question, he informed them all that Rebecca was fine, amazingly.

"Who found her?"

"Peter Starr on his way home from the pub."

"A star man for once in his life," said Len, but although it was mildly funny nobody laughed.

"How's Thelma?" asked Mick

"She was absolutely gutted. She blamed herself. It wasn't really her fault. It was just that one thing had led to another and if Rebecca's friend Pamela had been in their house, she would have only been away until it was time for her tea."

Sometimes when an issue or event like this happens, it affects everybody in the factory in one way or another. For the next few days whenever he strayed away from his drawing board, Alan was conscious of people looking at him. Even on the bowling green at lunchtime it was the same. And the following Friday people all over the town would see a photograph of him along with Thelma, Rebecca, Robert and the cat on the front page of the Ashurst Reporter.

By the end of the week everything was back to normal, both at work and at home. And there was also something to look forward to. The four Greenalls all had something to celebrate and they decided to do it in the shape of a party. The reason for Rebecca's celebration was obvious; Thelma had her birthday coming up and Robert was soon to start school. And what of Alan. Well there was the fact that his package of drawings for the Rosario power station job had been complemented highly by Tony Robledo; that shouldn't go unnoticed, he felt. And of course there was the start of the new season to celebrate as well.

A general invitation went out to all and sundry to attend the do which would be held upstairs in the Manor Hotel in Hemsley on the Saturday night starting at seven o'clock. There would be a few speeches at eight o'clock, after which the entertainment would start. By half past seven the place was nearly full, with Mick providing the first laugh of the evening. He came in wearing flared trousers and a jumper with the words Beach Boys emblazoned across it. Then Charlie appeared in a genuine Teddy Boy outfit. It looked like being a good night. At eight o'clock Alan stood up already a bit worse for wear, thanked everybody for coming, reminded them just who the celebration was for, and pointed to his daughter Rebecca who was sat in the corner with her Mum eating an enormous ice cream. Then he announced the name of the first entertainer of the evening, Mick Ellison, a chargehand in the Refinery. He proceeded to do his party piece which was impersonations of Eddie Waring, Harold Wilson and James Cagney and he finished up singing Rawhide and sounding just like Frankie Lane. Then he told the audience that he was working on two new characters and proceeded to impersonate first Alan and then Charlie.

The next on stage was a magician from Gillarsfield who put Rebecca inside a large wooden box and then appeared to cut her in half, but not before Thelma had run on the stage and tried to stop him. Then it was la piece de la resistance, an international star of stage, radio and television: yes a blast from the past, the one and only Les Earnshaw.

"Good evening mates, estimates, and degenerates. I am very pleased to be appearing here tonight having just returned from my latest world tour to Rhyl (what a thrill) and Colwyn Bay (what more can I say)."

He then cleared his voice and announced that he was going to do some impersonations. He indicated that he wanted complete silence, which was a little difficult, but finally achieved. He asked the audience to listen very carefully and after about thirty seconds of silence he imitated what sounded like a pig snorting, then another thirty seconds of silence followed by a similar noise. When asked what did the audience think it was, noone answered, so he replied with a big smile on his face, "That was an impersonation of Mr Michael Henderson O.N.C. (failed) at work in the morning after the tea break."

He then did another, although the gap between the snorts was twice as long, and before anyone could say what it was, he told them that that was an impersonation of Mick working overtime on a Saturday morning.

Next came an obvious impersonation of Alan trying to explain why he was late into work followed by one of David Frost. Then came a Churchill Redman lathe cutting a groove in brass, a steam train pulling coal wagons out of Ashurst station and the five to, three to, one minute to and twelve o'clock hooters at Wilkinson's.

Then he proceeded to read the football results in a John Snagge style Boat Race Voice:

"Forfar Four, Stenhousemuir More
Cowdenbeath Two, Bullenbeath Three
Ayr One, Wind and Water None
Hearts Two, Livers Two
Alloa Two, Goodbyea Two
East Fife One, West Fife One
North Fife One, South Fife One
Third Lanark Three, Fourth Lanark Four
Hamilton Academicals Two, Dumbarton School of Hard Knocks Seven
Stirling Albion Three, Stirling Moss Nil

"I now have the results of the Boat Race. First was Oxford University" ….. and then he shuffled a piece of paper, scratched his head, turned the paper upside down, back to front and then went on …. "oh yes, and the second was Cambridge University.

"There was also one cricket match today and it finished up Lancashire Nine Hundred and Eighty Seven for One declared, Yorkshire Twelve All Out and Twenty Six for Nine. Rain Stopped Play. Match Drawn. Two points each."

Then he walked to the back of the stage, pretended to use a telephone and then came forward again and continued:

"Finally we have one Rugby League result:

"St Helens Two, Wigan Ninety Two"

At this point there was an enormous amount of booing and clapping, and then above all the noise Les shouted out, "and that was only the half time score."

He then walked to one corner of the stage, held up his hand and asked the audience to watch him very carefully. He crouched down, imitated a bowler letting go of an imaginary bowl and then walked slowly across the stage, but with his third step jumped up, walked two more steps and jumped up again and repeated this until he reached the other side of the stage. It was Roger Ellison on the bowling green being attacked by every other bowler on the green.

Then he walked off the stage and came back carrying a cup and a large sheet which he had acquired from the little canteen at the back of the stage. He then lay on the floor under the sheet with the cup alongside him in silence for about three minutes while everybody else was just laughing.

"What's this?" he shouted out.

"It's my Dad," shouted out Rebecca, who was beginning to get the hang of Les's entertainment.

He stood up and said, "No, It's Roger Ellison after having been presented with the Ashurst Hospital Bowling Cup....... in hospital."

Then partly egged on by her Dad, Rebecca went up on the stage and asked Les if she could do an impersonation.

"Aye go on then, since it's you," he said.

So she whispered something in Les's ear, he went out and came back with a tin and some cutlery. She then held the tin and walked round the stage before dropping it:

"Rebecca, I'm sick and tired of it. I've just hoovered the place, go and tidy it up and go to bed you naughty girl. Get out of my sight. I'll tell your Dad when he comes home and he'll give you a big smack on your bum, you naughty girl."

It brought the house down. It also brought tears to Thelma's eyes, but made all the more worthwhile as Rebecca ran over to her, jumped on to her lap and threw her arms around her. And she hadn't finished yet. She went back on to the stage and interrupted Les, who had just started on his next bit of tomfoolery. She then sang the first three verses of 'Money, Money, Money' by Abba, did a couple of handstands and ran back to her Mum who was still wiping tears from her eyes.

The next to appear on the stage was Charlie, who announced that he had personally arranged for a stripper to entertain them. It seemed a little unusual bearing in mind the reason for the party and the age of the person involved. He walked off the stage and returned carrying a small box. He opened the box and took out something that looked like a tin opener.

"Ladies and Gentlemen, may I introduce you to tonight's stripper, a Critchley 1967 cable stripper to be precise," but his joke fell on deaf ears, unappreciated by many of those in the room.

At this point Robert rushed up to the stage and whispered in Les's ear. Les then announces that the world's youngest and best impersonator in the world, the internationally renowned Robert 'Hercules on a Bike' Greenall, would now perform his latest trick. He brought a chair from the back of the stage and Robert sat on it and closed his eyes and proceeded to behave as though he was asleep. After about three minutes Les shook him and shouted out, "Tell us who it is, maestro."

"It's my Dad watching the Nine O'Clock News" said the little 'un, totally inebriated now after having drunk five orange juices and had a sip of his mother's Babycham. But before much longer the fingers on the clock had raced round to half past ten and the barman was shouting 'Last Orders'.

What a good night out it had been. The only bad bit was right at the end when Rebecca began to complain when her Mum said that she couldn't go for a curry with Les and

Charlie. But she accepted her mother's last word on the matter, although she was heard to say in a very loud voice that if she couldn't go she would run away again. But she never did.

25.

I THOUGHT MURPHY
WAS THE REFEREE

The following Monday morning, as they were all slowly preparing to start work, in walked Colin, still wearing the same clothes he had been wearing on the Saturday night.

"You look as though you haven't been home for a bit," said Yorky.

"I haven't, I've been somewhere else for a bit," he said, and then he continued with a big grin on his face, "I think you could say I've just re-lived some of the Beatles greatest hits."

"What do you mean?"

"Well, who did I bump into at the do on Saturday night but the lovely Donna, who used to go out with our kid. Well 'Lady Madonna' was only with her brother and his girl-friend, so I brought her upstairs. It was soon obvious that 'I Want to Hold Your Hand', and after a couple of pints and while you were all listening to Les Earnshaw, she gave me 'A Ticket to Ride'. So off we went on 'A Magical Mystery Tour' back to her place. By the time we got up for breakfast I think that I had had 'A Hard Day's Night' but all I can say now is that 'I Feel Fine'."

Charlie laughed, "Aye and I bet next door will remember the weekend by that Dave Edmund's song 'I Hear You Knocking'."

"Look at the state of him now," chipped in Yorky. "He reminds me of that Clive Dunn record."

"Which one is that?"

"Grandad."

"Was there any place for Chuck Berry's 'My Ding-A-Ling'?" asked Alan in a very dead-pan voice.

As they all burst out laughing again, Len said that he had heard that Donna had the reputation as a bit of a gold digger and so Freda Payne's 1970 hit 'Band of Gold' might prove to be how she would be remembered.

> *"Some one broke into my world and stole my heart away*
> *The finger of suspicion lies on you, da di da"*

"What the bloody hell is that, Mick?"

"Dickie Valentine in 1955."

"1855 by the sound of it."

Then Colin started humming another Beatles hit, 'Come Together', just as Alan Groves walked into the office to see which one of them would be the first to draw a line that morning.

Two hours later, as they were enjoying the best part of the day, the morning tea break, Charlie said:

"I'll tell thee what, old lad, they could have picked a bloody good team from all them who were there on Saturday night."

"How?" asked Alan. "I didn't see that many stars there, present company excluded."

"That's only because you were pissed. Eric Fraser was there for a start so we'd have him at full back."

Eric Fraser had not only played for Warrington; at one time in his career he had also been the captain of the Great Britain Rugby League team. During the day he worked as an estimator in the Accessories Division at the BICC factory at Prescot.

"We'd have Ken Large at centre. You must have seen him, he was talking to John for ages."

Ken Large had played for the Saints in the Sixties as a centre to the legendary Tom Van Vollenhoven. He also worked at the British Insulated Callenders Cables factory in the Technical Publicity Department.

"On the right wing we'd have the ginger-haired lad who came with Keith Sanderson: he's just signed for Rochdale, and on the left wing that lad from Rainhill who had a few games with Huyton last season."

Billy was a capstan operator in the Machine Shop, not quite world class thought Alan, though a lot better than he ever was.

"Wilf Smith was there for a bit so we would have had him at scrum half."

Wilf Smith was another former Saints star, though usually eclipsed by the one he frequently played alongside, the one and only Alex Murphy.

"I never saw him either."

"He didn't stay long. Then we'd have my mate Frank at stand off; he had a couple of games with the 'A' team at Leigh last year, and in the forwards we could have your next door neighbour Ken hooking, Phil Singleton and John Meredith as props; and in the second row John Key and Jack Stone who play for Dob Lane: and at loose forward, Kel Coslett."

Kel Coslett was a Welsh star from the current Saints team. How he had got invited, Alan had no idea, though it didn't really matter.

"Not a bad team Charlie, but I've got two questions for you. Firstly, why did you miss out left centre."

"Modesty, my friend. You see it would have to be that superstar from the Fifties, the man who made Uno's Dabs the international force they once were. In words of one syllable, me!"

They all knew that in any team chosen by Charlie there would always be a place for a representative from the amateur team that for the short length of its existence had played down Parr in St Helens and had once got to within five matches of appearing at Wembley. And they all knew that that representative of the amateur game would have the surname Eccleston.

"And what's the other question?"

"Why is there no place in this great team for me?"

"Well it was a bit difficult. I did have you pencilled in along with another star."

"Which position?"

"Ball boy, but in the end I gave it to your Robert."

"Who would be the referee, Charlie, would it be Mick?"

"Not if he was wearing that Bleach Boys pullover."

"I thought it was very fetching," laughed Yorky.

"Aye, but only if you were fetching spuds in it," said Len.

"Well I thought Mick was very well turned out, he was very sociable and most important of all he stayed awake for the whole evening," said Alan.

There was general agreement that it had been a very good do and three things had stood out for most of those who had had the good fortune to be there. Obviously Les Earnshaw and his performance on the platform was highly memorable, as was the magician and his tricks, particularly when Thelma, under the alcoholic influence of three Babychams, had rushed across the room to wrest the saw from his grasp when she thought he was going to cut Rebecca in half. But pride of place went to Rebecca herself when she had imitated Thelma telling her off.

"Your wife was looking pretty smart on Saturday, Alan," said Len, "and I noticed that her accent is changing a bit, not quite so sing songy, eh?"

Alan laughed. "You wouldn't say that if you heard her shouting at the kids."

Then he put his hand over his mouth and went on, "Well I mean when she used to shout at the kids. She doesn't do that now."

"I think we'll have to inform the NSPCC," said Yorky

"Is everything all right between her and Rebecca?"

"Fine, there never was a problem. It was just unfortunate what happened that day, but I don't think Rebecca will ever be able to get out of the house on her own now. Not unless she can unbolt the six locks we've got on the front door," he laughed.

"I think that you must have missed it, Sam, when she was doing her imitation of Thelma," said Mick, "but the way she rushed off the stage when she'd finished and gave her Mum a big hug, well it nearly brought tears to my eyes."

"You know Alan I can remember when you first started going out with her," said Yorky. "I thought to myself that if she ever had any children she would love 'em to bits. I'm right, aren't I?"

Alan nodded. The sadness his wife must have experienced in her childhood days, she would never allow to happen to her own children. It's not that it was bad in the home. It wasn't. It was just that when she was at school, all her friends had mothers to go home to each night and she didn't. And then when she was nineteen and preparing to spend Christmas on her own she had had one brief stroke of luck and as a result everything in her life had changed and she had acquired first a lovely caring grandmother and soon after a whole new ready-made family.

"I can still remember when she first started working here," said Charlie. "She looked thrown together and you could never get a word out of her. I remember one morning she came in with her hair in a right state, that thin green coat she used to have with that ripped tartan skirt and her tights all laddered. And fool me, I said to her one day: "Has your Mother let you come out of the house without combing your hair?" I wasn't being nasty or anything. I mean I would never have said that if I had known about her situation."

"You know when she first started watching the Saints, do you know who her favourite player was, Charlie?"

"It was Wilf Smith, wasn't it?"

"That's right."

"I thought it would've been Murphy," said Colin.

"Why? Let's face it, she hadn't the first clue about Rugby. She wouldn't have known the difference between Murphy and the referee."

"I didn't think there was one," said Mick. "Every time I ever saw Murphy play, I thought he was the referee."

"It was against Oldham, her first game," Alan continued. "I hadn't a clue what she would make of it, and then at half time when I asked her what she thought about it, she said it was really great. But then she might have said that just to please me."

"So how did you know that she didn't?"

"Early on in the second half Austin Rhodes created a bit of space and then passed to Dick Huddart. He sidesteps round their hooker and sets off on a fifty yard dash for the line. Well you know how it is, everybody is urging him on and I looked at her and there she was, jumping up and down and shouting 'go on, go on, go on'. I knew then that she was going to enjoy watching the Saints."

"I can remember when she first started wearing that red and white scarf."

"Wearing the scarf. I thought it was sown into her neck," laughed Charlie. "She always had it on. Did she have it on in bed?"

"I couldn't get anywhere near her bed in those days. Not with Granny within a hundred yards of it."

"It used to make me laugh on a Monday morning to listen to her and Big Joan discussing the finer points of the previous match."

"I'll tell you what is interesting about someone like Thelma. You know, someone new to the game. She's got no history. All her appreciation of the game, all her knowledge started in 1963. If you mention names like Harold Wagstaff, Louis Baskerville, Smith, Fildes and Mulvanney, Wigan Highfield or even Belle Vue Rangers it means absolutely nothing to her."

"Why should it?"

"No, the point I'm making is that most Rugby League fans who are brought up in Rugby League areas have the game's history bred into them. Like I never saw Warrington and Halifax draw at Wembley and then take part in that famous replay at Odsal. I never saw Broughton Rangers play, or Streatham and Mitcham, or Alf Ellaby, or Ned Bacon but I know about them."

"Who's Ned Bacon, when he's at home?"

"Albert Edwin Bacon, he played for the Saints in the very early days, one of the fastest sprinters they've ever had and a distant relative of that mate of mine from Eccleston. He was always going on about him."

"I suppose this point could be put in a philosophical framework."

"Eh?"

"Well the more you move into the future, the greater opportunity you have to discover aspects of both your own and the collective past."

"You haven't joined that Open University have you, Charlie?"

"The thing I like about Rugby League is its contact between the players and the supporters," said Alan. "You'd never get that link in soccer or cricket."

"How do you mean?"

"Well on the field the players are like Gods, but off the field they are just as ordinary as the next bloke. They all have to work for a living, live in ordinary houses and travel around on the bus."

"I think most of them have probably got enough money to buy a car now."

"You're probably right, but I remember a few years ago I got on a bus going up to Eccleston to see that mate of mine. It was a Tuesday night about six and the only free seats were right at the front. Well they were really only half free. There were two enormous blokes sat on them. So I plonked myself down on one of them as the bloke moved up a bit. I looked up at him to nod thanks and do you know who it was? Ab Terry in a boiler suit. He'd obviously just come off work and was going training. Then I looked across at the other enormous sized bloke in a boiler suit and do you know who that was? Vinty Karalius. Two international stars on a number five bus."

"Well what's wrong with that?"

"Nothing, but you wouldn't get that in many other sports."

"I'll tell you, what I like is when the away team turn up at the ground and the players walk from the coach through the crowds and it appears that everybody knows them personally and starts chatting to them."

"Famous Rugby League players turn up in the most ordinary of places. One of the tracers at Mathers once told me that she found one in her bed on a Sunday morning."

"Was he offside?"

"Frequently."

"My sister-in-law used to be a referee," said Colin. "She once had a famous Salford player in her bed, but in the end she had to send him off."

"What for?"

"Lying on."

"There's been some great characters in this game."

"Aye, on the field and off it."

"Do you remember that Cup tie at Swinton when that old woman ran on the pitch and laid into the Dewsbury front row?"

Minnie Cotton was a red hot Saints fan and well into her sixties. She also had a lodger in her house, John Warlow, a second row forward who had joined the club from Llanelli in South Wales. John was more than capable of looking after himself, but in the 1966 Challenge Cup semi final against Dewsbury at Station Road he appeared to be getting the worst of things. Then, after a particular heavy period of play with Dewsbury getting closer and closer to a Wembley appearance, an almighty brawl had started with John fending off the affections of most of the Heavy Woollen pack.

Minny had always been very protective of her lodger and when she saw him under attack and with little apparent assistance from his own team mates, she rushed on to the field and attacked the uncouth Yorkshire hordes with her brolly, much to the amusement of the large crowd.

Another tale was told of the visit of an amateur team from Leeds to one of the top Cumbrian clubs for a Cup tie. The Yorkshire club had a new coach who very much believed that phsycological preparation was just as important as physical well being, fitness and ability. When his club went into their dressing room he saw that all the hooks for their clothes were set about seven foot high, just to make the visitors feel small. In order to get one over on his opponents the coach decided on a plan that would unnerve the home team. One of his team had a British Rugby League amateur International badge on his blazer. So Ernie told him to walk through the opponents' dressing room to visit the gents. As a result the 'marras' immediately knew their visitors included one international. Then he told another to don the jacket and do the same thing, and of course not to say a word as he walked through the other changing room. After that the third one did the same, then another and another. When the sixth one returned, he told his team mates that by now their opponents were looking really worried. It had been the coach's intention to leave it at that number, but just before he could call a halt to this pre-match war of nerves, the referee had asked him to step outside. Really keen to play his part, the left winger had then put the blazer on. Unfortunately all the previous wearers of the blazer had been of similar size and stature, around five foot ten, five foot eleven and around thirteen, fourteen stone. But the winger had only been chosen for his speed and goal kicking, which explained why at only five foot five and under ten stone, he was in the team. Needless to say the whole of the Cumbrian team collapsed in laughter when they saw the next visitor to the toilet with his blazer nearly down to his knees and the arms hiding the lad's hands. And when he had taken exception to their guffaws, he had thrown the first punch and finished up in the Workington District Hospital, according to ten witnesses, because he had banged his head on the ground after tripping over his blazer!

"Thirty four minutes. If you lot go on much longer you'll be late for your dinner." It was their section leader Alan Groves, reminding them in the most polite of ways that it was time to do a little bit of work and earn their pay for another week. But somehow it seemed that talking was what they wanted to do, although they had to wait until they were all sat in the canteen before they were able to continue their chat about Saturday night's do.

"Did you and Mick go for a curry with Les, Yorky?" asked Alan.

"Did he say anything about his next book?"

"Oh, aye."

"His wife called it a futuristic assembly of unsubstantiated untruths," said Mick.

"She sounds as daft as him."

"She is."

"So what's the book about?"

"It's set in the future, in the mid Eighties, with the main character Albert Entwistle again. You remember that he left Bridget Bardot on her own in his second book and goes off with his childhood sweetheart, Elsie. Well that doesn't last long, not when he discovers she's got three kids. So he goes back to France and gets his old job back as her bodyguard. She gets him into the film industry and he soon becomes a bit of a cult figure. So the first part of the book is about his debauched life as an actor, first in France and then Hollywood. But before long he gets homesick and comes back to Garsdale. By this time, it's 1985. Scotland and Wales have both become republics and there's trouble brewing throughout England. Computers have taken over most of the jobs and unemployment is around 30%. To keep the masses from revolting, the Government has poured millions of pounds into sport, providing facilities for soccer, boxing, and Rugby Union but nothing for Rugby League because it refused to be run from Twickenham.

"Back home Albert joins the North of England People's League and becomes one of its leading figures. They get help from Scotland and Wales and before long England gets split into two with Albert the Prime Minister of what is now called The Northern State of Great England. But then there is a new twist to the story: on the state opening of the new Parliament, which is in Rochdale Town Hall, a spaceship lands in Garsdale. Shortly after that time begins to go in reverse and the longer most people live the younger they become."

"This sounds like a typical Les effort but it seems a bit serious."

"Oh, there's plenty humour in it, like when Ted Heath gets kidnapped and brought up North by a hit squad from the Peoples' League. Knowing of their reputation, Heath fears for his life, but they tell him that they don't intend to torture him or even punish him. It wasn't their style and never had been, despite what the Fleet Street press said. They tell him that he has to stay with them for a month until other negotiations had finished, but more as a guest. They ask him if he would like to work on a boat and live in an olde worlde 19th century cottage. Of course he agrees. So they take him to the seaside and put him to work with a gang of dockers and he lives in a terraced house in Bootle."

"Is there much Rugby in it?" asked Alan.

"I don't know," said Charlie. "All he said was that Wigan were relegated to the Fourth Division in 1984 and Saints went ninety two games without losing a match."

"Obviously a fairy story," snorted Mick.

"Oh and there's one sad bit in it when an old age pensioner who can't swim, drowns in the urinals at Central Park."

"What's he going to call this book?"

"Wilson's Folly."

"What, after Harold Wilson?"

"Not quite. It's named after the Labour Prime Minister who takes over from Harold Wilson as leader. It's just a coincidence that his name is also Wilson, Charlie Wilson."

"I bet he's based him on you, Charlie?"

"Or the other Harold Wilson."

It was another coincidence that two people involved in politics on Merseyside in the Seventies had the same name. One once had been, and was hoping to become again, the Prime Minister. Born in Huddersfield in 1916, he had been elected Leader of the Labour

Party in 1963 on the death of Hugh Gaitskell. Born in Ashurst in 1920, Wilson the Lesser, as he was first known, had manipulated and connived his way into a position of slightly lesser importance on Ashurst Council in 1971.

Issues of international importance or of intense local controversy he always managed to avoid. Nobody really knew where he stood on any major subject. He just played to his audience, emphasising his wish to help those in greatest need to be rewarded fairly for their endeavours on this earth. He also made it quite clear that he did not want to hold any high position, certainly not Mayor which would appear to be the pinnacle of ambition of many of his contemporaries. As a result he was considered safe but dull, and so managed to get elected to the Housing and Planning sub committee of the Council.

Soon after his election to that committee, deals were done between Ashurst Council and a rather dodgy building firm called Cheshire Construction. Not much later, Harold the Lesser, still living with his mother in Cadishead Terrace, obtained a passport and then began to use it to travel widely, viewing housing schemes all over England and further afield in France, Spain and on the Greek island of Rhodes.

At home he saw his mission being to rid Ashurst of its slums, but while some of the property that the Council put a compulsory purchase order on were unfit for human habitation, there were others that had nothing wrong with them, and particularly Rose Street, where Les had once lived. It was an action that Les had opposed vehemently at the time but without success. Now he was going to get his own back, or so he hoped. And he worked out that he couldn't be sued for something that happened in the future, particularly since most of what his character Charlie Wilson said and did had a basis in fact and could be shown to be true anyway.

And so was 'Wilson's Folly' described to Charlie and Mick and their two wives by Les and his wife Eileen. And two years later the book was published, although by this time the landing of a spaceship on Billinge Lump, the melting of the Artic and the sighting of a Loch Ness Monster in Pennington Flash all helped contribute a few more bizarre twists.

In addition, there were quite a few stories about one Bartholomew Williamson which many people around Ashurst would laugh about. After the Northern Peoples' League had formed the new Government, all the big factories were taken over by those who worked in them. And at the Williamson Engineering Works, the former owner was made to suffer many indignities. At first he was put to work in the Foundry Pattern shop, working at a bench between two fat ladies who blew smoke over him all day and discussed at great length the social events that had occurred at the Empire Bingo Club on the previous night. And after that, he fell ill both from utter boredom and from eating too much pigeon pie in the works canteen and died on Christmas Day in the workhouse after suffering with intense stomach pains for months.

26.

POPPEL DOOMER MINI-STARS

"Do you know what always baffles me?" said Charlie.

"Electricity," laughed Mick.

"Paint drying," said Alan.

"How the light always comes on just as you open the fridge door," said Len.

"Whenever you come away from a match, even if you're the first one out of the ground, there's always somebody coming towards you from the opposite direction who's been to the match."

"What do you mean?" said Alan.

"Yesterday I had to leave with about five minutes to go. I walked up Dunriding Lane, and just as I got to the top, this guy comes out of Moxon Street."

"How do you know he'd been to the match?"

"He had a red and white scarf on."

"He might have been a Wigan fan who was lost."

"What, in Moxon St?"

"Wigan fans get lost all over the place. Look at Mick, you have to admit he looks lost and he's been coming here for over ten years."

"I'll tell you who I saw on my way home yesterday," said Alan, "coming out of the YMCA. Peter Sefton, with a woman that looked like the blonde out of Abba."

"It might have been his wife come up to see how he's coping with life in the frozen North."

"Had he been to the match?"

"I doubt it, he looked as though he'd just got out of bed."

"He probably had," said Mick.

"What! In the YMCA on a Sunday afternoon."

"Well he wasn't breaking any of the commandments if it was his wife, was he?"

"How did you know it was his wife. Did she have a ring on her finger?"

"No, but she did have a big smile on her face."

Early in 1976, Peter Sefton had come up to Ashurst along with two other employees of the Jarvis Engineering company, a Croydon-based firm that Wilkinson's had recently taken over. Peter was a whizzkid in the field of industrial electronics but otherwise a total nonentity. He had spent his first month working in the Drawing Office, at the end of which they knew as much about him as they knew when he had first walked into the place.

After that he was put into the Research Laboratory where he proceeded to fiddle about with numerous electronic components. He also made regular visits to see one of the mechanical draughtsmen, who was detailing a control box to house one of his inventions. Rather surprisingly, he had formed a sort of friendship with Charlie. It was a one way relationship really; Charlie couldn't stand him.

Whenever Peter passed through the office, he would stop and chat to Mr Eccleston, not about anything interesting, in fact not about anything in particular, except perhaps for an in-depth analysis of the weather over the last couple of days and the forecast for the weekend. Charlie's conversations with him were the biggest non event of the day.

Finally Charlie decided that he couldn't put up with it any longer and decided to bring their relationship to an end by using one of Les Earnshaw's tricks - daft language. The following morning Peter shuffled through the office and walked over to Charlie's desk and with a big smile on his face announced that he had just heard that the forecast for the weekend was for sunshine all day Saturday and Sunday morning, then broken clouds across the North West in the late afternoon.

"When they say that we'll be having broken clouds, Peter, who actually breaks them?" Charlie replied.

With a totally straight face Peter said that as far as he understood it, it was a result of their general position with relation to the ground and the amount of humidity that resulted in the particular make-up of the cloud formations.

So Charlie decided on a different tack.

"Do you know that a lot of the cloudy weather we've been getting this month comes from Belgium. I just wish we could get some of those Dutch clouds instead. They're of a much clearer disposition. Well they always were when I was in Amsterdam."

"No, the clouds are created in relation to the land mass below them. You can't actually say they have a national character, Charlie."

"The last time I was over there, I discovered that they're known as hoppel dinger clouds."

Peter had never heard of hoppel dinger clouds before and felt that their name had almost certainly been mis-translated for him.

"No, they were definitely hoppel dinger clouds," said Charlie, "because if they occur on a hot day, invariably the following night the sky will be full of vladitch poppel doomer mini stars."

The only straight face in the office was Peter's. He just did not have one shred of a sense of humour. Fortunately the phone went at that moment; it was a call for Charlie from Ronnie Garner asking him to come down to the Refinery. Ronnie was always very curt on the phone, the very opposite of when he was in their presence in the office. But of course no one else in the office knew that for the next five minutes Charlie would be giving the impression he still had Ronnie on the other end of the line.

"It's no good doing it that way, Ronnie," he said. "The furgel breakers won't synchronise with the poodle domps and then we'll have to add more capacitance to get the voltage down the pipe into the primary control circuits."

He waited a while then continued: "While you're on, you know that cubicle for Dubai you've just built, we forgot to put a rabbit trap in it. Do you think that you can fit one in before it goes to the Paint Shop?"

He waited a while then carried on: "It's because they're overrun with rabbits.. With all the sand in Dubai, I suppose our cubicles are the nearest they will get to a field, even though it's a magnetic field."

He waited for a couple more minutes then said, "Well we've got Peter here with us now. I'll just ask him." He put his hand over the phone and asked Peter if he had the B.S. Standard for the Poodle Domp Contact Breakers in his office."

Peter indicated that he didn't and disappeared quickly before Charlie could finish his conversation with nobody.

"He hasn't any sense of humour, has he?" said Alan. "Are they all like that down South?"

"No," said John. "When I was at Thompson's in London, the draffies there were alright, well most of them."

"Let's face it, I bet he's never worked in a place like this. Some of the things that have gone on here over the years are unbelievable," said Mick.

"Well I think somebody should write a book about this place," said Colin. "It would be a best seller."

"Well, why don't you do it?" asked Len. "You wouldn't be the first writer we've had here. Les Earnshaw, Yorky, Greeno, Tony Robledo with his expenses."

"Have you heard much about Les recently?" asked Mick.

But before Charlie could reply, the door swung open and in walked Basil with a visitor. As usual the place went quiet immediately and stayed so for the next hour while Basil and the visitor were seen laughing and joking with Alan Groves. And later that morning their section leader called them all into his office to inform them that the firm had just won a large order from Belgium, one which would keep the Drawing Office busy for the next two months.

There was little time therefore for much fooling about in the office during March and April. But this was also a time when the Saints fans among them were becoming excited at the prospects of another Wembley trip. And after the semi final against Keighley at Fartown in Huddersfield, possibility became certainty with their opponents their close rivals from the picturesque olde worlde seaside town of Widnes. Despite being labelled Dad's Army there was no lack of conviction that the Cup was coming back to Knowsley Road for another year. One person who was convined the 'Sintelliners' were going to be victorious was the former Saints star Alex Murphy, who announced that if they didn't win, he would jump off Runcorn Bridge. But success was there for the glass blowers in a temperature that at one stage reached an incredible one hundred degrees Fahrenheit. And two weeks later there was more joy as the men from Knowsley Road defeated Salford fifteen two at a packed Station Road at Swinton. Needless to say the month of May was not enjoyed by Mick.

Between them Charlie and Alan had missed no more than six matches all season, but both had to miss the next one, not surprisingly since it was held at Long Park in Brisbane against Queensland. But Wilkinson's Drawing Office were represented at the event and also one week later when the Saints met Eastern Suburbs at the famous Sydney Cricket ground. Colin, the recipient of quite a large win on the horses, decided to blow it all on a trip Down Under. But before he returned to regale them all of what life was like in Australia, a little baby girl came into Alan's life.

As he opened the front door one evening after work, he could hear the sound of crying. It certainly wasn't Rebecca or Robert. Who could it be? As he walked into the living room he saw a young girl about the same size as Rebecca sat there with a baby on her lap, his wife holding a feeding bottle and his own two children looking on in curiosity.

As he walked in, Thelma gave the bottle to the young girl, then indicated to Alan to come into the kitchen.

"Who is she?" asked Alan straightaway.

"Alan, we've got to help her."

"Yes, but who is she?"

"I don't know yet." She brushed her hand across her eyes and went on. "I thought I heard somebody crying in Mrs Pilkington's yard about an hour ago. So I looked over the wall and saw this young girl sat on the back doorstep. I went round to see what was the matter and to tell her that Mrs. Pilkington had probably gone to her son's for the afternoon. Then she told me that she thought her Auntie Ada lived there. It was clear she had got the wrong house."

"So I brought her round here and made her a cup of tea and asked her where she had come from,. Alan. She's from Chorley and her family have thrown her out now that she's got a baby. She's come all this way thinking her auntie lived here and she's only a kid, I don't even think she's sixteen."

Then she went on as he knew she would, "Alan, can she stay here tonight and we'll sort something out for her tomorrow. She looks absolutely exhausted, poor thing."

Her name was Allison and she was just turned sixteen. Her mother had died three years earlier and, as she later told them, she had then acted as a skivvy for her permanently drunken father and her two older brothers. Then earlier in the year the fair had come to the town. She and some of her friends had gone there every night and on the last night, she had done what she didn't quite know what with a young man from Scotland who worked on the dodgems. Some time after, when she had forgotten all about him, she discovered that she was going to have a baby.

As soon as the other three in the house discovered this, their attitude to her changed and shortly after the baby came into the world, she decided to run away and go to her auntie's in Ashurst. Unfortunately she had only been to the town once, just after her mother had died, and had stayed for a week with a kind old lady. She thought she knew where the house was. But she didn't and even if she had found it, she would have discovered that Auntie Ada had been put into an old people's home over three months earlier.

Allison was a little on the short side and clearly malnourished. Rebecca was quite tall for her age. Stood next to each other it seemed amazing that there was such an age difference between them. That night Allison and her baby slept in what used to be known as the spare back bedroom. On Christmas Day 1962 it was the room that Thelma had first slept in when she had fallen ill after her first ever family Christmas Day dinner. She remembered again vividly how an old lady had cared for her for the next two months. And now she had the opportunity to help someone else, some other young girl in trouble.

Allison stayed with them for three days. In that time Thelma was able to give her some idea on how to look after her baby. During those three days she spent a lot of time talking to the young girl, in a way similar to how Granny had first talked to her. And finally it was decided that it would be best if Allison and her baby went to live in Blackpool with another auntie, the younger sister of her own mother. Telling the rest of the lads about the issue over the next few days certainly brought out the best in them. Keith Sanderson began the ball rolling by telling Alan that Allison could have a packet of nappies they had never used. Then John Meredith brought in a couple of baby grows, soon to be followed by others who wanted to help so that by the time Allison left she had acquired an enormous collection of clothing and baby toys.

The day of her departure was quite sad for everybody. Allison had clearly enjoyed being looked after, maybe for the first time since her mother had passed away. Thelma had enjoyed doing a Granny and the two children had both enjoyed holding the baby and playing with it. But when they all had their first sight of Auntie Marlene it just didn't seem right to let Allison go to live with her. But there was not much else that could be done, and as it turned out their first impressions were wrong. But it was still sad for them to wave goodbye to what was still a young child.

For a long time after, Allison wrote to them every few months to let them know how she and her baby were doing. And then, when the baby was about five years old, as often happens, the correspondence came to an end and no more was heard of her until Rebecca met Allison fifteen years later in rather strange circumstances in New York.

A couple of weeks later Len began complaining of pains in his chest. Although not a smoker himself, the many years spent in smoke-filled rooms trying to sort out wage claims and fight redundancies were beginning to take their toll. He soldiered on for the rest of the week but they all knew that something was wrong when for the first time ever he had to send his apologies to the Divisional Council monthly meeting. And the following Monday his wife rang in to tell them that the doctor had put Len on the club for a month and told him to take things easy or he wouldn't live to see retirement.

That same afternoon Alan and John were told to go up to Basil's office. It looked ominous. Was he going to declare them redundant and so put the Office Committee under pressure without the ever thoughtful Len to guide them. But as soon as the two draughtsmen saw their boss, they could tell by his suave, self-effacing manner that he wanted something from them.

"John, is it correct that you can speak Serbo-Croat?"

Strange as though the question might have seemed, it was right. He could, well a little bit. Before he had first met his wife Sandra in Camden Town, he had gone out with a Yugoslavian girl. Petra Ibrisomovic was spending the summer of '67 working as a waitress in London, primarily to improve her English. John was keen to speak another foreign language in addition to the French and German he had learned at school. For four months, every time they were together, they would spend time speaking each other's language, usually when they were in bed he would laughingly tell them. And even after they had finished and she had gone back to Zagreb, he would often flick through the Teach Yourself Serbo Croat language book that she had given him on their final amicable parting.

"We have three engineers from the Yugoslavian State Railways visiting today. I'd like you two to show them round. I know you don't speak their language Alan, but you looked after that French visitor we had very well. I'm sure you will be more than useful. And there could be quite a bit of work coming from them, if they are impressed with what they see."

Shortly after the two lads met their visitors for the day. In Basil's presence, communication with the three men was difficult. But as soon as they were free of Basil, things were easier. Unfortunately for Alan, he couldn't use Rugby League as a way of breaking down any barriers like he had done with Jean Pierre from Lezignan. But despite their initial conversations being held in various noisy parts of the factory, they got along alright. They spent the morning in the Refinery and Rolling Mill. After they had eaten in the canteen, they went over to the bowling green, where their guests seemed to thoroughly enjoy themselves. They took their visitors round the Winding Shop, Tinning Shop and the two foundries in the afternoon, again all noisy places, and then just before they were due to deliver the three back to Basil, Alan asked them where they were staying. It was at the new Fleece Hotel in Hemsley that had been built on the site of the old Beswick colliery. Conscious of the fact that they hadn't really been able to converse much with their visitors, Alan suggested that they went out for a few drinks round the town that evening.

Amazingly, when Basil heard about it, he told Alan to collect an expense form on his way out. And so Kemal, Hamza and Vlado, along with Alan, John and Charlie, visited the Colliers' Arms, the Raven and the A.E.U. club in Fountain Street. It is amazing how being even slightly drunk enables some people to acquire a better understanding of a foreign language. And so by the time they got back to the quiet atmosphere of the bar in the Fleece, they were chatting away as though any language differences had disappeared. There they discovered that the following day their visitors were returning to London on the train, then flying out to Budapest to visit a refinery before returning home.

"So how long have you been away from home, Kemal?" asked Alan.

"One months."

"Have you got any family?"

"Yes, my wife and my childs."

"Children."

"Oh yes."

"How many have you got?"

"One boy and two girl."

"Girls."

"Oh yes."

"And where do you live?"

"My town is the capital of Yugoslavia. I think you will hear it. I am in Belgrade."

"And where do you two live?"

Kemal nodded at his friend Vlado, who was now on the point of falling asleep. "He is from an island who is near Split. His name is Hvar."

Alan knew where the island of Hvar was, his friends Ronnie and Dorothy had been there a couple of years earlier. Then he turned to Hamza, who hadn't said very much after the fifth pint had been drunk. At the time Alan thought little about the significance of the man's answer. It was just another place in another country. He had never heard of it before, but maybe twenty or so years later, it would fill him with horror and revulsion when he saw it on the television.

"Alan, my friend, I am from Bosnia-Herzogevinia. My home town is called Srebrenica."

27.

HANKY PANKY IN SMART STREET

"How long did you stay in the Fleece after I'd left you?" asked Charlie as he threw his empty cigarette packet about ten yards straight into the waste paper basket.

"It must have been about midnight," said Alan.

"So what did they think about the Western world then?" asked Len.

"They were a bit disappointed."

"Why?"

"Well they'd heard all about the free market economy. So they were very surprised that they had to pay for their own beer. They thought it would be free."

"Didn't you buy them a drink?" asked Keith. "You tight bugger."

"Well actually Basil told us to look after them and he gave me an expense form to show he meant it."

"Oh, I'd have come with you if I'd known the beer was free," said Yorky.

There then followed the usual discourse about Yorkshiremen always being in the front of the queue when something that was free was on offer.

"You didn't spend all night talking about the Saints with them, did you?"

"No, two of them were soccer fans. Hamza had seen some Rugby when he was in France last year, but I couldn't work out whether it was League or Union."

"So what did you talk about, it wasn't the new annealing process in the Tinning Shop was it?" laughed Yorky.

"We started off with Vlado, the blonde-haired one, trying to chat up that barmaid in the Raven. I had to laugh when he told her that she had a beautiful pair of pigs."

"What did he mean?"

"I think he meant her legs, or maybe her eyes. His English wasn't too good."

"You can say that again" said Charlie.

"I think he meant her legs, or maybe her eyes. His English wasn't too good"

"You are getting boring."

"He's been boring ever since he's been here."

"You can say that again, but don't," laughed Yorky.

"Kemal was an interesting guy to talk to; he was a lot older than the other two. He told us a bit about his war record fighting with the Partisans. He was only thirteen when he joined them."

"A bit young wasn't it?"

"The day he joined was the day he found out that the Gestapo had tortured his brother to death."

But before they could hear any more about Kemal's experiences in the war, the fire alarms sounded and they all trooped out. Fortunately it was a false alarm and once back in the office, work proceeded to grab their attention for the rest of the morning. The high-light of the afternoon occurred when Charlie found half a crown tucked inside an old drawing register book that had been 'lost' for over three years at the back of a shelf in the Technical Library. Otherwise nothing of note occurred. In the good old days, when things were boring, they had always had the arrival of their tea lady Joan to look forward to. She invariably had some juicy bit of gossip or story to tell that would liven up the rest of the day. But with her departure and the arrival on the scene of the new breed of tea girls somehow it just wasn't the same, even though the latest one, Melanie, had a beautiful pair of legs to drool over.

The following day started as the previous one had left off. It looked as though the sparkle of being in the company of a good bunch of lads all day at work was becoming a thing of the past. No one could put their finger on it, it was just a period of social inac-tivity and relative boredom. Then Yorky was moved to the Research Lab for a month, Mick went out on site to Eggborough Power Station in Yorkshire for a couple of weeks and Charlie was rushed into hospital to have his appendix out, and so for the next few weeks, there was only one thing on the minds of those who were still working in the office: home time.

But by the end of September all was back to what was now considered as normal, though it was definitely not as good as it used to be. But then it never was. It was like with the current Saints team. The players were alright but nowhere near as good as those who had played in the Fifties and Sixties. The game was alright but never as exciting as ten or twenty years ago. And the crowds were lower than they used to be. But then they were all ten years older than they were in what many considered to have been the golden age of the game. And generally the longer ago something happened, the better it seemed to be. The taste of the chips in the canteen was considered inferior, the quality of the bowls played every lunchtime was lower and the view from the office window was not as good as it was, particularly now that they couldn't see into the bedroom windows of the hous-es in Smart Street.

How that particular street had come to provide the draughtsmen with an enormous amount of entertainment was down to a pure stroke of luck. The terraced houses, twelve in number, were about a hundred yards away. They had no special architectural signifi-cance. There were hundreds if not thousands like them all over Lancashire. One morning Mick had brought in a pair of binoculars that he was lending to Alan to let Rebecca use for looking at birds, her latest hobby. Alan had immediately put the cord round his neck and focussed on a motorbike at the back of the end house. It looked like one he had con-sidered buying when he was seventeen but never did. Then he had moved the binoculars around, focussed on the first floor window and seen a naked couple romping away on the bed. Not surprisingly they all had to have a look. Maybe an hour later, Alan noticed a man getting onto the bike. He quickly had a look through the binoculars to see if he recognised him, but didn't. The following day around half past nine, Yorky noticed that the bike was there again. Unfortunately the binoculars were now in Rebecca's bedroom ready for Saturday's trip to Carr Mill, much to everybody's annoyance.

Monday saw them back on Alan's reference table and around ten o'clock the bike arrived. A look through the window indicated that the visitor had soon removed his crash helmet, leather gloves, Dr Marten boots and all his other clothes, and five minutes later was observed riding round in the bedroom. Every morning that week it was a similar performance. Then on Friday, horror of horrors, although it didn't seem so at first. At ten past ten the bike arrived with two people on it this time, the passenger a woman with long blond hair carrying a large parcel. A few minutes later three people were seen in the bedroom. By now Mick had decided that since they were his binoculars, he would have first call on them but, as a compromise, he offered to describe what he could see. As he told them of the shenanigans, his voice sunk.

"The bastards," he said, "Do you know what was in that bloody parcel?"

Nobody did.

"Curtains!"

"So it's curtains for us, is it?" grimaced Yorky.

Shortly after the man came into the yard, jumped on his bike and drove off.

"So what's your prediction for what happens next, Yorky?"

"I think he'll come back with another bloke."

Mick continued to look through the binoculars. His earlier promise to their section leader, Alan Groves, that he would finish the drawing on his board by the end of the day now looked unlikely, unless of course the curtains were permanently drawn.

"Bloody hell."

"What's happening now?" Charlie asked.

"The two women. They're both getting into bed."

By now the curtains had been hung up, but fortunately they were still open, though the view was a little restricted. Then the motorbike reappeared, but with no extra passenger.

"This should be good," laughed Mick. And five minutes later the old adage that three's a crowd was shown to have been constructed on a very shallow philosophical interpretation of the concept of pleasure and inter-personal relationships between people of the opposite gender. Inevitably word began to circulate around the factory about the goings on at number two. Then, at lunchtime, instead of going bowling, or sitting on the wall outside the Iron Foundry on Warrington Road, many of Wilkinson's employees began to go for a little walk. Invariably this included going down Smart Street, lolling about at the end before returning round the back. On one particular occasion Alan had stayed in the office and had counted fifty seven people walk by, and that was on a day when no motorbike had appeared.

Then one afternoon a man wearing a boiler suit came down the back of the street. Alan had a quick look and recognised him. It was Peter Starr, the UFO man and also the rescuer of his daughter, Rebecca. Not long after he was seen at the window, from which he proceeded to wave to the Drawing Office. Then he put a large piece of cardboard up against the window on which he had written 'No Peep Show Today' and closed the curtains. Unfortunately he must have done it with a little too much force, because the next thing they saw was the curtain rail at something like sixty degrees to the ground.

Next Alan saw an almost naked woman remove the curtains and the cardboard. She wrote on the cardboard and then placed it up against the window again. And on it she had written 'Peep Show at 11'. Later they discovered that the young lady was Vicki, who had just returned from her travelling around the globe. If the names of the places she had visited indicated anything, it was that Vikki had developed a particular interest in architecture and particularly in bridges. Her first move away from Ashurst was to Marus Bridge in Wigan, where she stayed for the fortnight that her cousin Stephanie's parents were away on holiday in Tenerife. During that time four parties were enjoyed, one that went on for three days solid. An hour before Stephanie's parents were due to arrive at Manchester Airport, Vicki left what was now a very untidy house with an empty fridge and moved back home for a couple of days before moving in with one of her old boyfriends at Gerard's Bridge in St Helens while the rest of his family were staying on a boat on the Norfolk Broads. She then moved out of the county, first to to Stalybridge and then into a hippy commune in Hebden Bridge.

She had then returned to Ashurst and set up the first commune that the town had ever known at number two Smart Street, the house of her auntie Janice, who was staying for a while in Colwyn Bay with her daughter and her husband, the parson Paul. Well actually Vicki had told her auntie that she would just keep an eye on the place and make sure that everything was kept in working order, and particularly the springs under the bed.

Peter continued with his obsession with the paranormal but then, in fact just after he got locked in Mossdale Library one night, he shifted his interest on to ecological matters that concerned the living planet. He began to study geology, weather patterns and seismic activity. Slowly he began to develop a reputation for being able to predict the occurrence of natural disasters and particularly earthquakes, floods and pestilence in all its assorted forms. Then he came out with his most outlandish one, but one based on a closely argued analysis that none of the so-called experts in the Engineering Department of Ashurst Technical College could refute.

Essentially, he predicted that within fifty years an enormous volcanic eruption would occur in the Canary Islands, one which would cause enormous waves to batter the coast of America and Europe. So strong was his belief in his own theory that he convinced his next door neighbour to move his caravan five miles inland from a site near Withernsea on the East coast of Yorkshire. Then, right out of the blue, he handed in his notice at Wallworks and headed out to Cape Disappointment on the West Coast of America to meet up with his new found friends.

Two months later he was back in town, with a story that was more like something out of a Les Earnshaw novel. Soon after he had been put in touch with the UFO watchers at Cape Disappointment, he had been given responsibility for sending monthly reports of spaceship sightings around Ashurst. Then his brief was extended to cover the whole of the British Isles, rapid promotion indeed. To protect his identity, both from the Zartracs and the British and American Governments, he was told to use the name Retep Rrats and pass himself off as a Finnish student studying geology at Liverpool University. Increasingly the magazine began to carry reports of UFO activity at Billinge, Rivington Pike and in Knowsley Park. Soon after he began to receive letters from his number one fan, Wendy, the group's International Press and Media Secretary.

It was around this time that Peter went on the night shift at work. This coincided with

Wendy's request for him to come to Cape Disappointment for special training. She also told him to phone her, not an easy task since Peter only had access to the phone at the bottom of Pemberton Street, the one that was invariably damaged by either the Zartracs or members of the Dob Lane Mafia (under nine's section).

During his third week on nights it was discovered that the door of the meeting room next to the Machine Shop was not locked. In the room was a phone which had a direct line out. During the first week, a couple of the turners had used it to phone home, then one of the millers had used it to ring his mother in Bolton. Then the labourer had rung a friend in Barrow-in-Furness, twice. After that the storeman decided that he would re-establish contact with his brother in Durban and the chargehand felt it necessary to tell his cousin in Alice Springs that their Auntie Alice had just died but left them nothing in her will. Soon after Peter thought he would try his luck and spoke to Wendy. By the end of the first week thirty eight telephone calls had been made. The second week this number had risen to forty two and then peaked at fifty one by the end of the month. In this way Peter began to get to know Wendy very well. Then, on perhaps the third or fourth occasion, she had told him that she wanted to give him some special night time training in the dark. And so, after she had told him that her full name was Wendy Wild and Willing, he decided he would hand his notice in and head for the New World. On this occasion his timing was perfection itself since the day he left Ashurst, Wilkinson's Accounts Department learned that their telephone bill had increased by 309%. And the following day, the meeting room door was locked permanently.

But by this time Peter had arrived at San Francisco airport. He took a coach up to Astoria, just north of Portland. He walked over to the wall behind Bay 17 where Wendy said she would be waiting at three in the afternoon and there she was behind it. The wall itself was probably about five and a half foot high and covered in graffiti. She waved and blew him a kiss. He recognised her from the photograph she had sent him, well it was actually just a photograph of her face. His first thought was that it was not a very recent photograph. He knew very little about her at that stage. He did not know that she was a very clever woman. Very brainy indeed; she spoke seven languages and had a degree in Engineering and another in Psychology, From this she well knew that first impressions were very important, which partly explained why she was behind the wall stood on a large box. As Peter walked round the back of the wall he discovered that not only was she was only five foot tall but nearly five foot wide as well. Still, she had a very seductive way of speaking and a nice face, even if it was over forty years old.

Over the next few days he was introduced to other members of the group. Shortly after meeting them he became convinced, not that the Zartracs were aiming to invade the Earth in the near future, but they had already landed and his new found friends were the Zartracs. Within a week he began to think his mind was being taken over by their daily rituals; within a fortnight he had the feeling that he was their prisoner. That was when he began to work out how to escape. So he made up a quite stupid story. He told them that it was clear that the group needed money to expand their activities and convinced them that he had access to large amounts of money which he had collected from sympathetic millionaires who lived at Dentons Green, Hindley Green, Goose Green and Lea Green, all places famed for their high concentration of wealth. To get access to this money all he had to do was go to the Manhattan Chase bank at San Francisco Airport, speak to one of the bankers there, fill out a form and answer some questions and then the money would be ready for their use. Although a little suspicious the other members of the group agreed that he could go but for his own protection (and their financial well-being), they would go with him.

They drove down in total silence the following day. It was as though they knew that he knew that he was their prisoner, or latest recruit to their intention to rule the world. They arrived at the bank early and, on Peter's suggestion, decided to eat in a nearby restaurant. Half way through the meal, he left to visit the john, climbed through a window and ran like hell to San Francisco Airport and two hours later was on a plane bound for Amsterdam, where he spent the next few days with some of the tallest, thinnest women he could find. And when he finally came back to Ashurst, nobody believed a word of what he said had happened to him in the USA.

To celebrate his return to the Old World, Vicki decided that it was time to make a fresh start to their relationship. And so a party was held at number two Smart Street on the Saturday night. It was a rather rumbustious affair, one that the members of the Drawing Office would have even paid to watch. About midnight, one of Vicki's friends came out of the bedroom to tell Vicki that a brick had fallen out of the wall. No one paid any attention to her, she was pissed but then so was everybody else. So little Stephanie went back upstairs where her boyfriend had in her absence fallen asleep and nearly set fire to the bed with his pipe. Five minutes later, she came down into the kitchen to tell Vicki that the curtain rail had just fallen to the floor. Her comments elicited no response. But half an hour later she was down again to say that the whole window frame had somehow broken free and now lay shattered in the back yard.

"You two must have been going at it pretty wild," laughed Peter. But then Vicki said that it was probably some of the draughtsmen from Wilkinsons throwing stones at the window. But as she spoke plaster began to fall from the ceiling.

"It's them bloody Zartracs," said Dave, a regular visitor to the house while Peter had been away.

"No, it's the ale," said Peter. "It's bloody strong, too bloody strong for me" and with that he went upstairs to pay a call. As he walked up the stairs a bigger crack appeared in the ceiling, and shortly after the underside of the bath was exposed accompanied by a trickle of water."

"Stop pissing in the bath," Vicki shouted out. "If that's what they do in America, I'm not having it in this house."

Then Jason, who had been in the shed with another of Vicki's friends, came rushing into the house to tell them that somebody was throwing slates off the roof. Vicki looked out of the window just as the chimney stack crashed into the yard. Was it the ale, was it the Zartracs, what the hell was going on?

Actually there was quite a simple explanation for all these rather strange happenings, not just at number two, but at all the other houses in Smart Street. Below the house lay the workings of the old Southport Edge pit. Now, due to some movement of the earth's crust on latitude minus three, longitude fifty two point eight, a little bit of subsidence was going on. By the following lunchtime all the inhabitants of Smart Street had been moved out for their own safety and by the end of November the whole street had been demolished.

It had been good while it lasted, unfortunately it hadn't lasted long enough. John then proceeded to tell them about the time he had worked in a drawing office in the centre of London, one that overlooked a long row of terraced houses. During the course of his stay there, the street had been the scene of two murders, one armed robbery, a four day long party to which many women in fur coats had been admitted but never seemed to leave and the arrival of a man on horseback who threw bricks through one of the bedroom windows. There had also been one incident when a young man wearing only his shirt had been chased out of a house by an older man carrying a shotgun, and another time when at least a hundred men all dressed in black had got into a fleet of cars and been driven away laughing and joking presumably either to the wedding of somebody they liked or the funeral of somebody they didn't.

After all the fun in Smart Street everything went quiet for a while. Winter followed autumn, and spring followed winter, but then right across South Lancashire, it always had done. Suddenly, right out of the blue, their section leader Alan Groves left. He literally walked out of the office after a long altercation with Basil one afternoon and never came back. It was well known that 'Grovesy' had never seen eye to eye with the boss over how his section should operate. Although he had kept telling the lads off for their rather lax attitude to time-keeping, he had always held the attitude that as long as the job was completed on time, it didn't matter if there was some tomfoolery as well. But then Basil was in charge, it was his factory and if he didn't like the way things were being done then he had the power to stop it. But despite whatever he tried, he never stopped the draffies having a laugh, playing tricks and from time to time baffling him and everybody else with rocket science. And so the days on which nothing humorous happened continued to be as rare as the proverbial rocking horse manure.

But as Charlie pointed out, always looking for the funny side in any situation was part of their culture. Like the time he had heard that his Uncle Joseph had been ordered to stay in bed for three months in order to recover from a serious injury to his spine, and Charlie had told him to look on the bright side as he wouldn't have to stand freezing at the bus stop every morning to go to work, or find an excuse to tell his wife why he hadn't washed up.

But nothing funny could be made of the disappearance of 'Grovesy', well not for a long time. He had split up with his wife a couple of months earlier, although that had been on the cards a long time. He had paid off his mortgage and seemed all right for cash. And he had often talked of travelling the world when he retired. Shortly after, his house in Grappenhall was sold and according to Keith Sanderson's daughter, who worked in the estate agents, the cheque for the sale was given to a very attractive middle-aged lady who until recently had worked in the Gas Showrooms. Soon after, her house at Gillarsfield was sold too and a large cheque posted to an address in the South of Spain.

A couple of months later, a postcard from Malaga was sent to Wilkinson's Drawing

Office. And on it was written: "I am very pleased to inform you lazy bastardos that my lunch breaks are now even longer than yours ever were."

28.

"DO YOU STILL PUT WATER IN THE BEER"

"Where's Charlie?" asked Ronnie Garner, who had just walked into the office carrying a bundle of marked up prints.

"Gone to a funeral," replied Mick. "He'll be in after lunch"

"Whose is it?"

"Tommy, one of his old work mates from Pilks."

"Well, if I want to get any sense out of him, I think I'll have to come back tomorrow when he's sobered up."

Charlie had worked with Tommy for much of his apprenticeship at Pilkingtons. He had taught young master Eccleston all the tricks of the trade, with special emphasis on repairing motors along with rewiring houses and how best to make it known around the town that he never charged for checking electric blankets in ladies' bedrooms.

Somewhat surprisingly Charlie did appear in the afternoon, although a little the worse for wear, but with a fine story to tell. It appeared that Tommy had known he was going for some time and so had made preparations, in a way only a person like he could. After his coffin had been lowered into the grave, all those in attendance had been invited to a soup and ham lunch in the Raven. There it was announced that the beer was free, thanks to Tommy's generosity, as were the cigars for those who wished to poison their lungs and pollute the atmosphere.

Then his eldest daughter Agnes stood up, thanked everybody for coming, and said how much they would all miss the old man and various other things that are normally said at events like this. This was followed by a couple of his old work mates paying their own tribute to him and then Tommy's grandson stood up. He proceeded to say that shortly before he had died, Tommy had given him a sealed envelope in which was a letter that he wanted read out. Every one went quiet as the lad boomed out Tommy's last words.

"Hoping that you are all pissed by now. Knowing how slow they are in The Raven, by the time you hear this read out, I will probably have started working on my first job up here, welding the Pearly Gates permanently shut so none of you lot can ever get in. On a more unfriendly note, I want to leave you with a few thoughts, which you are all permitted to pass on to anyone you meet in the gutter on your way home.

"First of all, to my dear cousin Alfred, the Sunday school teacher. I know that in the Bible it says Love Thy Neighbour. Well are you still loving that lady at number fifty nine every Thursday night when her husband goes to play billiards. Secondly, to my other dear cousin, Councillor Todd, your little secret about being in prison for thieving is still safe with me. To Ronnie Preston from The Eagle and Child and who I am sure isn't present, have you still got that fiddle going on with the brewery drivers and do you still put water in the beer.

"To everybody else: I loved you all and especially most of my apprentices, without whom today the world would be a much safer place. If Arthur Gray is present, when you have no matches with you and you want to light the gas, do you still use silver paper to get a light from the electric fire. If Dave Critchley is there, have you told your good wife about Mrs Sinclair yet, and finally for Charlie Eccleston, could you tell everybody what you meant when you said 'Bloody Hell, it's a man.'"

At this point Agnes stood up again and to avoid any embarrassment to anyone present, she suggested that her other sisters might like to say a few words about their Dad and after that another round of free drinks would be ordered. And as she spoke the two cousins and Dave Critchley left the room to visit the Gents and then go their separate ways.

"So what did you mean when he said that about you, Charlie?"

"It's embarrassing," laughed Charlie.

It was definitely not something he was proud of or pleased about, but it was funny in a way and it had happened a long time ago. So out of respect for Tommy, who had set it all up, he told them.

"I'd only been working at Pilks a few weeks when they had this trip to the Illuminations at Blackpool. We'd been supping all day and I was really pissed. Well I was only sixteen. Then about ten o'clock we went to this right seedy club, about six of us. Two of the lads started chatting up a couple of birds straight away and then I noticed a right brassy blonde keep looking at me. There were some spare seats next to her so we went and sat with her and her mate. She starts talking to me in a real deep voice, she was really friendly and sexy too. I just thought she had fallen for my good looks and charm. Soon Tommy and the other two disappear and I'm left on my own with her. She buys me a drink, though I thought it was a bit funny when she came back from the bar with a pint of bitter for me and a pint of Guiness for herself. She chats a bit more and then asks me what time my coach was leaving. When I told her midnight, she asked me if I'd like to go back to her place for a bit when I'd finished my drink, which I then did in about five seconds flat. Again I thought it a bit unusual for a woman, but she finished her pint off with one gulp too. Still with me being a bit naive, I just thought that that was what Blackpool women were like."

"Well she was all over me as soon as we got back to her place. She put my hand on her knee and asked me to stroke her leg gently because I had such beautiful soft hands and it made her feel so relaxed. Then she starts kissing me again and undoing my shirt and all the while my hand is slowly moving up her leg. She then tells me that I can stay the night if I wanted to. Well I couldn't believe my good fortune. So she starts kissing me again, telling me how lovely I was and how she wished that I lived in Blackpool. And then I moved my hand a little bit more and then, horror of horrors, I discovered that she was a bloody man."

"What did you do?"

"I ran away. I've never run so fast in my life and when I got back to the coach, they were all pissing themselves laughing. I didn't know what sort of a pub it was, but Tommy did."

"And what was that about the others?"

"Well it must have been something from the past. Alfred is well into his seventies but he still went bright red when Tommy virtually accused him of messing about with his neighbour's wife, and of course Councillor Todd, you couldn't meet a slimier character."

"And I wonder who Mrs Sinclair is."

"Ask Dave Critchley. He must know her."

It seemed strange seeing Charlie dressed in a dark suit, wearing a white shirt and black tie. He actually looked very smart, especially when he stood next to Mick. But then he had once come into work on a Saturday morning to borrow a drill from the Maintenance Shop wearing what he called his gardening outfit. And stood next to Mick that day, he still looked the better dressed. But quite soon after, the man from Platt Bridge managed to get one over all his work mates.

It happened a couple of Mondays later. Wigan had lost the previous day, the Saints had won, usually a recipe for Mick to keep out of the way as much as possible or get his head down as early as possible. But this particular day he had been walking round with an enormous smile on his face. Unfortunately, Basil and then John Barker had been in and out of the office like a fiddler's elbow, so it was turned ten before they could find out the reason. Charlie first had to ask Mick why he kept humming the Abba hit record 'Money, Money, Money' and what was wrong with Winifred Attwell. And then, getting no answer, he asked him directly why he was so happy.

"Why am I happy today? Because I'm here with all my friends. I've just successfully redesigned the controls for a large power station in Brazil. And I follow the greatest team in the world."

"Mick," laughed Charlie, "you don't have any friends. That power station in Brazil is actually in Argentina and all you've done is add two relays and a push button. And yesterday your finest team in the world nearly got beat at home by Barrow."

"All right then I'll tell you why I am happy. A wrong has been righted. A financial mistake has been corrected and the Henderson family honour has been re-established."

"Mick, what are you on about?"

"Well, you'll all remember when my Uncle Ernie died, he didn't include me in the will, so all the others got £500 each and I got nothing. Well my Auntie Ada died a few weeks ago and on Saturday morning I got a little letter from the solicitors. She must have thought that I had been badly treated, because in her will she left me the house, the garage with two vintage motorbikes in it, two thousand Premium Bonds and five thousand pounds in cash."

"It couldn't have happened to a nicer bloke."

"You deserve every penny of it."

"Do you want me to get you a cup of tea, Mick?"

"Would you like a bit of this cake the wife has baked?"

"Are you going to get a new suit?"

"You'll look really smart in a new suit."

"How are you going to celebrate it and what time should we be there for?"

In this moment of enormous financial gain, humour as always dominated the proceedings. And no more so than when Mick replied by stating that he was going to buy them all a drink and proceeded to pull a large bottle of Vimto out of his drawer, place it on his reference table and then stick a dozen straws in the top.

He then told them he would be buying all the ale on Friday lunchtime, a new suit on Saturday morning and inviting them all to a do in his local in Platt Bridge on the Saturday evening.

The following Monday morning found them all talking about the Saturday night experience in the Platt Bridge Hotel, all except for Len that was. He hadn't ventured out of Ashurst on the Saturday night and it was the third day he had been off sick in the last month. It was clear that he was not his usual self and something was wrong with him. And when he turned up on Tuesday he told them all that he was going to have to finish work on doctor's orders.

He had been the Office Committee chairman for over thirteen years, going back to 1963 when they had first got them all organised into the union. He had been an excellent negotiator and had put his neck on the line, or took a great gamble to call Basil's bluff, on a number of occasions. Now, approaching retirement and with his wife seriously ill, the latest upset was the Council's decision to place a compulsory purchase order on his street in Hemsley. And so, on health grounds he had decided to call it a day.

"So what will you do with all your spare time?" asked Alan.

"He'll start playing bowls, I reckon," said Yorky.

"Fishing; that's what he'll do," said Charlie, "after all, he was always fishing for information when he was chairman of the Divisional Council."

"Well, you'll be pleased to hear that I'm going to write a book. It'll be a nice easy way to spend the time, and no stress to it either."

"What will you call it?"

"The Contribution made by the Working Class in Ashurst to the Overthrow of Feudalism in 1728."

"Len, until 1750, Ashurst was made up of twelve houses built round that blacksmiths in Kiln Lane," laughed Charlie.

"I know, that's why it won't take me long to write it. Then I can get started on my major project as an established writer."

"What will you call that?"

"Ashurst Between the Wars. The Hidden Story."

"Seriously?"

"Yes. I know loads of people older than me who can tell me what they did and saw. And I've also got the motivation"

That was largely due to him having read the book that had been written by Cynthia Porter, the town's self-appointed literary sage. Called "Ashurst's Past Reclaimed", it was an idyllic, nonsensical, inaccurate account of life in the town between 1919 and 1939. It ignored completely the way that 99% of the locals lived in those harsh times: the unemployment that the soldiers had come back to at the end of the Great War, the Montagu pit disaster, the Town Hall food scandal of 1923, the General Strike of 1926, the incident at Mather's when two apprentices had been killed, and the jailing of the Town Clerk in 1934 for financial misjudgement and the uproar when he had been released a week later. All these were ignored. Instead the town was presented as though as it was some twee little country village with social gatherings aplenty, picnics, rambles and visits to the Free Trade Hall in Manchester and the Walker Art Gallery in Liverpool.

There was no doubt that Len would set the record straight, and many would buy it as well because, knowing Les, they knew he would tell the history as it was and not as Cynthia had experienced it growing up in her parents' large house in Cheshire and before she had been sent to a public school in Devon.

"Will it make me chuckle?" said Len. "Will it be in the Les Earnshaw mould of literary ambivalence and fantasy?"

"There'll be some funny bits in it. There'll have to be if it's going to be true to life. But to be honest, I don't think that the Thirties were a great time for laughing and joking when you look back on it."

"My auntie has got a load of photographs of Ashurst in the Twenties," said Alan. "You can use them if you want to."

"There you are. Another prospective old age pensioner to help you and you haven't even started yet."

"Len, how old are you now?"

"Sixty three, and if you're really interested I'll be sixty four on my next birthday."

"Len, you know in the future when we want a wage increase, will you still come in and negotiate it for us," asked Alan with a big grin on his face.

"We're going to have to find someone to take over as Office Committee Chairman," said Mick.

"I know who it'll be," said Charlie, "the last one out of the room at the Annual General Meeting."

"Well it's your problem now brothers. You've only got another three weeks to find somebody."

"Why does it have to be a man who does it?" asked Rita, now in charge of the Print Room after Big Joan had left to look after her sick mother.

"It doesn't. I'm sure you could do it just as well as anybody else," said Len.

And at his going away do in the Horse and Jockey later that month, Len was presented with two books and a Best Wishes card that had been signed by over a hundred employees. And then he was kissed by the new Office Committee chairman, which was actually very pleasant since the new holder of that exalted position was Rita Martlew. And the two books the collection had bought him were "The Civil War in France" by Karl Marx along with a biography of the Marx brothers.

And as Rita put it so eloquently, "We always knew you were a Marxist, Len, but we were never quite sure which sort."

With Len no longer with them, it was expected that Basil would use the opportunity to have a go at them. But somehow it appeared that he was a little unsure of how to handle their new leader, Sister Martlew. She had quickly come to realise that with a little power at her command she could now do something about righting the wrongs that women had faced over the years. It was also clear that she had learned a lot from the way Len had done things before, for she was soon sending sheets round collecting money for various groups of workers who needed support, whether financial or moral. Then, she surprised the Office Committee by announcing that she was going to start attending the monthly branch meetings. And she also let it be known that her friend, Norma Sykes, a tracer at the Gas Board and often referred to as Nymphy Norma, was going to come with her. And for the next few months, the branch attendance shot up by around 300%.

"I thought it were a good meeting last night," commented Yorky a few weeks later and the morning after the branch A.G.M.

"I thought it were a good meeting," said Keith very pompously. "What sort of English is that?"

"Well it certainly isn't the Queen's English," said Mick, "not what like I speak."

"Who rattled your cage, Keith?" said Charlie.

"I was just passing comment on Yorky's misuse of our cultured tongue."

"Yorky is from Yorkshire, so why shouldn't he speak like a Tyke?" said Alan. "Why should he speak like the Queen. He's not a woman"

"Hell, he's a bloody man," laughed Charlie.

"Why do we all have to speak like the Queen anyway?" asked Alan. "And why does she speak like she does?"

"It must be how people speak where she was brought up," said Charlie. "It was Balmoral, wasn't it?"

"But Yorky wasn't brought up in Balmoral," said Alan.

"I think he was brought up in Immoral," laughed Mick.

"And why are you getting so concerned about Yorky's English, Keith?" asked Alan. "For a Yorkshireman I think he's mastered the subtle nuances of our native tongue quite adequately, though I have to admit he sometimes gets his tenses mixed up."

"What do you mean?"

"Well he often jumps between the past historic, the perfect and the imperfect tense when he is describing something that he has done or heard about in the past."

"How can a tense be perfect?" asked Mick. "I've never heard ewt so daft."

"You know when you say 'I have walked to work' or 'I have eaten my pie' then that is the perfect tense, by definition. But if you say 'I was walking to work every day until I started to catch the bus' or 'I was always eating my pie when the ITV News was on' then that is the imperfect tense. The perfect tense relates to an action that maybe just occurred once in the recent past whereas the imperfect tense relates to a thing that was going on for a while, while the past historic relates to something that happened in the past, maybe just once a long time ago."

"Greeno, that is absolutely amazing. I never knew all that. How ever I managed to get here on time or feed myself at home, I'll never know," laughed Charlie.

"Here's another one, what is the definitive article and what is the indefinite article?"

"I know the answer to that," said Colin. "It's to do with the past and when you went shopping. The definite article is when you knew exactly what you had gone to buy in a shop before you got there, whereas the indefinite article is when you went in a shop and were just looking round for an idea of something to buy."

"Ha ha, very clever, so does anybody else know?"

"Go on, Shakespeare, tell us."

"The definite article is the word 'the' and the indefinite article is the word 'a'. The definite article is more specific, the match, the player, the referee, whereas the indefinite article is less specific, a match, a player, a referee."

"What a load of old rubbish," said Mick, "that's why half the kids in school can't read properly if all the teachers are doing is telling them all that before they are allowed to open their mouths."

"Mick, you Wiganers have no appreciation of the English language. I bet you can't tell the difference between a noun and a verb."

"A noun is the name of something, like match or referee, and a verb describes something that you do, which in your case isn't very often."

"I bet you don't know that sometimes a word can be an adjective, and at the same time it can also be a noun, or even a verb."

"I do," said Colin. "My brother teaches English and last week he was introducing some of these ideas in his class. So he asks one of the kids to give him a sentence with an adjective in it. So this little lad says, 'My mother has a charming broach on her frock'. So then our kid asks someone else to use the word charming but not as an adjectice and this other lad says, 'On the telly last night James Bond was charming all the women on his boat.'

"Then he asks if somebody else could give the class a sentence with the word charming used twice and a right little handful at the front sticks his hand up, much to everybody's surprise, and blurts out: 'Last night my sister was sat in front of the telly when my Dad came home from work. When he sat down she told him that she was pregnant and going to have a baby. And my Dad looked at her and said 'Charming, Fucking Charming.'"

And while he was eating his tea later that evening, Mick's wife asked him what he had been doing at work that day. And when he told her they had had a discussion on linguistics and the role that the adverb and the noun played in contemporary social verbal interchange, she shook her head and turned to her sister Martha who had just called in and said:

"Ee, they are a funny load of blokes in that Drawing Office. They don't half talk about some daft things." Then she turned back to Mick and asked, "Are they all like that in Ashurst?"

And he just nodded.

While he was having his tea, Alan also recalled the discussion. He had always been interested in language and its relationship to the way the human race had developed. He had also been interested, even fascinated by, the different accents found around South Lancashire. Every day he heard good examples of the Wigan accent and the St Helens accent from Mick and Charlie, in addition to the accent of his native Ashurst, which bore similarities to both. Then there were a couple of Warrington lads in the Assembly shop and his mate John Meredith who came from Widnes, and their old section leader Alan Groves, who had been brought up in Salford, with each one speaking with quite different accents.

Then there was the accent of his two children, Rebecca and Robert, clearly influenced by having a mother who had lived in South Wales in her early formative years. He also noticed a difference in the accents of some of his older relatives and how some words they used were disappearing. And he could also see or hear that with the greater mobility of people and the impact of television and its domination by American culture, how that was making an impact on the way people in Ashurst, and indeed throughout the country, spoke.

Then, having finished his tea he settled down to watch the television and the first person he saw was good old Eddie Waring being interviewed in his own distinctive vernacular.

Back in work the following day, however, there was no more discussion on the subject. In fact the only reference to language was the bad language that many of Wilkinson's employees used when they heard that Basil was again on the warpath, aiming once again to reduce the number of employees on the payroll. And back in the Drawing Office, a number of the older ones began wondering if it might be an idea to go for voluntary redundancy and get out while there was work around elsewhere. But in their hearts they knew that it was not a good time to be voluntarily giving up a job, even though it would mean having to put up with Basil five days a week.

And not surprisingly the future was discussed at great length over the next few weeks. Various people put forward different thoughts on the matter. Keith considered forming a new band and heading off to America. If it wasn't for his wife and her child having nicely settled in the town, John would have left to go contracting in Holland. And then Charlie told Alan that there was just the job for him less than twenty minutes walk from his house in Silkstone Street: as a bouncer at Mothercare in Bridge Street.

Then Yorky piped up to say that he had heard that Mick had now decided to leave and was going to become an entrepreneur.

"That's the first I've heard of it."

"Well I've just heard from one of the lads on the shop floor that you're going to start minding your own business."

But fortunately for them all he didn't leave. He stayed at Wilkinson's and was among the very last to walk out of the Drawing Office when the place was finally closed down. But a lot more incidents, packed with drama, tragedy and, of course, humour, were to occur before that happened.

RUGBY LEAGUE BOOKS FROM
The PARRS WOOD Press

BAMFORD - Memoirs of a Blood and Thunder Coach
- paperback £9.95

THE PETITION - Rugby League Fans Say "Enough is Enough"
- paperback £8.95

THE CUP - Passion, Murder and a Quest for a Sporting Grail
- paperback £8.95

ONE WINTER - Romance, Rock 'n' Roll and Rugby League in the Swinging Sixties
- paperback £7.99